KT-167-697

8000332715

80003327154

Praise for Robert Wilson

'Wilson's plotting is intricate, his detective endearingly
human . . . this is crime fiction of a high order'
The Times

'Few writers mix tension and action as effectively'
Guardian

'Action-packed and scarily plausible. A cracking thriller
from one of the best in the business'   Mark Billingham

'Like most of Wilson's novels, this one occupies the
shadow territory between the crime novel and the intelligent thriller . . . it's dark and powerful stuff. And the ending
has a kick like a horse'   *Spectator*

'Fast-moving and breathlessly exciting, this is the first
of a series to feature Charles Boxer from award-winning
author Robert Wilson'   *Irish Independent*

'Full of action and tension, a guaranteed great read from
this CWA Gold Dagger-winning author'
Lovereading.com

'Gripping from start to finish, this intricately plotted page-
turner will keep you transfixed'   *Choice*

'Mr Wilson writes with elegant vigour as he describes the
shoot-outs and emotional crescendos that result from the
political and criminal intrigue at the heart of the book'
Wall Street Journal

Robert Wilson has lived and worked around the world, including spells shipbroking, tour guiding and exporting bathrooms to Nigeria. After escaping car crashes, civil wars and angry baboons, Rob turned to writing novels. Since then, he's written twelve acclaimed crime novels, including the CWA Gold Dagger-winner *A Small Death in Lisbon* and the Falcón series, recently adapted for television. *Capital Punishment* was shortlisted for the CWA Ian Fleming Steel Dagger award. To find out more visit www.robert-wilson.eu

By Robert Wilson

The Ignorance of Blood
The Hidden Assassins
The Silent and the Damned
The Blind Man of Seville
The Company of Strangers
A Small Death in Lisbon
A Darkening Stain
Blood is Dirt
The Big Killing
Instruments of Darkness
Capital Punishment
You Will Never Find Me

CAPITAL PUNISHMENT

Robert Wilson

Typeset by Deltatype Ltd, Birkenhead, Merseyside

Printed and bound in Great Britain
by Clays Ltd, St Ives plc

The Orion Publishing Group's policy is to use papers
that are natural, renewable and recyclable products and
made from wood grown in sustainable forests. The logging
and manufacturing processes are expected to conform to
the environmental regulations of the country of origin.

An Orion paperback

First published in Great Britain in 2013
by Orion
This paperback edition published in 2014
by Orion Books,
an imprint of The Orion Publishing Group Ltd,
Orion House, 5 Upper St Martin's Lane,
London WC2H 9EA

An Hachette UK company

1 3 5 7 9 10 8 6 4 2

Copyright © Robert A. Wilson Limited 2013

The moral right of Robert Wilson to be identified as the
author of this work has been asserted in accordance with
the Copyright, Designs and Patents Act 1988.

All rights reserved. No part of this publication may be
reproduced, stored in a retrieval system, or transmitted,
in any form or by any means, electronic, mechanical,
photocopying, recording or otherwise, without the
prior permission of the copyright owner.

All the characters in this book are fictitious,
and any resemblance to actual persons, living
or dead, is purely coincidental.

A CIP catalogue record for this book
is available from the British Library.

ISBN 978-1-4091-3902-7

Northamptonshire Libraries & Information Services NC	
Askews & Holts	

For Jane

and Marian and Steve
Billy, Calum and Adelaide

But the line dividing good and evil cuts through the heart of every human being. And who is willing to destroy a piece of his own heart?

Alexander Solzhenitsyn. *The Gulag Archipelago 1918–1956*

1

The leaving party's last team effort: climb out of the tapas bar basement, up through the bottle-neck of the spiral staircase, everyone off their faces. Alyshia, their twenty-five-year-old manager, caught her heel in the grid of the cast iron steps. The scrum below, sensing a blockage, surged upwards to force it out. The rubber on Alyshia's expensive heel was ripped clean off as she was belched out of the stairwell, the room above reeling as the ragged band staggered out of the bowels. Bar stools rocked as they ricocheted through the savage crowd of baying drunkards, voices pitched louder than traders in the bear pit.

They were out in the street, Alyshia clip-clopping around in Maiden Lane like a lame pony, the freezing night air cooling the patina of sweat on her face. Was it the extra oxygen doubling her booze intake? Focus, refocus, as faces of atrocious ugliness loomed in and out of the sickeningly flexible frame of her vision.

'You all right, Ali?' asked Jim.

'Lost my heel,' she said, her knees buckling. She hung onto him.

'She's *pissed*,' said Doggy, always on hand to tell you the obvious. Jim shoved him away.

'We're *all* pissed,' said Toola triumphantly, whose legs went as if felled and she dropped hard on her bottom, legs akimbo.

'I told you,' said Jim in Alyshia's ear, 'you'd end up in Accident & Emergency if you went out with this lot. Last piss-up before jobseeker's allowance.'

It was the only decent thing to do, she thought, as the street tilted up and her head felt as huge and tight as a barrage balloon.

'You all right, Ali?' asked Jim, holding her shoulders, his face frowning in her pulsing vision.

'Get me out of here,' she said.

'Where's Doggy?' said Toola.

Doggy got pinballed towards her.

'Give us a hand here, amigo,' said Toola as she staggered to her feet.

'Give us a kiss,' said Doggy, pulling her up, tongue out.

A cry of disgust as the group stumbled down the street, hollering like school kids.

Alyshia grabbed Jim's arm, the street now a heaving deck.

'Find me a cab,' she said, neon blinking and blurring in her tearful eyes.

Bedlam in the Strand. Barking in Charing Cross.

'It's kicking off!' screamed a voice in the distance.

Teenage kids were running riot, careening down the street, running up and thumping off shop windows, taking down passersby. Hoodies doled out kickings. Two girls tottered on stilettos in the gutter, fists in each other's hair. A shout went up, the crowd split, shadows in all directions. Across the Strand, back to a pillar of scaffolding, a black boy on his arse, legs out, head bowed, hands on stomach, holding it all in.

'That kid's been stabbed,' said Alyshia.

'Come on,' said Jim. 'You're not going to get a cab down here.'

'Got to call the police.'

She fumbled in her bag for her mobile, asked for police, ambulance, the lot, through lips gone fat and rubbery, refusing to form the words.

Sirens hurtled through the night. Jim swiped her mobile, clicked it off, chucked it in her handbag.

'Let's go,' he said. 'They're onto it.'

'We should *do* something.'

'We're too *pissed*,' said Jim savagely.

He took her arm. Not a cab to be seen on Wellington Street. He led her up towards the Royal Opera House.

Glad you're here, Jim, she thought to herself. Older than the

2

others. Did I drink that much? A gin and tonic before. Wine with the paella. Doggy had flaming Sambuca. He would. What's up with this pavement? Got a steep ridge down the middle. Am I going to be sick right outside the temple of opera? The paella yawn in the cruella dawn. My head's coming untethered from my shoulders. Breathe deep.

Out of the corner of her eye, a floating orange light in the drunken blur.

'Taxi!' she yelled, flinging out an arm. It swerved in to the pavement.

She wiped her cheeks. Sucked in air. Hung onto the window ledge. Tried to look like someone who wouldn't projectile vomit. Gave the cabbie her address: Lavender Grove. Near London Fields.

The cabbie looked jaundiced in the street lighting.

'All right, love,' he said, tongue flickering between grey lips, 'in you get. Madhouse back there, innit? You coming, too?'

Jim shook his head, swung the door shut, waved her off.

The driver checked his mirror, pulled out, wheeled round in a tight U-turn. The doors' locks shunted to, startling her. The lights dimmed, went out. She sank back into the darkness of the cab, tried to stop her head from lolling.

Don't black out. Tell him the route and he'll know you're all right.

'Down here, left onto Tavistock Sreet, left again onto Drury Lane. Straight on … yeah, keep straight …'

'You're all right, love, we know where we're going.'

Couldn't wet her lips. Flinched at the swish of lights overhead. Her heartbeat was in her head. Her breathing in her ears. Never been drunk like this before. Her head tilted. Throat tightened. Nodding dog on the back shelf. Come on, blink, suck in the air. She lurched to the side, clicked on the intercom and thought she said: 'My drink's been spiked.' But the words, shapeless, fell to her feet.

'Don't worry, love,' said the cabbie. 'You're all right.'

I'm all right? she thought, face crushed into the seat, staring at the carpet, mouth slack. If I'm all right, what do ill people feel like? Dad? What's that, Dad?

'Always take a cab in London after eleven o'clock, a black cab, mind, none of those furry dashboard minicabs driven by those Bangladeshi bastards.'

What do *you* know? You're in Mumbai. I'm here in the Smoke. In the black …

Coffin dark. The only light from the demi migraine splitting her cranium. She blinked twice, confirming eyelid mobility and a total absence of illumination. She ran her hands over the seat; it was the same ribbed seat of the cab she'd taken, but it wasn't moving. She couldn't see the hands of her Cartier watch. No idea how much time had passed. She felt for the door. Stuff slopped to and fro in her head. It was locked. She fingered around the window for cracks. Knelt on the floor, spidered her hands over the sliding window of the driver's compartment. Shut. Immovable. The first tremble of panic fluttered beneath her rib cage. The other door. Locked. Window shut.

She listened, eyes wide open, trying to tune into the faintest sound. Nothing. She put her hand to her mouth; the fingers trembled on her lips and her breath pattered with the hyperventilation of phobia. A sudden surge of adrenaline through her system cleared the mess from her mind. She was no longer drunk. Her thighs quivered in her kneeling position. She tried to calm what was building inside her but couldn't. It was multiplying too fast, rapidly becoming unmanageable, bursting up from her lungs, screeching in her ears, and with a bright flash of light that illuminated nothing, she hurled herself at the window, threw herself to the other side, lashed out with her feet and fists and screamed so loud her larynx shredded.

Four cracks of light appeared around a door next to the cab. It must be in a garage joined to a house. The door opened. Light flooded into the dark interior and froze her solid. She waited, transfixed. Two silhouettes. Male. Heads shaved. One of the men split to the other side of the cab. She leaned back, sat up on the seat, clenched her fists, got her high heels ready. Knees up to her chest. Elbows braced against the back of the seat. Lips tight across her sharp white teeth. The faces floating outside were wearing white plastic smiling masks. She'd seen them before somewhere and they terrified her.

The doors' locks shunted back. Hands came in from either side.

She kicked out with one leg, then the other. Heard one of them grunt with pain. It motivated her. Until she felt her foot in the other man's hand, a terrible grip which twisted her ankle so that she had to roll with it or have it torn off. He dragged her towards him. Her other leg trapped beneath her. He got her face down on the floor of the cab, both ankles secured, knees bent and heels jammed against her buttocks. He leaned over and grabbed her hair, pulled her head back until her throat was stretched so tight she couldn't even squeak. She lashed out with her fists. One was caught and then the other and forced behind her back. A man's crotch was now in her face. He pinned her wrists with one hand, reached into a pocket, put a handkerchief to her nose and mouth and her world narrowed and collapsed.

Two men, both tall, well-built, mid-thirties, eerily lit in the cab of a white transit van, crawled the streets of East London. The taller, slimmer one, who called himself Skin, was baby-faced, blue-eyed, with a shaved head. He was getting testy, kept straightening his white cap, which had panels of the Cross of St George on its sides and the West Ham United crest on its front. He was staring down at the map in the A-Z guide, which was flashing orange and black as they passed under the streetlights. The spider in the middle of the web tattooed on the side of his neck and up his right cheek seemed to be crawling into his ear. Dan, the driver, was a different breed: short hair, side-parting, blandly good-looking and neither pierced nor painted. It was only their second time working together.

'We're late,' he said calmly, looking left and right at street names.

'I know we're fucking late,' said Skin. 'What are we on now?'

'It looks like ... New Barn Street.'

'New Barn Street?' said Skin, perplexed. 'Where the fuck is that?'

'I can only tell you what it says on the street sign,' said Dan equably.

'Nobody likes a smart arse; remember that, Dan.'

'Just tell me where the fuck to go. We're coming up to the end of it now. Straight on? Left? Right?'

'Fuck should I know?'

'You're the one with the map.'

'How come we got no SatNav?'

'Give it here.' Dan ripped the book out of Skin's hands. 'You're not even on the right fucking page.'

'Once I'm east of Limehouse, I'm lost.'

Dan chucked the book into Skin's lap, eased across the road, carried on for a few hundred yards and turned left.

'Grange Road,' said Skin, as if it was hardly a miracle. 'I wasn't that far off.'

'What number?'

'The one with the cab outside it.'

'You didn't bring the number with you, did you?'

'Just look for the fucking cab.'

'The cab's going to be in the garage,' said Dan. 'That's what Pike told us.'

'Fuck. You fuck …'

Skin started rooting around in his pockets, came up with a piece of paper, gave the number. It was an end-of-terrace house. They reached the driveway. Dan reversed up to the garage door, turned off the lights.

'Right,' said Dan. 'Let's chill for a few minutes.'

'Put this on,' said Skin, throwing him a hood, chucking his West Ham cap in the glove compartment. 'Make sure you get the eye and mouth holes facing the right way.'

'Thanks for the instructions.'

'And cop hold of that.'

Dan looked down at a handgun with the fattened barrel of a suppressor attached.

'I thought we were just going to pick up the girl?' said Dan.

'You're the one asked Pike to work with me,' said Skin.

'He didn't say anything about *guns*.'

'This is what I do.'

'What?'

'Take care of things.'

'We don't need *guns* to pick up the girl. How am I going to hold a syringe *and* a gun?'

'You'll work it out,' said Skin. 'Take one of these 'n' all.'

He handed Dan a ligature.

'Jesus Christ.'

'And put these on,' said Skin, handing him a pair of latex gloves.

'What's this all about?' said Dan, dangling the ligature.

'If we get any trouble, the guns'll shut them up, make them concentrate and, if we have to, you know, Pike said he didn't want any noise or mess, so we use these.'

'Them?' said Dan. 'I thought Pike said that we were going to meet the cabbie. He hands over the girl, I sedate her and we leave. Give him five grand down and the other five to come later.'

'That's what he said to *you*,' said Skin, snapping on the gloves. 'What he told *me* was that he hadn't done business with the cabbie before and we should take precautions in case he's got other ideas.'

'Other ideas?'

'Other friends who don't want to give us the girl and want to hold out for more money. The cabbie is connected ... know what I mean?'

'Shit,' said Dan, seeing the whole thing reeling out of control.

'Take it. Stop being a fucking fairy.'

Dan stuffed the ligature in his pocket, put the gun inside his jacket. They pulled on the hoods, got out the van and walked down the side of the garage to the back door.

Three men sat around a table: two plastic horror masks on elastic, a clogged ashtray, a thermos flask and two Styrofoam cups of crap coffee. The cabbie didn't allow drinking on the job. Things always went wrong, especially with a pretty girl involved. He'd caught the younger one having a good look up her skirt and got the older one, who spoke a few words of English, to explain that he'd have none of that. He looked at them now in silence. They were illegals, these two. Tough, stocky little bastards from Fuckknowswhere-istan. They had round, shorn heads, all scarred and dented, probably from some mad horse game they played on the steppes or, more likely, prison violence. The younger one looked unconcussable – a word he'd invented for the numbskulls that found their way to his door.

'Long time?' said the one who spoke a little English, cracked plaster caked down the front of his sweatshirt.

The cabbie didn't answer. Glanced at his watch and the curtained window. Yes, late.

The young one nudged his mate. The older one leaned forward, rubbed thumb and forefinger together in the cabbie's face. The cabbie licked his lips with a white-coated tongue, which did not darken them. He held up his forefinger. The gesture dumbfounded them and they communicated in gobbledygook for a full minute. The cabbie sat back, certain now that 'bollocks', minus its vowels, was the same in their two wildly differing languages. He batted his hands down as if calming a couple of kettle drums.

'They'll be here in a tick and you'll get what's coming to you,' he said, smiling, grey teeth all crossed at the bottom. 'More moolah than you've seen since your sisters' weddings.'

The words fell onto their nicked and dented heads like debris from a shattered piggy bank. They searched the fragments for valuables and found nothing. They talked at length. The cabbie looked from one to the other with a face of practiced cheer. He'd learned to love listening to foreigners over the past two decades in London, fascinated by how each race dug the words out. Arabs reaching down their throats as if they might gag on them. Indians bubbling away as if speaking Welsh underwater. Chinese fizzing, popping and wowing like indoor fireworks. These two sounded like goats farting in a field.

'Money,' said the older one, reaching out a hand, beckoning the cash forward.

A van pulled up outside. After some minutes, two doors opened and shut, footsteps down the side of the house. The cabbie got up, pulled the door to behind him, but it eased open, so that the backs of the two illegals were visible from the kitchen, where he unlocked the rear door.

'All right?' said Skin, face now hooded, with just eye and mouth holes.

'Took your time,' said the cabbie, taking in their white latex gloves.

'Any trouble?' asked Skin.

'Who from?'

'Who do you think?' said Skin, looking down the corridor, seeing the illegals. 'And who the fuck are *they*?'

'The help for when you're late.'

'Pike didn't say anything about … help.'

'I know he didn't, but I couldn't carry her on my own and she went nuts when she came round.'

'Where is she?' asked Skin.

'In the back room.'

'*How* is she?' asked Dan.

'Haven't looked for the last fifteen minutes,' said the cabbie. 'She was asleep.'

'Did you use chloroform on her?'asked Dan.

'I had to. She went nuts. Must be claustrophobic or something.'

Dan kept glancing up the corridor at the two illegals, who were talking.

'I'm going to have to call Pike,' said Skin.

'Fucking hell,' said Dan, under his breath.

Skin pulled Dan out with him, made the phone call, had a muttered conversation, Dan waiting, looking as if he wanted a piss. Skin hung up, drew a finger across his neck. Dan felt his guts shudder, mouthed: 'Fuck'.

They eased out the silenced hand guns from inside their black coats, went back into the house, holding them down by their sides.

'What the fuck is this?' said the cabbie, seeing them immediately.

'Wake the girl. Get her ready,' said Skin, taking him by the arm, pushing him up the corridor.

'Ready for what?'

'To go. What do you think?'

'What are you going to do with the guns?' he asked.

'You didn't follow the fucking instructions,' said Skin, red lips from within the black cloth hole. 'Now we've got our orders. Wake the girl.'

'For fuck's sake,' said the cabbie.

'Just do it,' said Skin, and pushed the cabbie towards the bedroom door.

The illegals turned and stood as Skin and Dan came in, to have their expectations suddenly reduced to a small black hole in a fat barrel, which kept coming until it was the eye's whole universe. White latex hands collared them, hauled them away from their chairs. They kicked the illegals to their knees, denting the undulating lino floor, the fat barrels pressed hard into the fuzz of their shorn heads. The illegals looked up, eyes desperate, lips drawn bloodless across their teeth, breathing quick as they realised their true value in the system that had brought them to the black, glittering mouth of the insatiable metropolis. Skin and Dan pulled the ligatures from their pockets, slipped the guns back inside their coats and looped the cords over the shorn heads of the men kneeling before them, tightened them around their necks. The cabbie closed the bedroom door behind him.

Alyshia was still asleep. The noise from the next room woke her. The fear came alive in her as soon as she saw the cabbie. The whites of her eyes quivered at the edges as she looked at the door. The animal noise of a terrible struggle came through it. She started as something thudded against the other side. The cabbie held onto his head with both hands, looking at the ceiling.

'What's going on?' she asked, her voice barely audible.

The cabbie didn't answer. Through the grunting and gasping of effort came the noise of heels clawing against lino. Then a rigid, pent-up silence, followed by a collapse. The cabbie let his hands drop to his sides, shook his head. Alyshia, back against the wall, stared unblinking at the door. No sound.

'All right,' said the cabbie, who couldn't wait any longer. 'Let's get you out of here.'

He opened the door. The room had filled with a shocking stink.

'Not yet, you fucking moron,' said Skin.

Alyshia saw the hooded men, looked down at the dead illegals' swollen faces, their new horror masks. She vomited. The cabbie pulled her back into the room.

'Get her cleaned up,' said Skin. 'Got anything we can roll these two up in?'

'In the garage,' said the cabbie. 'There's some plastic tarps.'

Dan left the room, staggered to the garage, dazed by what he'd just done. He came back with the tarpaulins. They rolled the illegals into them, secured them at both ends, coughing against the stink in the room. They took them into the garage. Dan went out the back and down the side of the house, checked the street. Empty. He tapped on the garage, opened the rear of the transit.

They lifted the bodies into the back, closed the doors, went back for the girl.

The cabbie had opened the window in the room and the stink was leaving, but slowly, because of the thickness of the blinds.

'Shouldn't have done that 'n' all,' said Skin. 'You're not paying attention to the fucking instructions.'

'Yes, well, I didn't know that was on the cards, did I?' said the cabbie. 'You got my money?'

Skin handed him a fat envelope. They went into the bedroom. Alyshia's skirt and blouse were on the floor, streaked with vomit and topped by a brown blur of tights. She looked up from the bed in bra and knickers, the fear streaming out of her.

'You got the alarm code to her flat?' asked Dan.

The cabbie shook his head, counting the money. Skin and Dan looked to Alyshia. She gave them the code. Skin made a call, gave the number, hung up.

'Get us a plastic bag for her things,' said Dan.

The cabbie went to the kitchen, came back with a bag, put Alyshia's discarded clothes in it. Dan removed a small black box from his pocket, took out a capped syringe filled with a clear liquid. Alyshia pressed herself against the wall and whimpered as he flicked the air out of it, eased off the cap.

'You done this before?' asked the cabbie, looking over Dan's shoulder.

'First time,' said Dan, rolling his eyes.

'I'll be quiet,' said Alyshia. 'Just don't …'

'This'll keep you nice and relaxed,' said Dan, and then to the cabbie, who was now looking at him intently: 'You fancy a vodka-tini 'n' all?'

'Who's going to clean this shit up?'

'There wouldn't have been any shit to clear up,' said Skin, hooded face up close to the cabbie's, 'if you'd done what you was fucking told.'

2

'Business or pleasure?' asked the receptionist from behind the black granite counter, unable to wrench herself away from Charles Boxer's light green eyes, which she'd only ever seen before on gypsies. He looked foreign in his black leather jacket, faded jeans and black boots; not the usual business client.

A flicker of irritation as he relived being stood up at Heathrow airport. No pleasure and no business here for a freelance kidnap consultant, although he'd arranged to meet an old client later that evening.

'Leisure,' he said, smiling as he handed over his passport.

She filled in the form on screen, saw that he wasn't far off his fortieth birthday.

'You have a reservation for two people with breakfast included,' she said.

'Sorry, it's just going to be me now,' he said.

'No problem,' she said, smiling, and he liked her for that.

Some minutes later, Boxer was lying on one of the twin beds in his hotel room, staring at the ceiling, going over the phone call he'd had at the airport with his seventeen-year-old daughter, Amy.

'I'm not coming,' she said. 'Didn't Mum tell you?'

'What do you mean, you're not coming? Jesus Christ, Amy. We've planned this since Christmas and *now* you back out,' he said. 'And no, Mercy didn't tell me. I haven't spoken to her since Wednesday.'

'She was probably too busy getting ready for that course she's on this weekend. She told me to call you.'

12

'And you left it to the last minute.'

He could feel her shrugging at the other end of the line, knew her timing had been critical. He wasn't about to go back into town and drag her out, kicking and screaming. This was the usual Amy *fait accompli*.

'So what's this all about?' he asked.

'I've got to revise for my exams.'

'At Karen's house?' he said, easing back on the sarcasm.

'No, I'm just sleeping here. I'm working in my room at Mum's. Call her. She'll tell you. We had it all agreed before she left.'

'But not with me,' said Boxer. 'And you know as well as I do that she's out of mobile contact until the course is over.'

'Oh yeah, right.'

'And what am I going to do with your hundred and fifty quid ticket to Lisbon?'

Silence. Aggression started coming over the airwaves. It didn't take much these days.

'You know why I didn't want to come?' she said, winding up to deliver.

'You said. Your exams. Although I don't remember you being such an assiduous student.'

'That's because you're never around.'

'Which was why we were going away together for the weekend.'

'Was it?'

'It was.'

'The reason I didn't want to come is that I knew you were going to leave me all night to go and play in one of your stupid card games.'

'That was absolutely *not* my intention.'

'So why did you book a hotel in the Parque das Nações, rather than in the centre of Lisbon?'

'First, because it's near an old client of mine, Bruno Dias, who wants to meet you, and second, because it's close to the Oceanarium, where you said you wanted to go.'

'Bullshit.'

'It is.'

'I looked it up online and, you know what, it's even closer to the Lisbon Casino. A hundred metres, I'd say, and I know you:

13

you'd come back at seven in the morning, in a good mood if you'd won and a bummer if you'd lost,' she said. 'And that was not how I wanted to spend my weekend: everything dependent on how the cards went for *you*.'

Boxer swung his legs off the bed, rested his elbows on his knees. The black hole was back, about fist-sized in his centre. He'd felt it there since he was a seven-year-old when his father had left him, disappeared, never to come back, never to contact him ever again. It was the rejection hole. Over the years he'd got it down to a point where he almost believed it had disappeared. But recently he'd found he had less control over it, especially where Amy was concerned. She was the one who could open it out in him with a look, a line, a curl of lip, and he'd feel the dark, swirling emptiness of something lost.

It was like this now. Eighteen months ago he'd given up his salaried job as a kidnap consultant with GRM, the private security company that ran seventy per cent of worldwide kidnap negotiations, in order to go freelance and give himself more time to spend with his daughter. And that had been the start of it. The loss of that corporate structure and the camaraderie of close colleagues seemed to have done something to his mind. Freed it up in a way – a bad way.

Amy had responded to his new ubiquitousness by reminding him for how much of her short life he'd consistently *not* been around. Standing him up for this weekend in Lisbon was her way of telling him that his little sweeteners were no recompense for more than fifteen years of abandonment. What opened up the black hole was that she was right.

He'd done mental battle with his inability to connect with her, thinking it was because he was too used to being a loner, holed up in Mexico City, Bogota or Karachi, reading thrillers, playing cards, waiting for a gang's next move. Now he knew it was far more dangerous than that; this feeling, the deadliness of it, and what he had to do to make it go away. Or nearly go away.

He needed help.

He had to learn a new way of being.

But not tonight. That was too much for tonight.

*

'How d'you like that?' said Skin, furious, Hammers cap back on, taking rip drags from his cigarette, cornered against the door of the van, foot up on the dashboard.

Dan said nothing, drove, still shaken from his first killing. Why did it have to be strangulation? He still had the feeling of it in his hands and forearms.

'Not "thank you very much for delivering the girl in perfect condition". Not "thank you very much for killing the two sheep who weren't in your fucking contract". Not "thank you very much for remembering to get the alarm code to the bitch's flat". Not "thank you very much for putting the whatsitsname in her arm". No. It's "fuck off and get shot of the mutton … and be careful about it". I fuckin' hate that.'

'What?' said Dan, barely thinking, irritated by Skin's ridiculous outrage.

'Offing people when I'm not jacked up for it,' said Skin.

'Right,' said Dan, thinking: 'offing people', is that what I do now? Why did I do that? 'It's called a cannula, by the way … the whatsitsname.'

'And where did you learn that fancy needlework?' asked Skin. 'You a junkie or what?'

Silence from Dan as they crossed the Royal Albert Dock, him thinking how easily he'd stepped over the line. What had made him do that?

'Hey, fucker?' said Skin. 'It's just you and me.'

Dan looked across at him and back out through the windscreen.

'I used to be a nurse,' he said.

Skin guffawed, took his cap off, scratched his shaved head with a thumbnail.

'You're a big fucker for a nurse.'

'You should have seen the girls,' said Dan.

'Fuck me,' said Skin, shaking his head. 'How d'you end up in this game?'

Good question.

'Had a girlfriend in the club scene, with a bunch of celebrity friends into prescription drugs. I lifted them, she flogged them until … *I* got caught. Did three years in Wandsworth. So here I am: in *this* game.'

'Ah right, is that where you met Pike?' asked Skin. 'He had the Royal Suite in Wandsworth.'

'I administered his daily medication,' said Dan. 'He didn't want some harebrained junkie doing it for him.'

Skin chuckled, playing with that bit of gossip in his head.

'Still see the girlfriend?' he asked.

'What do *you* think?' said Dan, making a big 'O' with his thumb and forefinger. 'That's how many times she came to see me inside. Anyway, where are we going to dump these two?'

'The only place I know,' said Skin. 'Keep going up here, take a right onto Barking Road.'

'I thought you were lost east of Limehouse.'

'I'll tell you when we get there,' said Skin, enjoying himself. 'No speeding. Don't want the cops stopping us with this lot in the back.'

'By the way, d'you know who she is?'

'Who?' asked Skin.

'The girl we just delivered.'

'No,' said Skin. 'She was pretty tasty, mind. Not Pike's normal line of work. You reckon he's moving into the sex business? Trafficking girls? There's money in that.'

'What do you know?'

'Been to a house in Forest Gate a few times. Nice girls from Moldova or Moldavia. I dunno. Belorussia. Those kind of places. Can't speak a word of English, mind. Who does with their mouth full?'

Dan looked across at him slowly, not impressed. Skin laughed to himself.

'Take a right under the flyover,' he said. 'Don't go up on it. There's a little road right next to ... that's the one.'

They drove past some factory buildings, the odd car flashing past on the flyover.

'Take a left here and pull up on the bridge,' said Skin.

Dan turned, slowed and stopped. They sat in silence. Dan still wrestling with himself. Skin leaning forward. The peak of his cap pecking at the windscreen.

'Now let's take a good look around,' he said. 'A gander. That's what my old man used to say. Let's take a gander.'

'I thought a gander was a *quick* look,' said Dan.

'You know fucking everything, don't you, Nurse?'

'I'd get shot of the cap if I was you,' said Dan.

Skin tossed it in the glove. They got out the van. No cars.

'What's this?' asked Dan, looking over the rail of the bridge, shivering.

'Don't know, but it ends up going past the Beckton Sewage Works,' said Skin. 'Looks clear to me. Let's do it.'

They lifted the first body out, humped it up onto the rail, Skin grunting with effort, Dan breezing it.

'Hold these tarps back,' said Dan. 'Our prints are all over them now.'

They held onto the nylon ropes at the corners, rolled the body forward. The tarp unfurled. The body dropped with a loud splash.

'Fucking noise of that,' said Skin.

They did the same with the second body. Folded the tarpaulins, stuck them in the back. Glanced over the rail, the bodies not visible in the black water.

Back into the van. Dan pulled away while Skin flexed his biceps.

'I suppose you did a lot of that, you know, when you were a nurse,' said Skin.

'Dumping bodies in the river?' said Dan. 'Did it all the time.'

'No, you twat,' said Skin. 'Lifting bodies, you know, *Casualty* – one, two, three, hup.'

'I did weights when I was inside. Helped pass the time.'

They got back onto the Barking Road, heading home.

'I fuckin' *hate* that,' said Skin, cap back on, taking rip drags from another cigarette.

'What now?' asked Dan.

'Those two,' said Skin.

'You mean, if it can happen to them, it can happen to us?'

Skin shrugged.

'The difference being,' said Dan, hopefully, 'they're not missed.'

'They will be, by somebody, somewhere,' said Skin. 'The older one had plaster down his front. Means he's working, so ...'

'So what?'

'You ask me, this isn't over yet,' said Skin. 'Not by a long way.'

Boxer got the call from Bruno Dias just before midnight as he was finishing a plate of sashimi at a Japanese restaurant near the Oceanarium.

Ten minutes later, he was walking through the modern development that had grown up around the Expo ground and passing the black glass casino where he knew he'd end up later. He headed towards the swooping roof of the new railway station and one of the landmark towers of luxury apartments in front of it.

Bruno Dias was a Brazilian businessman who had been Boxer's second client as a freelance kidnap consultant for the private security company Pavis Risk Management. Boxer had conducted the kidnap negotiations for the return of Dias's seventeen-year-old daughter, Bianca. Everything seemed to have gone perfectly. The kidnappers had appeared to be calm and non-violent and only interested in the money. At six hundred thousand dollars, they'd agreed a ransom larger than Boxer would have liked to pay, but Dias had been desperate to settle. A final proof of life had been received and verified. Dias's brother had driven Boxer out of São Paulo and dropped him at the side of a country road. The chief kidnapper had directed him to a deserted farm building where he'd left the money.

In the two hours after the ransom delivery, Bianca had been brutally raped, beaten and left for dead on a deserted stretch of road a few hours outside São Paulo, where she was found by a labourer the following morning. Subsequently, two of the gang were caught, tried and given life imprisonment in a Brazilian jail, where sex offenders were not tolerated by the other inmates. They survived less than six months. The third, who the other two had named as Diogo Chaves, was never found and it was assumed he'd fled the country with the money, had plastic surgery and disappeared.

Boxer took the lift up to the eighteenth floor of the São Rafael Tower where the maid was waiting for him. She took him into the stupendous living room, whose glass walls showed the lights of the city spilling out towards the leathery blackness of the Tagus. The glowing causeway of the Vasco da Gama bridge stretched out across the wide river estuary towards the far glittering shore of

Montijo in the south. Dias dismissed the maid and the two men embraced. They'd become very close during the kidnap because of their daughters' similar ages and Boxer's evident empathy and willingness to stay up drinking late into the night. Dias had been adamant that no blame should be attached to Boxer for what had happened; rather, he seemed to take all that on himself.

The last sixteen months had not been kind to Bruno Dias. His fitness regime had been unable to iron out the care that had piled into his face from the moment Bianca had been taken. He went to the drinks tray and poured a whisky on the rocks for Boxer and a brandy for himself. They stood in front of the glass doors, looking out onto a wooden-decked terrace.

'How's Bianca?' asked Boxer.

'No improvement. She's still in a wheelchair, can't move from the waist down,' said Dias, shaking his head at his ghostly reflection in the sliding doors. 'She hasn't said anything coherent either. I'm told it's psychological. She could come out of it. She might not. We're doing everything we can. She's just had a whole bunch of neurological tests at the UCLA Medical Center in Santa Monica. We're waiting for their findings.'

'I'm sorry, Bruno,' said Boxer, resting his hand on the tall Brazilian's back. 'There isn't a day that goes by that I don't think about her. She's one of those that never leaves me.'

'Where's Amy?' said Dias, to change the subject. 'I thought she was coming with you?'

''Fraid not. Pressure of exams,' said Boxer. 'Apart from that, she's fine.'

Dias checked him in the dark glass, didn't believe him.

'We're going through a difficult time,' said Boxer, giving in.

'Be thankful,' said Dias, putting an arm around Boxer's shoulders.

'I know, I should be.'

Silence. The wind buffeted around the high apartment. Dias withdrew his arm, sipped his drink, breathed in. He was gathering himself as if there was something big inside that he needed to get out.

'I didn't tell you,' he said, 'and I wasn't going to mention it because I thought Amy would be with you. I was here on business last September. I went out jogging one morning, down by the river. I'd just gone past the Camões theatre and there were some people sitting outside a café having breakfast. There was a guy on his own, smoking a cigarette and drinking a *bica*. You know who it was?'

Boxer shook his head, not ready to believe it.

'Diogo Chaves,' said Dias, nodding. 'The only change to his appearance was a moustache and goatee. I tripped, almost dashed my brains out on the cobbles.'

'You told the police?'

'I had to be sure,' said Dias. 'So I brought one of my security people over from São Paulo, Cristina Santos. She found out everything about the man I'd seen, got to know him. He has a nice apartment overlooking the river above the café where I first saw him, which he owns. He wasn't working, didn't need to, and he'd changed his name but, luckily for me, his face not quite enough.'

'And what are you going to do about it, Bruno?'

'I've seen him again, you know,' said Dias, turning to Boxer, sidestepping his question. 'I've been as close to that son of a bitch as we are now.'

'How's he doing?'

'It's a relief to find that tainted money stains the new owner's life with a bitterness they barely understand,' said Dias. 'I'm told the least of his problems is that he misses home.'

'Cristina got that close?'

'The poor little bastard's fallen in love; sees her as his saviour.'

'What about extradition? There must be an agreement between Brazil and Portugal.'

Dias moved away from the window, drank some more of his brandy, helped himself to a cigar from a box on the drinks table and took a seat in a white leather armchair.

'What do you see when you look at me, Charlie?'

Boxer squinted at him, as if down a gun sight; appraised him... kindly.

'An urbane, successful, handsome man – who's been profoundly hurt by what's happened to his daughter.'

'Not just hurt, Charlie. Ruined. I am not the same man. My wife knows it,' said Dias. 'Everybody knows it. And you know what's ruined me?'

Boxer nodded. After his Gulf tours in the army, he had an understanding of men who'd survived extreme experiences. It wasn't just their faces that were creased. If he were a believing man, he'd say their souls had shrivelled, too.

'You thought you were a civilised man,' said Boxer.

'It's been a terrible lesson,' he said, nodding. 'To find myself as bitter as Diogo Chaves.'

'And how did you get yourself into that state?'

'I blame myself for what happened. I'm tortured by what I might have done in my life that could have made these men do that to my little girl. I've asked myself too many unanswerable questions and I'm smaller inside for it,' said Dias. 'You didn't know me before. I was a happy guy, but now ...'

Dias clenched his fist, gritted his teeth.

'So, what are you going to do about Diogo Chaves?'

'You remember one of our conversations back in São Paulo, about retribution?' said Dias, clipping the end off the cigar.

'I might do.'

'You told me that the only shortcoming of your job was that you got the hostage back and then left. You were never involved in any retribution. The victims and families had their closure, but there was none for you. You never saw the criminals punished. Isn't that right?'

'Something along those lines,' said Boxer, remembering their talks long into the night, but not the detail. 'I probably told you that most victims don't like to testify. They just want to get on with their lives. But the problem with kidnappers is that once they've felt the *easiness* of that money, they always do it again.'

Dias leaned forward, put his glass down on the table and stared intently into Boxer's eyes.

'Exactly,' he said. 'How would you like to make sure that Diogo Chaves never does it again?'

Silence. The poker player in Boxer suppressed the jolt of adrenaline that whitened into his bloodstream. That *was* something he wanted. Or worse, since leaving GRM and finding this dark hole opening up inside him more frequently, *needed*. But he'd learnt something about his terrible cravings: never snatch.

'I think it should be *you* who goes to the police,' said Boxer, playing it carefully.

'I'm not talking about the police,' said Dias, leaning back, lighting his cigar with a gold Zippo. 'I'm talking about *you* … taking Chaves out.'

He snapped the Zippo shut, puffed on the cigar.

'What makes you think I'd be prepared to do that, Bruno?' he asked calmly.

'I have a friend, a Russian businessman. You did a job for someone he knows. He told me that you got this guy's son back unharmed from a gang in Kiev, and then you followed up on some information he received about a Ukrainian member of that same gang who was later found frozen to death in a forest outside Archangel.'

'He was inappropriately dressed for the conditions he found himself in,' said Boxer.

'Look, Charlie, you know what I'm talking about,' said Dias. 'I'd do it myself if I could, but I'm not up to it.'

Boxer wondered if Bruno Dias was expecting this to make him feel better. The Brazilian misinterpreted his silence.

'I don't expect you to do it for nothing.'

'I wouldn't be doing it for nothing,' said Boxer. 'I told you, Bianca is on my mind every day.'

'What about your charitable foundation?'

'How do you know about that?' said Boxer.

'It's out there in the ether somewhere,' said Dias, waving his cigar vaguely. 'The LOST Foundation. You help people find missing persons when the police have given up. Is that world-wide?'

'Just the UK at the moment,' said Boxer. 'I only have two ex-police officers working for me right now. I need more funding to be able to go worldwide.'

'What sort of contribution would you be looking for?' asked Dias.

'I need more trained investigators,' said Boxer, letting Dias make his assumptions. 'I also need a proper office.'

'How about two hundred square metres of office space in a quiet mews off Marylebone High Street?'

'Unimaginable.'

'Start imagining,' said Dias, hunched forward now. 'Do we have a deal?'

Boxer blinked, swallowed hard. Each time he'd found himself in this situation, he'd tried to analyse what was driving him across the line. He knew it was something to do with his father, what his father had done, but there was always a gap, an abyss over which the logic could never leap.

'What about access to Diogo Chaves and ... method?' said Boxer. 'I'm not exactly prepared.'

Dias left the room. Boxer turned to see his reflection in the window. As always, he couldn't quite believe what was happening to him, but was powerless to stop it. He switched his mind into professional mode as Dias returned with a roll of plans, a small box and a briefcase that had weight.

'These are the plans to Diogo Chaves' apartment,' said Dias, enthused by his project, unrolling the plans and then flicking open the box. 'This is the key to the building and this is the key to his apartment.'

'Your security woman, Cristina?'

'She's very thorough. Chaves is a creature of habit. He goes drinking every Friday and Saturday night in a Brazilian bar called Ipanema, on Rua do Bojador on the river front. He stays until late, three in the morning usually, and he walks back along the river to his apartment. He never gets up before midday at the weekends.'

'Photo?'

'This is a recent photo taken in the café underneath his apartment,' said Dias.

'Are you expecting me to do this *tonight*, Bruno?'

'Now that your daughter's not with you, I was thinking ... why not?' said Dias. 'Tonight, or tomorrow night?'

'No weapon.'

Dias opened the briefcase, took out a box, which held a Glock 17 and an AAC Evolution 9mm suppressor.

'I understand that this is one of the handguns used by the British police's authorised firearms officers,' said Dias. 'You don't have to use it, but I'm sure it will get Diogo Chaves' attention if you do.'

'Let me look at the plans again. I don't want to take those with me.'

Boxer memorised the layout, pocketed the keys.

'I'll do a recce tonight,' said Boxer. 'Check him out in the Ipanema, see how he behaves.'

'I hope I didn't ruin your weekend.'

'That's already ruined.'

They walked to the door, Boxer with the briefcase.

'Is there anything you want me to bring ... from Chaves?' asked Boxer.

'No, nothing physical,' said Dias. 'But you might ask him why he had to ruin my daughter's life.'

Flat One, 14 Lavender Grove, Dalston, London E8, in the Borough of Hackney, was silent until a key entered the lock, the door opened and a man dressed in black clicked on his headlamp and disabled the alarm. The flat was warm after the chill of sub-zero outside. The man moved quickly to the bedroom at the back.

The light from his headlamp wandered over some photographs on the wall and stopped at an old movie poster. The light travelled from the face, down the lithe body of a handsome Indian man in a white shirt and trousers, teeth to match, charisma blasting from every pore, with eyes staring down the sight of a revolver held out in front of him. His stage name, Anadi Kapoor, was emblazoned beneath.

The intruder moved in closer, focusing the light on a shot alongside of the same man, but taken twenty years later in his early fifties. His hair was still black but the body had thickened and was now encased in an expensive grey suit, open white shirt, gold chain around the neck. Despite gravity's terrible work, the face was still handsome, the charisma intact and the eyes still had it, which was why, but maybe not the only why, holding onto his arm was a stunning Indian woman three inches taller. She was dressed in an ivory blouse, with the tops of her breasts exposed, a short skirt and high heels that accentuated the length of her slim legs. In front of them were two young children, who stared ahead like two little sphinxes.

This same man appeared in another photo wearing a DJ, but

this time accompanied by a white woman with long, dark, wavy hair, rather girlish for her age of around forty. She was wearing a ball gown. In between them was a very beautiful honey-coloured girl in a long black dress and a dazzling necklace. On the frame of this photograph was a small brass plaque engraved with the words, *On the occasion of the 21st Birthday of Alyshia D'Cruz*. A latex-gloved hand tapped the glass over Alyshia's abdomen. *That* was the outfit he wanted.

The beam of light shifted around the room to the fitted wardrobe. He opened the doors, ran his hands over the clothes hanging in desolate flaps, until at one end he found several full length dresses. In a plastic dry cleaner's sheath was the same black dress from the photograph. He draped it over the bed.

He went through the drawers in the chest by the bed, sorting through the underwear until he found exactly what he wanted. He put the matching strapless black bra and knickers on top of the dress. He returned to the drawers but couldn't find what he was looking for. He searched under the bed, lifted the mattress, crawled around the room, peering and feeling under the furniture. Nothing. He went back to the fitted wardrobe. Instinct was telling him that, for psychological reasons, she would keep it here rather than in a safe-deposit box.

Underneath the clothes in the wardrobe were ranks of plastic shoe boxes. He went through each one, removing the shoes and feeling around inside the box before replacing them. At the bottom he found a pair of old, scuffed Ugg boots with their tops turned over. He felt inside the left boot and found it. A slim box with the words *Asprey London* printed in gold on the top. Inside was the diamond necklace from the 21st birthday photograph. He slipped the box into his pocket, replaced the Uggs, chose a pair of black, strappy, high-heeled Prada shoes, which he put with the lingerie, and rolled them up in the plastic sheath around the black dress. He gave the room a final check and left.

A sucking sound in her ears. A sense of being dragged down into a vortex but without spinning and, with a deep intake of breath, Alyshia came awake into the velvet blackness pressed to her face. She picked her head up off the coarse cotton of the pillow and wiped the drool from the corner of her mouth. She breathed back the nausea, brought a hand tentatively to her face and touched the sleeping mask.

A calm yet commanding voice, which had been amplified and distorted, said, 'Don't touch. Hand back down by your side.'

She responded immediately. Realised as she rested her wrist on her hip, on the waistband of her knickers, that there was something taped to her arm: a cannula. And she had no tights. She still had her bra on but her Cartier watch was gone and her feet were bare. She remembered vomiting down herself and what had caused it. She shuddered at the memory of the two purple, bug-eyed faces.

'How are you feeling?' asked the voice.

'Sick and disorientated,' she said. 'And I need to go to the loo.'

'Everything has to be earned.'

'Earned?'

'Yes, earned. I know it's not a concept the entitlement generation are familiar with,' said the voice. 'Now roll over onto your back, rest your hands on your stomach. Breathe evenly and deeply.'

'I'd like some clothes. I'm cold,' she said, but she wasn't, she just didn't like to be this vulnerable.

'You can't be cold, it's twenty-five degrees in the room,' said the voice. 'Stop whining and do as you're told.'

'I'd like a sheet.'

'Everything has to be earned.'

'Then tell me how I earn these things.'

'By answering questions.'

She thought about this. Privilege had given her a natural resistance to control by others. On the other hand, she needed to pee. Adapt. Fight from a position of comfort.

'OK, this is for the right to go to the loo.'

'Tell me something that only you or your mother could possibly know.'

The request made her emotional. Despite their recent difficulties, the idea of her mother being drawn into whatever this business was choked her up. She swallowed it down, felt she shouldn't show her feelings at this early stage. She concentrated on her breathing. Tried to bring some analysis to bear on what the voice wanted from her.

'Is that difficult?' asked the voice. 'We only need it for proof of capture. It will help to keep her calm.'

She hated the calculation in the voice, could feel a belligerence rising in her throat.

A door opened. Feet crossed the floor grittily. She flinched. Her hands were torn from her stomach and cuffed to the metal bar above her head. Someone else cuffed her ankles to the corners. The feet retreated. The door closed. Her exposure and helplessness doubled her vulnerability.

'Piss the bed, Alyshia. Lie in your own urine until it dries,' said the voice. 'And then your next question will be for a wash and the one after that for a fresh pair of panties. Do yourself a favour.'

'I call my boss "The Sacred Cow".'

'Not good enough,' said the voice. 'Anybody could know that. I want something deeply personal between you and your mother. Think.'

She didn't want to reveal personal things to this voice. She wanted to keep them inside, for her own strength.

'It's just so that we can prove to her without a shadow of doubt that you are alive and well,' said the voice. 'It's a part of the process.'

'What process?'

'The kidnap process.'

'You mean for ransom?'

'Well, ransom is rather a simplistic way of putting it,' said the voice. 'You've probably realised from the elements of the process that you've experienced so far that we're not in this for a few hundred thousand.'

'So what *are* you in it for?'

'You're trying to earn your right to go for a pee, if I remember correctly,' said the voice. 'You're very close to your mother, aren't you? Or at least you were. You still see her once a week. You're due there for lunch tomorrow. I think she should know that you're in good hands before you put in an uncharacteristic no-show.'

'If I don't show,' said Alyshia, 'and I don't answer my mobile, my mother will go straight to the police.'

'Well, there's some extra motivation for you.'

'Why?'

'If your mother goes to the police, we'll have to kill you,' said the voice. '*You'll* be all right because you'll be dead. Maybe your father will be able to handle it because he's got a new family now. But your mother? I think it would destroy her.'

'My mother's mother is Portuguese,' said Alyshia. 'The Portuguese for granny is *vovó*. She's always had a lot of energy, so when I was small I called her *vo-vó-voom*.'

It was two-thirty in the morning but he wasn't tired. The players agreed to take a break. Boxer went for the door.

'That's some pretty good cards you been getting, Charlie,' said Don, the American. 'Where d'you get them from?'

'Down my boots, Don,' said Boxer. 'The old tricks are the best.'

'Yeah, right. Don't you run away now.'

'Just going to breathe some air, Don. Back in half an hour.'

He left the other players smoking and drinking small bitumen coffees in the bar of the private room hired by the syndicate, and went out into the cold night air. Almost as if to spite Amy's absence, the cards had been good to him. He checked his watch, walked fast down the Alameda dos Oceanos, turned left towards the river, cut diagonally in front of the ticket office to the Oceanarium, through some gardens to the Camões theatre and along the river to Diogo Chaves' apartment building. Seven minutes.

He opened the front door, confirmed Dias' security woman's report that there were no cameras, went up to the first floor and listened hard at the apartment door. Nothing. He let himself in. No alarm system, no security chain. He moved through the rooms, committing the furniture to memory. He checked the sliding doors to the balcony, the railings around it and the drop. He preferred to do it inside but there was nothing suitable. He went into the hall and noticed that the ceiling there was lower than in the living room and bedrooms.

The light from Boxer's mobile phone found the tell-tale lines in the ceiling, three metres from the front door. He took a step ladder from the kitchen, opened the trap into a narrow crawl space. He heaved himself up with the mobile phone in his mouth. At the back were two empty suitcases and a used shoebox packed with $50 bills in sheaves. What was left of the ransom? He took a note of several serial numbers. Finally he found what he was looking for: a steel rod, partially exposed from the concrete.

Five minutes and he had everything back to normal and was outside on the path next to the river. There was nobody around. He jogged, keeping to the river. Skeletal cable cars hung empty in the dark, swaying in the wind, ghostly and threatening as he made for the huge sea-slug dome of the Atlantic Pavilion. He felt driven, all doubt as to the madness of this mission banished from his mind. He didn't notice the black hole in his centre anymore.

Ten minutes later he was at the Ipanema, listening to the music of Bebel Gilberto and drinking whisky on the rocks. Diogo Chaves was at a table with a group of lively Brazilians, sucking on a caipirinha, which looked as if it was his tenth of the night. His laughter was delayed by the fuzziness in his brain. The slackness of his face meant that his smile never completely made it. His eyes were rheumy and charcoal-smudged. The group suddenly got up, said their goodbyes. Chaves was still struggling out of his seat as they all left and dispersed out of the door in both directions. By the time he got outside he was alone for the walk home. He stuck his hands in his pockets and set off into the dark, drifting down to the river in the direction of his apartment. Five minutes later, Boxer was back in his seat at the poker table.

'Nice of you to show, Charlie,' said the American, looking at his watch. 'You had me worried.'

'What sort of a person do you take me for, Don?' said Boxer.

'I don't know, Charlie. I ain't never been able to read you.'

3

Isabel Marks was shopping for food for her lunch party on Sunday. Two writers from her publishing house were coming with their wives. A case of Bourgogne Aligoté and another of a Portuguese red called Cortes de Cima, along with two bottles of Taylor's twenty-year-old tawny port, had already been delivered to her Kensington home. She'd bought a bottle of cachaça and a bag of limes to make the opening caipirinhas in a way that would, hopefully, give the party a lift without smacking the uninitiated into catatonia. It seemed like a lot of drink but, in her experience, Sunday lunch parties in London with writers, who didn't have to be up early on a Monday morning, expanded to consume the hours and booze available.

She'd also invited Jason Bigley. He was a young screenwriter who'd tried to persuade her to take on his new serial killer novel but she already had five women on her list turning out horrors like that and she didn't need any more. He was, however, good-looking and she'd always been a sucker on that score and she hoped, in that hopeless, motherly way, that Alyshia might take to him.

No, she thought, be honest with yourself: she'd sniff Jason Bigley out in seconds.

Isabel had an uncomfortable understanding of Alyshia's taste in men, which she wanted to change. There had been very few, as far as she knew, but the ones she'd seen had not exactly been eligible. Initially, she'd had high hopes for Julian, a PhD student from Oxford, until she saw a photo and could tell from his sheer arrogance that he was bad news. Fortunately he'd been dropped when Alyshia had gone to Mumbai. Her father had said she hadn't taken to any of Mumbai's richest bachelors, which didn't surprise Isabel. Since Alyshia had come back, there'd been no one. For a twenty-five-year-old dazzling beauty, with a billionaire father, that was not normal.

Isabel shrugged away the monotonous cycle of maternal pre-occupations. Couldn't help herself. She'd been married and had had Alyshia by the time she was twenty.

She concentrated on the food. She was going Portuguese for this lunch. Prawns in her mother's sauce, followed by *arroz de pato,* shredded duck with rice cooked in its own stock with spicy sausage and black olives, and the Portuguese version of crème brûlée to finish. She loved shopping in the Whole Foods Market in the old Barker's building on Kensington High Street. Everything under one roof, all nationalities catered for, from Armenian to Zimbabwean. Despite being American, it was the perfect London store – apart from the ridiculous prices.

Her mobile rang. She hated taking calls when she was out and on the move, but the screen told her it was Chico, which meant it was her ex-husband, Francisco D'Cruz, Alyshia's father. Isabel always called him by the Portuguese diminutive, Chico. Everybody else called him Frank.

'Don't tell me you're in London,' she said.

'Are you OK?' he asked urgently, panting.

'Are *you* OK?' she asked. 'Where are you?'

'Bombay,' he said. He rarely called it Mumbai.

'Doing what?'

'I'm on the bloody fucking exercise bike, what do you think?'

Chico swearing somehow never sounded like swearing.

'It must be nine-thirty at night with you.'

'Try telling that to Sharmila. She has a preternatural ability to divine the precise moment my arse hits the sofa and I start watching a movie.'

'You must be getting too fat,' said Isabel, who could hear the TV in the background

'No, no, no, Isabel,' he said. 'I'm not too fat. I'm slimmer than

31

most men in their fifties. It's just that I have a younger wife who thinks I should still look like I did when I was in the movies.'

'She's good for you, Chico,' said Isabel. 'How are the little ones?'

'Spoilt to buggery,' said Chico, who still had access to a lot of Isabel's father's expressions. 'We're creating monsters with voracious appetites but with no sense of value. I love them to distraction. Name me a parent who doesn't have the same problem.'

'Me.'

'Yeeees,' said Chico thoughtfully, 'that's true. You're sure you're all right, aren't you?'

'Don't be ridiculous, Chico. I'm fine. I'm out shopping for a lunch party for tomorrow. Alyshia's coming.'

'Ah, yes, she's not answering her bloody mobile when I'm calling.'

'She was out last night,' said Isabel. 'A leaving party. I don't think she'll surface until much, much later.'

'So who's coming to the lunch party?' asked Chico.

'Just some writers.'

'You know what I mean.'

'A screenwriter called Jason Bigley.'

'I knew it,' said Chico. 'But Bigley? She can't marry someone called Bigley. Alyshia Bigley. She'll be a laughing-stock.'

'You're calling me because you're bored, Chico. Leave me alone to do my shopping.'

'No, no, Isabel. I'm calling you because I had one of my things.'

'A premonition?' said Isabel. He was famous for them.

'Yes, you know, that something somewhere is not good. So I'm calling the people closest to me to make sure they're all right.'

'You're too stressed, Chico,' said Isabel. 'It's nothing to do with us; more likely to do with business.'

'No, no, this was something close to my heart ... right in my chest.'

'*Before* you started cycling?'

'Oh yes. I had my check-up last month. My doctor says I have the constitution of a bull elephant,' said Chico. 'No, no, no, you see business hits me in the stomach and I can't eat. But I'm eating very, very well. Too well for Sharmila, which is why I'm always running, running, running.'

'Call me tomorrow but about five hours earlier. Alyshia will be at mine by midday.'

'Look at these bloody people.'

'Chico?'

She heard the volume come up on the TV.

'These bloody, fucking people ... these slum dwellers in the middle of Bombay ... they're on the BB bloody C.'

'I think you've just had the answer to you premonition, Chico.'

'Tomorrow,' he said. 'Bloody fucking people.'

The door opened. Two pairs of feet across the floor. The cuffs on wrists and ankles removed. Her feet swivelled off the bed. Large hands under each armpit. Men's hands. They lifted her.

'What's happening?'

No word from the men.

'You've earned your right to pee,' said the voice. 'They'll walk you to the bucket.'

They took her four or five yards from the bed. Alyshia was unsteady on her legs. Dizzy. Something to do with the drug they'd given her. They turned her. Her heel hit the metal bucket. One of the men bent down, lifted a lid.

'Squat,' said the voice.

'Do these men have to be here?'

'Yes, they do. You can't see. They have to guide you.'

'I'll take off the sleeping mask.'

'You haven't earned the right to remove the mask.'

This new world tightened around her. Her bladder creaked under the pressure. She shuddered, steeling herself against the humiliation. She pulled her pants down to the tops of her thighs, squatted. The relief was ecstatic. Toilet paper was pressed into her hand. She wiped herself, dropped it in the bucket, yanked up her pants. They took her back to the bed while she thought about the last time she'd peed in front of anyone, which was her mother.

'Please don't handcuff me.'

'Do you agree to leave the sleeping mask on until you've earned the right to remove it?'

'Yes.'

The feet retreated. The door opened and closed. She lay back down on her side, brought her knees up to her chest.

'Be kinder to yourself, Alyshia,' said the voice. 'You can't put yourself through that every time you want to have a pee.'

Every time? She began thinking her way around this new regime, checking her instinct for rebellion because, for the first time in her life, she was up against a system of management that would not easily give way. Her teachers at St Paul's in London had called her 'opinionated' to her face and 'single-minded' in their reports. Her psychology tutor at the Saïd Business School in Oxford had referred to her as 'fiercely independent', but that was because she didn't like him, had smelt his vanity and sexual interest on the first day. A managing director of one of her father's companies in Mumbai had been astonished by her immediate boldness. And 'The Sacred Cow' wasn't in her league. But this? This was a force of total ruthlessness and the strange thing was that the only other time she'd come across a regime like this was when she was working for her father. He was a dictator and not always benevolent.

That tapas bar, the kids from Bovingdon Recruitment, drunk, Toola on her bum on the pavement, all that mayhem in the Strand, seemed like a different era – a strangely innocent one by comparison. She played it all back to herself like news footage or CCTV product. Not quite real. Not as real as the images she didn't want to see flickering behind her dark, velvet mask.

'What are you thinking about, Alyshia?' asked the voice.

Silence. The two men had terrified her in their white smiling masks, but nothing had been as ghastly as their brutally engorged faces in death.

'Alyshia?'

'What are the rules?' she asked.

By ten o'clock that evening, Boxer was seated once again at a table for two in the Japanese restaurant in the Parque das Nações in Lisbon and was eating a set meal for one of sushi and sashimi.

After playing poker until six o'clock in the morning, he'd slept late. At midday, he'd hired a car and spent the rest of the day going to the sights he'd planned to see with Amy. Despite the clear, sunny, warm spring day, he felt bleak, lonely and cold. He missed her, hated this loneliness, which was different to being a loner with purpose.

Later, sitting on the beach with a cold wind from the Atlantic battering his face, it hit him that he'd had every intention of playing cards while Amy slept. The reason for the ferocity of the row was his anger at being found out. He was disgusted by himself: a man who lied to his own daughter. There was something missing in him. Maybe the same thing that had been missing in his own father, who probably hadn't spared him a moment's thought in thirty-odd years. A failure to connect. An inability to reach out. He held himself by his sides, not through the chill of the wind, but because he felt the hole inside him expanding.

His thoughts made him edgy. He needed to reel himself in. He drove back to the Parque das Nações to prepare for his night's work.

He finished his meal and went to the underground car park near the Camões theatre, where he'd left the car and picked up his afternoon's purchases. He let himself into Diogo Chaves' apartment building and listened at the door. Silence. He unlocked the apartment, checked the rooms. Empty. He took the step ladder and heaved himself up into the storage area and looped the rope he'd bought that day behind the exposed steel rod and secured it. He placed the shoebox full of the ransom cash by the trapdoor. He paid the rope out and measured it, took a knife from the kitchen and cut it to the right length. He replaced the trap with the rope coiled over it and the money on top. He put everything back in its place, found a broom in the cupboard and swept the hall. He walked through the rooms, committing everything to memory one last time.

Isabel Marks was in bed, make-up removed, the dull sheen of night cream on her face. She had an iPad propped up on her knees, reading an author's typescript, with her mind only partially on the job. The smell of duck stock filled the house. She'd boiled the birds with an onion stuck with cloves, bay leaves and peppercorns. Now the stock was in the fridge, the fat congealing on top for her to skim off in the morning.

She'd shredded the meat and put that in the fridge, too. All the time she was working, she was subliminally conscious of a sense of unease. Stripping the skin off the duck and tearing a fork through the flesh had left her feeling apprehensive. She fingered the mobile phone on the duvet. Alyshia couldn't stand phone calls concerned for her safety. Her voice had the terrible scathing edge of someone who'd never known the fear of loss. Isabel toyed with using the excuse of Chico's premonition. That might amuse Alyshia in a way that maternal worry wouldn't. Isabel knew now that she wouldn't sleep unless she called. What the hell.

The phone rang once before it was answered by a male voice, slightly distorted.

'Hello, Mrs Marks.'

'Who is that?' she said. 'Is Alyshia there?'

'She's here.'

'Can I speak to her, please?'

'She can't come to the phone at the moment.'

'Is she all right?'

'She's perfectly all right.'

'This line is terrible,' she said.

'There's nothing wrong with the line, Mrs Marks,' said the voice.

'And who are you?'

'You can call me Jordan. Why be formal when we're going to be talking to each other over the next few weeks, months ... possibly years?'

'Are you a friend of Alyshia's?' she asked stupidly, knowing there was something about the tone of the voice that she wasn't prepared to face up to.

'Not yet. I'm working on the relationship side of things. Men aren't so good at the initial getting-to-know-each-other phase. Not like women.'

'I want to speak to Alyshia,' said Isabel, irritation rising in her voice.

'Understandable, but not possible.'

'Why not?'

'She's been kidnapped and there's a whole process for us to go through before you'll get the chance to speak to your daughter.'

Silence. Mental paralysis. Words that had been on the way

jammed in her throat. Pure emotion took hold. Her blood turned to ether: thin, cold, unable to transport oxygen. A swoon, replete with nausea, walloped through her head.

'Mrs Marks?' said the voice. 'Can you hear me?'

The word 'yes' fell from her mouth like a loose tooth.

'Listen very carefully. Your daughter has been kidnapped. I know this is a shock,' said the voice gently, but then the tone changed. 'You must not go to the police and you must not talk to the press. If we believe that you have done either of these things, you will never hear from us again. And, I'm quite serious about this, Mrs Marks, you will only see your daughter if you are extremely lucky, but it will be some months later, and she will be in an advanced state of decomposition and forever troubling the mind of the unfortunate hiker, farm worker or gamekeeper who has chanced upon her remains. Do you understand me?'

'No police, no press,' said Isabel, on automatic.

'You can talk to Alyshia's father about what has happened, but—'

'What do you want? He'll want to know that.'

'Well, that's not so easy,' said the voice. 'That will have to be discussed over—'

'Money? Is it money you want? How much money?'

'I wish it could be as straightforward as that. Of course, rich people always believe that all anybody wants from them is their money. And that the kidnap of someone as precious as your daughter can be sorted out with a bit of negotiation over a few days or, at worst, a few weeks. I start at fifty million, you come back at twenty thousand and, after a bit of good old Asian haggling, we agree at, say, half a million. This is not about money. I am not going to be so crass as to demand that you put a price on your only child's head. Your ex-husband will try to dismiss our little endeavour as a mere money-making exercise and it's up to you, Mrs Marks, to persuade him to take it much more seriously than that.'

This man's talk had a strange effect on Isabel. His calmness earthed her. After the initial shock and the terrible, chilling constriction it had inflicted on her, his chattiness, even the severity of his articulate threat, had restored some normal flow. Her brain finally started to function.

'Do you know my ex-husband?'

'Frank D'Cruz is in the news so much these days you could go anywhere in the world and find people who *think* they know him. The difference is, Mrs Marks, that you know him better than anybody.'

'Do I?' she said. 'We've been divorced for twelve years and we weren't together much for three years before that.'

'That's what happens when you become very wealthy: you make sure people know you as little as possible. It leaves you greater leeway for ruthlessness,' said the voice. 'One last thing before I go, Mrs Marks. I will only speak to *you*. Understand? Nobody else is acceptable. Not your husband, not a friend, not a lawyer. Only you. If anybody else answers the phone, I will hang up. Three strikes and you're out.'

'What does that mean?'

'If somebody other than you answers that phone more than twice, you won't see Alyshia again,' said the voice. 'Goodbye, Mrs Marks.'

'Wait,' said Isabel, surprised at what had just come to her. 'How do I know you're holding her? That's the first thing my ex-husband's going to ask.'

'No physical proof, although don't expect her at your lunch party tomorrow.'

'That won't be good enough.'

'Alyshia asked me to remind you that when she was small, she used to call her Portuguese grandmother *vo-vó-voom*.'

The phone went dead, leaving Isabel Marks with the sensation of a double pulmonary collapse.

4

The phone calls had already started. Each one more complicated than the last.

The first was between Frank D'Cruz and the special risks underwriter at Lloyd's of London, who'd told him that the syndicate would not be liable for the kidnap for ransom insurance claim unless the Metropolitan Police were informed that his daughter had been taken. Not many people told Frank D'Cruz what he could and couldn't do. So his next call was to the Secretary of State for Business Innovation and Skills, who was put in no doubt as to the future of a major investment in the UK car industry.

The Secretary of State for BIS put a call through to the Home Secretary, Natasha Radcliffe, and he explained what Frank D'Cruz had brutally outlined to him, with added detail he'd gleaned from the special risks underwriter at Lloyd's.

'Just remind me which Indian friend Frank D'Cruz is,' said Radcliffe.

'He's the one with the new battery technology. The ferrous ion one that *can* be recharged from the mains in less than an hour and has battery switching capacity for longer journeys.'

'Sorry, yes, of course. I'm not quite up to speed on that,' said Radcliffe, who remembered now that the promise was for a major investment in two car factories in the Midlands with a roll-out of switching stations all over the country, creating lots of jobs and giving them the perfect mid-term announcement.

'He made it quite clear that, were the police to be involved, it would affect his inclination to invest,' said the secretary of state. 'I was wondering if there was a way that we could satisfy him without treading on anybody's toes?'

'You mean inform the police but ask them to keep their noses out?'

'If you think that would be possible.'

'Difficult to say without asking them, but my instinct tells me they wouldn't like it. There isn't quite the free flow of personnel and contracts between the private and public sectors here that there is, say, in the States,' said Radcliffe. 'Would Frank D'Cruz be prepared to use a kidnap consultant provided by the Met? The kidnappers wouldn't have to know he was a policeman.'

'He wants to use a specific kidnap consultant: Charles Boxer, who works for a private security company called Pavis Risk Management, which is run by an ex-army major called Martin Fox.'

'Is that non-negotiable?'

'The way he put it, yes.'

'The only way to find out if this is workable is by talking to the police themselves. If we don't tell them and something goes wrong and, God forbid, the girl is killed, there will be an investigation, it will all come out and we will *not* look good.'

'Is there any leverage you can bring to bear on the Met Police Commissioner to ensure that we get a sympathetic ear?'

'Leave it with me. I'll have to talk to Mervin Stanley, you know that.'

'Needless to say, Natasha, this is somewhat urgent.'

By midnight, Charles Boxer's brain had come back to the diamond sharpness he was accustomed to when playing poker and he'd found himself seated at the table opposite Don and getting the cards. The money had flowed back to his side. The American had started to get frustrated.

'It's getting on for three o'clock,' said Don. 'Maybe we should take a break.'

'You looking to get lucky like last night?' said Boxer.

'Don't know what happened,' said Don, open-handed.

'I emptied my boots,' said Boxer.

Don's face didn't crack; he just pushed himself back from the table.

Boxer left the casino, moving fast. He went straight to the hire car in the underground car park. He put the Glock in the back of his trousers and the suppressor in his pocket. He walked down towards the river and came up sharp when Diogo Chaves shambled across his path. Late. Damn. He'd have to give him some time.

The river lapped and gurgled as he stood in the darkness under a line of pines. The odd bit of traffic pulsed across the bridge towards the lights of Montijo on the far side. He looked up to the balcony doors of Chaves' apartment. The lights were on. He waited. The lights stayed on. He watched for movement. Ten minutes passed. It should have been all over by now. Still nothing. The tension built inside him as the minutes ticked past. He pushed himself away from the tree, went into the apartment building.

Up to the first floor. Listened at the door. Music. He listened harder. Nothing beyond the music. He fitted the key in the lock, eased in each tooth silently, turned it, opened the door. The music was louder than he'd expected. Brazilian. The sort that reminded you of the beach, the heat and string bikinis. He fitted the suppressor to the Glock by the light shed from the empty kitchen into the hall. On the sideboard was a bottle of rum, a tin of coke on its side, a brown puddle next to it. The bedroom at the end of the hall was in darkness. He moved towards the living room, peeked through the crack at the hinge of the open door. Couldn't see anyone in either of the two armchairs, the sofa was empty. He looked around for light elsewhere in the apartment. Not a crack beneath any door.

Boxer decided that Chaves had turned the music on, poured himself another drink in the kitchen, gone back to the living room to dream about Brazil, fallen asleep and sunk down into an armchair out of his line of vision. He couldn't check in the reflection of the sliding doors to the balcony without his own reflection from the doorway appearing there too. All he could see were the lights of the stereo system. He went down onto all fours and crept to the other side of the door. He checked the two bedrooms and bathrooms: all empty. He stepped into the living room, gun at waist height.

Diogo Chaves was fast asleep in one of the armchairs, with a half empty glass in his crotch. Boxer took a seat in the other armchair and swivelled it so that he was sitting opposite Chaves' unconscious form. He kicked him on the point of the ankle so that Chaves came awake with a terrible jolt and a strangled cry, spilling the contents of his glass into his crotch. Chaves held onto his ankle, the air hissing between his teeth. He saw what Boxer had in his hand, blinked at it in a way that told Boxer he was a man who'd had a gun pointed at him before.

'*Porra*,' said Chaves, '*o que quer, seu cuzão?*'

'I know you speak English, Diogo,' said Boxer.

'Diogo?'

'Don't piss me around.'

'My name is Rui Lopes.'

'Close your eyes and listen to my voice,' said Boxer. 'You and I have spoken before, Diogo Chaves.'

Chaves shook his head, things occurring to him.

'I was the one who delivered Bruno Dias's money to you. That's how I know you speak English.'

Chaves struggled to cope with the import of that short sentence as the horror of being discovered closed in on him and the fear rose in his chest.

'I can see you're beginning to remember now,' said Boxer. 'Couldn't forget what you did to that poor girl, right?'

'I don' know what you talking about.'

'Bianca Dias?' said Boxer. 'She was only seventeen and you ruined her, left her for dead on the side of the road. Beaten and raped.'

'Still don' know what you talking about.'

Boxer kicked him on the knee.

'*Porra*,' hissed Chaves, clasping his knee now, tears coming to his eyes with the booze and the pain.

'I've seen the money you've got hidden in the ceiling.'

Chaves sat back, his fingers trembling away from his damaged knee.

'You wan' that money, is that it?'

'How much you got left now, Diogo?'

42

'Maybe one hunner fifty thousan',' he said, more hopeful. 'It's yours.'

Boxer shrugged, shook his head.

'If I'd wanted it, I'd have taken it before, wouldn't I?'

Chaves was confused for a moment, then got it.

'Why d'you do it, Diogo?'

'Do what?'

'Ruin the girl,' said Boxer. 'You got what you wanted.'

'Not my idea. The other two. They wanted it. Nice little rich *menina*. Wanted to do to her what had been done to them all their lives. What am I gonna say?'

'Tell them no.'

'Maybe you don' understan' how Bruno Dias make his money.'

'I know how you made *your* money.'

'You on the rich man's side now?'

'I'm on the girl's side, always have been.'

'I didn' do *nothing* to her.'

'She can't walk. She can't talk. And you were the gang leader,' said Boxer. 'You're responsible. And you didn't give a damn about that seventeen-year-old kid, did you? You got any last words for Bianca? For Bruno Dias? Or for the lovely Cristina he sent to check you out?'

Chaves' eyes widened as he realised the extent of the set-up.

'You tell that bastard Bruno Dias …' he started, but then all the fight went out of him. 'Fuck it, man. Just do it. I'm finished.'

Natasha Radcliffe called the Mayor of London, Mervin Stanley, affectionately known as Merve the Swerve for his brilliance at extricating himself from the political and personal life catastrophes that had so far been the signature of his time in office. She outlined the problem to him while he held his finger to his lips and glowered at Svetlana, who'd just poured a glass of champagne over her naked, enhanced breasts and was licking it off with a surprisingly long tongue.

'Who?' he said, cutting in on something he'd been only half listening to.

'Frank D'Cruz.'

'I know that name.'

'Electric cars, Mervin. He's going to build two factories in the Midlands. I know it's not London but his daughter *has* been kidnapped in your city.'

'We can't have that,' he said in his robustly, fruity Old Etonian accent. 'Electric cars? That's why I know him. I secured permission for him to display some prototypes in the City and out at Stratford in front of the Olympic Stadium. I think they're going to drive them around the country in the run-up to the games. What's his daughter's name?'

'Alyshia D'Cruz,' said Natasha Radcliffe, shaking her head.

Stanley reached over for his iPad and went into Facebook, found the girl. A little more class than old Svetty Betty at the end of the bed, he thought, running his hand through the brilliantined rails on his head. He Googled Frank D'Cruz.

'What do you want me to do, Natasha?'

'We need some sympathetic treatment from the relevant department of the Met.'

'So, although Frank D'Cruz doesn't want the Met informed, you want *me* to tell them and then ask them to keep a low profile on the matter?'

'Not just a low profile.'

'A no profile?'

'What are the chances?'

'What do *you* think?' said Stanley, irritably. 'How would you like it if a private company, over which you had no control, started operating in the Home Office? They're policemen. Their lives depend on trust and hierarchy. They are very suspicious of people who do what they do, but for money. Not that theirs is a voluntary force, it has to be said.'

'So a compromise is in order?'

'That's what we're good at,' said Stanley. 'Look at it this way, Natasha: just by pulling all these strings, Frank D'Cruz has let a whole bunch of people in on his secret. One wonders, given his evident acumen, whether he did it on purpose. If I was you, I'd be wondering what his game is.'

'His game, Mervin,' said Radcliffe icily, 'is that his daughter has been kidnapped and he's using his high profile investment to persuade us to bend the law so that she doesn't get killed on day one of her ordeal. He's also letting everybody know that he has power, there's ministerial muscle behind him, and he's prepared to use it.'

'Quite so. I'm just saying it's as well to know who you're getting into bed with, Natasha,' said Stanley. 'Not that you would, of course; just a figure of speech, you understand.'

'Oh shut up, Merve,' she said, to Stanley's husky laughter.

'One thing is for sure, Natasha: he knows what *he's* doing and he'll know what *we're* doing.'

'Just get the best compromise you can, Merve,' said Radcliffe. 'Remembering that this Charles Boxer as consultant is the non-negotiable bit.'

'That's going to be tricky.'

'Will you call the Commissioner now, please, Mervin?'

Stanley saw that it was 3.30 a.m. and Svetlana was snoring quietly at the foot of the bed. He shrugged.

'This *is* my favourite time to call him, Natasha. You've just made my night.'

Boxer didn't watch Chaves' final struggle. He went into the living room, decided to leave the music playing and the light on. He checked the logic of the scene: the empty glass fallen on the floor, the man hanging in the hallway above the money spoke of a depressed drunk's realisation that he wasn't going to be able to put right what he'd done wrong and that suicide was the only solution.

When Chaves was finally still, Boxer couldn't help but feel pity; not for the dead man, only for a young woman's ruined life. He brushed past the body, pressed his ear to the front door of the apartment, heard nothing, opened it and left.

The night was silent, the river black.

He made his way back to the casino, feeling solid again, the hole in his centre collapsed to a pinpoint.

Detective Chief Superintendent Peter Makepeace, the head of Specialist Crime Directorate 7, which contained the Met's Kidnap Unit, sat at the top of the stairs, listening to the Metropolitan Police Commissioner and becoming more unimpressed by the moment.

'So what you're telling me, sir, is that, despite being the Met's best performing department with a 99.5% recovery record, we've got to let the highest profile case we've had in the last five years go private,' said Makepeace, quietly savage with fury. 'All these years we've been handling ugly little crimes with Yardies, Albanians, Chinese and the like, and now, when the big number comes along, we've got to hand it over to some tosser with a fancy office in Mayfair.'

'I know,' said the Commissioner, sympathising, 'all they have is a single client from whom they're trying to make a buck, while we have the safety of eight million people to consider. It's just politics, Peter.'

'And that's another point, isn't it, sir? What if they're terrorists, these kidnappers? We have defined procedures; what do Pavis Risk Management have? Probably just a bonus structure.'

'They won't be performing without supervision,' said the Commissioner. 'We're not giving them free rein.'

'And what's their experience in running a London-based kidnap?'

'That I don't know.'

'All these guys are experts in Colombia and Pakistan, but what do they know about London? We've got all the informers—'

'The kidnap consultant they want to use, like most of these private security company guys, is ex-army. He fought in the first Gulf War with the Staffords,' said the Commissioner, glancing down his notes, cutting through the fury, edging towards the compromise now, 'but afterwards he joined the Met as a homicide detective.'

'Name?'

'Charles Boxer.'

'I know him.'

'You *do*?'

'I didn't know the PSC he freelanced for was called Pavis,' said Makepeace. 'His ex-partner works for me in SCD7. Her name is Mercy Danquah. She's Ghanaian. They had a daughter together but split up straight away.'

'Badly?'

'No, no, very well. They're still good friends,' said Makepeace.

'He left his salaried job with GRM the year before last because he was out of the country all the time. The daughter was becoming a bit of a problem, you know, like all teenagers. Mercy was taking the brunt, so he quit.'

'Are you thinking what I'm thinking?'

'It's possible. I could live with Mercy being a co-consultant,' said Makepeace. 'I'd still like to have someone else in there to do some groundwork. And we'd want access to Pavis's operations desk.'

'In a supervisory role?'

'In an ideal world I'd like to run it.'

'And if they're not amenable to that?'

'We'd like to be consulted on all operational matters with the right to veto,' said Makepeace. 'And if we suspect *any* terrorist connection, we take over the whole show.'

'That's fair enough,' said the Commissioner. 'Let's see what we can do.'

Boxer looked from his mobile screen to the two kings and two fours in his hand, weighed it: Martin Fox with a job possibility or the potential for a full house.

'I'm going to have to take this,' he said, folding.

He left the room, stood in the granite-tiled corridor between two uplighters.

'Martin. How's it going?'

'Hello, Charlie. Where are you?'

'Tierra del Fuego.'

'Pity,' said Fox. 'I can tell I didn't wake you up. Is it windy?'

'It sounds as if you've got a job for me.'

'I do, but the initial meeting is over here, not Argentina.'

'What is it?'

'A girl's been kidnapped in London. The client asked for you by name.'

'How did he know me?'

'You only find that out face to face.'

'I'm in Lisbon.'

'I know. I just tracked you,' said Fox. 'It didn't sound like Patagonia in the background. Business or pleasure?'

'In London, you said.'

'Are you interested?' asked Fox.

'When's the meeting?'

'Two this afternoon in the Ritz.'

'My flight's not until this evening.'

'I'll book you an earlier one, business class.'

'London?' said Boxer, not letting that detail get away from him. 'What about the Met?'

'We're entering into a collaborative arrangement with them.'

'And now comes the small print,' said Boxer. 'Go on.'

'You have to work with them. I have to work with them. The client mustn't know.'

'He's important then?'

'Ministers of the realm are involved.'

'Who am I going to have to work with from the Met?'

'Mercy is going to be your co-consultant.'

'And how's *that* going to work?'

'I haven't got all the details yet,' said Fox. 'That was all the special risks underwriter at Lloyd's was prepared to tell me.'

Silence, while Boxer thought it through.

'I'll double your daily rate, given the circs.'

'Now you're making me suspicious.'

'There's more work for Pavis where this comes from.'

'Well, I've got to keep my hand in somehow,' said Boxer finally. 'And you'll owe me one.'

'Will I?' said Fox.

5

Alyshia lay on her back, still with the velvet underside of the sleeping mask pressing against her cheekbones. Her eyes were open and desperate to see something other than the swirling colours that zero visual stimulation sent to her retina.

The house rules had not been difficult to understand. Privileges had to be earned by answering questions and would be withdrawn for minor infringements such as doing anything without permission. Refusal to answer questions would be punished by being cuffed to the bed in increasingly more uncomfortable positions. Any assault on staff would incur corporal punishment. Any attempt to leave the room would be considered an escape and punishable by sexual violation.

'Rape?' said Alyshia. 'So you wouldn't kill me?'

'No point. There's considerable investment tied up in your detention,' said the voice. 'And don't think it's a soft option. If you try to escape, you'll be gang-banged by thugs. So, not only will you fail, but you'll be scarred for life. Don't even think about it, Alyshia. Just concentrate on giving us what we want and improving your quality of life.'

The sleeping mask was making her claustrophobic. Not in the way that the closed cab in the dark garage had made her panic, but more anxious than she'd like to feel. She needed a horizon. She had always avoided situations that might put her out of sight of land. She also did not like the abstract, preferred the figurative. In her state of sensory deprivation, these were the fragments of truth about herself that she was facing up to. But there were other fears, of a more personal nature, that would normally have remained subliminal but were beginning to nudge at the surface of her consciousness. This was why she wanted to see. Darkness encouraged doubt. Light would give her balance. But she didn't want to show them that darkness was a weakness. She was forcing herself to endure this state for as long as possible to show them that being blindfolded was no problem.

The formulation of this minor strategy gave her some small strength. She raised her knees, crossed one leg over the other and set her foot nodding as if she was connected to her iPod. She would not ask anything of them, but rather force them to come to her as often as possible and this would give her the opportunity to negotiate.

Her brain calmed down. She could concentrate. She sifted through memories for unlikely things that might help her. The rare afternoons of cable TV, watching survival stories. People in impossibly extreme situations and how they coped. Survivors all talked about giving themselves things to do and think about, so that they didn't get overwhelmed by the direness of their circumstances. They focused on immediate problems, like making their rations last. What did she have? What was the equivalent of making her rations last?

She needed something more active than the passive strategy of waiting for them to ask her questions. There might be long hours of boredom to get through. Prioritise your needs. That's good. A top ten of what would improve her current situation. Number one was obvious: removal of the sleeping mask. Number two: wash. Feeling clean had always been important to her, especially when she had been in Mumbai. Number three: how about a JCB digger? What sort of question would you have to answer to get one of those? Something really, phenomenally intimate about her father. Yes, well, she knew a few things that nobody else knew about her father.

'You're smiling, Alyshia.'

She shouldn't have smiled. That was bad. Must have been the thought of the JCB.

'I was just imagining myself elsewhere,' she said. 'I have to keep myself amused.'

'Like where?'

'On a beach in Goa.'

'With anybody?'

'A friend.'

'A friend like Duane?'

Silence. How did he know about Duane? Nobody knew about Duane.

'Who's Duane?' she asked, but she knew the beat had blown it.

'Try again, Alyshia.'

She uncrossed her legs, planted her feet to steady herself. All the strength she'd just built up dissipated. These people knew her.

'I wasn't thinking about Duane, no.'

'He'll be sad about that, but Curtis won't. Curtis will be happy, even if you weren't thinking about Curtis.'

'Have you spoken to Curtis?'

'*I* haven't, no. We don't do that sort of thing,' said the voice. 'Did you know that Curtis had an unfortunate accident the other day?'

'No,' she said, concerned. 'You didn't hurt him, did you?'

'No. *You* did,' said the voice. 'He saw you with Duane. Young guys like that find it hard to take. They get jealous. You might think it's all fair in love and war—'

'And kidnapping.'

'Good one, Alyshia. You're one tough cookie. But then again, secretive people are tough. Knowing things that others don't gives you strength. Your father's the same.'

'Nobody gets ahead by letting others know what they're thinking.'

'Did Frank tell you that?'

'My father always used to say: "If you're straight with people, they'll take every opportunity to block you".'

'That includes Frank's most loyal employees.'

'Are *you* one of his *ex*-employees?'

'It's probably better that you don't know who I am,' said the voice. 'That way, you stay alive.'

'You've forgotten about the return on your investment.'

'There's no return if I'm in jail. The moment I think, or even suspect, the game's up, you're finished, Alyshia,' said the voice.

51

'Your father took off from Mumbai some hours ago. He'll be in London soon. We want to call him with a welcome gift, to show him that you're alive and well. You should find it easier to give us something on your father than your mother.'

The voice was right there. Her mother had nothing to hide: *vo-vó-voom* was the level of *her* family secrets. Her father was different. The trick was to select the secret that would be least damaging. But she also wanted to protect the personal things. The names they had for each other when it was just them in the room and they were talking, father to daughter. Why should these people know the sort of thing that not even her mother knew?

'My father gives a lot of interviews. He used to be an actor. Whenever they asked him his favourite book, he would always give an Indian author's name, because he said it was important to be patriotic. But really his favourite book of all time is *The Great Gatsby*.'

'A very interesting character, Alyshia,' said the voice. 'I'm not surprised. Your father has always had tremendous powers of re-invention. So much so that nobody could ever possibly know him.'

The flight from Lisbon landed late at Heathrow, around 11.30 a.m. Immigration was packed. While he was waiting, Boxer thought about working with Mercy. It had never happened before, although they had compared notes on cases. Despite their separation, they were still very close, and not just good friends, more like siblings. They knew each other better than lovers, which was probably why it hadn't worked out on that front. But he did love her. More than anyone he'd met before or since. He felt nobody else saw what he saw in Mercy. Where strangers saw a tall, slim, erect, utterly driven cop, he saw the long limbs, the high cheekbones, the almond-shaped eyes and the rare but dazzling smile that showed the deeply buried sweetness of the heart within. He knew they would work well together, because they had that most indestructible of human connections: trust.

He called her, thinking if she'd been given this job, she'd have left the course she was on and would now be at home with Amy. He needed to start repairing the damage.

'Is that my new colleague?' said Mercy, irony on full.

'Who'd have thought it?' said Boxer. 'They told you anything yet?'

'Not much. I'm getting a full briefing later today. All I know is that you're the lead and I'm the supporting actress,' she said.

'You think this'll work?'

'Between you and me? Sure,' said Mercy. 'As for the rest, once Whitehall's involved, the Home Sec and all that, who knows? We're pawns, while the kings and queens do their little dance. How did you get the job?'

'Martin Fox said the client asked for me by name.'

'So who recommended you?'

'He didn't say.'

'You should find out. It might tell us something if you were put up by someone like Simon Deacon, for instance.'

'Simon?' said Boxer, incredulous. 'MI6 don't go around recommending people and certainly not people like me.'

'What's that supposed to mean?'

'Look, just let me talk to Amy quickly.'

'Yeah, very funny.'

'Come on, Mercy, don't mess me around. We parted on a bum note and I want to start patching ...'

He ran out to silence as things started dawning.

'What do you mean by "parted", Charlie?' said Mercy. 'She's with *you*.'

'Oh, shit.'

'I gave her her passport so that she could go to Lisbon *with you*.'

'She called me, said she had to revise for her exams and was going to stay at Karen's,' said Boxer. 'And that she'd spoken to you about it.'

'She told me she was going to hang at Karen's and then meet you at Heathrow for the flight at seven,' said Mercy. 'I even managed to call her at about six and I heard airport noise in the background. She said you'd gone to the loo.'

'Jesus Christ.'

'I'm serious, Charlie, when I spoke to her there *was* airport noise and she did have her passport with her. You don't think she's ...'

'I don't know,' said Boxer. 'I think she's capable of anything.

I mean, she had the nerve to take your call. Christ, the girl's got balls.'

'Leave it with me,' said Mercy, furious and galvanised. 'I'll find her and when I do, I'll handcuff her to the bloody radiator. She'll wish she'd never—'

'Clapped eyes on Merciless Danquah,' said Boxer. 'You know what gets me? How easily she plays us. We're the professional lie detectors. I mean, are all seventeen-year-old girls like this?'

'So I'm told,' said Mercy.

Frank D'Cruz's flight had been delayed so Martin Fox and Charles Boxer didn't turn up at the Ritz until four-thirty in the afternoon. A young Indian man let them into the Berkley suite, poured tea and provided a tiered tray of biscuits and cakes. He told them D'Cruz was on his way and left them to it. Martin Fox stood straight-backed at the window, looking out over the black and leafless trees of Green Park towards Constitution Hill, as if performing some military inspection.

'So who recommended me for this job?' asked Boxer.

'The client didn't say,' said Fox, turning into the room.

'It wouldn't be Simon Deacon, would it?'

'Why?' asked Fox. 'I haven't seen Simon Deacon since the test match against India at Lord's last July. Haven't even seen him at the Special Forces Club. Is he all right?'

'As far as I know,' said Boxer. 'He's just very busy with security in the run up to the Olympics. You know he's on the Asia desk?'

'Ah, right, I see the connection now,' said Fox. 'You'll have to ask Frank D'Cruz. It was the Lloyd's man who said he'd asked for you by name.'

Fox ran his hands through his sandy hair before shoving them into his pockets. He gave Boxer some background on Frank D'Cruz, his Bollywood past and Konkan Hills Securities, D'Cruz's holding company. He walked around the sofas as he talked, keeping an eye on Boxer from all angles. There was definitely something different about the man since he'd left GRM a couple of years ago; nothing dramatic, more a matter of perception. Fox wondered if others saw it. Boxer was watchful, patient and grasped all the detail he was giving him, all of which was normal in a consultant of his calibre. It was just that now those qualities seemed to be married to a man with the eyes of a sniper, rather than someone who was merely determined to understand a new situation.

Frank D'Cruz came in and immediately his charisma filled the room. He ignored Fox and went straight to Boxer, shook his hand and looked into his eyes. Boxer returned the intended intrusion and, after some long seconds, D'Cruz parted from him, feeling that he'd got the right man.

'I'd like to speak to Mr Boxer alone,' he said, shaking hands with Fox.

'Maybe it would be a good idea if we all sat down together to start off with,' said Fox. 'You give us a recap of the developments so far. We can formulate an approach, discuss terms and conditions, and if you and Charles would like to continue, then, of course, I would leave you to do that.'

D'Cruz was irritated but he also realised that Fox held the key to Charles Boxer. D'Cruz opened his hands to the sofas and took a seat in the armchair at the head of the coffee table.

'My ex-wife, Isabel Marks, called my daughter's phone at around eleven-thirty on Friday night and had her first contact with the kidnappers,' said D'Cruz, giving them a recap of the phone call, including the kidnapper's name and his calm, authoritative state of mind.

'Is that the only contact with the kidnappers so far?' asked Fox.

'No, they called me when my flight landed at Heathrow, using Alyshia's mobile. An electronically distorted voice said, "Welcome to London, Mr D'Cruz". I wasn't even off the plane. It was three o'clock.'

'Any demands made directly to you?'

'No. He said there was plenty of time for that. The point of the call was to confirm what I already knew. In case I doubted Isabel, I suppose.'

'But they didn't say that,' said Boxer.

'No. They gave me the same instructions about not contacting the police and press, and said they wouldn't be talking to me again. All further discussions would be through my ex-wife.'

'Did they offer you proof of capture?'

'They told me my favourite book, which I don't admit to anybody, but Alyshia knows.'

Boxer and Fox wanted to ask the same question but didn't.

They discussed the two lines that had contained some kind of demand. What could be 'more complicated'? What could the kidnappers mean by it not being 'a money-making exercise'? If D'Cruz knew, he wasn't letting on. Of course he had business enemies.

'Name me a billionaire, apart from perhaps Warren Buffet, who doesn't have a line of people they've trodden on to get to where they are now,' he said. 'I had a brutal battle to gain control of the steel works I wrested from the hands of the Pitale family in 2007. I'm in a big fight now with Mahale Construction to get the contract to remove the slums from central Bombay and replace them with a major inner city development. They are also furious because the government has asked me to advise on the building of some nuclear reactors. But these are business battles. I know these people. They will try everything but they draw the line at family.'

'Are you sure?' asked Fox.

'I am *dealing* with members of their families. I don't just talk to the patriarch, I speak to his sons and daughters. I know wives, husbands and their children. I know them socially. My wife, Sharmila, is very close to several women in the Mahale family, for instance.'

'Have you increased security on your family in Mumbai?' asked Fox.

'They're not to leave the compound until this is over. Screened tutors will come in to teach the children. Sharmila will only allow people she knows into the house. I've doubled security at the compound.'

'What about foreign business dealings?' asked Fox. 'I understand you've moved into the Chinese market. You're getting raw materials from Africa.'

'Yes, well, it's possible that the Chinese could be more ruthless than, say, the Europeans, but I haven't antagonised anybody … yet. I'm selling steel to them. I'm buying parts from them. I'm growing two companies in the Special Economic Zones around Guangzhou and Shenzhen. I'm creating jobs and I'm paying in hard currency – if you can call the dollar hard.'

'What about in London?' asked Fox. 'Do you have anything here?'

'Property,' said D'Cruz. 'I've been buying commercial property over the last four years with the market being so low. Now I'm selling it.'

'And in the UK generally?' asked Fox.

'I'm about to make a major investment in building electric cars and a network of battery recharging stations,' said D'Cruz. 'Some prototypes were delivered here from India last week for display in the City and out at Stratford. I'm trying to raise money for the project on the stock exchange. And if you're asking, I haven't had any death threats from Nissan or Toyota.'

'Presumably you're going to get some UK government support for this initiative,' said Fox. 'Tax breaks?'

'Of course, just like anybody else would who's making this kind of investment,' said D'Cruz.

'I think we'll see from the "complicated" nature of their demands whether this is a business enemy,' said Boxer. 'If it really isn't a "money-making exercise", then it's less likely that this is a criminal gang and we'd have to look more closely at business, political or maybe even Bollywood enemies. They're not amateurs. Voice distortion, lack of panic, articulateness and the timing of this last call to you is intended to show that we're dealing with professionals with resources.'

Fox could see that D'Cruz was impressed with the way Boxer handled himself. They agreed to come to terms, subject to Boxer's acceptance by Isabel Marks. The meeting ended. Fox left.

'Let's have a drink' said D'Cruz, moving over to a trolley laden with every conceivable liquor.

'Famous Grouse on the rocks, please,' said Boxer.

D'Cruz poured it out and made himself a pink gin.

'Isabel's father was an English diplomat,' said D'Cruz. 'He introduced me to this drink. I like it during the day. Whisky at night.'

'Martin Fox told me you asked for me by name,' said Boxer. 'Not many people wander the world with a list of kidnap and ransom consultants in their wallets.'

'I did my research,' said D'Cruz. 'I've always done my own

research, whether I'm targeting a company to buy or trying to find the right person to do a job. I know a lot of people. They talk to me and I listen. I know rich people but I also know poor people. I come from poverty myself. Poverty can dull the senses, but if you want to get out of it, it can heighten them, too. I've never been wrong about the people I employ.'

Boxer didn't interrupt. He knew this was the rich man's moment.

'That's not true,' said D'Cruz. 'I was wrong about Alyshia. Ever since she showed me her intelligence from a very young age, I was absolutely certain that she would work for me, learn from me and ultimately take over from me. I'm not a patriarchal kind of person. I have a small boy, but even at six years old I can tell that he doesn't have what Alyshia's got. But I was wrong about her. She walked away from me. I underestimated her.'

D'Cruz swallowed hard against the emotion. Boxer watched and wondered how much to believe it.

'*Under*estimated her?' said Boxer.

'I thought she would be happy to take over what I had created, but no. She wants to make her own way in the world, do everything on her own terms. She wants to learn things for herself, see how things work with her own eyes. She doesn't want to be told. She said this to me a few years ago: "Other people's experience is very valuable, but only half as valuable as your own". Not bad for a twenty-one-year-old.'

'That's good,' said Boxer. 'She'll cope well with being held in captivity. Is she physically resilient? Has she ever been in difficult circumstances before?'

'No, she's led a charmed life, of course. That's what she's fighting against. She found the poverty in Bombay very difficult to take. She was appalled that people lived in such squalor while others, like herself ... well, you know the story. The culture shock stayed with her longer than most; in fact, it never seemed to lose its horror for her. That's one of the reasons she came back to London, Mr Boxer. Can you see that being a problem?'

'If you've already been tested, you know what to expect of yourself. If you've *never* been tested, you might be surprised. People who think they're tough, crumple like paper; while others who imagine themselves weak, find some steel inside.'

'So what type of person copes best as a hostage?'

'Someone who accepts their situation and is able to adapt to it. A lot of people react to fear by denying it. It's not bravery, just paralysis. An emotionally-controlled person will fare better than an hysteric. Emotions consume lots of energy and volatility is not a good platform for thinking straight.'

'She's not highly strung,' said D'Cruz. 'Not like her mother.'

'Intelligent people cope well because they know how to occupy themselves,' said Boxer. 'They don't need outside stimulus. They can amuse themselves, think, observe and calculate. All good things. Having said that, you don't want to be too intelligent, because you have to be able to get on with people. Persuade your guards to give you things and not mistreat you, for instance. You have to be able to form a relationship with your kidnapper so that in the ups and downs of a negotiation process, you can always maintain some kind of contact.'

'She's very bright,' said D'Cruz, ticking off her attributes against Boxer's list, 'and well-liked.'

'On the other hand, you don't want to be too friendly. That can lead to the complications of Stockholm syndrome, when the victim begins to identify with the cause of their captor,' said Boxer. 'So you see, Mr D'Cruz, a delicate balance is required to be a hostage. You're not born to it. You learn on the job, adapting your behaviour accordingly and developing survival techniques.'

'I don't know what I would do if any harm came to Alyshia.'

'To me?' said Boxer, deadpan.

'No, no, no, no, no,' said D'Cruz, nearly summoning a laugh, 'with myself. She is everything to me. I am a driven man, Mr Boxer. I hated being poor. I made a name for myself in the movies. I have created enormous wealth for myself and my country. And yet nothing has affected me more in my life than looking down on Alyshia sleeping when she was small and realising that my happiness depended on her.'

Boxer wished he'd never been told that D'Cruz had been a famous actor. He found himself examining everything for emotional veracity. He was also aware of a circling motion in this conversation. D'Cruz wanted to get to something, but not directly. It could have been a cultural difference, Asian versus Anglo-Saxon, but somehow Boxer thought it more to do with delicacy. The man was listening and responding to him, but there was something big and pressing concentrated elsewhere.

'I see that you have a business yourself,' said D'Cruz.

'It's a charitable foundation,' said Boxer, thinking: now we're getting to the deeper research.

'I understand you started it because your father disappeared,' said D'Cruz.

'He went missing when I was seven years old,' said Boxer, avoiding that phrase 'on the run'.

'But you didn't name your charity after him. Normally, foundations are set up in memory ...'

'I've no reason to believe he's dead,' said Boxer. 'But that's beside the point. I set the foundation up because when people disappear, most of the time it's those who are left behind who really suffer. I called it The LOST Foundation because it describes the state of those still desperate to know what happened.'

'And how do you finance this foundation?'

'Donations. Fundraising events.'

Boxer was feeling the pressure of the man's interest but didn't shift in his seat. D'Cruz's mind swooped and banked away.

'Do you spend any time on your father's case?'

'No, not now,' said Boxer. 'When I first gained access to the police file, I spent all my spare time following leads.'

'Trying to prove his innocence?'

'To see if I could find him.'

'Where and when was he last seen?'

'He was seen by his neighbour in Belsize Park late morning, August 14th 1979,' said Boxer, wondering if D'Cruz was genuinely interested or if this was just a 'getting to know you' process. 'Twenty years later, I found the Indian "bucket shop" owner who'd sold him the ticket to Crete, and later I found the hotel where he'd been staying on the south coast of the island *and* its owner back in '79. He showed me the beach where they found his clothes and passport. And that's where it all ran out.'

'It can't be easy,' said D'Cruz, 'to pay two full-time employees in London, even if they are retired policemen.'

'We manage,' said Boxer, undisturbed by D'Cruz's jolting interview technique. 'Maybe you should tell me why you asked for me by name?'

'I was told about you by a Chinese businessman in Shanghai. You performed a very special service for him, for which I understand he makes a substantial monthly payment to The LOST Foundation.'

'Zhang Yaoting,' said Boxer. 'And did he tell you the nature of this special service?'

'He said that after you'd negotiated the return of his son from the gang holding him in Nigeria, you tracked them down and shot all four men,' said D'Cruz. 'I'd like you to do the same for me.'

'Does that mean you know who we're dealing with?'

'No, it doesn't. I have no idea. I am, of course carrying out my … research, but I have no leads.'

Silence from Boxer while he looked hard at D'Cruz's face, searching for any tell-tale signs. All he saw was a powerful determination. But it did give him a breathing space to recover from the shock of D'Cruz being the second person in twenty-four hours who knew about his dirty secret. Something somewhere was leaking and he didn't like it.

'I'm serious,' said D'Cruz. 'Once you've negotiated Alyshia's release, I want you to find the gang who were holding her and kill them all.'

'There's a big difference between doing that sort of thing in the Niger Delta and the banks of the Thames.'

6

'Found Amy,' said the text.

Boxer called Mercy on the way down to D'Cruz's limousine, which was waiting outside the hotel to take them to Isabel Marks' house in Kensington.

'She's in Tenerife with Karen and some other girls,' said Mercy. 'She flies back tonight.'

'And what the hell is she doing there?'

'Sun and sea. Clubs and bars. What else does a group of girls get up to in Tenerife?'

'How did she pay for it?'

'I'm working on that. Karen's mother assumed *I'd* paid for the ticket,' said Mercy. 'What riles me more than anything is that she doesn't care. Amy knew we'd find out in the end and yet she still went ahead and did it. What are we going to do with this kid?'

'I suppose she's not taking calls on her mobile.'

'I can picture her face when she sees "Mum" coming up on her screen every two minutes. I tried the hotel but they're not in.'

'Tenerife for the weekend? It doesn't make sense,' said Boxer. 'There's something else going on.'

'I'll be at Gatwick this evening to meet her off the plane,' said Mercy. 'How's the job?'

'I'm just about to meet the mother,' said Boxer. 'I'll get back to you.'

Boxer got into the back seat of the Mercedes. D'Cruz sat behind the chauffeur. He'd already told Boxer not to say a word about their business in front of the driver. They drove down Piccadilly, through the tunnel under Hyde Park Corner and crawled into Knightsbridge. It was cold, barely above freezing, the winter lingering through March. Londoners walked at their usual break-neck speed, hands thrust into coat pockets, collars up, merciless with dawdlers. D'Cruz stared out of the window at the darkening scene outside the Royal Mandarin Hotel and the new development of One Hyde Park.

'I've always looked after Isabel,' he said quietly. 'She works in publishing but she doesn't need to. A couple of years ago, I moved her into this new house in Kensington from where she used to live in Edwardes Square because her neighbour, some divorced banker, kept pestering her. It was supposed to be temporary, one of my residential investments, but for some reason she's still there. She's never been interested in anyone else since we split up. I was the only man she ever wanted. I feel responsible for her.'

Boxer nodded, said nothing, surprised at the intimacy.

'Does she have a relative or a close friend she can rely on?' Boxer asked, after some moments. 'Someone who can support her ... through all this?'

'It won't be me,' D'Cruz said. 'We're close but there are limits. Her younger sister, Jo, is with her now. They'll be all right for about a day but don't be surprised if she gets rid of her after that. Her closest friend, Miriam, is a diplomat's wife in Brazil. She might be able to come over.'

A scooter pulled alongside the passenger window on the driver's side. The rider wore a black helmet, visor down, and a bulky, black anorak, but what Boxer noticed was the lack of gloves in the freezing cold, and that there was no good reason for him to stop. The helmet did not turn. The rider's right hand flipped the visor up and then reached inside the black anorak. Boxer didn't wait to see what it came out with. He hauled D'Cruz out of his seat by the collar of his coat and threw him in the footwell, rolled on top.

'Drive,' he roared, as the window shattered with an explosive pop and he felt the diamonds of glass shower over his back. A thud.

'U-turn,' shouted Boxer.

The limo lurched forward, made an arc in front of the on-coming traffic, which had just come through the green light. Cars swerved, braked and honked. Boxer pushed himself up, twisted his torso and looked out of the window in time to see that the Vespa, which had peeled away from the line of traffic, was heading back towards Hyde Park Corner.

'Follow that scooter.'

The Mercedes dug into the tarmac and powered forward, heading for Hyde Park Corner. D'Cruz grunted underneath Boxer, who tried to keep his eyes focused on the scooter's tail light up front. Then the tail light went out.

'Where the fuck is it?' said the driver.

The traffic slowed to a crawl up to Apsley House. They had no chance.

'We've lost him,' said Boxer. 'Take us back through the park.'

Hyde Park, dimly lit, stretched out beyond Rotten Row to the deeper darkness of the Serpentine. The freezing night air buffeted through the car. Boxer checked behind, pulled D'Cruz up from the footwell, put him in the corner away from the smashed window, swept the glass off with his arm. He ran his hands along the back seat, found the bullet hole. D'Cruz would have taken it full in the chest.

'What now?' said the driver.

'Get back onto Kensington Gore,' said Boxer. 'Slow down. We're all right here in the back.'

The gold of the Albert Memorial flashed past in the gloom. The high-rise lights of the Royal Garden Hotel welcomed them from the darkness of the park. D'Cruz brushed himself down, shivered in the cold. After a few more minutes they pulled up outside a new development on Aubrey Walk. The Mercedes parked in the street. D'Cruz told the driver to take a walk.

'Maybe there's something you want to tell me before we go any further,' said Boxer.

D'Cruz was still in a state of shock. His hands trembled, his breathing came quick.

'Thanks for that,' he said. 'That was above and beyond the call of duty.'

'Martin Fox can organise a bodyguard for you.'

'Yes, I'll speak to him about that.'

'Who wants you dead, Mr D'Cruz?'

'I think you can call me Frank now,' he said, and hit the inside of the car door with the side of his fist, trying to pull himself together.

'Frank?'

'I don't know.'

'It looks as if you've upset more than one person.'

'Why do you say that?'

'If the people who've kidnapped your daughter want to get paid, or want you to take them seriously, they wouldn't kill you, the paymaster general, on your first day.'

'I don't want you to talk to Isabel about this,' he said fiercely. 'It will frighten her half to bloody death.'

'It hasn't done a bad job on you; or me, for that matter,' said Boxer. 'I'd have expected this in Karachi, but not here.'

'I'm going to have to think this through,' he said.

'I'll be your sounding board,' said Boxer. 'I'd like to know what I'm getting myself into.'

D'Cruz stared into the middle distance, flicking off bits of glass stuck to his wool coat.

'Is this an Indian mafia problem?' asked Boxer.

'What do you know about that?' said D'Cruz sharply.

'Nothing. It's just a question. Martin Fox told me you were a Bollywood actor. There are connections.'

'Keep to the work you know,' he said, looking hard into Boxer's face.

'I'm trying to,' said Boxer. 'But I found myself in the personal security business instead.'

'Sorry,' said D'Cruz. 'I'm still shaken. Sorry for that. Yes. Let's go and meet Isabel.'

'You still haven't told me anything, Frank.'

'Only because I don't know,' he said.

D'Cruz opened the car door. The driver ran over to help. He waved him away, went to the intercom, pressed the bell, spoke. The barred gate opened. They walked through a parking area into a fake Georgian square which, at its centre, had a landscaped garden, whose plants were bagged against the frost. There were very few lights on in the other houses. It didn't look as if D'Cruz was the only one using this upmarket estate as a haven for foreign investment.

A woman opened the front door, threw her arms around D'Cruz, pressed her face into his neck. She was crying and saying 'Chico', over and over for about a minute, a tissue balled in one of her fists. Boxer stood back, let them have their privacy. D'Cruz extricated himself and walked her into the warmth and light of the hallway. They stood, silhouetted, and talked, their mouths inches apart. She nodded as he explained, their heads turned in Boxer's direction. Isabel Marks went out to shake his hand, apologised for her state, brought him in.

It was always a tense moment to be introduced to the mother of a kidnapped child. If she didn't like the look of you, no matter what the husband might say, you'd lose the job. Boxer elicited extreme feelings. He either inspired total confidence or profound dislike. He'd noticed that the wives of very rich men generally fell into the second category. They did not like it that he was self-contained, unimpressed by wealth, not overawed by status or celebrity, and didn't have a molecule of subservience in his nature. He'd been fired on doorsteps in Miami, São Paulo, Nassau, Manila and Johannesburg.

Boxer had, initially, been concerned by the kind of residential development where she was living. But as soon as their eyes met, hands connected, Boxer knew that Isabel Marks was not the sort of person he usually came across in the hallway of a ten million pound home. There was no artifice, no attempt at disguising her terrible suffering. The barriers were gone and he fell straight through to the person inside. He had the strange feeling that a child might have, on looking into its mother's eyes: total trust, absolute belief, complete certainty. The meeting had a seismic effect on him because these were convictions that had been absent from his own life. He was surprised to feel a distant yearning, made even more poignant because it was for something he'd never experienced himself.

She withdrew her hand, went back under the arm of her ex-husband, who steered her down the hall, but she couldn't restrain a perplexed look over her shoulder at the light green eyes following her every move. They went to the kitchen at the back of the house, which gave out onto a patio garden and some huge lime trees beyond. Isabel excused herself to wash her face and repair her make-up.

'Where's Jo?' asked D'Cruz, when she came back.

'She had to leave,' said Isabel.

'Had to?'

'We were getting on each other's nerves,' said Isabel. 'I'm probably too raw to be with at the moment.'

'Bollocks,' said D'Cruz, surprising Boxer with his idiomatic English. 'She's self-obsessed, that's all. No sympathy. No empathy. She's probably seeing it all from the point of view of Alyshia's aunt.'

'Don't wind yourself up, Chico,' said Isabel. 'Pour some drinks.'

She set out tumblers and ice, while D'Cruz poured the whisky. Boxer was drinking her in. She was probably a few years older than him. The dark hair, still worn girlishly long. The brown eyes under straight black eyebrows, permanently on the brink of concern. Those eyebrows unbuckled something in him. High cheekbones with the slightest declivity beneath. He imagined men wanting to … he imagined himself kissing her on that spot. Then the full mouth with pronounced Cupid's bow. Her sallow skin, a strange hybrid of Mediterranean olive and London pallor that would go instantly golden in the sun. Her figure was almost old-fashioned, compact, as if it was used to work, but with a waist cinched by a belt that emphasised her high bosom and round hips. She was wearing a coffee-coloured cashmere wool dress, with a wide chocolate belt and suede high heels with the same cocoa content.

They sat with a bottle of the Macallan and a bucket of ice in the middle of the table, and Isabel insisted on first name terms. She had been working over the conversation she'd had with the kidnapper and had some notes in front of her.

'He seemed relaxed about time,' she said. 'When he told me I could call him Jordan, he said, "why be formal when we'll be talking to each other over the next few weeks, months … possibly years".'

'A tactic. He wants you to think he's got all the time in the world,' said Boxer. 'We'll see what sort of a hurry they're in as time goes on.'

'I stupidly asked if he was a friend but I could tell, even with the voice distortion, that he wasn't. He waffled on about "working on the relationship side of things", which annoyed me. I wanted to talk to Alyshia, not listen to his crap.'

'Don't be annoyed. He's showing you that he's rational, reasonable, even sensitive,' said Boxer. 'It's good to try to make that attitude last as long as possible.'

'I just wanted him to shut up and let me talk to my baby, but he said that wasn't going to be possible because she'd been kidna—'

Isabel broke down. D'Cruz got up and put his arm around her. They were very tender with each other, despite D'Cruz's mention of 'the limits' earlier. This gap in their lives was their only creation and they were each other's sole comfort. It always moved Boxer to see how parents were forever pregnant with the presence of their offspring, wherever they were in the world. And when they were taken or just gone, how that exquisite fullness turned to black. He couldn't help but think of Amy; his wayward, crazy child – gone, but at least not disappeared. Had his own mother been like Isabel Marks when she'd been told he'd run away from school? Three weeks he'd been gone, aged fourteen, when they'd picked him up in Valencia, and all she'd done was given him a rocket when he got home.

'Do you have children?' asked Isabel, jolting Boxer out of his thoughts.

'A daughter. She's seventeen.'

'Do you have a photo?'

He handed over his flipped open wallet.

'She doesn't look seventeen.'

'That's because she's fourteen there and sweet and innocent,' said Boxer. 'Now she doesn't allow photographs. She's in the process of derailing her life and I suspect she doesn't want anybody to see it in pictures.'

'They're a constant worry,' said Isabel, handing back the wallet. 'What else did Jordan say after he told you he'd kidnapped Alyshia?'

'He told me not to go to the police or press, but it was delivered with such a terrible threat ... I mean, so graphic I'm not sure I can bring myself to repeat it.'

'Try,' said Boxer. 'We need to know the psychology of the man we're dealing with.'

'He said we might be extremely lucky to see her some months later but she would be in an advanced stage of decomposition and forever troubling the mind of the person who'd "chanced upon her remains". I can't imagine the sort of person that would be prepared to stick that kind of image in a mother's mind. It's inhuman.'

'Yes, it is,' said Boxer, worried by what he was hearing. 'What about the demands?'

'I managed to ask him what he wanted and assumed, because Chico is such a well-known businessman, that it would be money. It's crazy, isn't it?' she said, momentarily diverted. 'I was so glad when Alyshia came back from Mumbai. I'd been terrified that this sort of thing would happen to her out there, but not ... not here. Not in England. Not in London.'

'It can happen anywhere in the world, Isabel,' he said, and realised that he'd enjoyed using her name.

'Jordan said it wasn't about money. That this won't be sorted out with "a good old bit of Asian haggling". He wouldn't "be so crass as to put a price on my child's head". He said Chico would dismiss this and I should persuade him otherwise. For some reason, that jolted me back to reality. It had all been *surreal* up until then. It made me think that Jordan knew Chico, so I asked him. He crapped on about Chico being in the media so much that everybody thinks they know him, but that I would know him better than anybody. And that again made me think he knew him personally. He also said he would only talk to me. If we tried to put anybody else on the line, he would hang up. Three strikes and you're out, were his words. After that, somehow, I had the presence of mind to ask for proof that he was holding Alyshia. And he gave me the nickname ... the nickname I haven't heard her use for ages. It used to make us laugh and laugh. The nickname for her grandmother ... my mother.'

Isabel broke down again, dropped her head onto her ex-husband's shoulder.

A phone rang somewhere in the house. Isabel went rigid,

sprang out of the chair and ran upstairs. Boxer followed, stood in the doorway of the bedroom. She looked at the screen, shook her hand at him and answered it. Boxer went back downstairs to the rare sight of a billionaire slumped and deflated by something beyond his enormous powers of control. D'Cruz dragged the whisky bottle across the table, poured a finger into his glass.

'If you're happy for me to continue,' said Boxer. 'I'll have to go back and pick up some equipment.'

'She likes you. There's no problem there,' said D'Cruz. 'You're hired.'

'While I'm away, you should think about where you want me to conduct this operation. From here? A rented flat? A hotel room? Isabel and I are going to have to be in close contact. A kidnapper's call can come at any time and I have to be on hand to help her with negotiations,' said Boxer. 'You should also make up a shortlist of trusted friends who you would be happy to negotiate on your behalf. The first thing we're going to do is try to take Isabel out of the firing line. The other thing to think about is this kidnapper knowing you and is that relevant to what happened earlier this evening? Is there someone who bears you some intense personal animosity, who would have the resources to conduct a professional kidnapping? Because with the flesh on the bones that Isabel's just given us, that is what I believe we have here: a highly professional, well thought-out, psychologically directed kidnapping. I'll be bringing some recording equipment back with me, but nothing that won't fit in a small suitcase. If Isabel would rather stay here, that's fine by me. I'll need a room to set up the computer and the recording equipment and a place for me to sleep, that's all.'

'I'm not going anywhere,' said Isabel, from the door. 'That was Jo, by the way. Apologising. She sends her love, Chico.'

'Bloody, fucking woman,' said D'Cruz.

'I've told her there's no need for her to come back. I'll be quite all right with Charles.'

Boxer had the use of the Mercedes. He sat up front with the driver, a thick-set Londoner with the customary shaved head, who'd used the last hour to install a sheet of plastic in the shattered window in the back. As they glided through the streets of Notting Hill, Westbourne Green, Maida Vale and Kilburn, the driver told him he'd only worked for Mr D'Cruz three times and nothing had ever happened before.

'You spoken to your boss yet?'

'Not on a Sunday evening.'

'Is he the nervous type?'

'Nah, he'll just tell me to take a car with bulletproof windows. We have them. I just didn't think that's what we were getting into.'

'Nor did Mr D'Cruz,' said Boxer. 'You'd better make sure your boss doesn't talk to the police about this until you get clearance from me. There's a delicate situation in progress.'

'I don't think my boss has very close relations with the police … if you know what I mean.'

'But don't try dealing with that bullet in the back seat yet. We'll organise some forensics to take a look at it.'

The car pulled up outside a large white stucco house in Belsize Park Gardens. Boxer took his small suitcase up to the top floor flat. He emptied out the clothes he'd been wearing in Lisbon, opened the case's false bottom and removed twenty-five thousand euros in cash – his poker winnings. He put the blocks of money in a wall safe behind a painting of a sixteenth century Italian businessman, which had a heavy rococo gilt frame. He took out two thousand pounds in cash, shut the safe and replaced the painting.

In the kitchen he went into a saucepan cupboard, removed the pans and a section of the base. He lifted a floorboard underneath and took out a Belgian-made FN57 semi-automatic pistol with a spare twenty-round clip. He liked this gun because, although it was light, at just over one and a half pounds fully loaded, the rounds could penetrate Kevlar vests. He put the gun, spare clip and one thousand five hundred of the cash in the false bottom of his overnight bag. He packed clean clothes. From the spare room he took a small, hard-shelled, silver suitcase, which contained the recording equipment, a laptop computer, memory sticks, note-pads, pre-prepared sign cards for use in telephone calls with the kidnappers, felt tips and Blu-tack. He took a pen torch and some metal tools from a cupboard and put everything by the front door and only then did he make his call to Martin Fox.

'I've been hired,' he said. 'Somebody on a Vespa took a pop at D'Cruz en route between the Ritz and his ex-wife's house in Kensington.'

'Jesus,' said Fox. 'Still, I can't say D'Cruz had the look of a virgin about him.'

'You'd better arrange for forensics to extract the round from the back seat and get the ballistics on it,' said Boxer. 'I've told the driver not to touch.'

'I'll talk to D'Cruz's insurers and I've got a DCS Makepeace coming to my office tomorrow to sit in my operations room. I'm sure he'll be interested in that.'

'I wouldn't think it's connected to the kidnap. Why kill the guy you want to pressurise?' said Boxer. 'You might get D'Cruz a bodyguard, too. The driver's calm, said he'll sort out a limo with bulletproof glass. Has D'Cruz spoken to you yet?'

'No. Was he shaken?'

'*And* stirred,' said Boxer.

The arrivals hall at Gatwick was busy. Mercy was standing well back from the mêlée of people crowding the barriers in front of the double doors from the customs area. She had a clear view down the channel where the arriving passengers would come. Amy's flight had landed.

There was a strong smell of fried food, which was contributing to the sickness in her stomach, although most of that was coming from her mental state. She couldn't help but feel that she'd failed as a parent. She thought her incapacity must have stemmed from the absence of her own mother, who'd died in childbirth when Mercy was only seven, and the insanely strict regime that her Ghanaian police officer father had imposed on her and her four siblings. Maybe she was just repelled by parenthood because, as the eldest, a lot of mothering had fallen in her lap. She'd never in-tended to have a child so early herself. Amy hadn't been planned, arriving, as she had, soon after she and Boxer had split up. She'd found herself with little to offer Amy, reluctant to impose her father's type of discipline, but with no alternative up her sleeve. Then again, she was dealing with somebody harbouring the suspect genes of Charles Boxer, and that was never going to be easy – a runaway boy with a 'missing' dad, a war veteran, a lone professional, a man who, as far as she'd known, had never loved passionately, and had now become someone, since leaving his job at GRM, worryingly detached.

The double doors opened and Amy came through alone, her blonde highlighted ringlets framing her wide face with its caramel complexion and her dark, full lips. Her light green eyes scanned the crowd confidently. She had a small rucksack on her shoulder and was dragging a very large sky blue suitcase, which Mercy didn't recognise and seemed far too big for a weekend away.

Mercy hung back, waited. As Amy reached the end of the channel, a black man stepped out of the crowd. He was around thirty, short dreadlocks, long black leather coat, white scarf. Not, to Mercy's practiced eye, a criminal. He kissed Amy once on the cheek and took over the suitcase. He gave her a quick hug around the shoulders and let her go. Mercy held up her mobile phone and took a photo of them. They walked together, chatting. It was like seeing an older brother meeting his sister.

They passed Mercy, who gave them twenty yards and fell in behind them. They headed off towards the short term car park and railway station. A surge of people from the station came between Mercy and Amy just at the moment when Amy peeled away from her partner and went down the escalators to the platforms. The guy continued with the suitcase. Mercy stuck with Amy. She already had a return ticket and went down the escalators to see her daughter sitting in the lighted waiting room.

She loitered on the gloomy platform, watching Amy through the window, intrigued to see her daughter as a person out of her normal sphere. Amy was chatting to a couple in their forties. She was at ease. The couple were laughing. It could have been … it should have been Charlie and Mercy, but it wasn't. That rush of failure swept over her once again. She felt drawn to the window as if to a screen she couldn't stop watching. She came closer and closer until her face was up to the glass. Her daughter continued, oblivious. She was telling a story, making faces, being entertaining. Then she looked up.

The first thing Mercy saw was fear, then anger.

'Oh fuuuuck,' said a voice behind her.

Mercy turned to see Karen approaching the waiting room. There was fear in her face, too. Was this all she inspired? Fear? No, no, there was always anger, too.

'What ... what ... are you doing here, Mrs Danquah?'

'I thought I'd meet you off the plane.'

The waiting room door slammed shut.

'That's typical, that's fucking typical of you,' said Amy, throwing her fingers out at her mother. 'You can't stop playing cops, can you? You have to play the fucking cop with your own daughter now.'

Mercy was momentarily shattered by the change in her daughter. The instant ferocity. And yet, seconds ago, she'd been so dazzling. Where's the dazzle? Let's have the dazzle back, girl.

But it was true what Amy had said. There was nothing she could do about it. Detective Inspector Mercy Danquah reasserted herself in moments. You don't do thirteen years in the Met and let a seventeen-year-old girl put one over on you.

'If I'd been "playing cops", I'd have organised a reception committee for you and your smooth friend and had you both arrested on smuggling charges,' said Mercy. 'Then where would you be, Amy Boxer? In fact, I might still do that with my photo evidence.'

She held up her mobile with her shot of the two of them on the screen. Amy stared with wide open eyes.

'You'd better tell me what was in that suitcase.'

Amy couldn't speak through her anger at being caught so red-handed. The humiliation raged through her. And all in front of her friend, too.

'It was just cigarettes, Mrs Danquah,' said Karen quickly. 'That's all it was. Promise. Just cigarettes.'

Isabel was cooking the duck rice that she should have done for her lunch party. D'Cruz took Boxer up to a spare room at the top of the house. He dropped his overnight bag on the bed and asked if there was a central room with a phone jack where he could put the recording equipment.

They went back down to the next level where there was a room with a desk, a chair and a single bed. D'Cruz watched from the door while Boxer plugged the recorder into the mains and phone jack. He asked for Isabel's mobile number, entered it into the computer within the recorder. He also booted up the laptop and tapped Alyshia's mobile number into the Pavis tracking software. No signal.

The pressure of D'Cruz's need to question him filled the room. Boxer carried on with his work. D'Cruz crossed the room, looked down into the dark gardens at the front of the development.

'What's it like to kill someone?' he asked.

'Why?' asked Boxer. 'You thinking of doing it?'

'I don't have it in me,' said D'Cruz.

'An interesting observation.'

'When I was in the movies I played gangsters who killed people, but I never knew what it was like.'

'Didn't the director introduce you to gangsters who *had* killed people?'

'Sure, but I could never ask that question,' said D'Cruz. 'The situation was never right. You know, there's an etiquette.'

'Are you asking me because of what happened to you on the way here?'

'No. I'm asking you because I can and you're intelligent enough to give me a reply.'

'I can only tell you one thing,' said Boxer, turning to face D'Cruz. 'That once you've killed someone, whatever the circumstances, it takes you out of the world of men. You are forever apart, because you have done the greatest possible damage one human being can do to another.'

They searched each other's faces for some time. The lamps buzzed in the room.

'You surprised me when I first saw you,' said D'Cruz.

'I found out when I was a homicide detective,' said Boxer, smiling ironically, 'that the most successful murderers were the ones who didn't go around looking like killers.'

'I only meant that I thought you'd be bigger,' said D'Cruz.

Boxer grunted a laugh.

'I used to be bigger,' he said. 'I got sick travelling in a remote part of Mongolia after I left homicide. A group of tourists picked me up just in time. I lost a lot of weight and never put it all back on.'

'What was wrong?'

'They never found out,' said Boxer. 'Do you ever *answer* questions, Frank?'

'Not often with the complete truth, I have to admit,' said D'Cruz. 'It's part of my job to keep people guessing.'

'I'm glad you told me that,' said Boxer.

'I won't *lie* to you,' said D'Cruz. 'Not to the man who's going to bring back my daughter.'

'This box here will record all calls to Isabel's mobile in the house,' said Boxer, and he handed D'Cruz an attachment. 'If she goes out and takes a call from the kidnapper, she should hold that to the phone.'

Boxer tested Isabel's phone to make sure her calls were being recorded.

'I asked you to think about something while I was out,' said Boxer. 'You got anything to tell me yet?'

'It's dog eat dog out there,' said D'Cruz, tapping the window. 'In Bombay, I mean.'

'Personal animosity,' said Boxer. 'Not business. Someone who would want to take revenge for something you've done, or been perceived to have done. Think visceral. This is someone attacking your *family*. They've taken your *child*.'

D'Cruz shook his head, pursed his lips.

'Women?' said Boxer.

'Women?'

'I imagine you get a lot of attention from women, Frank.'

'You think this is the work of a *woman*?'

'No, but women can inspire men to extreme behaviour,' said Boxer. 'Where do the big human emotions come from? What makes men behave irrationally? Jealousy. Betrayal. Humiliation. If Jordan is serious about not wanting money—'

'It will come down to money in the end,' said D'Cruz. 'You'll see.'

'I'm not so sure, which is why I want you to think and, more important, tell.'

D'Cruz blinked at the possibility of his enormous capacity to pay becoming an insignificant factor. The fear spread out from the whites of his eyes and he turned to face his insubstantial reflection in the window.

7

'Tell me about Hackney. Tell me about London Fields,' said the voice. 'You could live anywhere in London. Notting Hill, Chelsea … no, maybe they're a bit too grown up for you. What is it about Dalston, Broadway Market? Why'd you want to live there, Alyshia?'

'What do I get for answering this question?' she asked.

'This isn't a question. This is a conversation. This is us getting to know each other.'

'You gave me the rules. I'm just playing by them. I answer questions. You give me rewards. Nothing comes for free, you said.'

'You're a hard little nut, Alyshia,' said the voice, without conceding it. 'Tell me what you want.'

She wanted to see very badly. She couldn't bear the disorientation of the constant dark. Seeing would give her a sense of power. It would give her possibilities.

'I want a shower,' she said.

'No, a shower is a very expensive item. You need a lot of air miles before you get a shower,' said the voice. 'I tell you what. I'll let you take the sleeping mask off if you talk to me nicely.'

'I live in Hackney because I want to be an ordinary person. I want to make friends with people who like me for who I am. You probably don't know what it's like to be born into wealth.'

'It must be terribly, terribly hard,' said the voice, mocking. 'Probably harder than it is to live in a Mumbai slum with no electricity, no clean water, shit running down the street and rats who don't knock at the door.'

'I wouldn't know. All I know is what it's like to arrive in a perfectly insulated life. To never have the opportunity to learn from experience, because there's none available.'

'So how did *you* turn out so nice,' said the voice, aggressive. 'Where did *you* get this special insight from?'

'My mother.'

'Another very comfortable person from a privileged background. I suppose she made you sit on chairs without cushions?'

'She let me see over the walls.'

'Oh, *very* nice, Alyshia. The prison walls of wealth. Yes, we know how high and thick they are,' said the voice. 'You're not being very persuasive. I'm finding it hard to feel sorry for you.'

'I don't remember asking you to feel sorry for me,' said Alyshia. 'You asked me why I live in Dalston. I'm telling you it releases me from my family background. When I'm there, I'm not a billionaire's daughter. It's a huge relief. I get the same treatment as everybody else. I'm liked, or loathed, for being who I am.'

'That's such bullshit,' said the voice. 'If you said you lived in Dalston because it's close to where Duane and Curtis live, I'd be more likely to believe you.'

'That's not where I met them.'

'No, that's true. You met in the Vibe Bar on Brick Lane.'

'You're changing the subject now,' she said, rattled by the extent to which he'd penetrated her life. 'If we're finished with "Why do you live in Dalston?", you should let me take off the sleeping mask.'

'I should, but I won't, because we haven't.'

'So your rules are arbitrary.'

'The rules only apply to you and I apply them. I decide when you've given me a strong enough reply. In this case, you haven't given me the real reason why you want to live in Dalston while your mother lives in a fancy development on Aubrey Walk. Such a relief to get away from that tiresome guy in Edwardes Square. Christ, he fancied your mum something rotten. She wasn't having any of it. I doubt she's had any since Chico, has she?'

'You're disgusting,' she started, but there was something else that really shocked her. 'How do you know that name? My mother's name for my father?'

'It's such a pity your mum couldn't put up with that over-inquisitive cock of Frank's, otherwise they'd still be together. I mean Sharmila is incredible, don't get me wrong, given the choice, but, you know, she's a bit "No Billionaire Should Be Without One", isn't she? Don't you think? Alyshia? You're not talking to me.'

'You've done your homework. It's impressive.'

'Yes, but there's only so much you can learn from careful ob-servation and working around your subjects. There comes a time when you have to communicate. You know, get inside. So cut the poor little rich girl crap and tell me the real reason why you moved to Dalston, which, let's face it, is not known for its brilliant transport links?'

'I wanted to live in a place where I knew my mother would never go.'

'But why's that?' asked the voice in mock surprise. 'You *love* your mother. She's the one who let you see over the bullshit walls of wealth. If anybody should be able to handle the reality of her daughter's life, it should be Isabel Marks, shouldn't it?'

'She sees things in a certain way.'

'*Things?* What are these things?' asked the voice, digging down deep into the mocking well.

'She tries to influence me.'

'Keep going, Alyshia. We're nearly there.'

'She tries to matchmake. She's not so different to an Indian mama. She's always introducing me to *nice guys*,' said Alyshia with some vehemence. 'Today. What day is it? Sunday? Well, Sunday, I bet you she was going to introduce me to another of her so-called "*cool* guys". They're all writers or TV people, actors or wannabe directors, but none of them, not one of them, feels like a real person with a real life. They're all the same; they've been manufactured by some system. I reckon with a bit of research, you'd probably find they're all within two people of knowing each other.'

'She just wants what's best for her only daughter,' said the voice. 'You can remove the sleeping mask now.'

They were sitting around the plain wooden table in the kitchen, eating the duck rice.

'How will this … this event,' said Isabel. 'I can't say the word. I can't bring myself to say it. Kidnap. There. It sounds so old-fashioned, like highwaymen or press-ganging. How do you think this *kidnap* will unfold?'

'The calls you've had so far don't say "express or credit card kidnapping" to me. They're not looking for a quick cash return for minimal investment. If they were, we'd already be negotiating the money, its delivery, the release and pick-up terms. It would all be over within forty-eight hours.'

'That would be the case for, say, twenty thousand pounds,' said D'Cruz. 'But what if it was for more serious money? I can get twenty thousand in seconds. For millions, I need time. So don't write off the money demand yet.'

'Frank is right. For a larger sum, they will have prepared themselves for a longer game,' said Boxer. 'Express kidnappers don't get complicated. They just keep their victim drugged in the back of a van until they get their money. To hold someone for any length of time takes investment and research. You need to investigate your victim, find a safe house, organise transport, hire people, buy equipment, arrange supplies. The kidnappers we are dealing with have shown their considerable reach. They knew when Frank left Mumbai and arrived in London. They're calm. They come to you with convincing proof of capture.'

'So how long would this sort of kidnap normally last?' asked Isabel.

'Between a week and two months, although, depending on their resources, it could go on indefinitely.'

'They did mention a figure,' said Isabel, desperate now. 'When Jordan was talking theoretically about the "good old Asian haggling", he said he would start at fifty million and we would come back at twenty thousand and eventually agree at half a million. So what league does that put him in?'

'Except that he said it *wasn't* going to be like that,' said Boxer. 'Now they've spoken to both of you and given you proof of capture, they'll make you sweat for at least a day or two before they come back with any sort of demand. If they're really looking for a large financial return, it's also possible that they will try to scare and/or upset you during this time as part of the sweating process. The fact that they've said all "discussions" – that was the word they used, wasn't it, Frank?'

'Yes, "discussions".'

'Not "negotiations". All *discussions* will be conducted through Isabel, who's already experienced a very ugly threat to undermine her equilibrium, means that we should not assume a quick resolution. I also think that they would expect Frank, with all his resources, to bring in some expertise. So they'll be expecting a consultant to be guiding Isabel.'

'You mean *you* won't be talking to them?' said D'Cruz.

'They don't want to talk to me. They have no leverage over me. They don't even want to talk to you. That's why Jordan said he only wants to talk to Isabel, because they can bring emotional pressure to bear more easily on her,' said Boxer. 'The way we normally handle this is to have what is known in the business as a Crisis Management Committee, which is a fancy term for a team consisting of family members, loyal friends or possibly a lawyer. The next time Jordan calls, our chosen negotiator will tell him that Isabel's incapacitated due to emotional stress and he'll have to talk to x, y or z. This distances him from—'

'No,' said Isabel.

'No?' said D'Cruz. 'Charles is our consultant, Isabel—'

'I'm not having that,' she said. 'Nobody's going to negotiate on *my* behalf for *my* daughter. I wouldn't give anybody that responsibility. And I'm not taking any risks.'

'It would be a collective responsibility,' said Boxer. 'I would provide the strategy and tactics and rehearse all the possibilities with whoever we decide to use as the negotiator, but *you* would be involved at all times. The idea is just to put up a barrier between the kidnapper and you.'

'I understand, but I don't want that.'

'For God's sake, Isabel—'

'Let's sleep on it,' said Boxer. 'Look at it again in the morning. You should also think about bringing someone in who can give you some moral support. Your sister, Jo, is obviously not a candidate.

There must be somebody else. Frank mentioned Miriam.'

'Miriam's in Brasilia. I've already spoken to her and she's got her own problems with one of her sons. I didn't even tell her about Alyshia.'

'Who does that leave?' asked Boxer. 'Frank?'

The ex-wife and husband looked across the table at each other. Isabel had moved her food around her plate without eating it. D'Cruz's plate was clean.

'You tell him,' said D'Cruz. 'He should hear it from you this time.'

'We handle things in very different ways,' said Isabel. 'It's probably best that we don't spend too much time together in these stressful circumstances. I want to see Chico, of course. But I don't want him as my constant companion.'

'Who else then?'

Silence.

'At this rate, it's going to be just you and me,' said Boxer.

'I can live with that,' said Isabel. 'I don't like having too many people around me. It'll just make me irritable.'

'Are you *both* happy with that?' said Boxer, looking from one to the other.

They nodded.

'All right,' said Boxer, thinking: slowly, slowly, they'll come round. 'Tomorrow I'll introduce you to Mercy Danquah. She's going to be my co-consultant, which means she has to know everything about Alyshia's case and be able to take over if, for any reason, I'm incapacitated. She will also do some basic investigation around the case.'

Isabel looked nervous.

'Don't worry. She's used to doing this. She's discreet. The kidnappers won't know, and if by some miracle they do, she'll back off immediately. You have nothing to fear on that score.'

'What will she be investigating?' asked D'Cruz.

'She'll find out where Alyshia was last seen and by whom, she'll make contact with Alyshia's friends and colleagues and she'll want to go through her flat, check on credit card and bank card use, that sort of thing. Does anybody have the keys?'

'I don't,' said Isabel. 'She hasn't mentioned spare keys. But look, I'm very nervous about Mercy. You know what they said. Anything that even looks like police and—'

'Mercy's worked on dozens of kidnap investigations; she's very experienced.'

'So many?'

'That's just in the UK,' said Boxer. 'And every time the hostage has been returned safely.'

D'Cruz nodded, patted Isabel's hand. They finished their food, drank the remainder of the wine and D'Cruz had an espresso coffee before leaving. Boxer stayed in the kitchen while Isabel saw him out.

'You probably think I'm a very strange person,' she said, coming back into the kitchen.

Boxer looked up, said nothing: an old technique.

'No friends or family in my hour of direst need,' she said. 'Just a complete stranger appointed by my husband through an insurance company.'

'It's happened to me before, but it's not normal.'

'Are you concerned?'

'I don't like the expression "emotional rollercoaster", because there's some implied thrill, but it describes what happens in kidnappings quite accurately. One moment you're up, feeling as if everything is positive and going in the right direction, and the next you're falling into the deepest hole, feeling depressed and demoralised,' said Boxer. 'There are some white-knuckle moments, too, but the big difference with this rollercoaster is that there's not one bit of fun in it. And that's why you need people close to you, someone you trust, who can put an arm around you. This is an emotionally and physically draining experience.'

'I've always faced the hard things in my life alone. When Chico and I split, I saw no one.'

'But you had Alyshia.'

'True,' said Isabel, foundering. 'But when my mother died, Alyshia was away in Mumbai.'

'And your sister, Jo, failed you again?'

'My mother and Jo did not get on. She was not the right person to be with.'

'Kidnapping is a mind game. We sit here. They sit there. We

have no visual to help us. They've already shown they are very capable in the psychological dimension. It really would be good for you to have someone who knows both you and Alyshia by your side.'

'There's no one I can rely on,' she said, sitting back down at the table, 'except Miriam and now you, Charles Boxer.'

'I'm the outsider, remember. The one who gives you the objective view. I distinguish between the real danger and the tactical ploy. I make sure that you don't make the very natural mistakes that emotional involvement can lead you to.'

'Then you'll have to retain all that professional expertise and become an insider as well,' she said. 'We'll have to get to know each other. You can start by telling me where you got those eyes.'

'My mother.'

'And where's she from? Afghansitan?'

'Sydney, Australia,' said Boxer. 'And not an exotic suburb. Parramatta. Her mother died young. Her father was an out-of-work drunk, prone to getting into bar-room brawls. My mother left home when she was eighteen, became an air stewardess and never looked back, or went back, not even for his funeral.'

'What's her name?'

'Esme.'

'That's an old-fashioned name.'

'It was her grandmother's name.'

'Where is she now?'

'Hampstead. She lives in a place that my daughter calls The Coughing Hospital.'

'Is she ill?'

'Not in that way,' said Boxer. 'She has a flat in Mount Vernon, which was the old Consumption Hospital. It's Amy's way of poking fun at my mother because Mount Vernon is a very luxurious development.'

'So how is she ill, if she's not ill in that way?'

'She's an alcoholic.'

'Like her father?'

'Maybe, but for different reasons,' said Boxer, swerving away from the complicated things. 'She was in an industry that demanded a lot of entertaining.'

'I thought air stewardesses *served* the drinks.'

'She met a TV commercials director on a flight and ended up as his producer,' said Boxer. 'It was a job that involved taking people out to lunch and dinner and drinking a lot at both. She never got out of the habit.'

'Do you get on with your mother?'

'She's a difficult personality,' said Boxer, thinking: women, they understand things from the very little you tell them. 'Her condition makes her … temperamental, by which I mean mental, with a bad temper.'

They laughed, even though, to Boxer, it was no laughing matter.

'She likes my daughter, Amy. She especially likes Amy now, which is impressive,' said Boxer. 'I hear them cackling in the kitchen like a witch and junior witch stirring the eye of newt, toe of frog stew.'

She laughed again.

'Why wouldn't Frank stay?' said Boxer, to get some of his own questions in. 'He told me you had limits, but this is an extreme situation.'

'I like him. I admire him. I even still love him … which is crazy, I know, given that he destroyed me with his constant betrayals, and not just sexual betrayals. I thought he was a man of great qualities, a man to trust, somebody worth believing in. But I forgot the most important thing about him. He's an actor. He can pretend to be anything. He can make women believe he loves them. He can make his employees trust him. He can make politicians lick his fingers. But, as I came to realise, there is nothing there. Or rather there is something there, it's just that … I didn't say this in front of him, because it would have sounded too brutal, but it was the real reason I thought that the kidnapper knew him. When I questioned whether I was the person who knew Chico best, the kidnapper said: "That's what happens when you become wealthy. You make sure people know you as little as possible. It leaves you with more leeway for ruthlessness". And that's what there is inside Chico, right at his core: a monstrous ruthlessness. And *that* is why we can't spend too much time together, because I can pretend for only a limited amount of time, and *he* knows I know.'

85

'What about Frank and Alyshia?' asked Boxer.

'I can answer that, but only to a certain extent,' said Isabel, uneasy now, getting up to clear things away, offering him things which he refused. The whisky bottle reappeared with ice and tumblers. She sat back down with a coffee. 'Alyshia has always been a special child to Chico. He saw something extraordinary in her and gave her his attention in a way that he hasn't to his children in Mumbai. I'd like to think he saw his better self in her. She, like him, is very beautiful. She's razor sharp up top, always exceptional at maths and did a degree in economics at the LSE. Chico wanted her to do an MBA before she came to Mumbai, but at twenty-one, most colleges were reluctant to take her. I don't know what Chico did but the Saïd Business School in Oxford offered her a place and after a two-year course, she went straight to Mumbai to learn the real thing at her father's side.'

'He wanted her primed to run a major global corporation.'

'That's what he's building. He already had the Bollywood studio, which he's expanded, and the films were, and still are, making huge amounts of money, not just in India, but because of Asian communities all over the world, globally, too. He was making the sort of money that meant he could buy whole businesses. He knew cars would be the next big thing out there so he bought a parts manufacturing company supplying TATA. Then he went into tyres and plastics and finally into making cars himself. He also bought a steel works so that he had the whole manufacturing process under his control.'

'He told us he's sent some prototype electric cars over to raise interest in a manufacturing base in the UK.'

'Oh, yes, he was very excited a few years back when he got hold of some new battery technology,' said Isabel. 'He's already making and exporting them all over the world.'

Boxer nodded, made a note. If this kidnap wasn't about money, maybe it was about forcing D'Cruz to stop a manufacturing process.

'What about Frank's family?' he asked.

'His parents died before I met him. He had two sisters. The eldest one died of AIDS after years as a prostitute. The other has disappeared and, despite his fame and fortune, has never reappeared.'

'That's a dark past.'

'That's Chico for you.'

'So for Alyshia to come back from Mumbai to live in London means that something must have gone badly wrong between her and Frank?'

'Neither of them will talk about it.'

'How long did she last at his side?'

'Two years.'

'And you've no idea what happened?' asked Boxer, not quite believing her.

'Alyshia stayed here for a couple of months while she sorted herself out. I couldn't help myself and I think I badgered her too much. She moved out, rented a flat in Hoxton and got a job in a bank, which is about as far from what she wanted to do as you could possibly imagine. Now she works, doesn't seem to contact any of her old friends and has a social life that I don't know anything about unless I invite her here. I'm pretty sure she has no love life, which for a beautiful girl like Alyshia is ... is extraordinary.'

'Was she happy before she left for Hoxton?'

Isabel sipped her whisky and thought for some moments.

'She's not *un*happy,' she said. 'If you met her, she wouldn't be withdrawn. You wouldn't think her obviously depressed. We're still very close. We have a nice time together as long as we don't touch on certain subjects. But ...'

'She's changed?' said Boxer.

'We all do, I suppose,' said Isabel. 'I was young and happy myself until at twenty-three I found out what Chico was doing ... what he was like.'

'Will Frank ever talk to me? I mean, really reveal stuff to me?'

'No,' she said mildly, 'but that doesn't mean you shouldn't try.'

'He's already told me he's not too clever with the truth,' said Boxer, 'but that he wouldn't *lie* to me.'

'At least he's told you that and you don't have to go through the painful process of finding out for yourself,' said Isabel. 'It must mean he likes you or, don't take this badly, he's got you to do his bidding and when it's done, he'll drop you like a hot rock.'

'How do you manage to despise Frank and yet still love him?' asked Boxer, thinking out loud, unchecked.

'He's the only man I've ever loved,' said Isabel, unbothered. 'Nobody else has come close. The memory of that is still very powerful. It means that—'

'Approximations won't do.'

She nodded, as if that was, at least, part of the answer.

'How old were you when you met him?' asked Boxer.

'Seventeen.'

'That's Amy's age,' said Boxer, holding his finger out to stop her pouring more than an inch of whisky into his glass.

'Meaning?'

'She's young, crazy and impressionable. How old was Frank?'

'Twenty-five.'

'Did your parents like that?'

'No, they didn't, until they met Frank and that was it. He won them over. They didn't want me to marry him until I was twenty-one. He persuaded them to let us get together two years earlier. By the time I was twenty, I'd already had Alyshia.'

Boxer did some calculations in his head.

'So you're telling me you got divorced from Frank when you were thirty-three and you haven't had a relationship since?'

She shrugged.

'There's been no lack of opportunity,' she said. 'It's just …'

The phone buzzed in his pocket. Mercy. Damn. He was going to have to take it. He excused himself, left the kitchen.

'I've got her,' said Mercy. 'We're at home. She's up in her room, sulking.'

'And? What was it all about?'

'Karen's new boyfriend is in a cigarette smuggling ring. They send groups of girls out to the Canaries where they give them suitcases full of cigarettes to bring back to the UK. The girls have a good time away, all expenses paid, and they bring back 8000 ciggies each. Price per pack in the Canaries three euros, price in UK seven quid. Even with the crap exchange rate and price undercutting that's three quid a pack profit. Twelve hundred quid a girl. Flight, hotel, clubs, drinks – can't come to more than a couple of hundred. Six girls, six grand. Thanks very much.'

'It's not going to take Customs and Excise too long to work that out.'

'I've told them they're lucky not to be banged up with a criminal record before their eighteenth birthdays.'

'How did Amy take it?'

'Badly. Very abusive,' said Mercy. 'But you know, I was watching her before she saw me. She was in the station waiting room talking to a couple our age. She was fantastic. Lovely. Entertaining. I mean, completely dazzling. I didn't recognise her. Perhaps it's just us, Charlie; *we're* the problem, or maybe it's just me?'

'It's both of us.'

'What are we going to do with her?'

'Whatever you do, don't lose it, Mercy,' said Boxer. 'The first thing is that somebody's going to have to keep an eye on her while we're on this case.'

'I've been calling round,' said Mercy. 'None of the usual suspects can do it.'

'Do you want me to talk to my mother?'

'The drunken hag?'

'At least they get on with each other,' said Boxer. 'And she doesn't seem to drink so much when Amy's around. It could be good for them both. Mum will calm her down and give her some self-respect back.'

'And Amy will do the cooking.'

'I'll call her,' said Boxer. 'Don't blame yourself, Mercy. We're all part of it. Amy, too.'

'I love her and I just get hate thrown back in my face. It's wearing me down, Charlie,' she said, and he imagined her, forehead against the wall, wishing it was easier.

'Where are you now?'

'At the girl's mother's house in Kensington,' said Boxer. 'You're coming here tomorrow to meet her?'

'I won't get there until 11.00 a.m. I'm seeing the DCS first.'

'I'll call Amy.'

'Good luck. I doubt she'll take your call.'

They hung up. Boxer tried Amy. No answer. He went back to the kitchen.

'Trouble at home?' asked Isabel.

'It's complicated,' said Boxer.

'I'm used to that.'

'Mercy Danquah isn't just my co-consultant. The photograph I showed you earlier is our daughter. She and I conceived Amy and then split up soon after, but we stayed good friends. It looks as if Amy is expanding her horizons a little quicker than we'd like,' said Boxer, and gave her a recap of his phone call.

'I can't believe you could sit here talking to me so calmly with all that going on in the background.'

'It's the nature of the job,' said Boxer.

'Never showing your emotional state?'

'Just controlling it,' said Boxer. 'And over the years, I've developed a nose for when things have gone really bad.'

'How did you meet Mercy?'

'I was in the army, she was at college,' he said, making mental notes of the lies that were building up. 'We had a fling, she got pregnant. We lived together for about a week until we found we were friends, rather than lovers. We separated and shared Amy.'

'How did you find out you were just friends?'

'We revealed everything to each other,' said Boxer, 'and found we were too alike. There was no attraction of opposites. We had nothing to hide and nothing more we were desperate to know. That doesn't mean I wouldn't protect her with my life if it came to it, but it means we could never be lovers.'

'And you found that out before Amy was born,' said Isabel. 'So what's Charles Boxer been doing for the last seventeen years?'

'I've had girlfriends, but being in the army, then homicide and then this job, which can send me to Mexico or Yokohama at a moment's notice, has made a home life tricky. Women don't like that. Or rather, they like it for a bit until they find plans destroyed, holidays in ruins, life on hold.'

'So why do you do it?'

'I've found that I need to be in situations where life really matters,' said Boxer. 'In the army I saw action in the Gulf War and after that normal life seemed monotonous and dull. So I became a homicide detective, which I soon realised was a mistake. Finding out why somebody had been killed was not the sort of intensity I was looking for. It was post-life. Historical. Redundant. The victim beyond help. Kidnappings gave me what I was missing. Everybody intensely wanting the victim to survive. The extreme pressure of ensuring that survival. The reward of the victim's safe return to life and their family.'

'And has that always happened?'

'Almost always,' said Boxer, mind shuddering at the thought of Bianca Dias.

'And what about Alyshia?' asked Isabel Marks, her face breaking apart with a sudden onslaught of fresh worry.

'From what you and Frank have told me about her, she has the perfect profile for surviving well,' said Boxer, serving up his professional patter rather than the brutal truth. 'The gang is professional. They won't harm her. All we have to do is keep calm, be patient and they will tell us what they want. We'll take it from there.'

She came round the table to him, stood by his chair.

'I know we hardly know each other,' she said, 'but would you mind holding me?'

He stood, put his arms around her. He was nearly a foot taller and her head fitted into his chest. Her arms hung by her sides at first, like a child in shock. Then they found his waist and she drew herself in.

8

'What did I tell you?' said Skin, who was wearing dark blue Umbro tracksuit bottoms, a red England shirt under his blue fur-lined jacket, and black trainers, which he had up on the dashboard of the van.

'What *did* you tell me? You've told me so much shit over the last few days,' said Dan, looking right, turning left, 'I can't remember.'

'About it not being over?' said Skin, smoking viciously. 'And here we are …'

'Tidying up loose ends,' said Dan.

'That's what I mean,' said Skin. 'Think about it.'

'You mean, at what point does someone decide that *we're* loose ends?'

'Got it in one.'

'That would mean Pike would have to find someone to do you,' said Dan. 'And then someone else to do his killing for him.'

'All I'm saying is that if he gets shot of us, there are no more connections to the leading players.'

'And all I'm saying is that it's not so easy for him,' said Dan. 'I know Pike likes having me around. Medical advice on tap.'

'What use is medical advice if you're back in the Royal Suite?' said Skin. 'Don't underestimate Pike. Underneath all that fat there's a skinny, ruthless little bastard, screaming to get out.'

'Have you taken something?'

''Course I have,' said Skin. 'We've been told what we've got to do this time.'

'What did you take?'

'What's it to you?'

'I just want to know what I'm dealing with.'

'A little dexy, that's all,' said Skin, lighting a cigarette from the one he'd just finished in less than a minute. 'Got to be sharp for this.'

'You worried about anything, Skin?'

'Like what?'

'I mean to do with this job?' said Dan.

'That fucker, the cabbie, he's not going to be alone, not after what we did to those sheep the other night,' said Skin. 'He didn't like that. *I* didn't like that. He was having the same thought we were when we dumped them in the river: I'm fucking next.'

'So you think he's going to have company.'

'I know he's going to have company. Pike does too,' said Skin. 'Are you as handy with a gun as you were with the needle?'

Dan shrugged.

'I thought not,' said Skin. 'In that case, you deal with the cabbie. Get behind him. Point blank in the back of the head. Don't think about it.'

'Don't *think* about it?'

'I can see we're going to have a problem,' said Skin.

'And you?'

'I'll deal with the help,' said Skin. 'The unexpected help.'

'Who's going to give him the money?'

'I will,' said Skin, beckoning it over.

Dan gave him the money taped up in a plastic bag.

'Just get behind him and *pop*. The money's in plastic, so don't worry about the mess.'

'Right. Don't worry about the *mess*?'

'You're thinking too much,' said Skin. 'Don't.'

They pulled up, parked in the street outside the house in Grange Road, got out, walked past the cab in the driveway and down by the garage to the back garden. Skin knocked on the door. The cabbie opened it. Skin held up the money package.

'Pay day,' he said.

'You're not wearing your hoods,' said the cabbie, unimpressed.

'Didn't think we had to now the girl's out of the picture,' said Dan.

The cabbie let the door fall open, saw the spider web tattoo on Skin's neck and cheek, shook his head.

'You should have seen the guy who did it to me,' said Skin. 'Had the spider crawling up his nose, the web all over his face. Everybody held the door open for that fucker, I can tell you.'

'Go through to the other room,' said the cabbie. 'I'll count it in there.'

'Cuppa tea would be nice.'

They went through the kitchen, round the table and chairs, didn't sit down. Skin dropped the money in front of the chair that had been pulled out, Dan stood behind it, leaned against the wall.

'You can sit,' said the cabbie, pointing to the chairs on either side of his.

'Been driving all day,' said Dan. 'Need to stretch.'

'Sit the fuck down, both of you,' said the cabbie, hitting the table hard.

The door to Dan's right flew open. A young guy stood there with a gun held out in front of him. Skin fell back as he reached inside his jacket. The young guy fired. There was a grunt as Skin hit the floor and he returned fire lying flat on his back. The young guy took the bullet full in the chest. It knocked him back through the door into the corridor where he hit the wall hard and slid to the floor. Dan had already taken out his gun, pointed the cabbie into the chair with it. He stepped behind him, put the barrel to the back of his head. His fist tightened around the grip. The cabbie's neck was shaking.

'Do him,' said Skin, through gritted teeth from the floor.

The muscles tightened in Dan's jaw. His ears were ringing because the young guy hadn't used a silencer.

'Don't think about it,' said Skin.

He fired. The cabbie slumped forward violently. Dan stood there blinking, couldn't believe what he'd just done.

'I'm hit,' said Skin. 'The fucker's got me in the shoulder.'

Dan snapped out of the horror, put the gun away, went into casualty mode, dropped to his knees.

'Left shoulder,' said Skin, hissing through his teeth.

'Bone?'

'Fuck should I know? You're the nurse.'

Dan inspected the torn leather at the shoulder, saw the blood on the carpet. He put on latex gloves, opened the jacket, felt with his fingers around the wound.

'Feels like flesh only,' said Dan. 'Let's get your arm out of your sleeve.'

'Fuck me,' said Skin, wincing.

'It shouldn't hurt yet.'

'You the one with the hole in his shoulder?'

Dan lifted Skin's arm out, peeled the shirt back from the wound, pursed his lips.

'What is it?'

'It's just a nick but you're going to need stitches.'

'A nick?' said Skin savagely. 'Fucking ruined my jacket.'

'I can do it,' said Dan, trying to tear a strip off Skin's shirt for a bandage.

'Leave off,' said Skin, slapping his hands away. 'That's my England shirt. Use your own fucking shirt.'

Dan went into the kitchen, found a clean tea towel.

'Look on the bright side,' he said, 'if it had hit the bone, I'd have spent the rest of the night getting fragments out of the muscle and you probably wouldn't be able to lift your arm above your shoulder for the rest of your life.'

'You're back to your old cheerful self now.'

Dan bandaged up the wound, pulled Skin to his feet. He picked up the dropped gun, shook his head. Skin's blood everywhere, in the carpet, soaked into the floorboards. Nothing to be done.

'How does it feel, Alyshia?'

'It's good,' she said.

'Seeing the world with fresh eyes,' said the voice.

'Fresh eyes,' she said, barely listening, wincing against the harshness of the light as she let her vision drink in the surroundings, which were nothing special, but after so long in the dark seemed visually palatial.

White walls, high ceiling with three caged strip neon lights. Her bed was in one corner. It was an old metal hospital bed with tubular legs and a bed-head whose thin bars provided complete discomfort for the human skull. The mattress was foam with a rubber covering and a white cotton sheet stretched over it. The wall next to the bed was solid but the one behind her head, a stud wall. The wall with the door in it had a large, full length mirror facing the bed. In front of it was the bucket latrine she'd used earlier. The floor was of roughly skimmed concrete. She thought she might be in a room constructed within a warehouse. Above her head was a vent of the sort seen in hotel rooms to provide heating or AC. She was not cold in just her bra and pants.

'We have too much visual stimuli in this world,' said the voice.

Now she saw what she'd missed. In two corners, about ten foot above her, were white speakers and, hanging in the centre of the room, a microphone.

'We're all in a permanent state of distraction, don't you think?'

'Could be,' she said, distracted.

'But now, for the first time, you've started to see things clearly.'

'For the first time?' she said, rolling her eyes.

'Don't roll your eyes at me, Alyshia.'

She started looking for the camera.

'You've overcome your instinct for denial.'

'I'm not a liar.'

'Maybe not, but you massage the truth to suit your purposes,' said the voice. 'It's quite a common psychological phenomenon.'

'Is it?'

'For some reason, you wanted me to think well of you. You wanted me to believe that, in moving to Dalston, you'd recognised the truth about your privileged life and rejected it. Whereas the real motivation was to get out from under your mother's beady eye.'

'What's wrong with that?'

'Why do you feel the need to be secretive with her?'

'She's made me the focus of her life. She wants to live her life vicariously through me. She wants me to go out with the sort of man that *she* would like to go out with ... or at least, I think she would. It's not healthy. All I'm doing is withdrawing a little from her world and trying to live on my own terms.'

'Is that so?' said the voice.

She shrugged her shoulders off the bed. The voice was annoying her.

'I think we should do a "before" and "after" comparison,' said the voice.

'Before and after what?'

'Let's start with the here and now. Why Duane and Curtis? You've never had any black boyfriends before and now you've got two.'

'I don't sleep with either of them. They're just friends.'

'Curtis is unemployed and Duane's a plumber's mate.'

'So what?'

'These aren't what you'd call natural mates for Alyshia D'Cruz BA, MBA.'

'I don't know what you're trying to get at. Perhaps you need to tell me your prejudices before we carry on.'

'*My* prejudices.'

'*I* don't have any.'

'You're not being very forthcoming, Alyshia,' said the voice. 'Maybe we have to look at the "before", which will inform the "after". Tell me about Julian.'

'Julian?'

'Yes, Julian Maitland-Smith, that boyfriend you had when you were at the Saïd Business School in Oxford. He was at Christchurch doing a PhD on some weird bit of history. Bit older than you, wasn't he? Twenty-nine to your twenty-three. Do you know where he is now?'

'No. We split after I left to go to Mumbai.'

'He's in prison.'

'What for?'

'He got used to a certain lifestyle when he was with you. Couldn't give it up. Had to finance a little addiction problem. He went to stay at a friend's parents' manor house outside Great Missenden, thought he'd lift a little Fabergé vodka cup from their collection to keep the bailiff from the door. He'd assumed he was alone in the house, but hadn't banked on the au pair. She caught him in the act. He beat the crap out of her, left her for dead. You didn't read about it?'

'No.'

'They did him for attempted murder,' said the voice. 'You were lucky there.'

'What's this got to do with anything?' she said, feeling cold, rubbing her shoulders with her hands. 'Can I have a blanket?'

'There was an incident in Oxford, wasn't there? Something that triggered your departure to Mumbai.'

'An incident?'

'Interesting,' said the voice. 'Before we had denial, now we have a classic case of *tabula rasa*.'

'What's that?'

'Didn't do Latin? What's the world coming to?' said the voice. 'Clean slate. In this case, you've decided to wipe an unpleasant memory from your mind. Politicians, historians, businessmen and neurotics do it all the time. It makes life more tolerable.'

'Remind me,' she said, turning to the mirror now, certain that it was a viewing panel. 'I've been through a lot tonight; my brain's not working well.'

'Abiola Adeshina. A Nigerian colleague of yours at the Saïd Business School.'

'Yes, the Nigerian guy,' she said, feeling something drop in the pit of her stomach.

'Did you like him?'

'He was all right.'

'He was rather in love with you, wasn't he?' said the voice, 'But then again, everybody was rather in love with Alyshia D'Cruz, weren't they?'

'He was out of his depth,' she said, not meaning for it to sound so cruel.

'Yes, I think that's fair to say,' said the voice. 'But was he arrogant, prejudiced, brutal and stupid?'

'No.'

'Some of your friends would say that was unusual for a Nigerian,' said the voice. 'Was that why you singled him out? You spotted his weakness? I suppose the Saïd Business School had a module on the Law of the Jungle.'

'*I* didn't single him out, *he* singled me out.'

'Oh, right, so *you* were the victim,' said the voice.

'I'm tired,' she said.

'You can go to sleep just as soon as you've told me what happened to poor old Abiola.'

'He was besotted with me. There was nothing I could do about it.'

'But you did do something about it, in order to get rid of him,' said the voice. 'You just *over*did it, that's all. Maybe you hadn't expected Abiola to be quite so sensitive, although I think it would have taxed most young guys, what you did. You and Julian.'

'The counsellor afterwards said it was *nothing* to do with me. If people are going to do that sort of thing, there's nothing anybody can do about it. Their mind is made up. They've come to their own decision. The flaw is in *their* character.'

'Hey, all right, Alyshia, all right. I can see this upsets you. So just tell me what happened. Maybe it will make you feel better to give me your version of events.'

'I don't want to talk about it.'

'It'll be on with the sleeping mask again,' said the voice, teasing. 'And I know how much you hate the dark. Folds you in on yourself too much, doesn't it? Let me talk you through it. He was in love with you. Let's start there. How did you respond to his attention?'

'I didn't.'

'I think you did.'

'How do you know about this?' said Alyshia, glaring at the mirror now. 'How do you fucking know?'

'Investigative journalism.'

She threw herself back, stared up at the ceiling. Tears came. Her mouth crumpled and cracked. She cried in wracking sobs that lifted her bodily from the mattress.

'What are you crying about?'

'I didn't mean for it to happen,' she said, through the snot and saliva.

'You meant for *something* to happen,' said the voice. 'I mean, there was premeditation. The design was for maximum humiliation. I assume it was Julian's idea, that. Only he would have the insight into the young male psyche. Or perhaps not.'

Alyshia rolled over, turned her back on the mirror, shoulders shuddering.

'There's nowhere to hide,' said the mocking voice.

'I told Julian that Abiola was becoming a problem.'

'Tell it to the mirror,' said the voice. 'I want you to look at yourself telling it.'

She rolled over.

'Julian told me he could solve the Abiola problem. All I had to do was lead him on, make him believe that I was interested in him.'

'You probably didn't have to work too hard, either,' said the voice.

'No, that's true, he was primed,' she said, and was immediately attacked by another stab of grief, which brought her knees up to her chest.

'So he believed you?'

'Of course he did.'

'Just so that we know how far you went, he was going to introduce you to ...'

'His parents.'

'And what were you going to tell them?'

'That we were engaged.'

'Serious stuff,' said the voice. 'And how did that go?'

'It didn't. We never met. They wanted to meet afterwards but I couldn't. My father went to see them.'

'Tell me how you worked it.'

'Julian asked Abiola to come to his rooms in Christchurch for afternoon tea. Abiola liked that sort of English thing.'

'And what did he find?' said the voice. 'Tiffin? Not exactly. Tell me what he found, Alyshia.'

'He found me having sex with Julian.'

'Whose idea was that?'

'Julian's.'

'Yeees, it sounds like one of his,' said the voice. 'What were you thinking?'

'I ... I don't know. I was just doing what I was told to do.'

'Following orders, yes; they get that all the time at the International Criminal Court,' said the voice. 'Do you ever think about why you did such a thing, why you allowed yourself to be manipulated?'

No answer.

'All right. We'll come back to that,' said the voice. 'Just tell me how Abiola reacted to this sight of you fucking Julian?'

'He ran.'

'Where to?'

'His flat.'

'What did he do there?'

'He hanged himself.'

Isabel Marks went to bed. Boxer had told her, as she'd extricated herself from his embrace, that she had to be rested, that the days ahead were going to be tough. Boxer stayed in the kitchen. He tried Amy again; still no answer. He sat there for an hour, sipping watery whisky and thinking: he had a reputation now. Why was he doing this? Killing kidnappers. Twelve years at GRM and not a thought of it. For no apparent reason, his father came to mind. The pain of that broken connection. But why so acute now? A few months shy of forty years old. He turned that over and over but, as always, couldn't seem to make the logic work. Time to move on. At least he'd had the presence of mind to explain to D'Cruz that on the three other occasions he'd provided his special service, he'd always known who he was up against before he'd acted. A single man was no match for the mafia or a terrorist organisation, so he would only give his final agreement once it had been established who the perpetrators were.

Since that handshake in the Ritz, there'd been the shooting in Knightsbridge and the revelations from D'Cruz's family history. He was relieved at his caution. D'Cruz was the sort of man who only cared about himself and his immediate family. Then there was 'Jordan', as he called himself. He was concerned by what Isabel had told him. This was not playing out in the usual way. There seemed to be intelligence at work here, both sorts, and not necessarily geared to achieving the greatest possible financial return. There was no solid evidence yet, but Frank D'Cruz's personality and Jordan's psychology gave him the disconcerting feeling that the motive for this kidnap might be punishment.

He went up to bed and listened in at Isabel's room on the way. Silence. He hoped she'd be able to sleep through the night. He continued to the top of the house, showered and got into bed, as he'd always done since the age of ten, naked. He turned out the light, closed his eyes and was immediately aware of his insulation from the usual roar of the metropolis. There was no whooping of sirens from police and ambulances. The roar of city turbulence was still there but muffled by the quality of the build. Why was she living here? Why leave the real thing in Edwardes Square to come to live in this fakery, with no life and the sterility of investment about it? His mind was trembling in the confusion at the edge of sleep when the door to his room clicked and his eyes snapped open.

Isabel Marks entered, wearing a satin nighty, floor length. She came to the edge of the bed and stood over him. He wondered whether she was sleepwalking, with the stress ravaging her mind, but she looked directly into his eyes with an indecipherable expression. She said nothing, but flipped the thin straps of the nighty from her shoulders. The satin fell to the ground in a rush. Her firm, high breasts quivered as her arms dropped back by her sides. She slipped under the duvet next to him. Her hands were cool on his stomach, possibly with apprehension at what she was doing. Her breasts pressed into his rib cage, her pubis brushed against his thigh.

'I couldn't sleep,' she said. 'I don't want to be on my own.'

This was the most unexpected complication of all. Boxer tried to think himself into the head of a different man; someone more professionally responsible, more emotionally prescient. It was a hopeless task; the physical reaction to her touch was instant, and a feeling of extraordinary tenderness towards her, too. Something he hadn't experienced with any of his girlfriends of the last seventeen years.

He let his arm fall around her shoulders and with that confirmation, she ran her hands over his chest and stomach, the tops of his thighs, grasped his penis with a touch that sent something live through his veins. She kissed his chest as she moved her hand slowly and with a certainty of its effect. She looked into his face, concerned at his ecstatic torment, and he loved her in that moment, because he saw what was so special about her: her extraordinary capacity to care. It was both her greatest strength and her most awful vulnerability, and it gave him a powerful desire to protect.

It had been some months since Boxer had been to bed with a woman and it took self-control not to unleash that masculine urgency which a long sexual drought can precipitate. He was more gentle than he ever remembered being. He was like a man unburdened from disappointment and betrayal, as if all his wounds had not just healed but never been.

They didn't stop there but came back to each other again like fascinated creatures. He looked up at her, amazed, as she arched backwards, driving herself down onto him, her whole torso trembling and, with a shout, collapsed forward onto his chest.

Afterwards, they lay staring at the ceiling.

'Tell me how you met Mercy,' she said. 'You didn't seem to want to tell me everything before.'

'It's a long story,' he said, 'and we need to sleep.'

'Give me the short version.'

'I met her in Ghana.'

'What were you doing there?'

'I was eighteen. I'd run away for the second time, looking for my father who'd disappeared when I was seven. He was wanted for questioning in connection with the murder of my mother's business partner. He'd absconded. I thought he might have gone to West Africa, because I'd read that people liked to lose themselves in that part of the world. I didn't find him, but I found Mercy instead. Her father was a senior policeman and a brutal disciplinarian. A friend in Accra had given me an introduction to him and he let me stay in his house while I searched for my father. He treated his five children like servants. They moved around the house silently, heads bowed, and wouldn't dare look me in the eye in his presence. He beat them. It was a sad, dark, miserable family and I helped Mercy run away from it. She came back to England with me. I joined the army, in the ranks, and she went to college. The first Gulf War came along and we didn't see much of each other for a couple years, but we stayed very close and then she got pregnant. By the time she had Amy, it was over.'

Silence. She kissed his hand on her shoulder. They went to sleep.

*

At six o'clock they woke up.

'The phone,' said Isabel. 'It's the phone.'

And for a fraction of a second, it was just that. Two lovers who were going to ignore the intrusion. Then, in one movement, she came up off the bed and was out of the door and down the stairs, with Boxer on her heels.

'It's Alyshia's phone,' she said, standing naked in her bedroom, staring at the screen.

'You have to take it,' said Boxer. 'You've just woken up. You're still drugged from a sleeping pill. Give yourself some time to sharpen up.'

He left the room, came back with a pen, pad and the laptop, sat close to her on the bed so that he could hear the voice, nodded.

'Hello?' said Isabel, with a crack deep in her throat. 'I'm … hello? Who is that?'

'Isabel Marks?'

'That's me.'

'This is Jordan. I'm sorry to call you so early but your daughter is not well.'

'What? What did you say? Alyshia's … what's wrong?'

'Yes, I thought that might wake you up. You're that sort of woman, aren't you, Mrs Marks?'

Boxer glanced at the laptop and saw that Alyshia's mobile had been tracked by the Pavis online system. It was travelling down the M4 in the direction of Reading.

'What's the matter with Alyshia?'

'You see, that's what I mean. You're different from Chico …'

'Chico? How do you know I call him that?'

'You're different from Alyshia.'

'What are you talking about? Just tell me what's wrong with her.'

'There's nothing wrong with her,' said the voice. 'She's bearing up under the strain.'

'Let me talk to her.'

'Still not possible, I'm afraid.'

Boxer held up a pre-prepared sign card with PROOF OF LIFE written on it.

'Then you must give me some proof that she—'

'You're going to have to take my word for it, Mrs Marks.'

'I don't think that's very fair,' said Isabel, running on adrenaline. 'How can we be expected to proceed in good faith if you're not prepared to give us—'

'Cut the shit, Mrs Marks. Life's not fair.'

'No, I *won't* cut the shit. You're holding my daughter. If you want this conversation to proceed, I want proof that she's alive.'

'Don't antagonise me, Mrs Marks. You know what can happen.'

Silence from Isabel.

'Yes, that's right, I just take it out on Alyshia,' said the voice. 'Turn the heating off in her room. Cuff her to the bed for a day. Let her lie in her piss and faeces. Slap her around a bit. No lasting damage but very uncomfortable.'

Isabel glanced at what Boxer had written on the pad, said nothing.

'How do you think I know that you call your ex-husband Chico?' said Jordan. 'Right. There's your proof of life.'

'It's not ...' said Isabel, her legs shaking uncontrollably, 'it's not proof of life.'

'It will have to do for now.'

Boxer shrugged, pointed to what he'd written before.

'What do you want?' said Isabel. 'You said it wasn't money, so what is it? If it's something more complicated than money, we're going to need time. Tell us what you want so that we can—'

'What? Negotiate?' said the voice. 'Is that it? I bet Frank's organised one of those for you: a ne-go-ti-at-or. There's nothing he'd like better. He's probably sitting next to you now, telling you what to say. But this isn't going to work like that. I'm not going to demand anything material from you. I don't need it. How do you think I know you left your house in Edwardes Square because of that tiresome neighbour of yours?'

Isabel didn't know what to say, just shook her head, frowned.

Boxer scribbled more words. She looked at them without seeing.

'And you're right about Jason Bigley; I mean, not to take him on as a novelist. These screenwriters, you know, they're great at structure but they can't imagine the whole world. And Chico was right. Alyshia Bigley? I don't think so. And she wouldn't have looked at him anyway. You know why, Mrs Marks?'

Isabel fell silent.

'Mrs Marks?'

'I am *not* Mrs Marks,' she said, and the chill in her voice froze Boxer's hand.

'Who are you?'

Boxer wrote: CAREFUL.

'I *was* Mrs D'Cruz, but now I'm just Isabel Marks. No Mrs.'

'I see. I'll call you Isabel then.'

'If you must.'

'Do you know why she wouldn't give Jason a second glance, Isabel?'

'No.'

'Because her interest lies elsewhere.'

'And what do you mean by that?'

'When I say she's quite well, I should be a little more precise,' said the voice. 'She is physically well, but mentally a little distressed. She's on a bit of a guilt trip; has been for a while. Since she left Mumbai, in fact.'

Isabel snatched at the bait.

'What happened in Mumbai?'

'I'm not surprised you were kept out of the loop on that one,' said the voice. 'But let's take it step by step. First, the guilt trip. Your ne-go-ti-at-or will tell you where to find it. Ta-ta, as they say in India.'

Boxer looked at the computer screen. The phone signal was now stationary and transmitting from a point on the A404 between the M4 and M40 motorways, in the Maidenhead and Marlow area. He called the operations room in Pavis.

9

As the phone went dead Isabel collapsed on the bed. Boxer called Pavis. He stood over her, still naked, feeling like a teenager caught *in flagrante* by a parent. Isabel, prostrate with guilt, pulled the duvet over her head.

Boxer left the room, went upstairs, showered. He was a changed man and it worried him, not least because Mercy was going to spot it with their first eye contact. He dressed. Isabel's door was still shut as he went past her room. He transferred a recording of the call to his iPod and sent another to the ops room at Pavis. He went down to the kitchen, made coffee and toast and played the call back to himself, again and again. He phoned Fox at Pavis.

'You heard that call yet?'

'DCS Makepeace and I have been listening to it.'

'Do you want to run it past a profiler?'

'I'm doing that now,' said Fox. 'We haven't had your situation report yet.'

'I haven't had time. I'm here on my own with Alyshia's mother, Isabel. She's turned down a Crisis Management Committee and she hasn't got anybody close to support her, or rather she doesn't want anybody around her, including D'Cruz.'

'That's a bit ... intense.'

'I'll work on her and D'Cruz, see if I can bring them round,' said Boxer. 'I'll get you your report as soon as I can.'

Isabel came in; he hung up. She was dressed and composed,

had come through her shame and was out the other side of it. There was nothing to be said.

'Pavis are getting a profiler to listen to the recording of that phone call.'

'He frightens me, this ... Jordan,' she said. 'He's worked his way into my life ... our lives.'

'He seems to know you all,' said Boxer. 'Or at least knows someone who does.'

'He's like a poisoner,' she said, 'who wants nothing more than to be amongst the people whose food he's laced.'

'How big is your world?'

'The wider circle is too big to know everyone in it.'

'And he knows both ends: Mumbai and London.'

'It also frightens me that he doesn't seem to want anything from us.'

'It's early days yet. It could still be a ploy for wringing the maximum money,' said Boxer. 'He's impressing upon you the power of his knowledge. He wants you to know that there's nothing he hasn't covered. It makes you feel vulnerable to have had your life penetrated to that extent.'

'And I can tell you it's working. That and the fact that he's holding my life in his hands,' said Isabel. 'Alyshia *is* my life. If anything happened to her, it would kill me.'

'It would kill anybody. Even if you were happy, fulfilled with a whole rich life of your own, it would still be unbearable,' said Boxer. 'That's what kidnappers do. They drag you to that precipice and show you what's over the edge. He's shaping you into the person who will do anything he asks. The so-called successful kidnapping is less about holding the hostage and more about the manipulation of the family. He is sweating you so that when the time comes, you will exert the maximum influence on Frank.'

'I hope you're right,' she said. 'But something's making me ... I feel it in my gut: doom-laden.'

'It would be unusual if you didn't feel that way. It's intended,' said Boxer. 'This is the rollercoaster. The mind game has started. My job is to make sure you win that game.'

She nodded, her jaw muscles twitched in her cheek as she

pulled herself together. He poured her coffee, gave her toast. She waved it away. He insisted.

'You can't do this on an empty stomach.'

She ate with no appetite for it.

'You handled that call very well.'

'I didn't think so. I hated him too much. I couldn't stop myself.'

'That's why, normally, we'd create a barrier between you and the kidnapper, because the emotional involvement is very strong and it's two-way: he's breaking you down, manipulating you, and you're hating him for it,' said Boxer, easing off as he saw the resistance in her face. 'He was throwing his weight around in that call. He hit you early, wrong-footed you. He was cavalier about the proof of life process, aggressive and threatening throughout, and showing off his knowledge – a classic undermining tactic. He wants you to feel unsafe, watched.'

'He knew about *you*.'

'He'd have guessed that Frank would have K&R insurance. That's all. If he knew me, he'd have called me by name.'

'He knew about my neighbour in Edwardes Square.'

'Gossip,' said Boxer. 'Unless you were keeping it a secret.'

'No, I talked to my friends about it. Everybody knew why I moved house.'

'And Frank knew, too, so it was something known in Mumbai and London.'

'What about Jason Bigley, the man I'd invited to lunch on Sunday to meet Alyshia?' said Isabel. 'He knew the content of my call with Chico.'

'He's listening in on your calls. He knows your mobile number from Alyshia's contact list. He has a tracking system so he knows where you are. People have been listening in on mobile phone calls since they were invented.'

'And the guilt trip?'

'Don't get involved in speculation,' said Boxer. 'It sucks up too much energy and it's unproductive. We wait until we pick up Alyshia's mobile. What I want from you now is more background detail on Frank's Mumbai world, as best you know it. I have to write a situation report this morning before Mercy arrives at eleven. I'll type while we talk.'

Boxer went upstairs, came back down with the laptop, set it up.

'You know I haven't been to Mumbai in years,' she said.

'Tell me what you remember of it,' said Boxer. 'For a start: who did you marry? A film star? Or did that happen later?'

'It was 1984 and I married a businessman,' said Isabel. 'He was in import/export. Mainly between India and Dubai.'

'There's always been a long-standing relationship between Mumbai and Dubai.'

'There's a big Indian Muslim community over there: people running hotels and small businesses, and lower down the scale, a lot of construction workers. There's always been plenty of movement between the two places,' said Isabel.

'And Dubai has always been open-armed to people with money and not too concerned about how they got it,' said Boxer.

'I was naïve in those days, but so were my parents,' said Isabel. 'That's not entirely fair. I was crazily in love and my parents were utterly charmed by Chico. He had a powerful network even then, right at the beginning of his career. Important people, politicians that my father recognised, would speak up for him.'

'Import/export covers a multitude of sins in that part of the world.'

'I can't say all the people he knew were the sort you'd introduce to your parents,' said Isabel. 'There were some rough types. I think there still are. I suppose it's always useful to have access to people who can do the dirty work, like persuading people to move from a site where you're planning to build, for instance. In the phone call the kidnapper was listening into, Chico was bellyaching about some slum dwellers who were protesting in downtown Mumbai about being moved out.'

'And when did Bollywood call?'

'He won't tell you this, because he always wants to be thought of as a big star, but he'd had bit parts in movies since he was in his early twenties,' said Isabel. 'Always been obsessed with film. But he didn't get his big break until much later, a few years after we were married.'

'It's well known that Bollywood and the Mumbai mafia are close.'

'Is it? My English friends don't know that,' said Isabel.

'I don't know whether English people of our generation have fully connected with Bollywood yet,' said Boxer. 'Do you know how he became a film star? In those days, I doubt you were spotted; more likely "sponsored", in the Frank Sinatra "I Did It Their Way" style.'

'Chico's version of the story was that he did brilliantly in a screen test with the director Mani Ratnam.'

'Who's he?'

'He made a very famous gangster movie called *Nayagan,* based on the life of a big mafia boss,' said Isabel. 'But I'm not convinced by Chico's version. It could be one of his fantasies. Sometimes he gets his own filmography muddled up with Anil Kapoor's.'

'Still, he got a part in a movie.'

'A big part. It was an underworld movie in which he played a likeable *goonda*, or mobster. That was at the end of 1985. He was twenty-eight years old and he changed his name to Anadi Kapoor.'

'Why the name change?'

'Frank is Christian, Catholic, like most people from Goa. Bollywoood was a Hindu/Muslim industry with Hindu/Muslim audiences, so he thought a Hindu name would help him. He was very friendly with Anil Kapoor at the time. They're about the same age. Of course, Anil is very famous now, but he wasn't so big then. So Chico took the Kapoor name and attached Anadi to it, which means "Eternal". He was never short of self-esteem.'

'Did you like it that Frank was famous?'

'Bollywood was appealing to mass audiences. I liked the dancing but I found it a bit naïve for my taste. It was difficult to get excited about something I didn't admire,' said Isabel. 'And you're right, the reason so many movies were made about the Bombay underworld was that there were a lot of them involved in the business. That and cricket, which I've always found tedious, were the main topics of conversation. So I didn't fit in very well.'

'So you didn't know much about what was going on with Frank's business?'

'It always helped that he was neither Hindu nor Muslim and that he was a movie star. It meant he could play both sides of the fence and had friends in both camps. He also had a bit more freedom of movement just at the time when the Indian government was liberating the economy. Chico could set up companies, buy and sell them, had all the top government connections to pick up all the best infrastructure projects, and so on. He was the right man, in the right place, at the right time and with the right network.'

'Was that when things started changing between you and Chico?'

'It wasn't just that I didn't fit in. I hated that world. It was a *nouveau* world, where the men competed over money and power, and the women were judged by their looks, clothes, lifestyle and, to use Chico's horrible word, fuckability. There was something particularly ugly about it in Mumbai, or Bombay, as it was then. While we danced on glass floors with everybody else looking up, in screaming envy, there were millions living in, literally, shit. There were days when I just couldn't face going out. The comparative scenario was too vile. Chico knew I was all wrong for it. He developed an escort agency for himself and his friends. By the mid-nineties, he and I were finished. I was spending more than half the year in London, in the house in Edwardes Square, which he'd bought for me in 1992. By 1997, I'd got a job and my life in India was over.'

'What about his new wife?'

'Sharmila? She came from a poor background but she's very beautiful. She was some gangster's moll and Chico brought her in to run his escort agency and then ... she replaced me.'

'No hard feelings?'

'None. Chico has always looked after me. We never fought over Alyshia. He wanted her educated here, but to know Mumbai. So she was here with me most of the time and went to India for holidays. Alyshia would have been the only reason for us to fall out, but we never let it happen.'

'Sleep OK?' asked the voice, concerned.

'Yes,' said Alyshia, groggy from the drug they'd given her, confused at where she was and the level of care in the voice around her.

'Ready for a brand new day?'

112

'No,' she said flatly, as the reality flooded in.

'Even if I told you that this would be your last day on earth ... would you be ready for it?'

The fear seized her but she managed a what-the-hell shrug against the bed.

'I'm stuck here,' she said. 'What's there to look forward to?'

'Yes,' said the voice, conspiratorially, 'what's life without freedom?'

'Exactly,' said Alyshia, sounding bored.

'It's just life, but you'd be surprised how attached you get to it.'

'Can I take my sleeping mask off?' she asked, and realised, as she'd said it, how subservient she'd become.

'Good girl,' said the voice. 'I knew you'd pick things up quickly.'

She reached her hand up to her face.

'But no, you can't, not for the moment. Keep your hand down.'

'There's nothing to see in this room.'

'It shouldn't bother you then,' said the voice. 'Relax into it. Concentrate. Try to reach those moments buried deep in your unconscious mind, which reveal so much.'

'What are you?'

'A mad psychologist? You'd better hope not. Just an amateur one. I'll try not to make too many mistakes and put you into irretrievable trauma.'

'I thought you might be my confessor,' said Alyshia. 'All this talk about dredging my subconscious mind and my last day on earth.'

'Well, you *are* Catholic, I suppose, technically. Ever go to Mass?'

'I was christened.'

'That's something, but you've never confessed your sins?'

'One moment you don't have any and the next ...'

'They've got away from you,' said the voice. 'How little those closest to you know who you really are. They see what they want to see when you're a child and then, as time goes by, and you spend more and more time out of their sight, they lose track of you.'

'You're not going to tell my mother about Abiola?'

'I'm sure every beautiful woman has a horror like that somewhere in her life.'

'I'm atoning for my sins.'

'How? By being friendly with black guys?'

'I saw a black kid stabbed in the Strand ... was it last night?'

'And you called the police,' said the voice. 'I'm not sure I'd call that atonement.'

'How do you know about that call?' asked Alyshia, pouncing. 'The only person who knew about it was Jim. Is Jim in on this?'

'You'd be surprised at the people who were prepared to help us. For some, it was just a question of money. We *are* in London, after all. Others were looking for no reward at all. In that particular case, we were just listening in on your calls,' said the voice. 'But yes, you were being a good citizen, and one with a little subconscious motivation, too.'

'Do I know you?' asked Alyshia, wondering now if she'd come across this person in her free life.

'Yes,' said the voice, 'you know me. I'm your conscience. It's just that we haven't formally met for the last twenty years.'

'What do you put in that situation report?' asked Isabel.

'Everything to do with the situation as I find it,' said Boxer. 'A report on the initial call you received. The mental and physical state of the participants – that's you, Frank and Alyshia. The relationships between the participants and their relationships to others. The biographies as they stand at the time of writing. The idea is to bring the Director of Operations up to speed on the kidnap. Think of it this way: I'm here to help give you an objective point of view. They're there, at a further remove, to give *me* an objective point of view. It helps us to get things right.'

'Do you tell them *everything*?'

'I won't tell them what happened last night.'

'Has that happened to you before?'

'Never.'

She nodded, happy with that.

'I'm not sure *why* it happened,' she said. 'I've never done anything like that in my life.'

'Under normal circumstances it couldn't have happened because there would have been other people around,' said Boxer. 'It happened because I wanted it to happen. My professional self should have held me back.'

'I needed you,' she said.

'And I you,' said Boxer. 'What it means, we'll find out later. This is an intense situation and you may find you feel very different afterwards.'

'I don't think so.'

'What I'm saying is that you're vulnerable because of Alyshia and I don't have that excuse,' said Boxer. 'I just fell for you the moment I saw you and that has never happened to me before.'

'I saw that,' she said. 'It hasn't been the first time, but it was the first time I wanted it.'

'From now on we concentrate on the important thing,' said Boxer. 'Let's sort that out and look to ourselves afterwards.'

'I don't know whether I'm strong enough for that.'

'I don't know whether I am either,' said Boxer. 'It's just an expression of intent.'

'That's what makes parents so desperate,' said Alyshia. 'They can't control the people you meet, your friends and the ones you fall in love with. They cannot control fate.'

'They can equip you.'

'My mother's father was a diplomat, her mother from an army family. They walked the battlements of their moral standards, as my mother used to say, but couldn't stop her from marrying a womanising foreigner.'

'Even though they knew she'd regret it.'

'She couldn't be helped; she couldn't help herself.'

'Is that what happened to you and Julian?'

'I don't know,' she said, playing for time, feeling him prodding around again after the lull.

'Come on, kid, you must know whether you fell for him or not.'

'I thought I was in love with him at the time.'

'That sounds retrospective,' said the voice.

'I don't know what it was between Julian and me. It was intense, but I'm not sure it was love.'

'So, what did he have that you liked?'

'He knew what he wanted. That was attractive. I thought he knew who he was.'

'That was probably why your mother went after Frank.'

'There was no question of that. My father went after her.'

'And why was that?'

'A whole bunch of reasons, but one of them was probably that she gave him respectability.'

'Why do you despise your mother and worship your father?'

'Because my mother loves me without knowing who I am.'

'And your father?'

'He recognises me,' said Alyshia. 'And I recognise him.'

'What was the first thing that attracted you to Julian?'

'Why do you come back to *him* all the time?'

'It'll lead you to talk about other things.'

'Julian was unaffected by me; at least, that's how it looked.'

'Physically?'

'Everything-ly,' she said. 'I had to work hard to get noticed by him. He didn't go to goo in my hands.'

'I still don't see why you fancied him,' said the voice. 'He knew what he wanted and he didn't take any notice of you: doesn't sound like a great recommendation. You got anything more positive than that?'

'It wasn't his looks,' she said. 'He had terrible teeth, said it was from doing too much speed.'

'I said positive, Alyshia.'

'He was intelligent; he saw things differently.'

'Like a few thousand others at Oxford,' said the voice. 'Come on, Alyshia.'

What was it? The question reverberated around her mind. What had possessed her at that time? And it was a possession.

'Did you know his real name?'

'What do you mean his *real* name?'

'The *Daily Telegraph* dug that one up around his court case. His real name is John Black. Did he talk about his parents, what they did, where they lived?'

'His father ran a hedge business for airlines and aviation gasoline. Mother was a lawyer. They lived on the Old Brompton Road. We drove past there once.'

'Bet you didn't go in.'

'He didn't get on with his parents.'

'By the time Julian was sent down, he was thirty-one. His father had been dead seven years from liver cancer. His mother still lives on benefits in Nottingham. Her age at the time of sentencing was given as forty-six. She's part of those statistics that stick in the craw of Little England – the highest rate of teenage pregnancies in Europe.

'And by the way, something else you might not know: Julian owed Abiola thirty grand. He'd run up some gambling debts to pay for his drug habit. Part of the deal was that he could get Abiola an intro to you.'

Alyshia felt herself buried in a hole, deep in the foundations of a building that had fallen around her.

'And before you ask, it's all in the public domain,' said the voice.

She stared out into the expanding dark. Her eyelashes brushed the velvet sleeping mask as she blinked it all in.

'Think about that,' said the voice. 'What was it about Julian that drew you to him?'

10

There was one more person in the room than the Home Secretary was expecting. He looked hard and lean with dark hair, high cheekbones, a small scar under his left eye and a permanent frown, which gave him the look of a man who was always curious about what you were going to say next.

'This is Simon Deacon, from MI6,' said Joyce Hunter, of MI5. 'I thought it would save time if he sat in on this meeting. He runs the Asia desk at Vauxhall Cross.'

Natasha Radcliffe, the Home Secretary, was annoyed to find that the small favour she'd done for the Secretary of State for Business Innovation and Skills had now become a ball in her court. She'd heard from Mervin Stanley early that morning that someone had tried to shoot Frank D'Cruz in Knightsbridge yesterday evening. That news had done the rounds and triggered a call to her from Barbara Richmond, the Minister for Security and Counter Terrorism, who was doubly nervous in the run-up to the Olympic Games. After that call, she'd decided that the safest course of action was to convene a meeting with MI5 to discuss any possible security issues around this kidnap and shooting. At least the press hadn't got wind of any of it.

'Have you heard of Frank D'Cruz?' she asked.

'Of course we've heard of him,' said Deacon. 'He's always in the news. He's that kind of businessman. And we opened a file on him once we were told about his interest in investing in the UK and one of my agents is researching him. So far his reports have been quite bland and they haven't been circulated because nobody has requested any information about Mr D'Cruz until today.'

'And what about MI5?' asked Radcliffe. 'Have you opened a file on Mr D'Cruz?'

'Because he's been meeting ministers and the PM, yes, we have,' said Hunter. 'We've also had him under light surveillance, but so far he hasn't done anything that would classify him as a security risk.'

'Have we got any more information on last night's shooting?' asked Radcliffe.

'Just the ballistics report,' said her assistant. 'The bullet they removed from the back seat of Mr D'Cruz's car didn't match any they had on their files.'

'Any further developments in the kidnapping?' asked Radcliffe.

'We're awaiting an update from DCS Makepeace of SCD7. He's in a meeting with the Director of Operations for the kidnap.'

'Barbara Richmond called me last night and she wants to be absolutely certain that we're not missing something,' said Natasha Radcliffe. 'This combination of an important Asian investor's daughter being kidnapped *and* an attempted assassination doesn't make sense to her. And when things don't make sense, it's usually because there's something missing, something we don't know about that's preventing us from making the link. I don't want that "unknown" to become a major security issue. So what I'd like you to do is to start filling those open files on Mr D'Cruz with valuable intelligence that will put the Minister for Security and Counter Terrorism's mind at ease.'

'I'm not going to have it, Charles,' said Isabel. 'So just forget it.'

'As I said before, it doesn't mean you'll be sidelined. It doesn't mean it won't be your responsibility. It just means you won't be taking the brunt of contact with Alyshia's kidnapper.'

'I'm not going to trust anyone with her life,' she said, walking away from him, showing the back of her hand over her shoulder. 'So stop talking about it.'

'OK. Will you give me the names of people who you would consider in the event of your being incapacitated?' said Boxer. 'We have to think ahead all the time. If you crack…'

'I'm not going to crack.'

'It's not just the pressure of the phone calls. It's all this "down-time" as well. The waiting. The way things play on your mind. Nobody with your level of involvement could expect to last longer than a week.'

'What is this about?' asked Isabel, a little venom creeping in now, showing her steel. 'Is this about something else?'

'There is nothing else. This is how life is until it's over.'

'I mean, is this about what happened last night ... between us?' she said. 'You want some distance now?'

'No. It's not about what happened last night. But you're right,' said Boxer. 'We already have a highly emotional situation, into which we've introduced ...'

'What? What has been introduced? Is there a word for it in the manual? Like getting friends to do your negotiating for you is called a Crisis Management Committee. What's having sex with your kidnap consultant called? A Crisis Manager Encounter?'

'My boss would call it a Crisis Management Disaster,' said Boxer. 'I'd never work again.'

'And you? What would you call it?'

'Look,' said Boxer, holding up his hands. 'Look at us. This is what I'm talking about. We've introduced a whole new level of emotional involvement. There's not just the enormous external pressure from the kidnap situation but also a powerful internal one, because of what's happening between us.'

'And what is happening between us?'

They were staring intently into each other's eyes when Boxer's phone went off.

'Tell me,' she said.

'You know what's happening,' he said. 'There's no mistaking it.'

The phone continued to ring.

'Answer it,' she said.

'It's the profiler,' said Boxer, looking at the screen.

'Tell him to call back on the fixed line,' she said, still riled. 'I want to listen to this on the speaker phone.'

Boxer gave the profiler, Ray Moss, the number. They sat back in silence, waiting.

'I'm sorry,' she said. 'I'm just—'

The phone rang.

'Hi Ray. I'm putting you on speaker phone now. Present in the room is Alyshia's mother, Isabel Marks, and me. You've listened to the recording. Tell us what you think.'

'I don't think he's a kidnapper.'

'Hold on a sec, Ray.'

'I know,' said Moss, 'but it feels to me like he's playing a role.'

'Whether he's playing a part or not, he's still kidnapped my daughter,' said Isabel. 'What's your point?'

'The first thing that struck me was the way you found out that your daughter had been kidnapped,' said Moss.

'You mean the kidnapper waiting for Isabel to contact *him*,' said Boxer.

'That's significant,' said Moss. 'If I remember correctly, you said your ex-husband had been calling Alyshia on Saturday and she hadn't answered his calls. Do we know when she was taken yet? If not, when did you last speak to her, Mrs Marks?'

'Friday afternoon.'

'So it seems likely that it was Friday night,' said Moss. 'It's pretty rare for a serious gang to wait twenty-four hours for the *mother* to make contact so that they can reveal that they've taken her daughter.'

'He *did* have proof of capture ready,' said Isabel.

'Which in itself is odd,' said Moss. 'Why prepare yourself and then wait to be contacted? A lot of gangs make initial contact *without* proof of capture. They've got their prize and they want you to know it as soon as possible. More often than not, it's the kidnap consultant who ensures that the first proof of capture is asked for, and rarely the gang that offers it up.'

'What else?' said Boxer.

'The detail of his threat if you dared to involve police or press was much more calculated that the norm,' said Moss. 'And I understand you felt that he knew the extent of your ex-husband's ruthlessness, which I do think indicates that he knows him and that there's something personal about this, too.'

'Yeees,' said Boxer, in a way that warned Moss off what he was building up to.

'The second call was quite different in tone. More teasing, offhand, arrogant and casually violent. This time he's *not* going to give you any proof of life. I would have expected a gang eager to make money to have issued a demand during this call. If she was taken on Friday night, then we are now talking fifty-four hours later. That there's still no demand, but rather the reverse – a statement of disinterest in financial gain – is very unusual. That he also seems to want to demonstrate to you his superior knowledge about every aspect of your life, including your daughter—'

'What do you mean, superior knowledge about my daughter?' asked Isabel, hackles rising.

'The kidnapper said: "Her interest lies elsewhere", implying that he knows about someone your daughter is involved with that you don't. And he also seems to know "what happened in Mumbai". Do you?'

'No.'

'These are fairly normal tactics designed to alarm and undermine, but they're usually accompanied by a demand for money.'

'So if he's not a kidnapper, what is he?' asked Isabel.

Moss breathed in, held it.

'I think we should listen to what's on the mobile as soon as it's been retrieved,' said Boxer.

'You think he's a killer, don't you?' said Isabel.

'I haven't said that because it's not clear to me what he is,' said Moss. 'All I know is that he's not behaving like a *regular* kidnapper.'

'But you think he bears a grudge against my ex-husband and in not making a demand, in fact dismissing my ex-husband's extensive ability to pay, it's implicit that his intention is ... to punish him.'

'Whatever his intentions are,' said Moss, 'they don't seem to be immediate. He seems to want to spin this out. He's expecting you to retrieve the mobile. He's talked about "what happened in Mumbai", which indicates to me that there are more revelations to come. He's enjoying this role.'

'You say this "role" as if he's *acting* as a kidnapper when, in fact, he's told us he *is* a kidnapper and that we *are* in a kidnap process,' said Isabel, desperate to arrange the facts as positively as possible in her mind. 'Is it conceivable that we are hearing someone acting on behalf of someone else?'

Boxer could hear the pity coming down the line.

'All Ray is saying,' said Boxer, 'is that Jordan has set up a situation with all the appearances of a kidnap, but that there are a number of oddities, which make his intentions unclear.'

'I'd like to listen to what he sends you on your daughter's mobile,' said Moss. 'Forensics will want to look at it first. Then we'll talk again.'

'Thanks Ray,' said Boxer, taking it off speaker, putting the phone to his ear.

'She shouldn't be managing this on her own,' said Moss.

'We're trying.'

'He's going to kill her . . . in the end. I've got no doubt about it in my mind,' said Moss. 'This teasing is just part of the torture. I'd get the Met onto it straight away, whatever that fucker, Jordan, says.'

Simon Deacon's phone call had given his agent, Roger Clayton, the sort of full day's work he wasn't used to and especially not in this terrible mid-March humidity, which had taken over after the hot dry winds from Gujarat had departed. The phone call had precipitated three meetings, which were all in different parts of a city that, for some mad reason, had taken Los Angeles as its template for modern living. The city sprawl was colossal. The only way to get to all these places was by car, along with ten million other road users in Mumbai. He estimated his travel time alone at around nine hours for the day.

Rajiv Tandon was a Deputy Central Intelligence Officer for the Indian Intelligence Bureau, known as the IB. They'd arranged to meet in one of the most dreaded places in Mumbai for Clayton: the High Street Phoenix Shopping Mall in Lower Parel, a development which had ironically incorporated the old textile mill's chimneys and was only a few miles south of his office in the Bandra Kurla Complex. Tandon liked to shop and, because Clayton had nothing to offer Tandon to make him look better to his superiors, and Simon Deacon had told him that he didn't want D'Cruz's daughter's kidnap openly known in the IB, Clayton knew what he had to do: produce the credit card at the right moment. Clayton didn't like this; not because it felt like corruption or bribery, but because he had to pay with his own card and reclaim on expenses, which used to take six weeks but, since HM government's austerity measures, now took close to ten. At least Tandon wasn't excessively greedy, and three hundred and fifty quid's worth of Ralph Lauren did the trick.

They sat in Costa Coffee. He was grateful for that. Tandon was fond of McDonald's and Clayton already had a bandoleer of Big Macs padded around his waist. Tandon maintained his gold-framed Persol sunglasses, whose mirrored lenses reflected Costa's bean logo and Clayton's resolute calm, masking subcutaneous irritation. A distant roar from the TV, replaying Indian Premier League 20/20 games in the build-up to the new championship, competed with the milk steamer for noise supremacy.

'So we're here to talk about Goldfinger,' said Tandon, using the highly creative codename they'd developed for Frank D'Cruz. 'And you don't just want recent material but historical, too.'

'We need to know if there's anything ugly in his past that might have an impact on a situation that's developed in London,' said Clayton.

'I told you this wasn't going to be easy for me,' said Tandon. 'You're talking about the pre-computer era. Nothing before 1992 has gone into digital format yet. I'm still trying to find out where his paper file is being stored, but I *have* been able to speak to some people.'

'About Goldfinger's interest?'

'Yes, and I've been lucky because his name has come up quite naturally in our offices.'

'And why is that?'

Tandon tilted his head so that the TV screen appeared in duplicate in his sunglasses.

'The Indian Premier League?' asked Clayton, amused by Tandon's practiced cool. 'So what's going on in the IPL? I thought it was a huge success story.'

'It's going off,' said Tandon, wrinkling his nose. 'The word in the office is that D'Cruz has gone to London because of it.'

'How's he involved?' asked Clayton, letting Tandon do his bit, even though this sounded off brief.

'He's a major investor and he, along with other investors, were responsible for the installation of the president and the board,' said Tandon. 'The IPL is the most lucrative version of cricket ever played. Hundreds of millions of people watch these games. We're obsessed with it. It is a source of pride for our new nation. If it is proved that the corruption has reached to the deepest depths, then I promise you, the howling of Indian rage will be heard all over the world.'

'What are we talking about?' asked Clayton, who couldn't think of any enterprise in this madly burgeoning country that wasn't corrupt and so needed comparisons. 'How bad on the Gangrene Scale?'

'An 8.4,' said Tandon, accurate to decimal points. 'If you're a billionaire in this country, you are one of a handful of people in a teeming mass of humanity. You feel elevated. But to give yourself that extra feeling of power, you like to know what everybody else does not. It's not about money. It's about complete control. To sit back, watching the hysterical millions cheering on their teams, whilst knowing with total certainty … the result.'

'Ah, yes, match-fixing.'

'We're not certain yet, but the hysteria is building.'

'Did these discussions about the IPL lead any of your senior officers to reminisce about the good old days with Goldfinger? Because much as we'd like his investment, we still have to be careful where it's come from.'

'Well, not exactly, but something else did come to my attention as I was about to leave the office, but I don't know whether it's relevant to you or not,' said Tandon. 'I came across a police report dated seventh of January twenty-twelve. There was a break-in at one of Goldfinger's car plants.'

'What did they take?'

'That's the interesting thing,' said Tandon. 'They don't appear to have taken anything. The only evidence was a large hole in the perimeter fence and broken locks to two of the storage warehouses, but nothing appears to have been stolen.'

'And what was in these storage warehouses?'

'Some prototype electric cars.'

'Industrial espionage?'

'Who can say?' said Tandon, holding out his empty hands.

They were in the Half Moon pub on Mile End Road. Dan brought the pints of lager to the table.

'What about the crisps?' said Skin, Dan's arse barely touching the seat.

'Fuck me,' said Dan. 'They do the full English if you want it.'

He went back to the bar, bought two packets: salt and vinegar, cheese and onion.

'Nice place, this,' said Skin.

'It used to be a theatre,' said Dan, looking around.

'Anywhere that serves a pint at nine-thirty in the morning has my vote,' said Skin. 'Pity about the fucking students.'

'How's the shoulder?'

'Not bad,' said Skin. 'You did a good job.'

'Don't drink too much with the painkillers and make sure you take the antibiotics right to the end of the packet,' said Dan. 'That shoulder gets infected and you'll have the cops at your hospital bedside and they won't be bringing flowers.'

'Yeah, right,' said Skin. 'So what's the news?'

'Why do you think I've got news?'

'What are we doing here if you haven't?'

'Socialising?'

'Oh, yeah. You're a bit poncey for me, Dan. You know, read too many books. My Dad told me: never trust a brainy bastard, they'll fuck you in the arse.'

'Did he tell you that all male nurses are gay, too?'

'He did. Are they?' asked Skin, pulling his pint away from Dan's. 'I know you fancy me.'

'Bugger off,' said Dan.

'Oh no, I remember now. The girlfriend who put you inside never came to see you,' said Skin. 'Maybe they turned you in Wandsworth. It happens.'

'The only thing that happened to me in Wandsworth is I did weights and put on two stone.'

'That says something to me,' said Skin, tapping his head.

'You're not my type, anyway.'

'What's wrong with me?'

'Don't get all hurt now.'

They laughed, supped a couple of inches off their pints, tore open the crisps.

'As it happens, I *have* got news,' said Dan. 'About the girl.'

'What about her?' said Skin, looking round the pub but listening hard.

'I got her name from Pike, said I needed it in case there was a health problem.'

'And?'

'Alyshia D'Cruz is her name. I Googled her and she's the daughter of an Indian billionaire who used to be an actor in the movies.'

'I hate that shit.'

'Bollywood?'

'Everyone breaking into song and dance routines,' said Skin, moving his head from side to side on his neck. 'And no tits.'

'A succinct deconstruction of the genre,' said Dan.

'You see, *that's* my problem with you, Nurse, I only understood three of those words,' said Skin.

'As long as they were the important three,' said Dan. 'Now listen, Skin, no fucking about. Her Dad used to be an actor and now he's a billionaire. And that's a dollar billionaire, not rupees.'

They looked at each other for some time, Skin's blue eyes unsmiling, penetrating. Dan let him do it, let him know he wasn't being too fly for his own good.

'And?' said Skin, after some moments.

'Well,' said Dan, making a forward motion with his hands.

'I want to hear you say it, Nurse.'

'We have knowledge, opportunity and, with a bit of work, we could have the capability, too.'

'In English, Nurse: single syllables.'

'We know *who* the girl is, and *where* she is: that's the knowledge. We man one of the three security shifts in the warehouse where she's being held: that's the opportunity. All we have to do is find some alternative accommodation: and that would give us the capability.'

'So you mean ... what exactly?'

'We take over the kidnap.'

127

'Right. That's what I wanted. I need to hear these things said, that's all,' said Skin. 'That way, we don't have any misunderstandings. So that when Pike tells his dwarf, Kevin, to arrange us with our balls in a vice, I can say with a clear conscience that it was the Nurse who came up with the idea.'

That stopped Dan's hand on the way to his pint. Skin grinned.

'Do I look like the type who's going to grass you up?' he said, babyface all innocent, only the spider web tattoo giving it away.

A long hard look from Dan, brain doing double time.

'Have you been thinking the same thing all the fucking time?'

'What I've been thinking, Nurse, is that *we've* done a lot of dirty work for minimum wage,' said Skin. 'Doing the illegals, then the cabbie and his mate, taking an injury and then still doing our shift at the warehouse is what I call heavy overtime. I don't mind doing a bit of extra as long as it's appreciated. I don't know about you but *I* don't feel appreciated, not in my pocket, and not in here, neither.' He tapped himself in the chest, drank some more lager.

'So I've been making my own enquiries, since we thought about the people clearing up loose ends becoming loose ends themselves.'

Dan grunted a laugh. He'd underestimated Skin, as a lot of people probably did. 'And you've found out who Pike's doing this for?'

'What I *do* know,' said Skin, shaking his head, 'is that the only one he's had any contact with is the English bloke, and I heard the Irish fucker call him Reecey. The American guy who calls himself Jordan and does all the talking to the girl, he's running the group and, as far as I can make out, he hired in Reecey to organise the kidnap.'

'What about the other American we haven't seen on our shift?'

'He's Jordan's mate. They work together. I haven't heard his name.'

'And "the Irish fucker", the security guy?'

'He's with Reecey.'

'And who's behind them?'

'Does there have to be anyone?'

'Jordan goes outside to make phone calls after his sessions with the girl as if he's updating someone.'

'You heard any of that?'

'Nothing,' said Dan. 'Do you know if Pike's been paid?'

'A hundred K,' said Skin. 'So far.'

'Does that sound like a lot of money to you?'

'It does when you think that the only outside supplier was the cabbie. The rest of us, doing all the shit work, are on the payroll.'

'It's Pike's warehouse,' said Dan.

'Which is always empty,' said Skin.

'And I doubt that refrigeration unit they're in has been turned on this century,' said Dan.

'Get us another couple of pints in,' said Skin, slapping a tenner down on the table.

They sat in front of their refills. More crisps. Skin was nodding.

'What?' said Dan.

'I'm thinking it through, beginning to end,' said Skin. 'The easiest bit is going to be taking the girl in the first place.'

'I only went into the refrigeration unit at the beginning to stick the cannula in her arm. What's the scene in there?'

'There's only two of them and Jordan's occupied with talking to the girl most of the time,' said Skin. 'All I'd have to do is distract Reecey and I don't think that'll be too much of a problem.'

'How does Reecey know Pike?'

'I dunno,' said Skin. 'But if you had muscle behind you, would you come to Pike for it? Why not do the job yourself?'

'Local knowledge. Access to the cabbie. Warehouse facilities.'

'And us, the security detail,' said Skin, chuckling. 'Tell me about the Indian billionaire.'

'After the movies, he turned himself into an industrialist. You name it, he does it. Steel, construction, cars, energy. A conservative estimate of his personal wealth, according to *Forbes* magazine's India Rich List, puts him at number eighteen with four and a half billion dollars.'

'Fuck me. How much does number one have?'

'Around thirty billion.'

'He got any daughters worth kidnapping?'

'In India.'

'So what do you reckon is in it for us?'

'If you've got four thousand five hundred million dollars, you shouldn't begrudge a million for a couple of lads from Stepney, should you?'

'That's the way you see it,' said Skin, stuffing crisps in his face, the greed making him ravenous. 'I think we should go for a mill each. Fuck Pike.'

'He'll come after us.'

'Not with anybody I'm scared of,' said Skin. 'He's not tooled up. Doesn't have that kind of business.'

'What about Kevin?'

'That fucking dwarf?!'

'What about Jordan's mate and the Irish bastard? You think they'll take kindly to you offing their comrades in arms?'

Skin shrugged, smiled.

'And what about Mister Big, who's hired Jordan and Reecey to kidnap the girl?' said Dan. 'He doesn't strike me as someone who's used up his last savings to pull off this stunt.'

'You getting cold feet now, Nurse?' said Skin, screwing his finger into Dan's gut. 'Gone all lily-livered on me, have you?'

'All right,' said Dan, batting Skin's finger away. 'Let's get practical. Where do we keep the girl once we've taken her?'

'Well, we don't make it easy for Pike and co.,' said Skin. 'We don't keep her at my mum's. We've got to find somewhere he won't look, which is where you come in. Pike knows me back to front. What does he know about you? Fuck all. He wouldn't know where to start. Different background, you see. Posh.'

'I'm from Swindon,' said Dan. 'Since when did that get posh?'

'And that's why you're important,' said Skin. 'Pike's never been further west than Wandsworth. He doesn't know the first thing about you.'

'He knows I'm a nurse.'

'I'll take care of Jordan and his mate,' said Skin, ignoring him. 'You'll look after the girl. We've got the transport. Now all we need is a place. Are you in?'

Dan hesitated and then picked up his beer.

'Are *you* in?' he said, chinking glasses.

It took Roger Clayton more than three hours to drive from Lower Parel down to Nariman Point for his next meeting, which was in the Sea Lounge of the remodelled Taj Mahal Palace and Tower Hotel. He was taken to a window booth, with a view towards the Gateway of India and the Ferry Terminal, where Divesh Mehta was sitting. Mehta was a Gujarati, who worked for the Research and Analysis Wing, India's equivalent of MI6. Clayton preferred this relationship with Mehta, who had been educated and trained in the UK, because they had a valuable information exchange, meaning no friction on his credit card.

The only problem with Mehta was that he made Clayton feel like a slob. Immaculately dressed in a bespoke suit, with a starched white shirt that, unlike Clayton's, would never crease or come untucked, and with his Vincent's Club tie (he'd been a cricket blue) neatly knotted, he looked and spoke like Englishmen used to when they wore the shorts that lost the empire. He also drank tea. The words 'skinny latte with an extra shot' had never passed Mehta's lips. Clayton felt his own off-the-peg jacket clinging to all the wrong places. His top button was undone, tie loosened against the atrocious humidity outside. His specs (with clip-on shades) swung over his chest on a chord, while the belt of his trousers dug into his gut. They shook hands. Clayton sat back and let the Taj's aircon deflate him back to normal size.

'Tea?' said Mehta, in a perfect imitation of a waitress in a south London greasy spoon.

They laughed. Clayton nodded, feeling the dinner plates of sweat under his arms cooling horribly, while a waiter put a menu into his hands.

'They've done a good job,' said Clayton, looking around him, flipping his specs on to read the menu. 'I haven't eaten here since before the 2008 attacks.'

'I don't think this bit was hit as badly as some of the other parts of the hotel,' said Mehta. 'Anyway, you asked to see me. Did I detect some urgency?'

'It's about our film star friend, Frank D'Cruz,' said Clayton. 'Did you know he's gone to London?'

'He's not high on my list of priorities at the moment,' said Mehta. 'What's the story?'

'Your friends in the IB think it's to do with something even more horrible brewing in the Indian Premier League.'

'He wouldn't run away from that,' said Mehta. 'That's his meat and drink. And anybody who's been anywhere near the hysteria generated by that game couldn't possibly imagine that it's being run by a council of virgins. So why has he run?'

'We know *why* he's run, or rather left,' said Clayton. 'But we don't know who's behind it.'

Mehta leaned forward, picked up his cup and saucer, and Clayton knew he had his undivided attention. This wasn't the run-of-the-mill information update they usually had.

'As you know, we are particularly concerned with intelligence about our next-door neighbours and since he took over the steel-works, D'Cruz has been travelling regularly to Pakistan,' said Mehta. 'He's desperate for export contracts.'

'Did he travel alone?'

'Alone, and with his daughter until the end of last year.'

'Do you know the quality of the people they were dealing with?'

'They were both seen meeting socially at the Sheraton Karachi, with a Pakistani military officer called Lieutenant General Abdel Iqbal.'

'I don't suppose he's got anything to do with Inter-Services Intelligence agency, by any chance?'

'Yes, he's a serving member, we've been able to confirm that, but we're still researching his connections which, given the thin-ness of our operational support, is not going as quickly as I'd like,' said Mehta. 'Those connections may be one of the reasons why D'Cruz's contracts were signed so rapidly, the licences granted, the product transported, released and paid for so smoothly.'

'But do you suspect that Iqbal is part of "an old boy network", so to speak?'

'He's part of it,' said Mehta. 'We know he's an old friend of Amir Jat's, for instance.'

'Who's he?'

'You'll need a full report on him. He's a monster of connections and affiliations from the CIA to al Qaeda. You'll put me off my tea if you make me talk about him.'

'I wouldn't countenance it,' said Clayton.

'All we're waiting for now,' said Mehta, 'is that last piece of the jigsaw that shows Iqbal's got the terrorist links we suspect he has.'

11

Boxer filed his situation report by email and sat back in the room upstairs where he'd put the recording equipment. He wasn't looking forward to the call he had to make. To his mother. The 'drunken hag', as she was so sweetly known by Mercy.

'Hi, Esme, it's me,' he said. She'd insisted on him using her Christian name since he was twelve.

'Charlie? What do you want?' she said, in that cracked radio voice of hers from too much smoking. She knew he didn't call unless he wanted something.

At least she wasn't drinking yet. He heard the cigarette being lit up, a reflex action from her days as a producer.

'Mercy and I have both got jobs on,' he said. 'Would it be all right for Amy to come and stay with you … please.'

'Nobody else'll take her?'

'There's been a problem,' said Boxer. 'I think she'd benefit from some time with you. You're the only person she gets on with in our family.'

He told her about Amy's Tenerife jaunt. He could hear Esme chuckling to herself.

'The girl's got nerve,' she said.

'She has,' said Boxer, 'but it's not how parents normally like it to be shown.'

'Then you should have been around for her more, Charlie,' said Esme, in that calculated way of hers, guaranteeing maximum irritation because it was so ruthlessly true.

'Well, you know how it is, Esme, from when I was a kid,' said Boxer; couldn't help himself.

'You turned out all right, and you made sure there wasn't a whole lot I had to do with it,' said Esme. 'And I'm sure Amy'll turn out fine, too. It might not be the way you *want* her to turn out, but she'll get to where she wants to be in the end ... no thanks to you, or Mercy.'

'Can I tell her to go straight up to your place after school?' asked Boxer, not rising to it.

'Sure,' she said, and her phone rattled back down into its cradle.

He took a deep breath, tried to call Amy; still not answering. He sent her a text about the arrangement with Esme, went back downstairs.

Isabel was in the kitchen, staring into a cup of cold coffee. He wanted to focus her mind on the next phone call, develop a strategy that would give her a foothold on the sheer cliff of their opponent's psychological advantage.

'You look sick,' she said, raising her eyes from the muddy cup.

'I just called my mother. That's the effect,' said Boxer. 'We should talk about the next call.'

'Tell me about Amy,' said Isabel, ignoring him.

Boxer looked at his watch; Mercy was due any moment. They'd have the strategy session later.

'Why is she so unhappy?' asked Isabel.

'The reason most kids get unhappy – absent parents,' said Boxer, still wincing after his mother's rapier thrusts. 'Mercy and I have tricky jobs, which means we can't always be around. When I was working at my old company, I was out of the country for a minimum of two hundred days a year. That's why I resigned, but ... I think it might have been too late.'

'And when did you notice things going wrong with her?'

'She was always a restless kid. Always reaching beyond herself, wanting to be older,' said Boxer. 'We went on holiday to Spain when she was fifteen and she developed a twenty-two-year-old boyfriend. I thought we'd never get her away from there. We're pretty sure she's been having sex since then. Maybe it was because we weren't able to give her a proper family life, but she wasn't that crazy about being a child. Always wanted to be more adult. Mercy wanted the opposite, tried to hold her back all the time. It was the start of real tension between them.'

'Was she a sociable kid?'

'Sure. Always been a popular girl. Always had friends and lots of people who wanted to be her friend but ... she's never retained them.'

'You haven't said anything that scares me yet. So what is it?'

'Apart from the usual stuff, like pathological lying and instant aggression, which is mainly directed towards Mercy, I think, for me, it's her detachment,' said Boxer.

'Like what?'

'I saw her once with a group of kids who were talking animatedly about the latest band, which in this case was The Killers. There was a concert coming up and they were all wild about it. But I could tell Amy wasn't interested. Later, I asked her why and she said of the band: "They're floaters".'

'Floaters?'

'A complicated word in Amy-speak. It means dead in the water, but also floating on the surface. It's music that doesn't get inside.'

'But that's good, Charlie. That's insightful.'

'It is, but it's disturbing too, because I see her loneliness. She's an odd mixture of boundless curiosity, suppressed by endless tedium. She's like the excited kid in the front row of a party with a magician, but her enthusiasm wanes as she sees how every trick is done. And there's nothing more disappointing than seeing how banal magic is.'

'What's your deepest worry? I mean ... she doesn't sound suicidal?'

'No, I don't think she's that,' said Boxer. 'I'm more worried that she's like me.'

'And what's that?'

The doorbell rang.

'That'll be Mercy,' said Boxer, relieved. 'I'm going to have a quick talk with her outside before I introduce you.'

'About us?'

'*That* would not be advisable.'

Boxer went to the front door, put on a coat, took a key.

Mercy was wearing a sober, dark suit and a roll-neck sweater under a black wool coat, leather gloves over her long, slim hands. No jewellery. She kept her hair cut close to her head, which accentuated her sculpted face – high cheekbones, long jawline, a fine nose that hinted at some sub-Saharan ancestry. Her eyes were narrowed against the cold and her mouth pursed – shrewd and professional. She was not alone. Standing five metres away was a young man, in his early thirties. Cropped thick black hair with that Mediterranean whorl that could polish floors, dark heavy eyebrows, deep-set brown eyes, long nose, over-pronounced mouth and, despite a morning shave, a shadow already visible. Under his black raincoat he wore a dark suit and tie, with lace-up shoes. Boxer was surprised he didn't have a blue light revolving on his head, seeing as his whole demeanour screamed 'cop'.

'Who's he?' asked Boxer.

'George Papadopoulos,' she said, and mouthed 'Detective Sergeant'. 'We call him George Papa.'

'Nobody told me about him,' said Boxer. 'Who's he supposed to be?'

'My trainee consultant.'

'And on whose authority is he here?'

'I think this goes right back up to the Commissioner of the Met,' said Mercy, finger on chin. 'Part of the deal.'

'That nobody thought to tell me about.'

'There was a manpower clause,' said Mercy, bringing her thumb and forefinger together. 'Small print.'

'So what's the idea?'

'George is going to do the footwork while I work my connections,' said Mercy. 'Have we got a time and a place of the kidnapping yet?'

'No.'

'Are we allowed in or do we have to set up a tent out here?'

'You got one?' asked Boxer. 'Ray Moss, the Pavis profiler, has been on the line, having listened to the call. He doesn't like it. Thinks we've got a killer rather than a kidnapper. He said, "Bring in the Met". How do you like that?'

'You don't often hear those words from the private sector.'

'There's no Crisis Management Committee, either,' said Boxer. 'Isabel Marks doesn't want one. She won't even give me names in the event of her incapacity. She's on her own in there.'

'What about the ex-husband?'

'They don't get on under "strained" circumstances.'

'No friends?'

'Only in Brazil, and with her own problems.'

Mercy sighed, ran a long, slim, gloved hand over the tight curls of her hair.

'Let's have the good news,' she said.

'Jordan, our kidnapper, is the playful type. A show-off and a tease. He's keen to spin this one out along the lines: "You don't know what your daughter's really like".'

'Been there, done *that*,' said Mercy emphatically.

'I spoke to Mum, by the way; she'll take Amy and I've sent Amy a text,' said Boxer.

'Did Esme love you for that?'

'Oh, I think so,' said Boxer lightly. 'The bad news about Jordan is that he's on the volatile side. One call he's calm and in control, the next he's arrogant and cavalier.'

'Right. So we'd better get on with it,' said Mercy. 'Can we do this inside, Charlie? I'm bloody freezing out here.'

Her eyes were now tearful, turning rheumy, and her normally dark, lustrous skin was going grey. She hated the cold, had never got used to it, even after twenty years in England. He opened the door, let them in, shook George Papadopoulos's hand as he came through. They shed their coats, went into the kitchen where Boxer introduced them to Isabel Marks, who poured the coffee. He hadn't doubted it, but he was glad to see that Isabel and Mercy liked each other on sight.

'So, Mercy, how will you and George fit into this ... this scenario?' asked Isabel.

'I'm Charlie's back-up,' said Mercy. 'If it's a prolonged kidnap, I'll take over after two weeks. That means I have to know everything.'

'And George?'

'He observes and learns. He's my trainee.'

'Mercy and George will also be doing some research around the kidnap,' said Boxer.

'Meaning what exactly?'

'We'll find out where Alyshia was last seen, at what time and with whom,' said Mercy. 'We'll build a picture of the lead-up to the event, in the hope that it might give us an indication of who we're dealing with. Someone alone or with a gang. A disgruntled boyfriend. Perhaps people in her everyday life can shed light on any strange personalities, difficult business interactions, that sort of thing. We also might find out stuff that we can use in our nego- tiations with the kidnapper, something to give us an advantage. As you've realised from your conversations with Jordan, knowledge, in this game, is power.'

'But you won't contact the police.'

'Don't worry, this is a very private investigation. We tread very carefully. We understand the threats that have been made,' said Mercy. 'Now, we'd like to start by hearing your story. We've had a briefing from the Director of Operations but there's nothing like hearing it in your own words.'

Mercy listened to Isabel's version of events. She got her to go back in time and, being a sympathetic woman and a clever inves- tigator, she dug deeper and was rewarded.

'Alyshia left and went to rent her own place because we weren't getting on so well. I was finding her reticence difficult to take,' said Isabel. 'Something had happened in Mumbai and, while I expect my ex-husband to be secretive, I don't expect my daughter to withhold. She's always told me everything.'

'Everything?' said Boxer. 'Is there such a thing as everything?'

'No,' said Mercy. 'As we find out all too often, and to our cost. Young people have their own lives.'

'I suppose you're right,' said Isabel.

'The kidnapper has dropped Alyshia's mobile phone somewhere off the M4. We're waiting for it to be brought in,' said Boxer, 'with more revelations.'

'About?' asked Mercy.

'About Alyshia's "involvements", I think,' said Isabel. 'A boy- friend, I assume, that she's never spoken to me about.'

Boxer put the iPod in the dock and they played the recording of the second phone call.

'All right,' said Mercy, 'let's build a picture, starting from the moment of the kidnap and working back. Where does Alyshia work?'

Silence.

'Isabel?'

'I don't know,' said Isabel, conscious of falling at the first hurdle. 'All she said was that she was working in a bank in the City. When I asked which one, she just said it was one of the big investment banks. I didn't pursue it because she'd already started to get quite scathing with me if I "intruded" on her life too much.'

'And where does she live?'

'She's renting somewhere in Hoxton. That's all she's told me. This was part of her need for her own space. Part of the separation process. Trying to stop me living my life through her. She had started to get quite brutal with me. I was feeling like the clingy lover.'

'Has she ever worked in the UK before she got this job in the bank?'

'Yes, when she finished school and after university, before she took her place at the Saïd Business School.'

'And she was living here?'

'Yes.'

'Did she leave any of her paperwork behind when she moved out?'

'There's a box file in my office full of stuff she didn't want to take with her.'

'Is there somewhere George can set up a computer?'

Isabel took Papadopoulos into the dining room before going upstairs with Mercy. They chatted non-stop. Boxer grabbed a notebook to start doing some forward-thinking, taking the opportunity to get some strategy together to draw a demand out of Jordan. This was the problem with no Crisis Management Committee. He was with Isabel all the time. He was everything to her: adviser, consultant, friend, consoler, intimate and, now, lover. It meant he had little time to do his work.

What he wanted Isabel to do, despite her loathing of Jordan, was to engage with him. There had to be a relationship. This would slow the phone calls down, open up more opportunities for Jordan to be revealing. The vague voices returned, louder.

Mercy reappeared in the kitchen, gave Boxer the nod. They had something.

Martin Fox called. Boxer took it in the sitting room, looking out into the grey, frozen garden.

'How's it going?'

'Tricky, on my own,' said Boxer.

'I spoke to Frank about that. He's going along with what his ex-wife wants, but he has given me two names. Her lawyer and the woman who runs a residential property consultancy he uses. Apparently Isabel and this woman got on well together when she moved her out of the Edwardes Square house.'

'Have you contacted either of them?'

'Frank said that I should only do that in the event of Isabel's incapacity, or on her specific instruction.'

'Well, it's a start,' said Boxer. 'Mercy's here, by the way – and George.'

'Sorry about that. We had to agree.'

'I can feel them muscling in on us,' said Boxer. 'Mercy's already assuming control.'

'You know how it is. It's in their nature to assume that the private sector is, at best, money-motivated and, at worst, venal, whilst we think of the Met as hobbled and incompetent.'

'The perfect working relationship,' said Boxer. 'I'd rather George didn't meet Frank.'

'Right. Got chevrons on his suit?'

'Have you spoken to Ray Moss?'

'That's why I'm calling.'

'Isabel knows what he thinks. She's taken it on board.'

'No breakdown?'

'Not yet. She rarely shows it, but she's got some steel in there. You might think she's just a warm, good-natured woman, but there's the right stuff holding her together.'

'While I'm trying to relieve the pressure on you, I'm also following a lead from a different source,' said Fox. 'A friend of mine at the *Financial Times* recommended that I talk to this guy who's a competitor in the steel business to Konkan Hills Securities. I haven't spoken to Frank about this yet. And I don't want it to reach him. So it's a name you shouldn't run by Isabel Marks, although I think she might have even met him once. I want more dirt and to get it verified.'

'Is this a disgruntled employee scenario?'

'Could be. My contact gave me the name Deepak Mistry. He's in his mid-thirties, although there's some question mark about his birth date. As far as we can work out, he was a computer science graduate who put together a group of programmers and started up a company in Bangalore. They developed most of the software used by Konkan Hills, and in one of those "I liked the product so much I bought the company" moves, Frank incorporated Mistry and his business into Konkan Hills IT department.'

'Did that make Deepak a rich man?'

'Not a multi-millionaire, but comfortably off,' said Fox. 'One of the reasons Frank did this was that he liked Deepak Mistry. He admired his entrepreneurial spirit, and within a year Deepak was head of IT for Konkan Hills. And, apparently, it didn't stop there. Deepak was brought into the inner circle. As head of IT he was given a place on the board and, in the space of a couple of years, became Frank's untitled right-hand man. And he was still in that position when Alyshia flew out to Mumbai a couple of years ago, with an economics degree, an MBA and no experience. My informer doesn't know quite what happened next, but he does know that Deepak Mistry has disappeared, not just from Konkan Hills Securities' board, but also from the southern Indian business scene.'

'Did your informer's company want to offer him a job?'

'Exactly that,' said Fox. 'And nobody knows where Mistry has gone. I've got some private investigators in Mumbai trying to track him down.'

'I thought you said Mistry was in IT. Why is a steel competitor looking to employ him?'

'Frank had a Chinese business friend who'd bought a steelworks in Germany, dismantled it and was shipping it piece by piece to China. Frank sent Deepak Mistry to Shanghai for two years on and off to watch the Chinese rebuild that German steelworks and make it twenty-five per cent more efficient. Then Frank had him use his knowledge to rebuild the steelworks he'd bought in India.'

'It sounds more intriguing than promising.'

'It sounds like both to me.'

Mercy appeared at the door, beckoned him into the kitchen. Boxer hung up.

Papadopoulos was in his shirt sleeves, capable hairy hands at his sides. Isabel was seated, puzzled.

'It seems that Alyshia wasn't working for a bank but a recruitment agency, called Bovingdon Recruitment. They have ten branches in central London and she was based at Tottenham Court Road. Her home address was given as Flat 1, Lavender Grove, London E8, which is in Dalston, close to London Fields. Not that far from Hoxton, I suppose,' said Papadopoulos, offering some mitigation.

'I find that so strange,' said Isabel, bewildered and hurt. 'Why lie to me about such ridiculous things?'

'It might just be a symptom of another problem,' said Boxer. 'You shouldn't take it personally. It's more about Alyshia, less about you.'

'What other problem?'

'Whatever it was that happened in Mumbai, maybe?' said Boxer. 'She came back here and hasn't been herself since.'

'Now I'm worried that, without my seeing it or wanting to see it, she's been having some kind of a breakdown,' said Isabel. 'I mean, recruitment? That's not her at all.'

Her mobile vibrated on the table.

'Chico,' she said, glancing at the screen.

Boxer moved the others out of the kitchen and into the living room.

'I don't want Frank D'Cruz, who she calls Chico, to see you,' said Boxer.

'Why not?' said Papadopoulos.

'Because he'll take one look at you …'

'At me?' said Papadopoulos. 'You think I look like a copper?'

Boxer looked at Mercy, eyebrow raised.

'Let's go,' said Mercy. 'We've got enough to be going on with.'

Papadopoulos picked up his jacket and computer, threw his mac on, with aggressive shooting movements of his arms. Isabel came in to say Chico was coming over. Mercy and Papadopoulos excused themselves. Boxer took them to the door. Mercy pulled him out into the street, told Papadopoulos to go to the car.

'So what's going on here?' she asked.

'I spoke to Martin Fox about it and he agreed that it wouldn't be a good idea ...'

'You know what I'm talking about, Charlie,' said Mercy. 'What's going on between you and Isabel?'

'We have no Crisis Management Committee, that's what's going on,' said Boxer. 'Which means ...'

'I can see the way she's looking at you,' said Mercy. 'I bet even George can.'

'I'm not sure what you're getting at.'

Mercy got her face up close, nose to nose. His cool, green eyes looked into the pitch-black wells of her wide pupils, her brown irises almost invisible.

'My God,' she said. 'I don't bloody believe it.'

'Don't bloody believe *what*?' said Boxer, annoyed.

'You've been there, Charlie. I can tell.'

Only long experience at playing poker enabled him to maintain eye contact with her, but even that gave away too much.

'I hope you know what you're doing, Charles Boxer. A girl's life is in the balance here.'

'I'll make sure you get a copy of whatever's on Alyshia's iPhone,' he said.

Mercy, dismayed and furious, turned without a word, headed for the car.

Boxer hovered at the front door, annoyed at being so readable by women, as well as speared by Mercy's professional correctness, but still burning with his new desire.

The traffic had been spectacularly bad, even by Mumbai standards, and it was 6.30 p.m. by the time Roger Clayton reached Vile Parle, close to the airport, where the taxi turned off the road and headed for Juhu Beach and his final meeting of the day. The crowds were gathering for sunset and the snack vendors were doing a huge trade. The taxi dropped him off and he wandered past the balloon-sellers, drummers, fun rides, shooting galleries, fortune-tellers and performing monkeys, to the food stalls.

He squeezed through the crush and uproar of a thousand snacking Mumbaikers, who seemed oblivious to the Rothko bands of dark blue, purple, violet, red and pink as the sun eased itself into the black waters of the Arabian Sea.

Gagan was waiting for him at his favourite *pani puri* stall. He was already on his third crispy doughball as Clayton joined him. They chatted and let the spicy madness in the *pani puris* explode in their mouths. They paid up and moved to the massive circular iron griddle at the centre of the *pav bhaji* stall. Clayton bought two plates of the potato and vegetable curry with bread on the side, shaking his head at the prospective calorific intake. He slipped a $50 bill under one plate and handed it to Gagan, who accepted the gift with a small bow.

They walked away from the brightly lit stalls and the din of the generators, and into the darkness of the beach. Gagan was in his twenties and rail thin, dressed in black trousers and a white shirt. Both were a size too big for him, so that the trousers had to be cinched at the waist and the shirt puffed out at the back. He had thick black hair with brown streaks and a side parting. His default setting was a broad white-toothed smile. It was easy to see why Sharmila D'Cruz had hired him: he was both pretty and uplifting to the spirit.

Clayton was relieved that Frank D'Cruz paid his staff so badly that $50 made Gagan a willing accomplice. He was doubly useful because, as a general servant, he went everywhere in the house. He could also rustle up very good snacks, too, and specialised in D'Cruz's favourite and fattening *pakodes*, croquettes, Goan pork pies and patties. He also lied to Sharmila about D'Cruz's intake, which made him just about the only servant D'Cruz spoke to, rather than barked at.

'So your master has gone to London,' said Clayton.

Gagan's eyes widened with astonishment at Clayton's knowledge. He was disappointed too, because this was to have been his opening nugget of remarkable intelligence.

'Yes, it was something very sudden. Not planned at all. Mrs Sharmila very upset.'

'Why?'

'They were supposed to be going to a big film premiere this

week and a big party to celebrate the start of the IPL cricket tournament. Now there is nothing for her to do.'

'Have there been any changes at the house and the compound here in Juhu?'

'Yes, yes. Much more security now. Everybody being searched before they coming in. Men with dogs in the gardens at night.'

'Anybody different come to the house before he left?'

'Oh yes, Anwar Masood.'

'Who is he?'

'The cook is telling me that he is a big Muslim gangster. An old friend of Mister Frank.'

Clayton squeezed some lemon over the buttery potato curry to cut its oiliness and scooped some up with his bread, stuffed it messily into his mouth and took some time to clean himself up.

'Was Sharmila involved with the meeting with Anwar Masood?'

'No, no, sir, Mrs Sharmila was out of the house. Just Mister Frank and Anwar Masood on their tods.'

Clayton smiled at Gagan's cheering English.

'Did you hear any of their conversation?'

'Oh, yes, sir, Mister Roger. Mister Frank telling me to make snacks but no pork. So I do the beef croquette, fish tart …'

'That's great, Gagan, but just tell me what you heard them say.'

'Mister Frank telling Anwar Masood to go to Pakistan to talk to their friend in Karachi.'

'Their friend?'

'That's what he said. Their friend in Karachi,' said Gagan. 'They not naming their friend, they know him already.'

'Are you sure there was no name? He must have a lot of friends in Karachi.'

'Now, I'm thinking,' said Gagan, and he did just that. 'It was a long night, many different parts and me coming and going.'

'Take your time.'

'Yes, at one point I think they saying Mister Iqbal. Yes, Mister Iqbal is the friend.'

'That's good,' said Clayton. 'What did Anwar Masood have to talk to Mister Iqbal about?'

'Something about Miss Alyshia. I don't understand it very well. They were not talking very straightly and I was in and out. I'm

145

thinking that she is not being very happy after leaving Mumbai.'

'It's important that you tell me what you heard, even if you don't understand it.'

'They having very long conversation and I'm making my beef patties. So one minute they talking about Miss Alyshia. The next minute I come back with the beef patties and they talking about Deepak Mistry.'

'Who is Deepak Mistry?'

'He is very close to Mister Frank,' said Gagan. 'I put the beef patties on the table and Mister Frank says, "Make some fish tarts for Mister Masood". So I have to go back to the kitchen straight.'

'What did you hear when you came back with the fish tarts?' said Clayton, who realised that the evening was structured culinarily in Gagan's mind.

'Anwar Masood already standing to leave and Mister Frank saying, "You must try one of Gagan's fish tarts. They not making them as good as this, even in Goa." And Anwar Masood is trying one and heaping praise on my head. And Mister Frank telling me to leave the plates and go. And I'm closing the door and Mister Frank says, "You *have* to find Deepak". And I'm staying to listen because I'm liking Mister Deepak and sorry that he is lost.'

'And what did you hear?'

'Anwar Masood telling him that he's not finding Mister Deepak. Mister Deepak not here in Mumbai and not there in Bangalore.'

'How long was Anwar Masood at the house?'

'He leaving soon after. He maybe there for two hours.'

They finished the *pav bhajis* and walked back up the beach towards the lights of the food stalls. Clayton bought himself a vivid, red ice *gola* in the hope that it would cleanse his palate without giving him diarrhoea.

As he travelled back into town, he called the consular researcher, who was still in the office.

'Tell me everything I need to know about a gangster called Anwar Masood, a Pakistani friend of Frank D'Cruz in Karachi called Mister Iqbal, who I assume is Lieutenant General Abdel Iqbal, and an employee of Konkan Hills Securities called Deepak Mistry and, if you can, whether Mistry is still in the country.'

12

'Well?'

'Well what?'

'Could Mercy tell anything about us?'

'I told you, she knows me very well.'

'So what did she intuit?'

'That we've been intimate and that we've been to bed together.'

'I like her,' said Isabel, a little stunned. 'She must be good at her job, too.'

'I'm glad you like her because she'll be the one to take over from me if it gets out that you and I are having ...' said Boxer, trailing off to nothing.

'What is it that we're having?' asked Isabel, teasing.

'A different relationship to the one that we should be having,' said Boxer. 'We have to talk, Isabel, about the job that I ought to be doing.'

'Which is?'

'Preparing you for your next conversation with Jordan,' said Boxer. 'You have to start forming a relationship with him.'

'Maybe that will be easier once we find out what he's been talking about to Alyshia.'

'No, I don't think so. We have to have our own strategy, not based on Jordan's narrative. We have to start trying to control him, rather than letting him manipulate us.'

'And how do we do that?'

'We have to manoeuvre him into giving us what he doesn't

147

want to give; namely, a demand. He knows as well as we do that the moment he makes a demand, he transfers some of his power to us. From that moment, we start to know something about him. While we have no idea of what he wants from the kidnap, we are in a state of maximum uncertainty and, therefore, helplessness.'

'But we think we do know what he wants,' said Isabel. 'To punish us. I mean, Chico.'

'So far, all he's declared is that he's not in it for any material gain. I think you have to demonstrate your understanding of that by approaching him on the "higher level" that he wants to be seen. You're no longer grubbing around in the filth of money and possessions. He disdains that.'

'So what is a kidnapper's higher plain?' asked Isabel sarcastically.

'He enjoys the psychology of the situation he has created. He is in control and cannot be bought by the man who can buy everything. So we have to work towards finding a way of admiring him. It mustn't be crass. He's too intelligent for that. It has to be subtle and sincere. He will despise flattery, so that's out. The one great advantage you have is that you're a woman and you work. And you probably work with men, intelligent men, but men who need their egos stroked.'

'Not my colleagues,' said Isabel. 'They're all women in publishing. But the writers ...'

'Tell me about the writers.'

'Intelligent but unworldly. Egotistical but insecure. Communicative but detached. Well-known but solitary. Talented but in their own eyes worthless.'

'Worthless?'

'That probably only applies to the more self-aware ones,' said Isabel. 'They recognise that they have talent but somehow think that "making up stuff", as some of them call it, is a worthless profession. Given their intelligence, they think they should be doctors or entrepreneurs or, perhaps, kidnap consultants. I have to tell them that people need stories more than ever, to make sense of this new and uncertain world, and remind them that without their "stuff", there'd be no publishing industry, a smaller TV industry, fewer films ...'

'So their sense of worthlessness springs from their insecurity,' said Boxer. 'They sound like very interesting potential criminals. You've had the perfect training.'

'So what do I talk to him about?' said Isabel. 'With writers you've always got their books.'

'And with Jordan it's obvious, too,' said Boxer. 'You've got a common interest: Alyshia. Talk to him about her. Get him to share in your concern over her mental state. See if you can make him care.'

'But how do I elicit a demand out of that kind of conversation?'

'You don't. You cannot be seen to have ulterior motives. Don't think of yourself as a saleswoman trying to close a deal. Never reveal your goal. Think of him as a difficult person you've met at a party who's revealed to you that he's having trouble with his daughter. I know, that sounds familiar. But that's how to do it. You want to identify with each other, but you should have no interest in trying to get something from him. You have to show *genuine* human interest.'

'That might be difficult.'

'Don't make me say it, Isabel. Even Mercy was dismayed.'

'Shut up about the bloody committee.'

'All right,' said Boxer. 'This is important, too: you have to imagine Jordan with a human face.'

Isabel blinked, unable to bring the necessary image to mind. All she found herself doing was suppressing a vast, nearly uncontrollable rage against this man who had kidnapped her child.

'It's absolutely crucial that you do not dehumanise him,' said Boxer. 'When you're talking to him, I want you to think of someone. Not necessarily someone you know. It could be an actor or a politician, but someone who, despite their difficult nature, you think you probably admire because, deep down, they're a good man.'

'Now you're just punishing me for not having a committee.'

'The other person you can talk about is Frank,' said Boxer. 'And there you might find yourself on common ground. You have no illusions about Frank. You don't love him any more and you know *why* you don't love him. You thought that Jordan knew him too, and he didn't like him either. You see eye to eye on the reason for that.'

Isabel stared into the table, nodding.

'Something else for you to think about, for you to focus on,' said Boxer. 'Something to give you strength. Although you still think of Alyshia as your child, you have to remember that she's a grown woman. She has experience of dealing with people, she is intelligent and confident, and that has been proven to her in her life. She can look after herself. She has resources.'

'Yes, you're right,' said Isabel, beating the table softly with her fist, as if drumming these things into herself. 'I *do* think of her as my little girl. I even find myself telling her off like one. That's why she gets annoyed with me.'

'That's how I think about Amy. Well, some of the time. Recently, that's become almost impossible, I have to admit. But you never lose that protective instinct; it's engraved into you at the moment of their birth.'

The doorbell rang.

'That'll be Chico,' said Isabel, getting up.

Still not enough time to prepare her, thought Boxer. Too many distractions. The situation kept slipping away from him.

He stood to shake hands with D'Cruz as he entered the room.

They listened to the early morning phone call with Jordan. D'Cruz shook his head, perplexed, asked where Alyshia's mobile was now.

'Pavis will send it round here, just as soon as they've carried out the forensics and made a recording of what's on the device,' said Boxer. 'Have you had any further thoughts, Frank, about who this could be? You might be dismissive of the disgruntled employee possibility but we should be considering every angle.'

D'Cruz said nothing.

'A profiler has listened to that call,' said Isabel. 'He didn't think Jordan was a kidnapper. He didn't want to say it but he thought he was a killer. Now why would Jordan want to do that? You must know something, Chico. You must have crossed someone badly for them to be doing this.'

'I've done a lot of terrible things in my time as a businessman,' said D'Cruz. 'I've fired people, that's for sure. I've taken over businesses aggressively, without approval of the families who own them. I've made ruthless decisions, I can't deny it. But this is the first time someone has kidnapped my daughter in retaliation.'

'And what happened in Mumbai?' asked Isabel. 'Why did Alyshia not go back after Christmas?'

'Why do you assume I know that?' said D'Cruz. 'I'm not like you, Isabel. Alyshia and I have a different relationship. When she arrived in Mumbai, she spent only the first weekend with Sharmila and me before moving into the apartment we'd arranged for her. From that day on, she had her own private life. I gave her responsibilities in the company. She had to learn about the steel business from scratch.'

'How did she do that?' asked Boxer.

'She worked in all the different departments. I sent her to Australia to meet our raw material suppliers. She worked in shipping, to see how those materials arrived in the docks. She had experience of all the different production lines – pipe, girder, roll – and then she went into marketing and sales.'

'Did any one person show her the ropes?' Boxer asked.

'That's not how I do things. I believe in people learning with their own eyes, from their own experience, not having everything filtered through the mind and opinions of one other person. So she met people from all the different departments, from the managing director to the crane operators, to the men on the foundry floor and back up to the sales director. But there was no one person telling her how to think about the business. She saw everything for herself and made up her own mind.'

'What was she doing by the time she left?'

'She was manager of the sales teams for the home market and Pakistan.'

'So she wasn't on the board?' said Boxer. 'There was no one who could have been envious of her position? She was where she was through merit?'

'She was where she was because she was my daughter, but she held on to her job through merit. Nobody was dissatisfied with her performance.'

'When the daughter of the owner comes into a business, there must be employees who interpret that in a certain way,' said Boxer. 'Did anybody leave because Alyshia had come on board and they could see the writing on the wall?'

'If they did, they didn't give Alyshia's appointment as their reason for leaving,' said D'Cruz. 'She had a long way to go before she could have made it to any directorial post. I deliberately started her off in the steel business because that was not her natural interest. She was always going to have to work hard to get anywhere. She was much more interested in the manufacturing sector, especially cars, but I wanted to see her prove herself in heavy industry first and to understand where all the components of the car industry came from.'

'What was the name of that young man you particularly liked?' said Isabel. 'You brought him over here once. We all had dinner together before Alyshia left the Saïd Business School. Deepak … I can't remember his family name. What happened to Deepak?'

'Deepak Mistry left the company,' said D'Cruz. 'It was very sad. I had high hopes for him, but he said he didn't want to work in a corporation anymore. He wanted to be an entrepreneur again. He left to set up on his own, although I don't know where he is now. I'm told he is not in Mumbai and he hasn't been seen in Bangalore, where I first came across him.'

'Any resentment on his part?'

'I made him a wealthy man. He could have done anything he liked in Konkan Hills, but he decided it wasn't for him. He was responsible for transforming the steelworks I'd bought into the business that it is today. I'd always thought that he would end up running it. Nothing I could say would persuade him to change his mind.'

'Would it be worth checking him out?'

'I could have his details sent to Pavis but I think they would be wasting their time. Deepak kidnapping Alyshia? It doesn't make any sense.'

'So why did Alyshia leave Mumbai?' asked Isabel. 'The kidnapper seems to think he knows why. You were so close to her, Chico. You must know something.'

'It was nothing to do with her work. There was no friction with anybody that I knew of. It must have been something to do with her private life. I assumed she'd had an affair and it had gone wrong,' said D'Cruz. 'I mean, *you* share everything with her and she didn't tell you anything, either.'

The doorbell rang. A bike messenger from Pavis with Alyshia's mobile.

George Papadopoulos went into Bovingdon Recruitment on Tottenham Court Road and asked at reception for Alyshia D'Cruz.

'She hasn't come in today.'

'That's weird,' said Papadopoulos. 'We arranged to meet here at eleven-thirty. I bumped into her on Friday evening. Can I speak to one of her colleagues?'

The receptionist made some calls and sent Papadopoulos up to the first floor to meet one of the other managers. He handed over a fake business card and explained that he'd met Alyshia with a group of people on Friday night.

'The leaving party.'

'That's right,' he said. 'We got talking about business. She was with another girl. I can't remember her name.'

'Toola. Toola Briggs.'

'That's the one,' said Papadopoulos. 'Maybe I could speak to her if Alyshia's not in?'

'It was *her* leaving party. She's not with us anymore.'

He left, fobbing off other people to talk to, asked them to get Alyshia to call him when she came in. He went for a coffee on Goodge Street and accessed Toola Briggs' tax details, home address and mobile number.

'Hi Toola, this is George,' he said.

'George?'

'A friend of Alyshia's. We met on Friday night at your leaving party.'

'Oh my God.'

'Yeah, right. You were all a bit bladdered. Alyshia told me to meet her in the office at Tottenham Court Road this morning but she hasn't come in today and she's not answering her mobile. When did you last see her?'

'We were all running away from Doggy down Bedford Street to the Strand to get the tube at Charing Cross. Alyshia, as far as I know, went off down Maiden Lane with Jim.'

'I don't remember Jim.'

'Jim Paxton. Tall, balding, a bit older than the rest of us. I've got his number if you want it.'

Papadopoulos took the number down, hung up, went back into the computer and got an address for Jim Paxton in Shoreditch. He called Bovingdon Recruitment, asked for him, and was told that he'd left the company. Papadopoulos decided that if Jim Paxton was the last to see Alyshia, he'd prefer a face-to-face conversation. He took the tube to Old Street and half an hour later was standing outside a block of flats on Purcell Street. No answer from Jim Paxton's bell. He rang the one next to it, got an answer from a girl.

'Hi, I'm Jim Paxton's mate. He told me to meet him here but there's no answer. You seen him?'

No reply. The door buzzed open. Papadopoulos went up the stairs, was about to hammer on the door.

'His bell's broken,' said a girl's voice from down the corridor. 'He expects the landlord to fix it, which is why it's still fucked.'

'You seen him at all?'

'I saw him over the weekend,' she said. 'But not since Saturday, which isn't so weird. He quite often doesn't surface on Sundays.'

'He left his job. We were out together on Friday night.'

'He said he was going to Thailand to get away from the cold.'

'I thought it was India.'

'That's Jim,' said the girl, shrugging. 'Never has any money. His travel plans are all up here.' She tapped her head, pulled her cardigan tighter around her body.

Papadopoulos pounded on the door.

'I'm worried about him,' said Papadopoulos, taking out his mobile, calling the number Toola had given him. 'He's not answering his calls.'

They heard the mobile ringing in the flat. A look of genuine concern came over the girl.

'Any ideas how I can get in here?' asked Papadopoulos.

'I haven't got any keys and the landlord's a wanker. You won't see him unless Jim's rent cheque doesn't turn up, and he paid that ...'

She stopped as Papadopoulos leaned back and hammered his heel into the lock. The door cracked back into the wall. The flat was in darkness.

'Well, that's one way,' said the girl, who'd walked up the corridor to peer in. 'It smells terrible in there, doesn't it?'

'Stay here,' he said.

Small, depressing kitchen on the right, window overlooking the razor wire around the yard next door. Washing up all done, clean cooker and floor. Sitting room, blinds drawn, vaguely aware of a battered sofa, two chairs and a table up against the wall, three shelves of books. Papadopoulos rolled the blind up to let in more light but there wasn't much to be had. He looked down into a grey yard piled high with white plastic furniture, as if tossed there by hooligans. He turned to see a large flat screen TV in the middle of the far wall, brand new. The room was very tidy, as if recently dusted and hoovered.

'I haven't seen that before,' said the girl, pointing at the TV.

'I told you to stay outside,' said Papadopoulos, unable to suppress his cop instincts, not wanting her to contaminate the scene.

'Jim's a bit of a control freak, you know, a compulsive cleaner. Doesn't like mess. Irons his underpants. Know what I mean?' said the girl. 'It never smells like this in his flat. He burns aromatic candles normally.'

'Don't touch anything, OK? Just wait for me outside. I don't like the look of this.'

'Are you the police or something?'

Fuck off, he thought. Not you and all.

The girl backed out slowly. Things more serious than she'd anticipated, but she trusted the guy, Jim's mate, who kicked down doors. Cop type, if not a real one.

The bedroom was a mess. Duvet on the floor, bedside lamp and table knocked over. Very bad smell, but no sign of Jim. Papadopoulos turned on the light. Huge wardrobe in the corner, massive for the room. Clothes on hangers were piled in the corner, shoes all over the shop. The right-hand door of the wardrobe was hanging open a couple of inches. Papadopoulos eased it open with his foot. Jim was hanging from the bar, stripped to the waist, trousers and underpants around his knees, but his feet in contact with the floor of the wardrobe. His head was drooped over the belt around his slack neck, lips swollen, eyes bulging out.

'Shit,' said Papadopoulos.

He backed out of the room, shut the door, called Mercy. The girl was on the threshold of the sitting room, hovering.

'You'd better go back to your flat,' he said, but she didn't react. 'Hey!'

'What?'

'I'm calling the police. Go back to your flat.'

'What's happened to Jim?'

'He's dead,' said Papadopoulos. 'Two secs, Mercy.'

'Jim's dead?' said the girl, puzzled. 'Suicide?'

'Why do you ask that?'

'He was a bit of a depressive ... a manic depressive,' she said.

'What about the flat screen TV?'

'What about it?'

'You don't buy one of those if you're going to kill yourself the next day.'

'I don't know what you're getting at,' she said, still in shock.

'Just go back to your flat while I speak to the police.'

She left. Papadopoulos followed her, made sure she went all the way, closed the door to Jim's flat.

'Mercy, I've just found the last guy to be seen with Alyshia D'Cruz on Friday night. He's dead, hanging in the wardrobe in his flat in Shoreditch.'

'Murder?'

'Looks like it to me, but with a half-arsed attempt to dress it up as auto-erotic asphyxiation.'

'I'll call the DCS, see how he wants to play this,' said Mercy. 'It's got to be connected to the kidnap.'

'Maybe we should start looking at CCTV footage around Covent Garden on Friday night. Alyshia was last seen by a girl in the leaving party group heading down Maiden Lane with this guy. His name's Jim Paxton.'

'Leave it with me.'

'How are you getting on?'

'So far, so nothing,' said Mercy. 'I've just been phoning around, but I'm about to go face-to-face with informers. I'm on my way to the East End now.'

'There's a girl here in the flat next to Jim Paxton's. She knows him. Do you want me to interview her or wait?'

'They'll probably want to put a full homicide unit onto it, so leave it until you hear from the DCS.'

'I'll get back to the girl in the leaving party who last saw Alyshia and Jim. See if I can get a bit more detail.'

Papadopoulos hung up, called Toola.

'Hi, Toola, it's me again. Don't know what's going on today. No luck with Jim and Alyshia's off work. No answer from their mobiles. When did you say you last saw them?'

'Alyshia wanted to get a cab. She was really out of it. I was surprised; she doesn't drink that much. Not like us. One moment she was all right and the next she was wasted. I thought afterwards someone might have spiked her drink.'

'Jim?'

'Not Jim. He was looking after her. He's not the pervy type. I think they just went off to the other side of the Garden to get a cab. It was mad on the Strand. Everybody off their faces and that kid got knifed.'

Another call coming in. Papadopoulos hung up on Toola, took the call from DCS Makepeace.

'Good work, George,' said Makepeace. 'You're at Jim Paxton's flat with the girl?'

'I've sent her back to her flat. I'm on my own here, sir.'

'There's no cloak and dagger way round this. It's got to be investigated as murder and the body has to be removed,' said Makepeace. 'We'll maintain your cover ...'

'I'm just a mate of Jim Paxton's as far as this girl's concerned, although I did put my foot through the door to gain entry.'

'Sit tight with her. I'll have a homicide unit round there in ten minutes,' said Makepeace. 'We're going through the CCTV footage now.'

'If it's any help on the timing, Alyshia's colleague at work told me that a black lad was stabbed on the Strand at the same time Alyshia would have been looking for a cab with Jim Paxton.'

13

'Bad news,' said the voice.

Alyshia thought she was awake. The sleeping mask was still on, but with all the drugs, she wasn't sure whether she was under or not. Her mind felt sharp but flighty. She reached out and touched the wall with her fingertips. She wanted consciousness but no interference. She wanted to think. Too much of her life outside work had passed by in a blur, with no contemplation, just a continuous stream of action and reaction in a twittering, facebooking, texting world, where everything was about speed and connection, but empty of content.

'Did you hear me, Alyshia?'

This kidnap, this voice, had forced her in on herself, to a place she'd rarely been before. He'd driven her to consider things that could possibly be true, but because she'd never been able to resist the momentum of life, she'd never had time to disentangle it all. Only now was she becoming aware of the ambivalence within herself. The need and the resistance. The wanting to know and yet fearing it, too. But what, exactly, was there to fear? She wasn't the fearful type. Who was it who'd said that ignorance and arrogance were the perfect combination for the fearlessness of the young?

Her mind was reaching for something, but with the uncertainty of a hand that had to go into a dark hole in the wall to grasp something. Her father had always told her: 'Courage is retrospective. You don't know you've got it until you've done it.' She knew now that she was reaching out for the answer to the voice's last question: 'What was it about Julian that drew you to him?' She knew none of her friends had been able to understand it.

'Anybody home?' asked the voice.

The door opened. Feet strode cross the floor. Four of them. They had violence in their contact with the rough cement. The coldness of the latex hands that touched her skin made her throat leap. They hauled her to her feet, pulled her across the floor. Her legs were not working properly. They got her standing, cuffed her hands behind her back, then swept her legs away. One of them grabbed a fistful of her hair, pulled her head back until her neck was taut. Her heart pattered in her chest like a bird baffled by a window. Two slaps. Left, then right. The inside of her cheek bled. Tears seeped into her mask. She had a vision of herself, blind and helpless before the chopping block.

'Bad news,' said the voice. 'Are you with me now, Alyshia?'

She tried to nod, couldn't speak.

'I want to hear your voice; you're on camera?'

'Yes,' she said. 'I'm with you now.'

'The negotiations with your parents have not worked out to our satisfaction.'

'What does that mean?'

'They've broken down. We can't seem to come to an agreement. We warned Frank and Isabel what would happen but they don't seem to believe us. We've decided to terminate the negotiations. This kidnap is now over. We are going to dispose of you as we see fit.'

'Dispose of me?'

'It's unfortunate. This is what happens when kidnap negotiations break down,' said the voice. 'But to show your parents that we're not completely heartless, we've decided to give you the opportunity to say some final words, to whomever you want. Perhaps you don't want to say anything to them now that you've realised how obstructive they—'

'But I've done everything you've asked. I've answered all your questions. Ask me anything. I'll … I'll …'

'No, no, Alyshia, don't get me wrong. This is not *your* problem. This is purely to do with a breakdown in communication with your parents. It's beyond your control, and ours too. I'm sorry it's come to this. We ... I thought we were getting somewhere with your ... what shall we call it? Treatment?'

'You're confusing me,' said Alyshia, white fear racing around her body, cold and fast as quicksilver. The pulse in her neck tapped faster than little fingers over a tam-tam. Her mouth was box dry, pins and needles in her lips, eyeballs searching the velvet blackness of the mask for an inkling of light, or meaning, or an exit.

'It's not confusing. You're understandably upset,' said the voice. 'I'm being crystal clear. The negotiations have failed. Your parents have not acquiesced to our demands. The kidnap is over.'

'But I've ... I've only been away ...'

'You've been a hostage for sixty hours now,' said the voice. 'Normally we'd expect to resolve this sort of thing in forty-eight. The longer we hold you, the riskier it becomes. We're in London, where everybody's watching, everybody's talking.'

'But you told them no police, didn't you? They won't go to the police.'

'I'm sure they didn't actually *go* to the police, but,' said the voice, 'we've had to be careful ourselves. You know, cover our tracks, as they say. We had to kill Jim, you see.'

'You killed Jim? Why? I thought you said he had nothing to do with this.'

'I lied to you. You were right. He was involved. He delivered you to us. Put a bit of a spike in your last drink and sent you to our door. We paid him very well, but you know how it is, you can never rely on people not to shoot their mouths off. There's a powerful need out in this anonymous city to make yourself the centre of attention, even if it is for Warhol's fifteen minutes down the pub.'

'But that means you've covered your tracks,' she said, grasping at the reeds flashing past on the bank. 'There's nothing for you to worry about. I haven't seen your faces. I haven't even heard your real voice. What do I know about you?'

'The police found Jim this morning. We made it look as good as we could. Pills, alcohol, bit of auto-erotic asphyxiation.'

'Don't tell me. I don't need to know. Why are you telling me this? I'm not going to tell anybody.'

'I don't think it will wash with the crime scene guys, though. They'll see through it in seconds. Even you'd see through it.'

'But it will still take time. You've still got time,' said Alyshia. 'Just go back to my parents ...'

'That has not been fruitful,' said the voice. 'Of course, they've got a negotiator there, a professional telling your mother what to say and how to say it. This has complicated the issue which, as we see it, is very simple.'

'Let me talk to them. I can persuade them.'

'It's too late for that,' said the voice. 'The police finding Jim's dead body has put us under pressure. We're getting out before we're caught. The decision has been unanimous. We've bought you some of your own clothes. Rather special clothes. We want you to get dressed, look nice and composed and say your final words. But Alyshia, this has to be done in ten minutes. If you try to string this out, we'll just shoot you like a dog. It makes no difference to the men holding you. As you've discovered, they've been a bit rough with you already. They're annoyed. They know they're not going to get their bonus.'

They pulled her up to her feet. One of the men holding her left the room. She heard a plastic dry cleaning sheath being stripped off. The other uncuffed her wrists.

'You're going to need a different bra for this dress,' said the voice. 'Take off your underwear.'

She stripped naked and covered herself, crouching. A pair of knickers was crushed into her hand. She pulled them on. A strapless bra was thrown over her shoulder. She slipped it over her breasts.

Someone knelt down in front of her.

'Left foot up,' said the voice. 'Down. Right foot up. Down.'

The dress was drawn up her thighs, over her waist. She knew the feel of it. It was the black mermaid dress. The figure-hugging one that shot out at the knee in a taffeta skirt. The one she'd worn for her 21st birthday in London.

She tried to jog her brain into thinking of some words, but all that ripped through her mind was a jetstream of fear.

The zip ran up the middle of her back. The design left her shoulders perfectly naked, ideal for jewellery. There was the dull click of a box opening. Her hair was sheafed and raised above her head. A man's arms came over her shoulders. The touch of ice on her clavicles made her throat catch and struggle as the settings were drawn up to her neck and the clasp fixed at her nape. Her hair fell back onto her shoulders. A brush was put into her hands.

'Do the best you can,' said the voice. 'Keep the mask on.'

The brush snagged through her unwashed hair, tore through the tangles; she pulled until the roots hurt and the tears came.

'Shoes,' said the voice. 'Bring her the shoes. Hurry it up. We've got seven minutes to be out of here.'

Her feet were fitted into high heels, the black strappy ones. She was elevated to a new height. The smell of alcohol came to her nostrils. Doused cotton wool dabbed at her tear-stained cheeks.

'No make-up. You should look as natural as possible. I want them to see the pure you. Remind them of what their intransigence has cost them. Are we ready?' said the voice. 'Close your eyes, Alyshia. Take off the mask.'

The cotton wool swabbed around her eyes. She cherished the coolness of its touch. The final stroke of care in this world. The light hurt and she squinted against it.

'Open your eyes,' said the voice. 'The camera is running. You may speak. Action.'

Her whole life tore towards the funnel of her mind. Twenty-five years cramming itself into a small sphere, like a child looking down binoculars the wrong way to see the improbable adult so far off. How to crystallise a life? Nothing had prepared her for this moment. Not even some of the most advanced presentation techniques she'd learned at the Saïd Business School were adequate to this monumental task. *Who am I?* she thought. *Who was I?* When they asked celebrities that question: 'What do you owe your parents?' they always replied: 'Everything'. Did that still apply when it also included your death?

She looked in the mirror and saw a further intensity to her beauty now that she was teetering on the edge. By contrast, the men on either side of her were deeply ugly, dressed in amorphous, thigh-length biker jackets, collars zipped up to their noses, hoods over their heads, only eye-holes visible. And the one on her right with a silenced handgun hanging loosely from an ungloved hand.

She trembled inside, felt her stomach muscles quivering against the fabric of the dress. Only then did she concentrate on the necklace: the diamonds given to her by her father on her 21st birthday. Three swallows to get the emotion back down.

'Come on, Alyshia,' said the voice. 'I'm going to start clearing this equipment away in two minutes. You've got—'

'I'm sorry for what I've done and I'm sorry for what I have not done. You mustn't blame yourselves for any of this. You gave me the perfect preparation, the best genes, the deepest affection, the greatest attention, the right instruction, and I have squandered it all. I regret my cruelty to you, Mummy. You did not deserve any of it. I know now that it came from my own sense of failure. I love you more in this moment than I have in my entire life. I am sorry I abandoned you, Daddy. You gave me opportunities. You've been giving but demanding, and loving without smothering. I wish I could have returned it to you, with the interest it deserved. I am going now. But I want you to know that I'm not ignorant, selfish, arrogant and indifferent anymore, but regretful, humble and wishing that I could see you both one last time.'

The last words were soundless, mouthed through saliva that had clogged her mouth. Tears streamed down her cheeks, drops hung at her jaw.

'Very nice,' said the voice. 'Surprisingly restrained, I must say. Now let's get it done and out of here.'

Hands on her shoulders, pressing her down into a position she did not want to be. She knelt on quivering thighs, facing the man with the gun. She looked up, desperate and pleading into the black, glinting pupils beyond the holes in the hood. The gun came up. The barrel came to rest on her forehead. She reached her hands up and clung to the lower edges of the man's jacket, while behind her the other man unrolled a length of plastic sheeting, which went over her heels. The man with the gun slapped her hands away and she dropped onto the plastic sheet on all fours, like a retching dog.

Mercy Danquah had just finished a fruitless meeting with the first of her informers, Busby, and was on her way to her second meeting with Nelson. She noticed that her gear-changing had become increasingly irritable and that she was leaning forward out of her seat and gripping the steering wheel tightly. She was angry with Boxer. He'd put her in a position. She was going to have to tell DCS Makepeace what had happened, or rather, what she believed had happened between him and Isabel.

'I can't believe it,' she said out loud, to God, Boxer and the traffic.

The sound of her own voice broke something open in her and she began to suspect her motives, caught a glimpse of something else she didn't like to admit. She smacked it down, thought about Nelson instead. Why he was the better bet. Yes, Nelson, he was more in the thick of it because he lived on disability benefits and spent most of his time in the pubs and clubs of Bethnal Green, Whitechapel and Stepney.

She parked up, not far from where they were meeting in a local café, E Pellicci, on Bethnal Green Road, just round the corner from the Kray twins' old house on Voss Street. The walls were lined with light brown wooden panels in which there were marquetry designs that dated from the 1940s. The windows had stained glass. People sat on wooden chairs at formica tables with the triumverate of brown sauce, tomato ketchup and mustard in front of them. The tea came in big cups from a large chrome urn by the till. The healthiest food on the menu was baked beans on toast. Mercy ordered a plate, seeing as she hadn't had breakfast that morning. Nelson, despite the hour, was taking advantage of her offer to pay by having the full English, whose centrepoint was a pile of inch thick chips, which he doused in salt and vinegar and dipped in ketchup before cramming them into his mouth, leaving red flecks at the corners.

Nelson was the codename Mercy used to protect his identity. He'd lost his arm in an industrial accident some time ago and only last year had compounded his codename by losing an eye to glaucoma. At least he didn't wear a patch, but had a glass eye with a disturbing clarity, which made Mercy think that he could see more out of that one than he could through the rheuminess of the good one. He was not a small man, with a bowling ball gut and a full head of grey hair swept back. He talked in a way that made Mercy think he'd spent a lot of time in libraries while absentmindedly shovelling eight teaspoons of sugar into his tea.

'You know, maybe it's something to do with the economic downturn or the government austerity measures,' he said, 'but I've heard more talk about kidnapping in the last couple of years than I have since—'

'What's the economic downturn got to do with it?'

'Fewer young people with jobs, no money to buy drugs, so the drug dealers have to look elsewhere to make their money.'

'You should be in a government think tank,' said Mercy. 'You're wasted here.'

'There's less money around at street level, that's all I'm saying.'

'I thought that's why they were bringing in plant food from China for the kids to snort.'

'Plant food?'

'Mephedrone,' said Mercy. 'Don't worry about it, admiral. Tell me why kidnapping's back in fashion.'

'It's mainly the quick twenty-four hour stuff. Nothing complicated. Track your mark. Stick them in the back of a van. Smack them about a bit. Put them under. Make your phone calls. Take your money. Tip them out and run.'

'What about longer term stuff, for big money?'

'You mean the new tax on the rich?' said Nelson, stabbing his fried egg viciously, as if it were the eye of a banker. 'Make them pay for all the shit they're putting us through. Steal their kids and give them an alternative education.'

'On what? Dog racing?'

'There's nothing wrong with the dogs, Mercy.'

'Let me know when these gangs start their Samuel Beckett workshops and I might turn up myself,' said Mercy. 'So have you heard of anybody getting involved in longer term stuff?'

'What? Like that Indian businessman they nabbed in East Ham a while back? Asked for a Fergie. Kept him on an industrial estate in Essex.'

'A Fergie?'

'That's half a mil.'

'You never forget, do you, admiral?' said Mercy. 'Yeah, that's the sort of thing I'm talking about. Long term. Safe house. Big ransom demand.'

Mercy recognised Nelson's methodology. He'd given some intelligence on the Indian's kidnap, which had been very useful in getting the hostage back. She felt the excitement kick in at the thought that he might actually have something.

'It's not that easy in this part of London anymore.'

'You mean with friends like you littering the place and listening in on the chit-chat?'

'Let me know how you get on when you lose your right arm, Mercy.'

'Only teasing.'

'Yeah,' said Nelson, disbelieving.

'What about somebody doing something to order?' said Mercy, trying to jog Nelson along. 'Like a businessman with money and resources but no expertise or manpower, who hires a gang to carry out a kidnap on his behalf?'

Nelson nodded, concentrated on his food, put together a forkful of bacon, egg, sausage, tomato and a chip.

'You've gone all quiet on me, admiral,' said Mercy, nervous that she might have pissed him off by reminding him of his snout status.

'I'm eating,' said Nelson, swilling down the last mouthful with the dark, brown, sweet tea that he sloshed around his dentures. 'You know why I like to come here?'

Mercy sank a little inside. More stroking was going to be required. 'Think of it as foreplay,' they'd said on the Met's informer course, but that, in Nelson's case, was just too disgusting.

'It's a nice place,' said Mercy, looking around. 'I go to the Winning Post down in Streatham every now and again. I'll take you there one day.'

'The thing about this place, Mercy, is that Nev, the owner, doesn't change anything.'

'Even the Ladies?'

'And out there,' said Nelson, ignoring her, pointing over her shoulder at the traffic pounding through the grey on Bethnal Green Road, 'it's changing all the time.'

'How's that?'

'We're getting squeezed by the Bees out there.'

'The bees?'

166

'The Bankers, the Brokers and the Bengalis,' said Nelson. 'There's not many of us left.'

'Which tribe are you?'

'The white working class,' said Nelson, brushing his front. 'Nowadays you go out there and there're Poles and Ukrainians, Lithuanians and Bulgarians, Chinese and Jamaicans, Punjabis and Pashtuns. We don't know who *we* are any more. But, at least, in here, I know: I'm English and I belong.'

'Even though Nev's Italian,' said Mercy. 'And by the way, you left out Ghanaians. I'm hurt.'

'You're not Ghanaian, Mercy. You're bleeding English,' said Nelson, pointing his fork at her across the table. 'You know what? Nev doesn't even know what a latte is.'

Mercy thought that unlikely, but let it go.

'It's Grade Two listed in here,' said Nelson, looking around at the marquetry and the stained glass windows. 'That's how English it is. It's become part of our heritage, an institution.'

'And you're all in it,' said Mercy. 'What's your point, Nelson?'

'Kidnapping is not an English crime,' he said.

'I think you might be forgetting that the bloke who kidnapped that Indian in East Ham was called Danny Gibney.'

'Irish,' said Nelson, weighing his fork. 'Most kidnaps I hear about are Yardies, nabbing someone's sister because they haven't paid their drugs bill. Or Ukrainians, grabbing illegal girls and sticking them in brothels.'

'Sweet,' said Mercy, finishing her beans. 'But what I'm talking about is different.'

'I hear what you're saying.'

That was when Mercy knew for certain that Nelson had something and he was just putting her through the negotiation process. Either that, or he had something on someone a bit too close for comfort.

'One of the things that concerns us about this kidnap is that we're not convinced that they're looking for a ransom,' she said. 'We think they're going to tease, torture and kill. You don't want to let people get away with something like that, do you, admiral? Not with a young woman.'

'How young?' asked Nelson, pushing back his plate, cleaning

167

the nooks and crannies of his front teeth with his tongue.

'Mid-twenties.'

'What nationality?'

'Half English, half Indian.'

'The only thing is,' said Nelson, playing the edge of the table with his remaining hand, 'this'll come back to me too easily. So, if I tell you, you'll have to find another way in. You've got to promise me that.'

'I don't know how easy that's going to be.'

'You'll see when I tell you.'

'All right. I'll guarantee you that,' said Mercy, cocking her head to one side. 'It looks as if there's something else, Nelson.'

'It's going to be pricier than usual.'

'Why?'

'I'm more exposed.'

'Is he a friend?'

'What sort of a bloke do you think I am?'

'So what's the problem?'

'He's connected. I could end up getting knee-capped.'

'How much?'

'Monkeys. Triplets.'

'Now I'm going to have to go out into the cold and call some-one,' said Mercy, kicking her chair back, annoyed.

She went out into the street, walked up and down outside the yellow Vitrolite exterior of Pellicci's café and called DCS Makepeace, told him Nelson was after £1500 for his grubby piece of information.

'That's pushing it,' said Makepeace. 'Doesn't he read the news? Reduction in police numbers, public sector cuts, wage freezes …'

'We've covered that already,' said Mercy wearily.

'Tell him we're working on the CCTV footage of where Alyshia was taken and we've got a time on it too, so we'll get there in the end with or without his expensive info. Five hundred's the max, or if we're quick enough, bugger all.'

Mercy went back into the café. Nelson was sitting in a food daze. Nev was clearing the plates.

'Anything else I can get you?' he asked.

'I'll take a latte, please,' said Mercy.

Nev looked completely clueless for a moment.

'All right, make it a white coffee,' she said, sitting down.

'I told you,' said Nelson.

'Bollocks,' said Mercy. 'You put him up to it.'

'Are we on?'

'We're nearly there under our own steam,' said Mercy. 'We're just checking the CCTV footage in Covent Garden of where the girl was last seen. The boss said you can have three hundred and that's it – or sweet FA if he calls me back before you spill your beans.'

Nelson shifted in his seat, irritated, and she knew they were on the right track.

'Make it up to a monkey and it's all yours.'

'Three hundred is tops.'

'Bloody hell, Mercy.'

'I've got it with me, too.'

'Have you ever heard talk of The Cabbie?'

'No.'

'He's not a cabbie, but he drives around in one: a London black cab. He runs a legit business off Violet Road in Bromley, buying and selling office furniture. He also employs illegals fresh in from Calais, pays them bugger all. They sleep in dormitories above the warehouse and he farms them out as cheap labour.'

'What's his name?'

'Jack Auber,' said Nelson. 'But if you're talking about killing people, Jack doesn't do that.'

'But he does exploit people,' said Mercy.

'All right,' said Nelson. 'I'm just telling you he doesn't kill people.'

'So what did he do and how do you know he did it?'

'There's a builder in Stepney called Fred Scully. The building trade is dire at the moment. So when Fred gets work, he has to make it count.'

'So he uses Jack's cheap labour.'

'Fred's using two of Jack's lads; been using one of the lads on and off for a year, trained him up good. Friday afternoon, Jack asks Fred to send the two lads over to his house on Grange Road, I don't know the number, but it overlooks the East London

Cemetery at the back and it's the only one with a garage. Fred knows the place because Jack lets him keep his gear there. They're working late and he can't drop the lads off until after nine. Jack says as long as they're there for midnight, he's not bothered.'

'So what time does he drop the lads off?'

'Just after nine-thirty.'

'Does he see Jack there?'

'Yeah, the cab's parked outside. Jack lets them in. Gives them some coffee. Tells them to clear the scaffolding out of the garage so that he can fit his cab in there and then stay at the house until he gets back. Fred leaves. The next day the lads don't show. When Fred calls Jack, he says: "No problem, Fred, I'm sending you another two. They'll be with you in an hour." Fred wants to know what happened to his two boys, and Jack says there was an accident. Don't ask questions.'

'When are we getting to the kidnap bit?' asked Mercy, looking up, head low down near the tabletop.

'Look, I'm just telling you how I know Jack was involved,' said Nelson. 'Jack's daughter, Cheryl, and Fred's son, Vic, are having a thing with each other. Jack's got Vic down as his future son-in-law. So Fred asks Vic to find out what happened to the two lads. This is the story that comes back. When Jack fetches up at the Grange Road house in his cab at around half past midnight, he parks the cab in the garage, because he's got someone in the back, asleep. He goes into the house and waits with the lads. Half an hour later there's screaming and shouting from the cab and he sends the two lads in there to dope the girl and bring her into the house.'

'The girl? What girl?'

'An Indian girl, in her twenties and a cracker,' said Nelson. 'The lads bring her in, put her in the bedroom at the back of the house. Then they wait. Half an hour later, two blokes turn up in hoods. Jack's expecting them but not what they do next, which is ... strangle the two lads to death. They put the bodies and the drugged girl in their van and left. Jack was shocked. Hasn't been able to get over it, which was why he spilled it to Vic, told him not to tell anyone, not even Fred, but you know how it is ...'

'Let's you and I go for a little walk, admiral,' said Mercy.

14

'Anwar Masood is a gangster,' said Roger Clayton, making his telephone report to Simon Deacon of MI6 in London, with the *pav bhaji* he'd eaten with Gagan on Juhu Beach still chupping quietly in his stomach, encouraging soft burps and worse. 'A big Muslim gangster who does what gangsters do: prostitution, girl trafficking, drugs, betting, protection and all the rest of it.'

'How far back does he go with Frank D'Cruz?' asked Deacon.

'Masood was in the gold smuggling business on the Dubai to Bombay run twenty or thirty years ago. Before Frank got his break in the film business he was running an import/export business between Bombay and Dubai, where there's always been a large Indian Muslim expat community. I'm sure that's how he knows Masood.'

'So what's their relationship now?'

'Difficult to know, precisely, but for some years he's been an alternative security department for Konkan Hills,' said Clayton. 'He doesn't pitch up at board meetings or work alongside Frank in any way that might link them publicly. But he makes sure that Frank is aware of all pertinent underworld intelligence, and he guarantees that nobody close to Frank will get kidnapped, as well as protecting his construction sites, warehouses and offices from being mysteriously fire-bombed.'

'I'm assuming that this "Mister Iqbal" and Lieutenant General Abdel Iqbal are one and the same. He was mentioned by your source in the D'Cruz compound and Divesh Mehta from the Research and Analysis Wing.'

'He's a serving member of the Inter-Services Intelligence agency in Karachi and is known locally as "Mr Steel". I think that's as in the metal rather than corruption. He's Frank's main introduction to most of the steel contracts he's picked up in Sindh province and there's been a lot since the floods of 2010 and 2011,' said Clayton.

'How clean is he, given the multi-layered tendency of the ISI?' asked Deacon.

'They haven't pinned anything on him – yet,' said Clayton. 'But they've got their suspicions based on the fact that Iqbal is known to collaborate with a retired ISI officer called Amir Jat.'

'I'm just working my way through a CIA report on him: a rather sinister combination of piety and sadism with connections to the upper tiers of US Intelligence as well as to terrorist organisations, such as Lashkar-e-Taiba and al Qaeda,' said Deacon.

'Divesh Mehta sent me an RAW report on him. Bloody hair-raising,' said Clayton. 'The man they're particularly looking at as a possible terrorist connection for Iqbal is a protégé of Amir Jat's called Mahmood Aziz, born in the UK in 1975 to Pakistani parents, left in 1987 full of ideas of joining the Jihad against the Russians at the age of twelve, for God's sake. Latest activities believed to include training the Mumbai attackers of 2008 and bombing NATO fuel convoys in 2010 and 2011.'

'So why don't the RAW pursue Iqbal?'

'Stretched resources,' said Clayton. 'I think if Frank D'Cruz is sending Anwar Masood to see Iqbal, it's probably because of his more piquant connections to people like, well, Amir Jat, who can actually tell him things …'

'Like?'

'Whether his daughter being kidnapped in London is an al-Qaeda-inspired action, for instance,' said Clayton, leaning back in his chair, giving his digestion a bit more room. 'Maybe you'll have to dig deeper across the border on that one.'

'I'll get someone digging around in Dubai, too. See if we can flush out any connections there,' said Deacon. 'Let's talk about your last bit of intelligence: D'Cruz's uber-apprentice, Deepak Mistry. Where is he? Why does D'Cruz want to find him?' And if he's got Anwar Masood on the job, Deepak must have gone underground. Why would an ex-employee have to do that?'

'Because Mistry doesn't want to be found?' said Clayton. 'So perhaps I should get out there and find him.'

'Maybe,' said Deacon. 'It's got potential, given this development in London.'

'If Anwar Masood can't find him it's because he's being hidden by a Hindu gang.'

'So what are your connections in the Mumbai Hindu gang world like?'

'I know a young gun from one of the Hindu breakaway groups from the old D-Company.'

'D-Company? That rings a bell.'

'That was the original gold smuggling outfit that operated out of Dubai in the 1980s. The Mumbai gang I'm talking about is run, in name at least because he doesn't spend much time here, by a man called Chhota Tambe – that means Little Tambe. Small in stature, big in reach. All I can say about his gang members is that they don't like the Muslims one little bit,' said Clayton. 'My contact knows all the other Hindu gangs. If Deepak Mistry is underground in Mumbai, he'll know where.'

Mercy had given DCS Makepeace her report on Nelson's information but had held off talking about Boxer and Isabel. She needed time to think, examine herself, before she did something as damaging as that. While she was waiting for Makepeace to come back to her with an independent sighting of Jack Auber picking up Alyshia D'Cruz on CCTV, she did a couple of drive-bys. One past Jack Auber's house on Southern Grove, which was as silent as the graves in the Tower Hamlets cemetery behind.

The second drive-by was past Auber's office furniture store on Violet Road, which looked closed. She parked up outside to watch and wait. Her mind immediately drifted onto the two people causing most turbulence in her life: Amy and Boxer. She couldn't get over that vision of Amy with the couple in the waiting room. She realised that it had more than just stung her to see how appealing her daughter could be. She was mortified by her failure. And once her anger had subsided after their confrontation and she'd got

Amy home, she'd felt sick at the atmosphere in the house. Yes, it had reminded her of her own family home in Kumasi, where even the most brilliant sunlit days, with the hibiscus flaming in the garden and the children singing on their way to school, had always felt dark.

She shook her head. Her father, the police officer. They were too alike. They even had the same posture. She knew it was why she was so driven. The guilt at having run away. And no man in her life to take the edge off. She hadn't felt a flicker of interest in men since she'd split from Charlie. Little social life to speak of. The pub with colleagues, coffee with neighbours was about it. Nothing to make her want to relent on the work. And now, in the quiet of Violet Road, she could admit the other thing that was bothering her. That look in Charlie's face. He'd found someone – and she was good for him. Yes, she didn't like to admit it: she envied him. No. Worse. She was jealous.

At midday Mercy got the call telling her that Alyshia D'Cruz had been seen on CCTV getting into Jack Auber's black cab on Wellington Street at 11.50 p.m. on Friday night. They gave her three possible addresses. The two she knew already, plus one on Grange Road. She hammered on the door of the office furniture warehouse: no answer. Back to the house on Southern Grove. The doorbell sounded a cathedral gong. A big girl answered the door in tight jeans, bare midriff hanging over the waist line, huge breasts in a creaking bra, one shoulder black with tattoos, blonde hair tied in a top sprout, blue eyeshadow, pink lips. She said nothing, chewed gum, having smelt cop from down the hall.

'Police,' said Mercy, holding up her warrant card, no pretence necessary now. 'I want to speak to Jack Auber.'

'Not in.'

'Are you his daughter?'

'What about it?'

'You got a name?'

'Cheryl.'

'Where is he, Cheryl?'

'I dunno. Gone to work.'

'His work's shut.'

'Then he's out buying.'

'Can I speak to your mum?'

'Out, too.'

'When did you last see your dad, Cheryl?'

'Yesterday.'

'What time?'

'About seven.'

'So he went out?'

'He likes a drink on a Sunday evening.'

'But he didn't come back?'

A shrug that sent everything atremble.

'You got a mobile number for him?'

'He never turns it on unless he wants to use it. Doesn't like them.'

'We're worried about him,' said Mercy.

'First time for everything,' said Cheryl, cramming her bosom behind the door as she shut it.

Mercy went back to the car, set the SatNav for Grange Road. Twenty minutes later she found the end of terrace house opposite a church. It also had a rear view over a cemetery, this time the East London. What was the matter with Auber: was he terminally morbid or something?

There was a cab parked in front of the garage. She touched the bonnet. Cold. She banged on the front door. Blinds down on all the windows. She went down the side of the garage and into a bleak garden piled with scaffolding poles, wooden planking, building detritus and mounds of dead leaves. The kitchen door was locked. She checked the windows: one of the sash windows was open at the top. She pulled it down, leaned a plank up to the sill and clambered into a small bedroom with a single bed up against the wall, with small pink roses all over it.

The next room wasn't so pretty. There was a man, grey-haired, slumped across the table, arms bracketing his head, like a kid crashed out over his homework. There was a black hole in the back of his skull and dark red, almost black, matter sprayed out over the formica of the table. Another man's legs were sticking out into the room from the corridor that led to the front door and the foot of the stairs. He was young, twenties, and had a gun in his hand, a Browning HP35. He'd taken his bullet in the chest, which had knocked him back against the wall where he'd slid to the floor. A dark red vertical smear rose up the wall a metre and half behind him, ending in a broad spatter, like a naïve painting of a tree.

The corridor was dark, barely any light from the glass in the front door panels. She checked the other rooms, went upstairs. All empty. She called DCS Makepeace.

'I think I'm looking at another two dead loose ends to add to Jim Paxton.'

'Two?'

'One is Jack Auber, I'm pretty sure. The other must be the back-up he brought for what he suspected was going to be an eventful evening.'

'After what he'd seen done to the two immigrant workers,' said Makepeace. 'I think we've picked them up now. Two unidentified bodies floating down Barking Creek on their way to the Beckton Sewage Works.'

'Five murders for the kidnap of one girl and still no demand,' said Mercy. 'What do you think we're dealing with here? Charlie said the Pavis profiler thought he was a killer. Told him to bring in the Met.'

'And here we are, but not in the cavalry role,' said Makepeace. 'There's some organisation behind these killings. Gang stuff. This is bigger than a disgruntled employee.'

'Has Frank D'Cruz offered any theories?'

'He's been almost totally silent,' said Makepeace, 'which, given that someone took a shot at him on his first night in London, might mean that he knows plenty but is too scared to tell. You should brief Charlie on what's happened to the labourers in this kidnap and see if he can squeeze any juice out of D'Cruz.'

'Yes, Charlie,' she said thoughtfully, and hated herself instantly.

'What about him?' asked Makepeace, radar well-tuned.

'He's got his work cut out, that's all,' said Mercy. 'He's on his own in there. No Crisis Management Committee. It's … intense.'

'I heard. Perhaps you should think of ways to take the pressure off him. But just you. Keep George out of it.'

'We've hit a dead end here,' said Mercy. 'With Jack Auber and Jim Paxton down, that's our main leads to the kidnappers gone.'

Boxer was sitting at the kitchen table between D'Cruz and Isabel, the MP3 player in the dock. They'd just listened to the Abiola recording from Alyshia's mobile phone for the third time. Isabel was stunned, incapable of speech.

'I've never come across a kidnap like this before,' said Boxer. 'Still no demand and the kidnapper putting his hostage through an extended psychoanalysis session. He must have done some heavy research. And the only reason I can think of for him doing that is to create some sort of dependency in her.'

'On what?'

'On him, the kidnapper,' said Boxer. 'He's talking to her about the most intimate events of her life: somebody committing suicide over her. He's forcing her to relive the experience and getting her to relate it to her current behaviour. He's creating a special bond with her and, in the process, revealing to you how little you know about your own daughter. Undermining on two fronts.'

'Yes,' said Isabel suddenly, coming out of her stupor. 'What *did* you know about all this, Chico? The Saïd Business School would have contacted you. You were … whatever you were doing for them, you must have been important to them and they … I'm sorry, I'm not thinking straight. Just tell me what you knew, Chico, what you didn't tell me.'

'I knew everything,' said D'Cruz. 'I was told about the suicide by the Dean. I spoke to her and that son-of-a-bitch, Julian – told him never to go anywhere near Alyshia ever again, not to contact her, nothing. I took Alyshia out of the course and straight to Mumbai. I told her not to talk about any of it to you, because I knew it would upset you.'

The tension in the room was audible, with a ringing intensity, like stress-induced tinnitus. Boxer's mobile vibrated across the table towards him. They were grateful for the distraction. He took the call from Mercy in the living room. She briefed him on the five murders they'd uncovered in the last twenty-four hours and told him how he should present them to D'Cruz, to show that there had been no police involvement until the discovery of Jim Paxton.

'How's it going otherwise?' asked Mercy.

'Otherwise?'

177

'Don't make me say it, Charlie.'

'The ex-husband is here. I'm discovering the limits of their endurance together.'

'Need any help?'

'You're my co-consultant.'

'Yes,' she said, unhappy to find him withholding from her.

They hung up. Boxer went back to the brutally silent kitchen, asked D'Cruz to join him in the living room.

'I know you wanted to keep the police out of this, but there have been some developments which make that impossible,' said Boxer.

'I have a guarantee from the Home Secretary,' said D'Cruz, jutting his chin.

'Not even the Home Secretary can prevent the police from investigating multiple murders,' said Boxer. 'The Pavis research team have found that, on the night of her kidnap, Alyshia was out drinking with colleagues at a leaving party of the recruitment agency she was working for.'

'What recruitment agency?'

'She left that party to look for a cab with a man called Jim Paxton, who was later found dead, hanging in his wardrobe. My colleagues reported that to the police.'

'Why?'

'Because you can't leave dead bodies hanging around. Excuse the pun,' said Boxer. 'In their subsequent investigation, the police found CCTV footage of Jim Paxton putting Alyshia into a taxi. In the follow-up, the cab driver has now been found dead, with another unknown man, in a house in East London. That's three killings, plus the pot shot taken at you last night. There are two investigations ongoing in the hands of the Homicide and Serious Crime Command. They will want to talk to you, as will the Head of the Serious and Organised Crime Command.'

'I expressly asked for the police to be kept out of this. Police and press. This is putting my daughter's life—'

'The police kept out of the kidnap, yes, but these are murders,' said Boxer, 'and the reason I'm having a private talk with you about this is so that you can start telling me things that are going to help us get Alyshia back. I know it's not in your nature. But it's clear to everybody that there is a level of organisation behind this kidnap that rules out loners looking for revenge. The fact that we have no demand and they have no interest in financial or material gain, but have asked you to take them seriously and applied maximum pressure to achieve it, means, to me, that you must have *some* idea who we're dealing with. Even if you don't know them personally, you must know the direction from which this pressure is coming. So let's have it, Frank.'

'I really don't know,' he said. 'I'm not being difficult. As you know, my affairs are, to put it mildly, very complicated. My background before I became a businessman was pretty damned spicy. I have my own internal investigations going on, trying to find out who could possibly be doing this. I have my suspicions but I don't want to reveal them and have people shooting off in, what could possibly be, wrong directions.'

'Look, Frank, you've asked me to do something for you and I've agreed in principle. If you want me to honour that agreement, you have to start revealing your suspicions and trust me to act on them.'

'But they must stay between you and me until I have confirmation, because if you tell the counter terrorist team at Special Crime Command about the sort of people we might be dealing with, they will launch a massive hunt and the heat will be so intense that I am sure the kidnappers will kill Alyshia and run.'

For the first time in this kidnap negotiation, the sweat came up on Boxer's palms. He was used to the rush, expected it, liked it even, but this was more like fear. He had to check D'Cruz for veracity but the billionaire's face told him only what he would expect to see in any man's eyes in this position: desperation and terror.

The man is an actor, pulsed through Boxer's brain.

'You haven't given me your word, Charles.'

'It wouldn't matter if I gave you my word,' said Boxer. 'I am bound by the terms of my contract with Pavis to keep the Director of Operations informed of all developments.'

'Then I have to keep my suspicions to myself for the moment,' said D'Cruz. 'And that's all they are. I have no proof.'

'So what do you expect me to do?' asked Boxer. 'You've hired me to get your daughter back safely.'

'All you can do is maintain negotiations.'

'But there aren't any negotiations,' said Boxer. 'We're in their hands. We have no way of manipulating the situation to our own ends. We can't even find out where they are, now that the people who've done the dirty work are dead.'

'This level of ruthlessness is not unusual, as I'm sure you know,' said D'Cruz. 'All you can do, for now, is sit tight, support Isabel, think positively—'

'Are you negotiating as we speak?'

'No, not negotiating, merely investigating – just as Pavis has done.'

The doorbell rang. Boxer got to his feet. D'Cruz grabbed his arm.

'Isabel shouldn't be told about these murders,' said D'Cruz.

'So what's the story?'

'I'll think of something. You follow my lead. Ask me if I'm involved in anything controversial that demands a decision in the near future. We'll improvise from there.'

Boxer stormed past him into the corridor and held Isabel back from the front door.

'Expecting anybody?' he asked.

'No,' she said.

He looked through the spyhole. Man in motorbike gear, behind him a Vespa with a box on the back and the legend 'Domino's Pizzas' and a telephone number.

'Anybody order pizza?' he asked, remembering the pot shot taken at D'Cruz the night before.

'No.'

'Go to the living room with Frank, close the door.'

Boxer sprinted upstairs, took his semi-automatic out of his case and put it down the back of his trousers. The doorbell rang again. He rumbled back down to the hallway, opened the door.

'Pizza delivery.'

'We didn't order one.'

'There's two.'

'We didn't order two.'

The biker checked the number on the door against the delivery sheet.

'This is Wycombe Square and my order says two pizzas for

number fourteen and that's the doorway you're standing in.'

'Who took the order?'

'I don't know. I do the delivery.'

'Let's have a look at you.'

The biker flicked his visor up. He was a kid with freckles. Sixteen at the most.

'You've got to pay for it, too,' he said, grinning.

'How much?'

'Nineteen quid.'

'Where did you pick up the pizzas?'

'Domino's on Westbourne Park Road.'

'How many stops on the way?'

'Four. You're my last,' said the biker. 'You know, you need to chill, man. You're way too tense.'

'You leave your bike in the street at any point?'

'Like, of *course*. This is the only house I can pull up in front of the door.'

'What's your name?'

'Darren Wright.'

Boxer gave him a twenty and a pound coin, took the pizzas, watched him go. He closed the front door, stayed out in the street, opened the first pizza box. Pizza: spicy sausage and chillies. He closed the lid, raised the box to a right angle to open the one below and saw the plastic slip case stuck to the underside with a DVD inside. Opened the next lid. Four seasons or something like it. Closed the lid. Went inside. Ripped the DVD slip case from the box, shook out the disc, went to the player in the living room.

'Another message from our friend,' said Boxer.

'Maybe just Charles and I should look at this first.'

'Forget it, Chico.'

'Just to make sure it's nothing disturbing.'

'It's an idea,' said Boxer.

'No,' said Isabel and ripped the DVD from Boxer's hand and stuck it in the machine. She picked up the remotes, clicked on the TV and the player, sat down. White noise and then Alyshia dressed in her long black mermaid dress. She started her speech. The camera moved in to pick up the tears on her jaw line.

The three of them stared unblinking. She finished, went down on her knees, grabbed the man's jacket. The camera held her head and shoulders. The gunman swiped her hands away. She fell out of the frame.

The sound of the gun discharging seemed to make the living room expand and contract. The gunman's shoulder jerked with the recoil, jolting them all. Isabel keeled over to one side, fell off the sofa to the floor and convulsed.

15

'How do you know about this place?' asked Skin.
'Friend of mine.'

'He's got friends. Who'd have thought it?' said Skin. 'Well yeah, Nurse, I gathered that, didn't I? What's the connection?'

'He was one of my prescription drugs clients in the bad old days.'

'He still on them?'

'No, he deals.'

'Hard or soft?'

'Everything. Mainly H, pills, bit of grass,' said Dan. 'He and a huge Jamaican called Delroy Dread, a crack dealer who pushes my mate's H to the black kids, run the estate, although they're not exactly friends. They keep a respectful distance. Nothing happens around here without them knowing it, or allowing it.'

Skin, hands in pockets in a new fur-lined jacket, looked up at the grey, bare brick exterior, which was in need of repointing. The building looked derelict.

'Has it got everything we need? Running water, electrics, heating?' asked Skin. 'We might be here for some time. Like a couple of weeks.'

'A couple of *weeks*?'

'You don't know,' said Skin. 'How long does it take to get a couple of million in cash together? How long does it take to persuade someone to part with a couple of million? How long will it take us to work out how we're going to receive a couple of million?

183

It's not something you want to do under pressure. You've got to let the people you're dealing with know you're very comfortable with all the time in the world.'

'Downstairs is a workshop which he uses as an art studio. Upstairs there's a small flat with everything we need, he says.'

Dan unlocked the double doors and they went into the studio. Huge windows divided into small panes overlooked the Regent's Canal at the back of the property. Pots full of brushes, tubes of oil paint, stacks of paper, books and a collection of old sunglasses covered a long table, which was backed up against one wall. In the open space, by the window, stood a couple of easels and leaning face in against the other wall were canvases of all sizes.

They went up some brick stairs to the flat above. It was furnished, but not by an interior designer. There were old armchairs, a battered leather sofa, some chrome, tubular kitchen chairs and a formica table in the living room. Coming up from the floor to the roof beams were the same windows as the studio below. The bedroom had a single metal-framed bed in it with a foam rubber mattress, some soiled sheets and a dirty blanket. Pieces of old fitted carpet, curling at the edges, partially covered the floor. The curtains over the window hung like scapegoats, as a warning to others.

'This is what I like about the place,' said Dan, looking out of the window.

'What's there to like?' said Skin, hands in pockets, looking up at the ceiling, a single bulb hanging from a flex, energy-saving.

'The canal,' said Dan.

'You got a boat?'

'No,' said Dan, 'but that's our escape route if it all fucks up.'

'I can't swim.'

'Then you'll have to stay and die,' said Dan.

Skin joined him at the window and took a wary look out.

'Fuck me,' said Skin, rearing back. 'It's bloody miles down there. I don't go for heights, you know.'

'But you're not afraid of anything Pike can chuck at you?'

'It's different when I'm on the ground with a gun in my hand.'

'We'll just have to do our best to arrange that scenario when the shit hits the fan.'

'Your friend have a name?'

'He calls himself MK.'

'As in Milton Keynes?'

'I don't think that was uppermost in his mind.'

'How much does he want?'

'He's offering a special rate for a mate. Five hundred a week.'

'I suppose it *is* a short let,' said Skin, meanly.

'And he knows ...'

'What?'

'I don't just want it for a fuck pad,' said Dan. 'We're up to no good.'

'How did you know him before you sold him drugs?'

'He was a patient on my ward. Broke his leg in a motorbike accident, had a lot of pain from skid wounds on his dick. Couldn't pee. Ended up addicted to painkillers.'

'Is he reliable?' asked Skin, leaving the bedroom, checking out the bathroom.

'I saved his life when he OD'd once. He always said he owed me one.'

'So we've got at least one life before he cashes us in.'

'He won't. It's not in his nature.'

'There's no seat on the toilet,' said Skin, 'and no curtain on the shower.'

'You looking for a discount now?'

'I'm just saying,' said Skin, putting his head round the door before moving off to the kitchen. 'No oven.'

'You planning a Sunday lunch?'

'Lamb, bit of rosemary and garlic. Lovely,' said Skin. 'At least there's gas in the bottle for the hob.'

'Fridge working?'

'The light comes on, no beer and there's something furry in the salad box,' said Skin, coming back to the bedroom. 'But ... I suppose we'll take it.'

'Been married long?' asked Dan.

'Another ten minutes if this is the best you can do,' said Skin. 'How about if we need the place for longer?'

'I'll have to ask.'

Skin collapsed on the bed. 'So where are you kipping?'

Frank D'Cruz was ashen, immobile on the sofa. The white noise played on. Boxer picked Isabel up off the floor, righted her on the sofa.

'Wait,' said D'Cruz. 'Look.'

The white noise ceased. The screen showed a bed in a room. There was the sound of whimpering, crying and the coughing up of excess emotion. Into the frame came Alyshia, squirming across the floor, dragging herself on her elbows in her long black mermaid dress, high heels hidden under the tail. A black carp out of water. She reached the bed and looked as if she might try to pull herself up onto it, but had second thoughts and crawled underneath, lay there shuddering, like an animal gone off to die on its own.

After some moments, the voice-over began.

'I had the distinct impression, and I doubt that I'm wrong, that you weren't taking me very seriously. That's you, Frank. I'm sure you're watching this. I know how your mind works. You're still assuming that, in the end, this can be sorted out with money, your unfathomable pocket. I can almost hear you saying it to yourself: "Even if it's ten million, I can handle that". That's the sort of loose change you've got fluttering around in your offshore accounts, I imagine.

'That little demonstration was, perhaps, a bit too graphic, but it was designed to show you just how powerless you are in this particular situation, Frank. You have no cards. What I want to see from you is how seriously you're taking me. I've given you a demonstration of my intent. Now I want a demonstration of your sincerity. I've shown you mine. Now you show me yours.'

The sound and picture abruptly cut. The white noise resumed. D'Cruz collapsed back onto the sofa, still transfixed by the screen as if there would be more. As if he wanted there to be more.

'What's he talking about, Chico?' asked Isabel, whose recovery had been accompanied by a hardening. 'You must know something, for God's sake. You have to act. You're just a spectator at the moment. You've said and done bugger all. You saw what she was wearing: that dress you bought her in Paris, the diamond necklace you gave her for her twenty-first. These people are goading you.

How many more attempts, how many more mock executions do we have to suffer before we get to the real one?'

She'd riled him now and D'Cruz leapt to his feet, rounded on the television, which still spewed white noise.

'I don't know what he's talking about. That's just the bloody point. He's talking in riddles. He doesn't want my money. I am powerless. I have no bloody cards. But somehow I have to show that I'm taking him seriously. Give him a demonstration of my sincerity. What is this bollocks?' he roared, shaking his fist at the screen.

'Are you involved in something controversial that demands a decision?' said Boxer.

'Everything I bloody touch is controversial. What isn't controversial out of construction, energy, manufacturing ... even the bloody cricket is controversial. And they all demand decisions instantly, all the bloody time,' roared D'Cruz.

'But is there something crucial happening right now?' asked Boxer. 'Where your decision to proceed or not will have an impact. A move you could make that would somehow show your sincerity to the kidnapper.'

'What does that bloody mean? What is sincerity?'

'Something politicians and businessmen are experts at imitating in order to get their own way,' said Isabel. 'But, when the time comes, find it impossible to deliver.'

'Ha fucking ha, very bloody funny,' said D'Cruz viciously. 'Why is it that businessmen are always cast as the villains of the piece, when all we do is create work, jobs, trade and prosperity? Why is profit always looked down on as an "ulterior motive", as if this isn't what everybody is trying to do when they see a bargain at the market, get a house cheap because of a foreclosure or make an offer for a steelworks because you can make it stop losing money and give shareholders a return?'

'Is that your main motivation when you buy a business for Konkan Hills Securities?' asked Isabel. 'Shareholder return? *That's* what Jordan means by "sincerity". You don't give a shit about shareholder return. You're motivated by adding wealth to your name. Climbing up the *Forbes* magazine India Rich List. Being number one. And you don't care how many people you tread into the mud on your way up to that supreme position. You can't even be *sincere* about your own ruthlessness.'

Isabel's rant finished on a high-pitched screech, with her ring finger rapping the glass top table in front of her.

A silence ensued while both parties fumed. Boxer decided to let it continue in the hope that it would eventually induce some calm. The outburst of emotion didn't surprise him after the gruelling horror of the mock execution and its aftermath: their daughter creeping under the bed, desperate for some semblance of protection.

'What about those slums you were talking about on Saturday?' said Isabel. 'When you had your premonition. Remember? They were protesting "on the BB bloody C", the slum dwellers.'

'What about them?' asked D'Cruz.

'Why were they rioting?' asked Boxer.

'Because the bulldozers are coming. They're squatting on prime real estate in the middle of the city and they think they can go on living there for eternity.'

'What he means,' said Isabel evenly, 'is they're rioting because they've got nowhere else to go. Some of these people have been living there all their lives. It's their home. Not much of one, it has to be said, but—'

'They *have* got alternative accommodation; they just don't want to live in it. They prefer to live in a shit hole in the city centre rather than move to a clean high-rise a few blocks away.'

'But there's too little housing for the numbers living there. A lot of them will have to give up their livelihood, because you can't have a pottery or a tannery in a high-rise apartment. They might be given a place for nothing but they know there will be fees on top. Like "lift charges": paying to use the lift, which an old woman on the fifteenth floor might appreciate.'

'All right, all right,' said Boxer, holding up his hands. 'This isn't the time for a major debate. I'm sending this DVD to Pavis and I'll talk to Martin Fox. In the meantime, Frank, you should think about what you can do to resolve this problem. You know your world better than anybody in this room.'

'It's just that the word "sincerity" doesn't appear in it,' said Isabel.

Boxer made a small hand gesture for her to quieten things down and left the room.

Mercy and Papadopoulos were sitting in the front of a Ford Mondeo behind the Crime Scene Investigator's van, in front of the Grange Road house. Papadopoulos had just given her a report on the Jim Paxton killing.

'And the girl, Jim's neighbour, did she hear anything?' said Mercy.

'It wasn't my job to interview her,' said Papadopoulos. 'What I know, just from chat, is that she works in a call centre, raising funds for charities. She comes home late and gets out of her head most evenings and, if she doesn't, she's not hanging around at home, which is a dump. She didn't even know he'd taken delivery of a flat screen TV, which apparently arrived last Wednesday.'

'Where was she at time of death?'

'That would be between two and four in the morning of Sunday eleventh of March. She said she didn't get home until seven from an all-nighter in a warehouse in Bermondsey. They're checking her story. I was told to fade away,' said Papadopoulos. 'What about this shooting here? Somebody must have heard or seen something?'

'The neighbour heard a bang, didn't think anything of it. Happens all the time.'

'You're kidding.'

'Of course I'm kidding. We're not in bloody Helmand.'

'Just one bang?'

'The young guy in the corridor – who, according to his wallet, is called Victor Scully – had fired his gun, which didn't have a suppressor.'

Knock on the window. One of the forensics. Mercy buzzed it down.

'We've found a bullet, which looks as if it comes from Victor Scully's gun. We've also found blood, which does not belong to either body. We're pretty sure there were two gunmen and one of them has been hit.'

'Enough for a DNA sample?'

'Plenty. Don't worry, it's been despatched.'

Mercy called DCS Makepeace, made sure the DNA sample was put on fast track. She called Nelson, asked for another meeting.

They drove down to the Old George on Bethnal Green Road. Nelson was already there, sitting in the cathedral gloom, staring into his pint, looking as old as the pub's interior. Papadopoulos went to the bar, ordered a ginger ale and a tonic water.

'Big night out?' asked the barman.

'Oh, go on then,' said Papadopoulos, 'give us a double Britvic orange on the rocks with lemonade and an umbrella.'

He came back with the drinks. Silence at the table.

'I was just talking to Fred Scully,' said Nelson. 'He's a broken man. The boy meant everything to him after he lost his daughter to meningitis. Terrible business. He's got no one now.'

'What was Vic doing there?' said Mercy, trying not to be too unsympathetic. 'With a gun?'

'Fred can't believe it. Didn't even know Vic had a weapon. And he can't believe Jack Auber was up to that kind of nasty stuff. Hard times, I dunno.'

'Have you managed to have a word with Jack's wife and daughter yet?'

'I called Ruby as soon as I heard. No answer,' said Nelson. 'They won't talk to you, I can guarantee that.'

'So if Jack wasn't up to this kind of action, who did he get involved with who was?' asked Mercy.

'I can't believe it was any of the old crews around here,' said Nelson. 'They wouldn't have you done unless you were asking for it. After what happened to the two illegals, Jack must have taken Vic along for protection. He'd only have been going back to collect on the job and he probably thought if you're going to get done, it'd be over the money. I reckon they must have been ethnic. You know, unpredictable. Black, Chinese or Albanians. You cross the street in front of some black kids these days and they'll gun you down for "disrespecting" them.'

'All right,' said Mercy, trying to keep Nelson's racism on the leash. 'Jack Auber couldn't have been running his illegals business without someone's permission, could he, Nelson?'

'No, but I doubt that was anything to do with it. If it was his home crew, he wouldn't have taken young Vic with him, would he? He'd have drawn on someone more experienced,' said Nelson. 'No, they approached him because of his cab. It was a deal on the side with an outside gang.'

'Who runs his home crew?' asked Mercy.

'Joe Shearing.'

'And what will Joe Shearing do about it?'

'If Jack went freelance, Joe probably won't see it as his responsibility,' said Nelson. 'On the other hand, you don't want to get on the wrong side of Ruby, and Joe might give her a hearing. If he does, she'll persuade him otherwise.'

'And you'll hear about it if she does?'

'The pubs'll be ringing with it.'

'I'm sorry about that, Alyshia,' said the voice. 'Believe me, it was absolutely necessary. I think we have your father's undivided attention now. Are you there, Alyshia?'

Alyshia was catatonic. No sleeping mask. She was staring up at the ceiling, having come out from under the bed after an hour or so. Her brain functioned in bursts. Life crashed in on her in savage cuts of intensity, like streaks of brutal news footage, and then she'd blank out, unable to process extreme emotions – hope and despair, relief and fear, faith and dread.

'Sit up on the edge of the bed,' said the voice.

She sat up, swivelled her legs over the bed, rested her hands on the edge of the mattress. Robotic.

'Drink some water.'

She drank water from a glass on the bedside table.

'Place your hands in your lap and breathe evenly and deeply.'

She did as she was told. She could find no trace of resistance or disobedience in herself. She was content to be in this narrow world with the sound of the voice's commands, which she found she enjoyed obeying as precisely as possible.

'We have just one more very important part of your life to discuss,' said the voice. 'We've talked about the relationship with your mother and how that has developed since you've been back in London. We've looked at your early adult life: leaving the comparative innocence of university before taking the more complex ride through the Saïd Business School. We've seen how the guilt at what happened there has erupted during this more confused period you're living through at the moment. What we're going to do now is look at the relationship with your father, what happened in Mumbai and why you left, never to return. Is that understood, Alyshia?'

She nodded.

'Say it out loud.'

'Yes, I'm ready to talk about that.'

'Do you know how your father managed to extract you from that difficult little situation at the Saïd Business School?'

'Not at the time. I found out later,' said Alyshia. 'The only way I could cope with what had happened was to deny it. My father told me not to talk to my mother about Abiola Adeshina. He developed an alternative story for me to tell her: the break-up with Julian and how that meant I had to leave for Mumbai as soon as possible.'

'And your mother bought that?'

'It wasn't difficult for me to be convincing.'

'Was that when you started despising her?'

'Probably, yes,' said Alyshia. 'Because that was the moment I stopped being the person I had been and started being someone else.'

'Who was that "someone else"?'

'That's a difficult question,' she said. 'I'm not sure. A lot of it was probably done subconsciously. For a start, I needed a platform of total confidence. You can't do business feeling vulnerable. That meant lopping off the unsatisfactory elements of my life. I thought I'd been successful. Now I see that all I'd done was push things down, for them to bubble up somewhere else.'

'So how did you try to control those unsatisfactory elements?' asked the voice.

'I realised I had to maintain a balance. If I let my emotional life get out of control, it would make me feel exposed again and I wouldn't be able to perform. That meant staying away from all relationships. Not an easy thing to do when you look like I do and have a wealthy father. That combination seems to be particularly intoxicating in modern India.'

'So you got a lot of interest,' said the voice. 'But you must be an expert at freezing men out.'

'I am and I was until I ran into Deepak Mistry.'

'Right. We know about him,' said the voice. 'Tell me about Deepak Mistry.'

'He comes from Bihar, India's poorest state. He has no family to speak of. And nobody knew how he could have come from that background to run a successful software company in Bangalore.'

'So the Mysterious Mister Mistry,' said the voice. 'Did that attract you?'

'It was intriguing, the kind of gossip that might make people exaggerate, but not especially attractive. I wasn't receptive on that score.'

'So you didn't even bother to find out?'

'I asked my father when we were having dinner alone one evening,' said Alyshia. 'He said it didn't interest him how Deepak had got there, just that he had.'

'So how had he done it?'

'He put himself through school, working nights at a call centre. He was already writing software programmes for the call centre by the time he left and set up on his own.'

'There's still a lot of gaps,' said the voice. 'How did he learn to speak English? In the village school in Bihar?'

'My father couldn't care less. All he saw was a capable young guy who reminded him of himself,' said Alyshia. 'And I suppose he took him under his wing because of that.'

'Had you met him by the time you were asking your father these questions?'

'We'd met before: a couple of years ago at a dinner in London. But in Mumbai we had no reason to meet. He was trying to maintain a level of production while implementing structural changes in the plant. He worked and slept. He had nothing to do with sales and marketing.'

'Did you think it odd, at that point, that your father didn't reintroduce you?'

'I hadn't met anyone on the board. My father said I wouldn't until I'd proved myself. His regime was strictly meritocratic, unlike a lot of other Indian industrial dynasties.'

'What was your first impression?'

'Serious. Preoccupied by his job. No time for life.'

'So he made no physical impact?'

'Not an immediate one,' said Alyshia. 'Only later. He was like one of those movie actors who don't look particularly remarkable and you wonder how the hell they got into the business, until you find that they have that elusive quality: watchability. Whenever they're on screen, your eyes follow their every move.'

'Charismatic?'

'No. He wasn't that,' said Alyshia. 'Not like my father. He didn't command a room. In fact, Deepak had the reverse of that. Stuff didn't shine out of him; rather, his intensity drew light to him. He had presence, but it was dark.'

'Not an obviously attractive quality,' said the voice. 'On the human scale of things, unless ...'

'Unless what?'

'It was around that time you discovered some dark matter in yourself?' said the voice. 'What was your social life like at the time?'

'Cricketers, Bollywood actors, industrialists and state administrators' sons.'

'Any friends?'

'Friendship is not on offer in that world,' she said. 'Contact is everything, but only to create a network. Real intimacy is not just rare but dangerous. Other things are so important that to reveal yourself would be a mistake. Intimacy makes you vulnerable. The mask has always got to be firmly in place.'

'Was this how Deepak made his first big impression?'

'The impressions he made were never big, but they were cumulative,' said Alyshia. 'He isn't a looker. He's not a great wit. He's not obviously brilliant, or worldly. But each time I was left with something indelible. I never felt myself being emotionally drawn in, which meant I never took fright and ran away. I watched him whenever he was in the frame.'

'So where did you first meet up with him in Mumbai?'

'On Juhu Beach. I was staying at my father's house nearby and I went to watch the sunset. It was a weekend. I found myself looking at someone standing in the water, trousers rolled up, a shoe in each hand. I don't know why I thought this, but I was sure that he was a man in a state of profound thought, as if he was contemplating his future, making a big decision or a change of course. Maybe the sea and the setting sun is the necessary cliché to bring that out in people. After the sun had gone down – and he didn't turn away until the whole red circle of light had disappeared into the black horizon – he walked back up the beach towards the food stalls. He saw me looking at him and blinked as if in partial recognition. As he came level with me I realised he wasn't going to stop, so I said, "You're Deepak Mistry, aren't you?"'

At that point Alyshia withdrew into herself and was back on Juhu Beach, mentally sitting on the sand after a sunset in the half dark, lit only by the food stalls.

'I think I know you,' said Mistry, uncertain, nearly embarrassed.

'I'm Frank D'Cruz's daughter. We work in the same place.'

Relief flooded his face.

'You know, I'm really happy you said that. I thought you might be an actress from the TV, or the movies, that I was so accustomed to seeing that I'd begun to think of you as an acquaintance.'

'You watch that much TV?'

'It's my sleeping pill,' he said. 'I turn it on low and the murmur makes me think I am with family. Then the colours float in front of my eyes and in ten minutes I'm gone. It's still on in the morning when I get up.'

'I'm surprised to see you here.'

'Me too,' he said. 'I hardly ever come here. I haven't taken a day off in a year. But I finished something today and I thought I needed somewhere different and, you know how it is, take stock. Are you … doing the same?'

'Not quite,' she said. 'I was just getting away from the crowd.'

He looked up at the food stalls, the thousands of people milling around, the tumult of their voices. He laughed.

'It's not easy to be alone in this country,' he said. 'But not so difficult to be lonely.'

'That was it,' said Alyshia, coming back into the room. 'The sum total of our first meeting. He said goodbye and was gone. As you can see, it made an impression. I remember it word for word. What struck me was this feeling of respect he left me with. I had respected his need to be alone, he respected mine. I can't think of another man I've met who would have done that, who wouldn't have tried to make something of that situation. It wasn't even a tactic.'

'So you were already thinking something was possible at that stage?' asked the voice.

'No, it didn't feel like that. It felt much more like the beginning of a friendship,' said Alyshia, feeling tired and dull now. 'After a blind date, people will say there was none of that "elusive spark". Well, there was no spark. No clenching of the stomach. No passion. There was something, but not what I'd expected, given what happened later.'

16

'If you told me there was a chance that Alyshia was being held by Muslim extremists, I would have to pass that on to my boss, Martin Fox, who would then have to decide whether or not the police should be informed,' said Boxer, trying to pressurise D'Cruz, who was still in a state of shock, to reveal the direction of his investigations, if nothing else. 'Given the number of killings so far, I think there's a high chance that the police would alert the Counter Terrorism Command.'

'And for how long do you think the terrorist community in the UK would remain ignorant of that?'

'All right, Frank. Let's analyse this theoretically,' said Boxer. 'That way you don't have to admit to the knowledge. If she is being held by terrorists, what is their motivation?'

'Well, it could still be financial. I know you dispute this. That this doesn't conform to your kidnap model. But there's a big difference in negotiating techniques if you're aiming for two hundred thousand or want to achieve, say, fifty million, which was the figure mentioned to Isabel in the first phone call.'

'I'm sure you've heard of that annoying corporate expression, "thinking outside the box", but that's what I want you to do for me,' said Boxer. 'You're firmly in the box of financial gain. We have to look at *all* the possibilities. The kidnapper's behaviour, with all his teasing and psychoanalysis, makes me think his ultimate intention is to punish you. Why would a terrorist organisation want to do that?'

'Because not only am I not being helpful to them, I am being obstructive,' said D'Cruz.

'Does that mean you know these people personally?'

Silence from D'Cruz. The stress chiselling lines into his forehead by the moment. He knew he had to reveal something now; the escalation of brutality in the kidnap demanded it.

'Look, Charles,' he said, both confessional and conspiratorial, 'before I was a businessman I was an actor, and before that, yes, I had a dodgy early career in the 1970s and 80s to pull myself out of poverty. I was, what *you* would call, a gangster. As far as I was concerned, that was just a name. I was taking advantage of a stupid situation, which is what all smugglers do. The government controlled the importation of gold into India. As you probably know, Indians are obsessed with gold jewellery – it's part of our culture. By smuggling it in fishing boats from Dubai, I made a good living and a lot of friends in high places, who wanted to buy my product. In order to operate, I had to have the backing of a gang and so … I became a gangster. If I'd tried to do that work naked, I'd have been killed.'

'And the members of your old gang have connections to terrorism?'

'Even you, as an outsider, must know that terrorism has connections in all worlds: business, political, criminal, religious, scientific,' said D'Cruz. 'I am in a unique position in that I have been a criminal, I am in business, I am politically connected, I am outside the religious argument, with friends in all camps, and I'm even in the scientific world, since I've been asked to advise on Indo/Russian nuclear reactor projects. I am what you would call "plugged in".'

'So in what way have you been unhelpful and obstructive?'

'I move an enormous amount of money and goods around the world. I have all the necessary resources to launder large amounts of cash and distribute, let's call it equipment, globally. I could do that for the people I used to be connected to in the underworld, but I don't. I refuse to do it.

'I am politically well-connected enough to be given valuable intelligence on matters of state. These nuclear reactors, for instance, are vital if India is to keep up the level of growth to raise millions out of poverty. There are people who would like to know how to ruin this project and send India back to the dark ages. I tell them nothing.

'I also do not react to their religious pressures because I am a Catholic, and a lapsed Catholic at that. So, you see, there are all sorts of ways I would be expected to be helpful but I am not. But recently I have been treading a fine line because I have accepted favours, primarily to ensure that my steelworks did not fail. These are people who expect favours to be returned. When they are not, I could be considered not just unhelpful but obstructive as well.'

'And taking Alyshia is the only way they can apply pressure and show their disapproval?' said Boxer.

'This is the least obtrusive and the most personal,' said D'Cruz. 'If it's who I think it is, I'm expecting it to get much worse. They are smacking me into line and they are from a culture where a smack draws blood.'

'It sounds as if you're ninety-nine per cent certain who these people are?'

'I am awaiting confirmation, but that is part of the game. They are bringing me to the edge of my seat,' said D'Cruz. 'They have always been good at this. This charade of Alyshia's psychoanalysis and goading me with her dress and diamonds is no surprise to me. They have a deep understanding of what makes people tick. The only thing that puzzles me is that they have still not asked me to do anything specific for them. They are applying pressure, but I don't know what for. What this "demonstration of sincerity" is, I have no idea, but I have to try to find out.'

It was six o'clock. D'Cruz had left, which was for the best under the circumstances. Boxer knew that Amy would be at his mother's flat in Hampstead by now. She was still refusing to take his calls or respond to texts. After Alyshia's farewell speech and mock execution, he had a powerful need to reconnect with her. He wondered what Amy's speech would have been like had she been in Alyshia's place. He went upstairs and made the call, looking down into the empty square.

'Hello, Esme.'

'Charles.'

'Is Amy there?'

'Yes, she is.'

'Can I speak to her?'

'Hold on.'

He hung on for a minute.

'She doesn't want to talk to you,' said Esme.

'I know that but I want to talk to her.'

More silence.

'She still won't take the phone.'

'Make her, Esme. Make her.'

The phone went dead. He called back.

'What happened?'

'She cut the line.'

'What's going on, Esme?'

'I don't know yet. I haven't had the chance to talk to her.'

'Ask her just to listen. She doesn't have to talk. It's just three words.'

He hung on.

'Here she is,' said Esme. 'She'll listen only.'

'I love you,' said Boxer.

The line went dead again.

He didn't call back.

A car pulled up on Aubrey Walk. Mercy came to the front door below him. More trouble, he thought, and went downstairs to let her in.

'Where's Isabel?' asked Mercy.

'Swimming. There's a pool in the basement.'

'Why aren't you down there with her?'

'I've been trying to talk to Amy,' he said, not rising to it.

'Any luck?'

'I spoke, she hung up.'

Mercy shook her head. He led her into the living room, said he had something from the kidnappers she should see. Mercy briefed him on the Grange Road killings. Boxer turned on the DVD player. Mercy watched, hardly daring to breathe. The shot came. She gasped and dropped her head into her hands. Boxer nudged her back up and they watched to the end.

'My God, how did she take that?'

'Badly at first, as you can imagine, but anger's brought her round. She's mad at Frank D'Cruz.'

'So she's tough, too,' said Mercy.

The door opened. Isabel stood there in a white towelling bathrobe, drying her hair with a towel. Isabel smiled. She was pleased to see Mercy, who crossed the room and, without a word, embraced her. Mercy felt all Isabel's strength and vulnerability pulsing under her fingers and now knew for certain that she'd lost Charlie to this woman.

Armed with a photo of Deepak Mistry, Roger Clayton was sitting in Leopold's café in central Mumbai with an ill-advised Kingfisher Premium beer in front of him. It was 10.30 p.m. and he was waiting to be taken to his contact in Chhota Tambe's gang, the Hindu breakaway outfit from the infamous D-Company. He was nervous, which was the reason for the beer, and it was ill-advised because he could feel the *pav bhaji* being horribly transformed in the excessive acid of his stomach.

Other things played on his mind. The situation had become more complicated in London. Simon Deacon had called back later on to ask him to follow up on the police report about the break-in to the warehouse storing the electric car prototypes at D'Cruz's factory. Deacon had also fleshed out more details of the lead-up to the kidnap, the profiler's report on the kidnapper and the fact that he had staged a mock execution of D'Cruz's daughter. Finally, Deacon told him that he'd spoken to the CIA about Amir Jat's protégé, Mahmood Aziz. Their primary concern was that he was ambitious, that after more than twenty years in the field in Afghanistan, Pakistan and India, he now had Western targets in mind.

Agents in Pakistan were now looking at the network of people around Lt General Abdel Iqbal and his links to Amir Jat and friends. Pressure had been applied on the Indian Research and Analysis Wing to help find any connections D'Cruz might have to other ISI officers with terrorist sympathies. They were on the hunt for information from Dubai. Clayton couldn't help but feel that a lot of this activity had been generated by his brilliant source: the idiot Gagan and his sublime fish tarts.

A taxi driver came into the café, signalled to him and saved him from the last of his beer. He was taken to the Bandra Fire Station and pointed into a black and yellow auto rickshaw. For once he was glad to be in one of these infernal machines, whose loud and obnoxious exhaust was marginally more toxic than his own. He rapidly gave up trying to work out where they were going and sank back into the enclosing darkness of the canopy, from where he could secretly observe the lurid city lights, which stamped back-lit vignettes onto his retina.

Half an hour later, the rickshaw driver stopped in a narrow lane of even more squalid squalor than usual and pointed to a green door with a red light behind it. He made a sign for Clayton to batter it with his fist. Clayton wiped the sweat from his face and put his foot daintily on an invisible black mush, which skidded away from him, and he landed awkwardly on the floor of the rickshaw, twisting his knee. He clawed his way up and out and hung onto the rickshaw's black canopy in agony. The driver took off and he just saved himself from ending up face down in the sludge that had reignited his old croquet injury. As the blatter of the engine receded, he heard an animal sound: the lowing of water buffalo, the stamping of their impatient hooves.

It's a bloody game, isn't it? he thought, as he limped towards the green door.

He hammered on its planks; the cracked paint stuck to his fist. The red light behind pulsed. The door opened onto an empty corridor. A girl in a lime green sari appeared through a curtain of muslin, beckoning him forward, and he thought he might be lurching into a dream.

The door creaked shut behind him. A hood of evil-smelling hessian came down over his head and was tightened at the neck so that he choked. His knees were kicked from behind and he went down heavily on the smooth cement floor, grunting with pain. His arms were pinned behind him and tied together at the elbows by a thick band of cloth, while some plastic flex was wrapped around his wrists.

Two men hauled him to his feet and the effort resulted in a monstrous fart, followed by a beat of silence and uncontrollable giggling. They said something in a language he didn't understand, not Urdu, and laughed again. They dragged him down the corridor, through the curtain and out into a courtyard, where women were chattering and there was the smell of frying food.

They ricocheted down another corridor, out into the open air and stuffed him into a car. It was a tight fit, so that the two men sat with a buttock on each of his thighs, their smell coming through his hood – soap, sweat, spice and something sharp on their breath, like *paan*. Another fart, this time low and growling, protracted and inaudible, as his fear multiplied the horrors of his guts. His two minders made exaggerated protests. Clayton was dismayed to find that the first remotely exciting thing he'd done in his two years in Mumbai was descending into farce.

Fifteen minutes later, he was dragged out and rushed in a loose ruck into another building, up some rough steps and more doors. A long corridor. He was handed over to someone else using the same incomprehensible language. The solid grip and presence of a big man guided him into a room. He was released from his constraints and pressed down into a small sofa. The hood came off with a flourish, as if he was the main dish at a restaurant with ideas above its station.

There was a man sitting in front of him on a wooden chair. He was wearing a white *kurta* over jeans, with pointed black leather shoes by which, Clayton thought, he would not like to be kicked. Littered around the room, on a mixture of low-slung chairs and benches, were an assortment of young men. They looked at him with eyes that were quite dead, either drugged or consumed by weariness at the prospect of further murder. The heat in the room was suffocating but no one seemed bothered by it. The sweat poured from his chest, trickled down his stomach and flanks.

'Who are you?' asked Clayton.

'I'm Yash,' said the man in the pointy shoes.

'Where's my friend?'

'I'm your friend's boss,' said Yash. 'He said you were looking for somebody.'

'I'm trying to find a man called Deepak Mistry,' said Clayton.

'Why?'

'I'm not entirely sure, strange as that may seem. He's a missing piece of the jigsaw. I hope that by finding him it will complete the picture and make things clearer.'

'Make what clearer?'

'Well, this, too, might seem odd, but I'm not entirely sure of that, either. I think his disappearance may have something to do with Frank D'Cruz and possibly ...' said Clayton, going for the big guess, 'something to do with his daughter, Alyshia.'

'Who do you represent?' asked Yash.

Clayton had thought about this. HMG's MI6 was not a card to be tossed lightly onto the table amongst this bunch of *goondas*. But he needed a cover that they could not easily check.

'Alyshia's mother's lawyer, in London. He didn't give me a very full picture for good reasons, I'm sure. I was just asked to locate Mr Mistry and put some questions to him.'

There was a prolonged exchange between Yash and another young man sitting next to him on a low chair, which Clayton didn't grasp, as they were speaking what he thought was probably Bambaiya, a strange blend of Hindi, Marathi, oddly pronounced English and slang.

'Why would a lawyer in London want to know where an ex-employee of Frank D'Cruz is in Mumbai?'

'It sounds to me, Yash,' said Clayton, looking him hard in the eye, 'that you know where Deepak Mistry is and that you're protecting him. So why not let me talk to him direct?'

'Only if you tell me what it's about.'

'It concerns Alyshia and that is all I am prepared to say.'

There was another exchange during which Yash did not take his eyes off Clayton. It was now apparent that the men were all nervous. The dead eyes were suddenly livelier in their heads. Rapid talk flashed around the room. Yash made a call, put his hand up and the cacophony stopped. He spoke rapidly and listened before closing down and making a small motion with his finger. The hood was fitted over Clayton's head again. They pulled him to his feet and cuffed his wrists. They led him back to the car. Forty minutes drive, the sweat coming out of him in stinking cobs. Shirt drenched, trousers and underpants too. No one spoke.

The car came to a halt and he was bundled out. The unmistakeable noise and smell of slum came through the hessian. He wondered whether it was Dharavi, which he could see from his offices in the Bandra Kurla Complex, across the stinking Mithi River, with its mangrove swamps being slowly destroyed by the industrial effluent and the combined detritus of the millions who lived along it.

They walked him for some minutes, holding his head down at various points. The howl of generators filled the night. Music, TV, radio and humanity fought for air-time. Then quieter and quieter. One arm released, the passages so narrow now they couldn't manage two abreast.

Finally they went indoors, uncuffed him and pushed him down into a chair. The heat was oppressive, even with the hood removed. He was left alone in a room with sky blue walls, all cracked. A framed and faded photograph of Rajiv Ghandi, festooned in garlands of marigolds, was hanging from a nail. There was a closed pair of wooden shutters opposite the door and one other chair. Clayton massaged his wrists where the plastic cuffs had left a reddened welt. He flexed his damaged knee.

The door was opened by a man in a white *kurta pajama*. He sat in the chair opposite, leaned back. Resting in his lap was a stainless steel Beretta with black plastic grip panels. The man flicked his long hair back over his shoulders and Clayton realised that this was Deepak Mistry.

'You're lucky,' he said.

'I don't feel it,' said Clayton.

'Yash thought you'd been sent by Frank.'

'I thought my friend had explained everything when he set up the meeting.'

'We are all a little paranoid and Frank is a very cunning fellow,' said Mistry. 'Yash was thinking he wouldn't take any chances, just kill you and tie you down in the mangrove swamp until you rotted away to nothing. That might still happen if we find you've been lying.'

'Why does Frank want to find you so badly?'

'Because he wants to kill me,' said Mistry, opening his hand.

'Any particular reason?'

Mistry thought about this for a moment as if he was trying to decide what story he would choose.

'With Frank, you're all right as long as you stay inside the circle. If you drift out and he feels he no longer has influence over you, your every move becomes a potential danger to him. He is no longer sure what you know and, worse, whether you will tell what you know,' said Mistry. 'I've seen men who want to get out, who just can't stand the pressure anymore. They leave and a few days later they get a visit from a *goonda* sent by Anwar Masood.'

'Who is Anwar Masood?' asked Clayton, transfixed by Mistry and only just remembering in time who he was supposed to be and what he couldn't possibly know.

'Yash tells me you have information for me concerning Alyshia,' said Mistry.

'I'm surprised to be sitting here in front of you,' said Clayton, realising now that the security tests were continuing, the paranoia level very high, and the only information he was going to get from Mistry would be before he'd revealed his bait, not after. 'I was only expecting a meeting with my friend to ask if you could be found. I didn't realise you were already connected. I'd never heard of Yash.'

'Yash and I go back a long way,' said Mistry. 'To the village. We left Bihar together. He wasn't very bright, academically speaking. He came to Mumbai and found that there was money to be made in a gang.'

'And you?'

'I went to Bangalore where I got a job with an English family. The father had come over from the UK to set up a company designing econometric software. He taught me almost all I needed to know and his wife gave me English lessons. When they left they asked me to come with them, but I said my future is in India.'

'I heard you ran your own company in Bangalore,' said Clayton. 'Did the English guy set you up?'

'He was kind, but not that kind,' said Mistry. 'I had to rely on Yash for that.'

'Ah,' said Clayton, getting things now, 'and did that come with strings attached to Chhota Tambe, for instance?'

Mistry could see Clayton's brain moving up a gear; it made him nervous.

'Does this have anything to do with what you're going to tell me about Alyshia?'

'It could do,' said Clayton. 'I'm just not sure *what*. Would you just tell me what was demanded of you? I assume that Yash is running things for Chhota Tambe.'

Mistry shifted in his seat, lifted the gun, held it over the side of the chair, still relaxed but aware now that Clayton's greatest talent was his lack of threat and how willingly people opened up to him.

'I think, Mister Clayton, the time has come for you to tell me this news about Alyshia,' said Mistry.

'The reason I was asked to make contact with you, if at all possible,' said Clayton, trying to sound lawyerish, but verging on the Dickensian, 'was to inform you that Alyshia D'Cruz has been kidnapped. You were both employed in the Konkan Hills steel works and you both left the company at more or less the same time. Alyshia's mother's lawyers were wondering if there was some connection, or if you could shed light on any possible reason for her kidnap.'

As he delivered this news, Clayton watched Mistry for the slightest reaction. Mistry's eyes widened by a few millimetres for a fraction of a second.

'When and where did this happen?'

'In London, late on Friday night.'

'Who by?'

'We were hoping you might be able to help us with that.'

'Have they made any demands?'

'Not yet,' said Clayton. 'And somebody tried to shoot Frank D'Cruz dead on his first night in London.'

Clayton noticed that the gun was no longer in a relaxed hand but had come up onto the armrest of the chair and was now in a fully tensed grip, pointing at his gut.

'I think you can tell from my situation here that I am in no way responsible, if that's what you're implying,' said Mistry.

'It's important under these circumstances to gather as much information as possible in the hope that we can find out who *is* responsible,' said Clayton.

'Why *me*?' said Mistry, his voice taking on a brutal edge.

'I'm not here to accuse you,' said Clayton. 'Just for insight.

Things have become very serious, very quickly. Mr D'Cruz has hired a kidnap consultant and a profiler has reviewed the conversations so far. They believe that no demand will ever be made, that the idea is to punish Mr D'Cruz and eventually kill Alyshia. He's even staged a mock execution.'

Each additional piece of information seemed to have the opposite effect on Mistry that Clayton was expecting.

'How do you *know*?' said Mistry, leaning forward, his eyes burning into Clayton.

'How do I know what?' asked Clayton, confused.

'How do you know to come to *me*?'

Clayton's sweat-drenched clothes had gone cold and this coldness penetrated his innards. His throat was constricted; air was scarce in the room.

'You … you are one of the participants, aren't you?' said Clayton. 'You left Konkan Hills at the same time as Alyshia. She returned to London a changed person. Something had happened, but nobody knows what. We're having to piece things together ourselves and we're under extreme pressure. You are a part of the jigsaw, Mister Mistry, but we don't think you're involved.'

The paranoia Mistry had mentioned earlier in such a calm way seemed to be more alive now in his body language. There was nothing languid about him anymore.

'I'm beginning to side with Yash now,' he said, using the gun to make his points. 'I'm thinking that you're not who you say you are, that you've been sent here to smoke me out. I'm thinking that you come here with such news to—'

He stopped at the unmistakeable sound of a gunshot. There was a beat of silence before a barrage of return fire broke open the suffocating night. Mistry looked at the door as if it might disintegrate into splintering holes. Clayton got to his feet, not springing into action, exactly, but more out of pure alarm.

'I should have listened to Yash,' said Mistry. 'You were so plausible.'

More gunfire and Mistry rushed at the wooden shutters, clambered out into the dark as two gunmen shouldered through the door. They trained their weapons on Clayton, into whose mind there suddenly flashed an earnest young face with a wake of betrayal flaming behind it: Gagan. Gagan and his supremely edible fish tarts. He could see Anwar Masood heaping more than praise on his wiggling head.

The shot, when it came, cannoned into Clayton's chest. As he thumped backwards over the chair and hit the wall with the flattening sound of a carcass of meat, he thought someone had taken a sledgehammer to him. The second shot nailed him to the floor. The blue ceiling crowded darkly in on his vision, his head fell to one side and Rajiv Ghandi's portrait was the final image he took with him into the vast black beyond.

17

'What did he make of it?' asked Boxer.

Conference call: DCS Peter Makepeace and Martin Fox in Pavis operations room, Charles Boxer from the house in Aubrey Walk. They were talking about the DVD of the mock execution, which Fox had shown to the MI5 psychologist that Pavis used to assess new recruits.

'Professional, not amateur,' said Fox. 'Devastating shock tactic in order to prepare hostage for more intrusive grilling, or the family for a heavy demand. He believes that the shooter was military trained, just in the way he held himself and his weapon, which was a Sig Sauer P220. He's undecided about their nature: criminal or terrorist. That will become clear only with a demand. If they are terrorists, there's also the possibility that they're being coy about demands because they don't want to unleash the Counter Terrorism Command, which would certainly turn the heat up.'

'And what do the two of you think?'

'It looks criminal to me, but with a highly trained group used to military-style assignments, with powerful research and psychological backing, looking to squeeze the maximum out of a wealthy man,' said Fox. 'They don't seem to be in a hurry, but they're ramping up the violence with this extreme demonstration in the DVD. I think the teasing will stop and we'll get a big money demand in the end.'

'Has someone been sent to investigate the pizza delivery boy?'

'George Papadopoulos is dealing with that,' said Makepeace.

'And you, sir? How do you feel about the kidnappers?'

'My major concern, as we close in on one hundred days to go before the Olympics' opening ceremony, is a terrorist attack,' said Makepeace. 'My analysis tends to come with that bias. There is nothing we've seen so far from these people that *overtly* indicates that they have terrorist intentions. I am uneasy about the apparent level of training. But, then again, if you're looking for a big pay-off, then this may be a necessary level of investment and professionalism. I'm unhappy at their insistence that this is *not* about money. I'm as concerned as D'Cruz is about the "demonstration of sincerity", because I don't know what it means. I'm worried that, despite their declared intention only to talk to Isabel Marks, they might confuse the issue by starting direct talks with Frank D'Cruz, who is their ultimate target. Having made their emotional point through his ex-wife, they're going to get down to the real business with him and exclude us. If they're terrorists, they'll know about you as a consultant and they'll probably assume our involvement and they won't want to trigger a major counter terrorism operation. What's Frank D'Cruz said about it all?'

This is where it started, thought Boxer, to lie for Frank ... or not.

'I've had a theoretical conversation with him about the possibility of the kidnappers being terrorists.'

'So he does suspect their involvement?' said Makepeace.

'That means he's not unaware that in his past he has been involved with people who've gone on to develop terrorist links,' said Boxer, who gave them a quick recap of D'Cruz's involvement in the gold smuggling business. 'He's also not unaware that, given his wealth and "plugged in" status, he could be in a position to help them, which he insists he doesn't.'

'All that could give the "demonstration of sincerity" a terrorist complexion,' said Makepeace. 'Has he got any theories about that?'

'The impression he gave me was that this is pressure being applied to him to make him more compliant. The nature of this compliance is unknown. To me, if it's got any terrorist connection at all, it feels like something in development, rather than the next step towards an imminent attack.'

'I don't like it,' said Makepeace.

'Don't like what?' said Fox. 'I thought we were still in theory here.'

'Theory based on fundamentals, like D'Cruz's involvement with people who've got terrorist links.'

'I've done some work in Pakistan,' said Boxer. 'Nothing is straightforward in that country. Government, business, politics, religion and terrorism have a way of blending together in surprising ways. You might think you're doing business with a retired army officer but, in fact, he may have tribal connections that demand his attention in ways that we would construe as criminal. None of this appears on their business cards. You have to work it out for yourself.'

'*If* you're so inclined,' said Makepeace brutally.

'There is that,' said Boxer. 'Taking on a steelworks during an economic downturn might make you less inclined to be investigative. Most businessmen want to find ways to sell, rather than reasons not to.'

'Is he operating at a comfortable level of ignorance, or a self-serving level of turning a blind eye?' said Makepeace.

'Can't help you there.'

'The real question is: how do we treat this?' said Fox. 'Criminal or terrorist?'

'D'Cruz would rather you kept an open mind while he gathers more information,' said Boxer. 'Unleashing counter terrorism could spook the kidnappers and result in the death of his daughter. We still haven't had a definite terrorist threat.'

'You, DCS Makepeace?'

'I don't think we should throw counter terrorism at it yet,' he said. 'I think we pass this information on to MI5. We've been told they've got a file on him. And see what they make of it.'

'Martin?'

'That doesn't jeopardise the safety of the girl and it potentially broadens our knowledge of both friend and foe,' said Fox.

'Who's the friend?' asked Boxer.

They laughed themselves to a quick silence.

*

Mercy was thinking about Isabel. She liked her, but she was scared by her, too. For the first time in twenty years, she'd met a woman who could take Charlie from her. She'd never feared any of the others. Even the supermodel types with legs that went on forever.

Charlie was the only person in her life who'd ever made her feel safe. And now he was going to give his undivided attention elsewhere. Her insecurity shivered through her like the cold waves of a viral attack as she saw herself on the brink of losing everything. Her daughter hated her and the only man she'd ever loved – and yes, still loved – had fallen for someone who was more than her equal.

And that was the other thing: Isabel was everything she wasn't. Or was it just that Isabel had the ability to show what she never could?

She had a vision of herself as a lonely person, which gave her a desperate need to put things right with her daughter. She didn't call Esme to see if this was all right and it was close to eleven at night when she pulled up outside the old Consumption Hospital on Mount Vernon. She rang the buzzer, stood in front of the video camera.

'Jesus, Mercy, is that you?' said Esme through the intercom.

'I need to see Amy.'

'Are you all right?'

'Will you let me in, please, Esme?'

Esme buzzed her in. She went up to the first floor. Esme was waiting and smoking outside her flat.

'What's all this about, Mercy?'

'I want to see my daughter, that's all.'

'It's late.'

'I've been working and she won't be asleep yet.'

'I'm not sure it's such a good idea,' said Esme. 'She's still in a rage at you.'

'I don't give a shit,' said Mercy. 'I want to see her.'

'Look, I can see you're upset, Mercy,' said Esme. 'Is this really the best time to be doing this?'

'I've just seen something terrible in my work and I don't want … I want to … I need to see …'

'Yes, OK, it's all right, Mercy. Let's go in. Have a cup of coffee.'

Esme took her into the kitchen, sat her down. Mercy was craning her neck to see the room where she knew Amy would be sleeping. Esme put a coffee down on the table in front of Mercy's clenched hands. Mercy leaned over and rested her forehead on her fists as her body was wracked with shuddering sobs. She leaned back, tears streaming down her face.

'Sorry,' she said. 'I'm losing it.'

Esme was transfixed, had never seen Mercy in such a state.

Mercy got up suddenly, wiped her face and walked across the living room into Amy's bedroom. The girl was sitting on her duvet in her pyjamas with an MP3 player plugged in. She glanced up, yanked the buds out of her ears and a look of such scowling mean-ness crossed her face that Mercy reared back.

'What do *you* want?' she said.

And Mercy didn't know. She didn't know what she wanted. Except for it to be all right. But not how to make it so.

'I just ...' she started.

'What?'

'I just wanted to tell you how much I love you.'

'Now you're all at it,' said Amy, mocking.

Mercy turned, left the room, straight past the smoking Esme and out of the flat.

'Are you sure you're not a poof?' asked Skin, standing in the middle of the room with its new blinds drawn, thumb hooked into one pocket, and a can of Stella hanging from his hand.

'You mean, just because I'm doing the hoovering?' said Dan, shunting Skin's foot so he lifted it, and then the other.

'There's that, and all the fancy ready-cooked meals you've bought, new sheets on the bed, a new blanket, *lah-vely* blinds *and* you've spent half an hour cleaning the crapper and putting a new bog seat on. The other fucker's keeping her stripped down to her undies on a bare mattress with hardly any food and pissing into a tin bucket. And here we are in the Colville Estate Hilton with room service.'

'Hyatt,' said Dan. 'For fuck's sake, the *Grand* Hyatt.'

Skin laughed wheezily into his Stella. 'It's cutting into my profit margin,' he said.

'For a start, it's coming out of the money we didn't give to the cabbie; second, we're living here, too; and are you really going to give a shit about a couple of hundred quids' worth of stuff when you're sitting on a million?'

'We're not sitting on it yet,' said Skin. 'And if this fucks up, we're down the rent, your seafood linguine times ten, whatever the fuck the blinds and bog seat cost *and* the hoover.'

'If this fucks up, we'll be finding out if there's a God or not,' said Dan. 'Anyway, the hoover's yours after the event. Whatever happens. It's a deal.'

'Don't use them,' said Skin grumpily.

'You put this end over your knob and it's great.'

'Never been that desperate.'

'Right. I've seen you fighting the girls off with a pitchfork,' said Dan.

'What do you know?'

'The shaved head and the tat probably don't help. What was the big idea behind that fashion statement?'

'I was called Gabriel at school.'

'Gabriel?'

'The angel,' said Skin. 'I had blond curly hair.'

'Sweet,' said Dan. 'Did you get the part in the nativity play, too?'

'Fuck off, Nurse,' said Skin, eyes gone dead.

'And the tat?'

'Then they called me Baby-face.'

'Can't win, can you?'

'The tat shut those fuckers up,' said Skin. 'And I stabbed a teacher in the leg.'

'What's the time?' asked Dan, thinking: that's enough history.

'Just gone quarter past midnight.'

'We're on at one.'

'Everything ready?' asked Skin. 'Restraints? You were going on about restraints as if, you know, you were into them.'

'Didn't want to get her back here and find we can't even tie her to the bed,' said Dan. 'Look like amateurs on our first night.'

'You got your knock-out juice?'

Dan took out the syringe from its box, flicked it so the liquid shook.

'Weapons?'

They took out their guns, racked the slides, showed each other they were loaded. They headed out to the van.

'You remember to put that carpet in the back and some cushions?' asked Skin.

'Now who's looking after her welfare?'

'Once she's in our hands, she's worth money. I don't want her knocking about like a piece of old furniture.'

Dan opened the back, showed him. They got in the front, looked at each other.

'What could possibly go wrong?' said Dan.

Skin looked up into his head as if performing an enormous calculation.

'All right,' said Dan, starting the engine. 'No need to go into it.'

'Thank fuck for that,' said Skin, foot up on the dashboard, ciggies out.

They headed south through the Rotherhithe Tunnel, then east following the curve of the Thames. They came into Deptford and some abandoned buildings around Convoys Wharf.

'Talk me through it one more time,' said Dan. 'Make sure we know what we're doing.'

'Do everything as normal. Park in the same place. Go in through the same entrance. Have a chat and a laugh with the previous shift. Check in with Jordan and his mate. Take up our positions. Me inside. You out. Everything as we've always done. The only difference is that I won't close the inner door to the refrigeration unit.

'I won't make a move in the first half hour so you can relax. Only after 1.30 will anything happen. You do nothing until you hear from me. Then you come in with the roll of carpet. We hood up. We go into the room and you sedate the girl. We roll her up in the carpet. We take as much of Jordan's set-up as we can. You go out and bring the van into the warehouse like you did when we first delivered her. We put her in with any equipment we've lifted. I drive the van out. You close up. We head back to the Colville Estate Hyatt. Couldn't be simpler.'

'You ever got anything out of Jordan and his mate?' asked Dan.

'Like what?'

'Who the fuck they are? What they're doing with the girl? Why the mock execution?'

'That was too fucking much,' said Skin. 'That Irish fucker, I could tell he was enjoying it. You don't want to get on the wrong side of him, or any side for that matter.'

'What if the Irish guy is backing up Jordan tonight?'

'We don't do it. I wouldn't be able to work it,' said Skin. 'He sits there cradling his gun like it's a newborn baby. Reecey is all right. He thinks I'm thick, but that's fine by me.'

'Do you hear any of what Jordan says to the girl?'

'Nothing. He speaks very quietly into a microphone and all her replies come through his headphones. The only time I've heard anything is when I've been in the room with her when she wants to pee or for that fucking business yesterday. And from that I can tell you all Jordan wants to do is break her down.'

'That should make it easier for you to deal with them then.'

'Did I tell you Reecey's armed?'

'No, you didn't.'

'Didn't I?' said Skin. 'I wonder why.'

'Come and talk to me when you've worked the weekend shift in A&E in a London hospital.'

'I know you can do blood and gore, Nurse, but this is different,' said Skin. 'I know Reecey carries because he's shown me, just as he's shown the other shift. He's letting us know he's no pushover if we start getting ideas. Yeah, exactly, now you're understanding it. He doesn't trust the situation he's in. He's trained, and in more ways than one.'

'Why are you telling me this just before we go in there?'

'Just so you know it's not going to be a piece of piss,' said Skin.

'Is Jordan armed?'

'Don't think so. Can't tell.'

'Your shoulder all right?' asked Dan, wanting to think about something else.

'It's fine and it's my left arm, not my shooting arm.'

Silence. All the new problems stacked up high in Dan's mind.

'Don't worry, I get on with Reecey,' said Skin. 'He showed me the laser device on his gun. So when the red dot falls on you, Nurse, you know when to run.'

'Thanks for the advice. I'm not sure I'll have time to register when the red fucking dot falls on me.'

'Look, Nurse, I'm the one in the front line, not you,' said Skin. 'Just try to keep calm. If I don't call you in by twenty-five to two, you can run like fuck.'

'With the red dot falling on my fucking back.'

'At least you won't see it coming,' said Skin, chuckling.

He tossed his cigarette butt out of the window and something cold settled in the pit of Dan's stomach.

'Tell me about your father,' said the voice. 'How did your relationship with him develop in this new world? You left England under a cloud. What happened in Mumbai? Tell me from the top.'

'One thing I noticed about conversations with my father: we never talked about the past. His or mine. In England, my friends' parents quite often talked about the past, you know, in a nostalgic way. That was something else I hadn't quite grasped at the time. They were, by comparison to the Indians I met on arrival, complacent. It was as if they'd done it all and were coasting into a life where they would do less and less and benefit more and more. They saw the future through their children. Whereas my father, and all those around him, were relentlessly moving things forward, looking to the future, imagining this new world they were in the process of creating. It was exciting. It was liberating. You didn't find any Indians sitting around reminiscing about the village and homespun. It was all about the latest shopping mall or the new cinema complex. So the past was out, which was fine by me.'

'You admired your father?'

'Yes, I was grateful to him for what he'd done for me in England and I was impressed by what he was achieving in India.'

'Were you happy?'

'I didn't have time to know what I was. I moved into a flat. My father said he wanted me to be independent from the beginning. I started work, being shown every aspect of the steel business by various expert guides.'

'But not Deepak Mistry?'

'No. I only saw the things that he was involved in after he'd moved on.'

'And when you weren't working?'

'I was invited to all the parties. I had a mad social life in Mumbai high society. I had no time to myself for the first six months. It was calculated. My father wanted to put a gap between my time in the UK and this new life in India. It was also his way of bringing me into his sphere of influence. He managed my work and the people I met, but always at a distance. To start with it was a blur, but gradually a pattern emerged. I was being directed to families where my father had little or no influence, but who he considered important for the trajectory of Konkan Hills Securities. Sharmila was complicit in this and, as we became more friendly, she would question me about my likes and dislikes and report back.'

'He must have found your attitude very frustrating.'

'I told him I wasn't interested in a new relationship. I told him through Sharmila, who he didn't believe. Then I told him to his face. He seemed to take it well, only because he thought I wasn't serious. It was just a question of finding the right guy.'

'That was true, though, wasn't it?' said the voice. 'It just wasn't somebody Frank expected.'

'Something happened before that,' said Alyshia. 'Something terrible and I needed somebody. Someone I could trust absolutely and he gave me that and more, which was why I fell so deeply in love with him.'

Dan parked the van where he always did, just in front of the previous shift's old BMW. They got out, walked back to the door to a small office in the side of the building. Skin unlocked the door and locked it behind them. He tapped on the door to the warehouse, looked up into the camera, waited. The previous shift opened the door.

'Everything all right?' asked Skin.

'Yeah, no probs.'

'Still haven't found the tunnel then?'

'You what?' they said, dull with lack of sleep or entertainment.

'*The Great Escape*.'

'No. Yeah, right. Don't think she's had much time for tunnelling. They've kept at her. See ya.'

They handed over the walkie-talkies. Skin took one and went

into the refrigeration unit. Dan let the previous shift out and waited until their BMW took off before going back in. He heard faint voices from inside the refrigeration unit as he closed the main door and sealed it with the handle. Now there was no sound except for the faint rush from the air conditioning. He pulled on a pair of latex gloves, took a bottle of ethyl alcohol and, in a fit of obsessive/compulsive behaviour, methodically wiped down every door handle and surface he could possibly have touched.

The cold air knifed through his thin sweater as he went to the van and lifted out the roll of carpet, which he took into the warehouse, locked up again. Enjoyed the repetitive activity. He stood the roll up by the door to the refrigeration unit. Waited. Looked at his watch. Only eighteen minutes had passed and he was ready. He paced the huge freezing space of the warehouse, hoping the plodding movement of his feet would banish all negative thinking. It didn't. For every vision he had of Skin and himself sitting on a bed with two sports bags and a million quid each, there were ten along the lines of: Reecey has probably done time in Baghdad looking for the tell-tale signs of a suicide bomber.

Time slowed down. He was convinced it had stopped. He had to listen to his watch to make sure it was still snickering past at its normal rate.

'My father has a house near Juhu Beach,' said Alyshia. 'He's had it for years, since his Bollywood days. Sometimes, if I couldn't be bothered to go back to the city, I would spend the night up there. There were some studio apartments in the compound. The gateman was an old friend I'd known all my life and he couldn't refuse me anything. He would let me in and I'd sleep there. One time my father found out and said I should always call him if I was going to spend the night there. Sometimes he had guests who wanted to be very private.'

'What did that mean?'

'I was no innocent by then,' said Alyshia. 'My mother had told me that one of Sharmila's duties was to run an escort agency for my father's business associates. There were parties at the Juhu Beach house. I knew about them. I just locked my door, slept and left in the morning. I wasn't going to call and tell my father every time I wanted to do that. But I didn't know what else happened out there.'

'Special, private parties?'

'Sometimes my father would make the house available on a *very* private basis. Just one person staying. No servants. Only the gateman.'

'Did you know who he did this for?'

'By this time I'd been travelling with my father on selling trips. He'd introduced me to his Pakistani network, mainly in Karachi, but also in Hyderabad, Multan, Lahore and Islamabad. They were all men and they were either military, retired military, or government officials. Most of them were prepared to accept me as an alternative to my father. But I was introduced to two of them who, my father told me beforehand, would never do business with me. They were very strict Muslims. I had to have my head covered at all times. Contact was restricted to the minimum. They behaved as if I wasn't there. I was glad I didn't have to deal with them, and one of them in particular.'

'Who was that?'

'Amir Jat. He was a military officer and officially retired, but he still seemed to me to be very active. There was something, I don't know, about the way he checked people out that made me think he was in intelligence. I took one look at him and thought this is the kind of man who could have you killed and it wouldn't bother him for a moment. I'm pretty sure my father was scared of him, too, or at least his power, if not personally. Amir Jat had tremendous presence, but it wasn't in the least bit attractive. He was a man who would not stop at anything. He would have you horribly tortured if it would serve his purpose. It was the only time I ever saw my father's charisma slightly diminished.'

'And was Amir Jat a special guest at the Juhu Beach house one night when you were there?'

'It was the only time that the gateman wouldn't let me in. Not only that, he said I wouldn't want to be there. I begged him. I couldn't face the trip back into the city. I promised to be silent and not turn on any lights. As I said, he couldn't refuse me anything, but he did take the main fuse out of the junction box in case I forgot about the lights. Of course, he didn't know who was staying, didn't know the guest by name. But I was intrigued and I stayed up to see who it was.

'It was terrible,' Alyshia said, face in hands. 'I mean, I didn't see anything truly awful, nothing … graphic. It was what it meant that was the true horror.'

'And what did you see?'

Skin sat on an empty shelf, knees up, looking at the back of Jordan's head, the red hair thinning, pretty well bald on top. Broad shoulders hunched over the desk, headphones clamped to his head. He was dying for a ciggie, but Jordan had a smoking ban. He was waiting for Reecey to start his exercise routine, thinking this would give him the slight advantage he needed. Time in here was battering on at top speed towards 1.30 a.m. and Reecey was taking his time reading a hardback with no cover, feet planted on the floor, both hands cradling the book.

'What's that you're reading?' asked Skin.

Reecey didn't answer, shook his head as if it was way beyond Skin's level.

Skin shrugged, swung his legs off the shelf, took off his jacket. Started doing the exercises he'd seen Reecey doing: lunges, squats, crunches and press-ups, but not the one-armed kind that were Reecey's speciality.

'You're a joke,' said Reecey.

'Got to start somewhere.'

'Do any more of those power lunges and you won't be able to walk for a week.'

'Know what you mean,' said Skin. 'Gets you on the inner thighs.'

'Build up to it,' said Reecey. 'You don't train to run a marathon by running marathons.'

'Right, so what should I be doing?'

'Warming up for a kick off,' said Reecey, putting his book down.

'I'm doing this because I'm bored,' said Skin. 'Warming up sounds more boring than sitting on my arse doing fuck all. So let's get straight down to the hard stuff.'

'If you don't warm up you'll have to be hoisted out of bed in the morning.'

'Go on, then.'

Reecey showed him some stretching exercises, which were quite a challenge to someone who hadn't touched his toes since football training when he was fourteen.

'My hamstrings feel as if they're going to snap up round my arse like roller blinds,' said Skin, face reddened, eyeballs pounding in his head.

Reecey showed him how to do the exercises properly. Skin did a full circuit with fifteen repetitions of each. After the stomach crunches, he lay on his back spreadeagled, his heart leaping in his chest like a dog going up for a ball.

'That's about a tenth of what I do every day,' said Reecey.

Skin rolled over, got himself up onto all fours, crawled back to the shelf, put his jacket back on, rested his head on his fists, playing at it.

'How much do you smoke?' asked Reecey.

'Couple of packs a day,' said Skin, to the floor.

'You're an idiot.'

'I like doing things I'm good at.'

'Smoking?'

'Always had a huge talent for it.'

'Blowing smoke rings out your arse?'

'Only if you ask me nicely,' said Skin. 'Show me how you do those one-armed press-ups. I want to be able to do them down the pub.'

'You weren't too hot with two arms.'

'Yeah, but it's not about strength, is it?' said Skin. 'It's all in the technique.'

Reecey got down on all fours, lay face down, legs outstretched.

'The first thing,' he said, 'is you've got to get yourself stiff as a board. You do that by tightening your thighs, buttocks and abdominals. Lift yourself up on two arms and bring your right hand—'

Those were his last words. Skin had him just where he wanted. At his feet. He took his gun out of the inside of his jacket and fired straight into the back of Reecey's head. No silencer. Too cumbersome. The noise exploded in the confines of the room.

*

'And what did you see?' repeated Jordan.

'At about midnight,' said Alyshia, 'the gates opened and a car rolled in. I knew the car—'

The noise of the shot blasted through Jordan's skull. He tore the headphones off his ears and, rising from his chair and turning, staggered back against the desk as he saw the gun barrel smoking and Skin behind it.

'Hands on your head,' said Skin.

Jordan looked down at the plume of blood emanating from Reecey's shattered skull, clasped his hands over his own pate.

'On your knees,' said Skin.

Jordan dropped heavily to the floor.

'Who are you working for?' asked Skin.

'How do you know I'm not doing it for my own amusement?'

'You make phone calls after the sessions. You're recording everything,' said Skin. 'So who's paying you?'

'You want to know who you've got to be afraid of?' said Jordan, smiling.

'I'm not afraid of anyone.'

'Try McManus when he finds out you shot his friend.'

'The Irish fucker?'

'He might not come for you tomorrow,' said Jordan, nodding, 'but he'll find you.'

Skin put a bullet through the glass panel in front of the desk. It shattered and fell to the ground in diamonds. Jordan instinctively ducked. Alyshia found that she was no longer looking at her own image sitting on the edge of the bed, with the horror of what she'd seen running through her mind, but rather the real world. A man on his knees and behind him someone with a shaven head, standing erect, arm outstretched, gun at the end of it.

'All fours like a dog,' said Skin.

Jordan fell forward on his hands.

'Grovel like you made her grovel,' said Skin.

Jordan put his nose to the floor, crawled around.

Skin shot him in the leg.

Jordan collapsed face first into the concrete and slumped to one side. Skin turned to Alyshia and shouted: 'Put the sleeping mask on *now*.'

She fumbled for it, found it by the pillow, pulled it on.

'Are you—?' she started.

'Shut up!' roared Skin. 'Hands on head. Do not move until you're told to.'

Skin went to Jordan, who was panting, holding onto his leg, eyes closed. He kicked him over. The sweat was standing out on Jordan's face. Skin put the second bullet into his head. Alyshia jumped up off the bed as if it were live.

'Sit!' roared Skin.

'I know your voice,' she said, couldn't help herself, brain fizzing with shock, thoughts tumbling out unfiltered. 'I think … I think you might have just done something very stupid.'

'But nobody's fucking laughing, are they?' said Skin.

18

Amir Jat's special agent never came through the main gate. He'd been given a key to a door at the back of the property, which gave into a small garden so that he could come and go in secret. He was nervous as he made his way to the house to see his boss. Nervous but excited at the cataclysmic nature of his intelligence.

Although Lt General Amir Jat was officially retired from the Pakistani intelligence service, the ISI, he still worked as he always had done, getting up at 4.00 a.m. to do paperwork before receiving guests at 6.00 a.m. Today he was up at his usual time, but not for paperwork. He was on the rear verandah to receive this special agent, who only ever came to see him at night with intelligence exclusively on Frank D'Cruz. It was always delivered verbally, never in a written report, and only when the house was empty of other people.

Frank D'Cruz had a special place in Amir Jat's world. He was the one person that the retired officer hated above all others. Not because D'Cruz was a non-Muslim, not because he was a vastly rich ex-actor, who was well worth envying, despising and resenting. No. He hated him because D'Cruz knew his one inadmissible weakness and Amir Jat was not in the business of being weak. He was a man to be feared and he knew D'Cruz was afraid of him, but Jat also knew, as a politically astute animal, that this could change in a moment and he could find himself hopelessly exposed. This was why he had to know everything he possibly could about Frank D'Cruz, even if it wasn't strictly ISI business.

It was the nature of the ISI that nobody, not even the head of the ISI nor its officers, actually knew how the agency worked, or who it was influencing. Constitutionally, it was supposed to respond to the prime minister as an army unit responsible for collecting foreign and domestic intelligence. However, that was not necessarily the reality on the ground, where a lot happened that was not written up in reports or circulated amongst politicians. Benazir Bhutto had called the ISI 'a state within a state', and this was true.

The ISI was composed of officers ostensibly under the control of the Ministry of Defence but in reality, while they behaved like military officers, they also represented, lobbied for, supported, gave access to and found funds for all the factions that existed in the complicated, tribally divided, religiously disparate state of Pakistan. How could the members of an agency that had helped the CIA create a mujahideen insurgency against the Russian occupation of Afghanistan in the 1980s, who were afterwards dropped like wet lepers when the operation had succeeded, then turn their backs on their fellow countrymen, who had shown their allegiance in blood?

Even after thirty-seven years in the ISI, Amir Jat couldn't pretend to know the inner workings of the whole agency, but he knew his own vital corner very well.

The CIA and MI6 would have been mystified by retired ISI officers retaining their power and influence, but to Amir Jat it was just life going on. He still controlled large amounts of money and, after thirty-two years in Joint Intelligence North, had powerful connections to the Afghan Taliban, al-Qaeda and Lashkar-e-Taiba. Why should his employment status have any relevance? He was the same man, with the same sharp mind and, of course, a person for whom the accumulation of power had been a life's work.

The special agent came up onto the verandah. Jat did not get up, but sipped his boiled water, waiting. The agent delivered his report, maintaining a steady, official tone despite his excitement at dropping the bombshell about D'Cruz's sudden departure to London because of his daughter's kidnap.

Amir Jat was a still man, but this news induced a different level of stillness that the agent immediately recognised as an intense interest. He was used to Amir Jat's capacity for self-control. Even before the D'Cruz job, when he'd given reports describing death and terrible injury, interrogations and tribal retaliations, none of them had drawn a flicker of horror from Jat. But this development in the life of Frank D'Cruz quickened Jat's blood so that the penetrating eyes became even more piercing and the hundreds of minor muscles affected by the adrenaline rush produced an increased tension, which made Jat's left hand grip the arm of his chair.

'Sources?' he asked.

The agent knew that one was never enough.

'I first got wind of this yesterday afternoon from my insider at the Indian Research and Analysis Wing. An enquiry had been made by a British MI6 agent as to whether an element of the Pakistani intelligence services could have been in any way responsible for the kidnap. And if so, were they using it to apply some kind of pressure on Frank D'Cruz.'

'And who else?' asked Jat, impossible to impress.

'Anwar Masood was in Karachi yesterday. He went to see Lieutenant General Abdel Iqbal, who then asked me to make my enquiries,' said the agent. 'Anwar Masood is D'Cruz's unofficial security head ...'

'I know Anwar Masood. He's a gangster,' said Jat, cutting him dead, his mind in overdrive. 'What else?'

The agent was used to this. Jat never gave him any picture. All he got was specific instructions. Curiosity was treated as suspicious. He always had to hold things back to maintain Jat's attention and to ensure that he was invited to return.

'There was one other thing,' said the agent, 'but I don't want to talk about it because the picture is incomplete. I am awaiting a final report to come from Mumbai.'

'Tell me.'

'I only have one source.'

'Which is?'

'The police.'

'Yes, and we know how reliable they are.'

'It will take time to get it corroborated by the Indian Intelligence Bureau.'

'Tell me.'

'A British agent was shot this morning.'

'Where?'

'In Mumbai, the Dharavi slum.'

'Who shot him?'

'The police are interrogating one of Anwar Masood's men.'

'Does that mean they think he was responsible?'

'That is unclear. The weapon used in the shooting has not been found.'

'Why would Anwar Masood be going after a British MI6 agent?'

This was the point at which the special agent decided to turn off the information tap. Always leave Amir Jat with a question to turn over and over in his endlessly machinating mind.

'This happened only a few hours ago. My police contact just phoned me. All I know is that Anwar Masood's men came up against a rival gang and this Englishman was killed. What he was doing there is not known.'

'And the rival gang?'

'Nobody has been caught. The police investigation is still in progress.'

'Find out more. I want to know everything,' said Jat. 'Go now.'

The agent stood, dithered in the customary way. Amir Jat gave him an envelope, dismissed him by looking out into the dark garden.

Amir Jat remained fixed in his seat behind the mosquito screens on the veranda. He sipped his now lukewarm boiled water, while his mind played in the three dimensional chess game of Pakistani politics and intelligence.

Questions seethed through his brain. Some were more straightforward than others: why had Anwar Masood gone to Lt General Iqbal and not directly to him? Unless there was some suspicion at his involvement in the kidnap. Perhaps Masood's enquiry was a roundabout way of giving Jat the opportunity to clarify his position. Or was it? He was always wary of the answer that immediately presented itself. In this world there was always another layer or two of subterfuge.

Jat realised very quickly that he needed information and unfortunately most of that information was only available in London. As first light came up he was conscious, too, of the irony of this situation. He was regarding this attack on Frank D'Cruz, the man he hated most in the world, as an attack on himself. This inevitably led him down the path of the continuing antagonism of the Pakistan Taliban to his authority, to his connections, to his control of vital drug funds from Afghanistan. He needed to find out what they were doing as well.

In his office, while he searched through his passports for one suitable for a trip from Dubai to Paris, he made arrangements for his inside man in the Afghan Taliban to pay him a visit. Once that was done, he booked a flight from Karachi to Dubai, but then decided against booking a separate flight in a different name from Dubai to Paris. Instead he sent an encrypted email to an operative in the United Arab Emirates, asking him to make arrangements.

Finally, he called Lt General Iqbal in Karachi and asked him to gather as much information as possible, either from Anwar Masood or directly from Frank D'Cruz, on the nature of the kidnap of Alyshia D'Cruz. He also told Iqbal that he would take the first available military flight from Lahore down to Karachi and that he should meet him there at the airfield before he proceeded to the international airport.

Only then did he sit back and wait for some more water to boil.

Dan was stunned to see the two dead men, the viewing panel shattered, the diamonds of glass mixed with blood on the concrete floor. Somehow he'd expected to find Skin tied naked to a chair, head bloodied, lips split, eyes swollen.

'Open the side door, get the van, drive it right in, close the door. You got that, Nurse?' said Skin, with extraordinary command in his voice. 'Nurse!'

'You did it,' said Dan.

'Just fucking do what I tell you to do and get back in here with the vodkatini.'

Dan went out, elated, amazed, impressed by Skin's sudden transformation into decisive hard man. He rolled up the side door, got into the van, reversed it into the warehouse. It was as if Skin was high on something. Yes, well, that's what he said he always did before a job. But this seemed like something different. A better high than a dexy gave you. A real high. Yes. That was it. He was showing off. And who would Skin be showing off to? Not to him. Not Nurse Dan. It was the girl. He hadn't thought about that possibility. He reversed the van in, lowered the door, took his syringe box, opened the back. On the way into the refrigeration unit, he grabbed the roll of carpet, dragged it along with him. This was an added dimension, he thought, as he looked through the empty frame of the viewing panel to find Skin, head cocked, appraising Alyshia in her underwear.

'Let's get her covered up,' said Dan, stripping off the old latex gloves, stuffing them in his pocket, pulling on a new set.

'With what?' asked Skin, looking around. 'Just put her out.'

'I know your voices,' she said, 'you were in the house … where the cabbie took me.'

'Shut it!' roared Skin.

'Don't put me out,' she said. 'Please don't put me out.'

'Can't take that risk,' said Dan, who injected her through the cannula in her arm. She slumped back on the bed. They lifted her onto the roll of carpet.

'She going to be all right in this?' asked Skin. 'Not going to suffocate or anything?'

'I'll open it out when we're in the back, put her in the recovery position for the drive. She'll be fine.'

'I'll go in the back with her,' said Skin.

'I thought I was the nurse.'

'You are, but …'

'But what?' said Dan, giving him a hard look.

'All right,' said Skin. 'What are we going to take from here?'

'Everything on that desk for a start.'

Skin dragged a couple of plastic boxes over, found one was half full of cheap mobile phones, SIM cards. He dumped the electronic equipment from the desk on top, opened the drawer, emptied that in there, too. In the other box, which had restraints, gags, cuffs, eye masks, he put some files and the notebook Jordan had been using.

'Check the bodies,' said Skin.

Dan did Reecey first, lying face down with one arm still behind his back. Empty pockets. Not a thing. Not even a coin. He tried Jordan next and came up with one mobile phone switched off, nothing else.

'Shit,' he said. 'These guys ...'

'What?'

'They've got nothing on them. No ID. No wallet. Nothing personal.'

'Take that box; we'll come back for the girl.'

They loaded the boxes, got Alyshia lying down in the back of the van, Dan sitting next to her, checking her vital signs.

'Take these,' said Dan, giving Skin a pair of latex gloves and the ethyl alcohol, 'wipe down everything you've touched. It might be worth it.'

Skin went back into the refrigeration unit, pulling on the latex gloves, took one last look around. Hung for a bit to fool Dan and left turning off the lights, closing the doors to the refrigeration unit.

'That was quick,' said Dan.

'Didn't touch much that would pick up prints.'

'So you're going to Rio with yours?'

'What?'

'This is a small island with a lot of people on it. You don't last long with the police on your tail,' said Dan. 'You want me to go in there and do it for you?'

'I'm fucked anyway.'

'And what about me?' said Dan. 'We're joined at the hip now.'

Skin started the van, pulled out, went back to shut the door, ducked underneath it as it came down. They left the warehouses, took a different route back through the Blackwall Tunnel, and then up north towards Mile End, where they headed west to the unit on Branch Place. It was 4.30 a.m. when Skin backed the van up to the double doors. They unloaded the girl, took her up to the flat.

'You'd better get that van out of here,' said Skin.

'*I'd* better get that van out of here?' said Dan. 'What about *my* patient? I'm not leaving her until she's conscious. Then I'll give her a full medical. *You* move the van, and not just round the

232

corner. We don't want any link between that van and us here.'

'You want me to spend a couple of hours wiping it down?'

'Not a bad idea,' said Dan. 'And we should clear it out, too. We're not going anywhere near that van again. They find it, they'll be watching it.'

'What are you worried about?'

'Time,' said Dan. 'Pike will know he's got trouble by nine this morning. The police? We don't know where they are yet.'

'Police?' said Skin, his brain stumbling a little, coming down from the dexy high.

'There've been a few murders, if I recall,' said Dan.

Amir Jat was packed and ready to go. His small case was in the back seat of his car and the driver was in position. Jat was on the veranda at the back, waiting for his last visitor. He was surprised to find himself in a state he'd rarely known: anxious. A situation had occurred which had wrested control from his claw-like hands.

He was aware that when two male animals were seen together as constant companions it was not because, in that sentimental western way of thinking, they liked each other. It was, rather, the reverse. They were inseparable because they had to keep an eye on each other, in case an advantage in mating or food rights should present itself. Hate was the binding factor. With the kidnap of D'Cruz's daughter, Jat now felt exposed, as if he'd lost sight of his loathsome mate and it would somehow lead to catastrophe.

His next guest was his protégé, Mahmood Aziz. He came sauntering up the garden path, as if he had no more care in the world than to score a few runs in a local cricket match. But Jat knew he had masterminded some particularly ruthless bombing campaigns since Benazir Bhutto's return to Pakistan, and had even claimed her assassination, which was not impossible, as he had long-established links with al-Qaeda. Jat and he had worked together closely since they'd planned the attacks on the NATO fuel convoys in retaliation for the US drone attacks.

Mahmood Aziz didn't even look Pakistani. He had short hair, was clean-shaven and had a Western cast to his handsome face. He was the last person anyone would suspect of radical Islamic views. But what Jat particularly liked about the thirty-seven-year-old

Aziz was that he had spent the first twelve years of his life in Upton Park. He even spoke English with a London accent. He thought that Aziz would have some very useful contacts for him.

Before they even uttered a word, Jat handed Aziz an envelope containing $10,000. He didn't say what it was for. It was just a clear indication of his support for whatever Aziz had in mind. Aziz received the gift with both hands.

'*As-Salaam Alaikum*,' said Jat.

'*Wa-alaikum As-salam*,' replied Aziz.

They had a protracted discussion for several minutes about the health of family and friends. Jat's demeanour was completely different with this man. He was full of the utmost respect. Finally, they sat, Aziz with tea made and poured by Jat.

'Are you aware of any operations in progress in London at the moment?' asked Jat.

'By my people, no,' said Aziz. 'The Olympic Games are too obvious a target. The security situation is impossible. MI5 have stepped up their recruiting since 7/7 and the level of watchfulness is very high in all our communities. We have only just managed to root out the three double agents, who betrayed our plans for co-ordinated attacks in London, Paris and Berlin in 2010. We don't want to give away any more of our structure than is already known to MI5, the DGSE and the BND. Our policy remains the same: look for weak targets, always launch with the benefit of surprise. I would be amazed if any other group had embarked on operations at a time like this.'

'The operation that's come to my attention was not a direct attack on an active target, but more of an auxiliary action, a diversionary tactic, a pressurising strategy,' said Jat.

'Are you able to be more specific?' asked Aziz. 'I mean, we are continuing a number of research projects, seeking targets for the future—'

'No, no, this is something entirely different,' said Jat. 'A kidnap.'

'For ransom?'

'Possibly.'

'Or obtaining information?' said Aziz. 'Forcing the government into an embarrassing position? Pressurising them to succumb to demands? But in London … that's never been done before, I don't think. I mean, it's not so easy to hold someone secure in such a place, with so many people and the police with all their informers on the ground, plus MI5.'

'So you think it unlikely that any of your groups would be involved in such an operation?'

'I would have to confirm that to you, but yes, I think it extremely unlikely.'

'Would you know of a group in London who could make something like that happen?'

'What sort of a figure are we talking about? A politician, a business person?'

'It's less about the person, who is not someone obviously important. It's more about the situation,' said Jat. 'It would be a question of finding the whereabouts of a hostage, and then taking over the kidnap from another group.'

19

'And where the fuck have you been?' asked Dan, looking up from the files he'd been reading, pulling out his earbuds and turning off the voice recorder. 'It's past six o'clock.'

'Growing my hair,' said Skin. 'My new disguise.'

He grinned, running his hand over his still shorn pate.

'Where d'you put the van, Skin?'

'Yeah, no, that's why I've been so long. I had an idea.'

'I don't like you out there thinking all on your own.'

'While you sit here swotting up for *The Weakest Link*?'

'*Mastermind*, Skin,' said Dan flatly. 'Specialist subject: Alyshia D'Cruz. Where's the van?'

'I took it to my mate.'

'What's he going to do? Paint it pink and put in some curtains?'

'No. I watched him stick it in the crusher. It'd fit under that table now.'

'You took it to a breakers yard?'

'That way they'll never find it.'

'What about the plates?'

'They're in the canal.'

'And where's your mate's breakers yard?'

'Three Colts Lane.'

'That's Bethnal Green,' said Dan. 'Nice and local for Pike to walk into. Does he know how to keep his mouth shut?'

'Course he does, and he's got some heavy help in the yard 'n' all.'

'It's a bit bloody close for comfort.'

'If I'd known a breakers yard in Watford, I'd have gone there, but I don't,' said Skin, annoyed. 'And even if I did, how do you think they'd react to someone like me asking them to crush a car like, fucking, now! I know this guy and he's reliable.'

'As long as he's more scared of you than he is of someone else.'

'Pike?' said Skin, derisively. 'Pike doesn't know where he is on this side of the river. His SatNav stops at the Thames.'

'So you keep telling me,' said Dan. 'At least you remembered the newspaper.'

'How's the patient?' asked Skin, chucking him a copy of today's *Sun*.

'I don't know, I sent her out to get some bacon sarnies half an hour ago and she hasn't come back.'

'Wasp got up your arse or what?' said Skin, opening the bedroom door a crack, enough to see a lump in the bed.

'She's sleeping,' he said. 'Blood pressure, temperature and pulse are all normal. She's in perfect condition. I handcuffed her to the bed. Is the *Sun* the best you could come up with? We don't want them thinking we're cretins.'

'They'd run out of the *Daily Star*,' said Skin, still looking into the bedroom.

'Why don't you make us a cup of tea?'

'All right,' he said, closing the door softly. 'And you can tell me what you've found out about our specialist subject.'

'Read it yourself.'

'It sticks better when I'm told,' said Skin. 'I only ever look at the pictures in the *Sun*.'

'You can't play the thicko with me,' said Dan. 'You're just being a lazy sod.'

'So what were you listening to?'

'The tapes of Jordan talking to Alyshia,' said Dan. 'That guy, I tell you, he was very highly trained.'

'How do you know?'

'Because I've worked in mental hospitals. I've seen psychologists and psychiatrists in action. He was more aggressive in his style, which makes me think he was maybe military, like PsyOps or something. But I'm looking at his research and listening to him and he's got all the interrogation techniques and a shedload of psychological profiling and analysis,' said Dan. 'And the notes he's taken: there's order to them. He scribbles shit down and then reorganises it into bullet points and then drafts questions to suit. Fucking brilliant.'

'So you reckon they were all military? Except for the Irish bastard; he was just criminal,' said Skin.

'Looks like we're going to have a bunch of mercenaries after us,' said Dan, trying not to sound too depressed. 'That's two East End outfits, the police and—'

'You'd better get on the phone pretty fucking sharpish and ask for the ransom,' said Skin, cutting in on him.

'Me?'

'Yeah, you. You're the negotiator. You're doing the reading and the thinking, so you're going to do the talking 'n' all.'

'And you? Where do you fit in?'

'I'm the enforcer.'

'You got that from *Goodfellas*, didn't you?'

'I'm just saying, I do all the physical stuff. I'll take all the risks.'

'So from now on you're doing fuck all.'

'Until you've negotiated the ransom. Then I'll be the bastard who goes and collects it. The one who sticks his head up over the parapet.'

'So having found this place, I'm now doing hostage care, research *and* negotiation,' said Dan. 'While you do fuck all, plus occasional violence.'

'I took out the two in the warehouse. You looked after the girl. You don't get killed, doing what you do,' said Skin. 'And anyway, I once heard Jordan tell Reecey he would only talk to the mother.'

'What's that got to do with anything?'

'I reckon you'd be good at talking to women.'

'Oh yeah?'

'You do housework.'

'Fuck off, Skin.'

'You listened to all the recordings yet?'

'No. There's a hell of a lot of material here.'

'Maybe Jordan recorded his phone calls, too.'

'Why do you think he'd be doing that, I mean, recording anything?' asked Dan.

'I asked Jordan that before I shot him and he said the only one we had to fear was the Irish bastard, who's called McManus, by the way,' said Skin. 'He said he'd be after us for killing Reecey. Maybe not tomorrow but, you know, in the end.'

'That's left me brimming with confidence and so totally relaxed I—'

'And I didn't tell you what Alyshia said to me when I shot Jordan, did I? She said: "I think you've just done something very stupid".'

'She was only recognising an evident characteristic.'

'Talk English, Nurse, for fuck's sake.'

'Time is running out for Amir Jat,' said the Director General of the ISI. 'The Americans have a dossier as thick as your arm, of which the last inch is dedicated to Amir Jat's involvement in the hiding of Osama bin Laden in the Abbotabad compound a hundred kilometres from my office.'

These were words the DG had directed at Lt General Abdel Iqbal in a secret meeting in Islamabad three months ago. Iqbal had left that meeting in no doubt as to what was required of him. He had to solve the Amir Jat problem. The Americans mustn't take him; it would be far too embarrassing for the government and the ISI.

How he was supposed to achieve this without having him assassinated on home soil was beyond him. Because that, in veiled language, was what the DG had implied to him had to be done. The only problem being that Amir Jat rarely left Pakistan and if he did, it was always in secret.

Then last month Iqbal had been approached by Mahmood Aziz, who he'd met through Amir Jat. Aziz had made a proposal that, if you didn't know the tortuous machinations that were possible within the ISI, would have seemed incredible. Mahmood Aziz knew what the DG had asked of him. How the content of such a secret meeting could have been leaked to a radical such as Aziz might only be comprehensible in retrospect. Aziz had offered not only to help but also to reward, which had left Iqbal with the flame of his ambition roaring from all cyclinders and yet torn by a range of complex loyalties to the service and his old friend, Amir Jat.

Now Frank D'Cruz had been fed into the mix and there was another complicated loyalty: D'Cruz had funded the life-saving surgery on Iqbal's son's brain tumour. That must have been re-paid by now, surely. But then again, can the life of your eldest son ever be repaid?

Iqbal paced the room, waiting for the phone to ring, his posture erect, shoulders back, stomach flat, hands behind his back, glancing out into his garden. Nervous. His eyes darted in his large square head, oiled hair swept back off his furrowed forehead but beginning to come unstuck. The call he'd been waiting for finally came through from a secure phone in another ISI officer's home in Lahore.

It was from Mahmood Aziz, who'd only just recovered his composure after that short conversation with Amir Jat in which he'd seen eighteen months of operational planning potentially go up in smoke because of some unforeseen kidnapping stunt.

Aziz calmly outlined the conversation he'd just had with Amir Jat.

'He's coming to see me later this morning,' said Iqbal.

'On his way to London,' said Aziz.

'He didn't say.'

'But that's where he's going.'

'He's crazy.'

'Definitely unbalanced,' said Aziz. 'But this will give us the perfect opportunity to bring about the change that we talked about last month.'

Silence. Aziz could feel Iqbal's tension coming down the line.

'You told me that the Americans were closing in on our friend,' said Aziz. 'I am telling you that I have now arrived at a solution. All you have to do is not deter our friend in any way from doing what he wants to do. I will be in constant touch with him throughout. Later, I will tell you when to release the information that he is due to arrive in the UK to Frank D'Cruz. At that point you will also persuade him that our friend is responsible for kidnapping his daughter.'

'Wait a minute,' said Iqbal. 'You can't give our friend over to MI5. That would be no different to the CIA taking him. And they'll be watching D'Cruz's every move. I already have MI6 sniffing around here. They follow Anwar Masood to my door every time he comes to see me.'

'Just as I am about to entrust you with the considerable financial power from our Afghan "agricultural" operations, a power held onto with such a tight grip by our former friend, you must have complete faith in my actions,' said Aziz. 'It is for our mutual benefit.'

'And what about Alyshia D'Cruz?'

'What is your concern exactly?'

Iqbal was going to say 'for her safety' but veered away from such sentimentality.

'Frank D'Cruz could be very useful to us.'

'I am afraid that has not been borne out by past events,' said Aziz. 'You will have to accept that his daughter is expendable.'

Jack Auber's wife, Ruby, was up early. She did not look good. Even before Jack got himself killed, she did not look that good. Now she looked terrible. Ill. Her hair, which had been blonde, hung down to her shoulder blades, but with no structure it looked like an ash pile hit by a north wind. She decided to wear it up on her head with a big toothy clasp at the back. Her face was wrecked from an early life of heavy drinking and smoking. Her cheeks had caved in and her dentures were loose in her mouth, but her eyes were still steely blue and could rivet a man to the spot from twenty paces. Nobody crossed Ruby Auber. She might weigh a little under seven stone but she was five foot nine and had nails that could claw a ploughed field down your cheek.

Nothing was going to help her look any better this morning, so when her daughter Cheryl shouted up the stairs that the taxi had arrived, she just stuck on a slash of lippy and left.

Fifteen minutes later, the cab had dropped them off outside Joe Shearing's house in Voss Street and Cheryl was ringing on the doorbell. There was an exchange through the frosted panes of glass and the door opened a crack. Cheryl beckoned to Ruby, who came in off the pavement, and they went into the front room.

Joe Shearing had been a boxer at the famous Repton Boys Club in Bethnal Green. The living room was a shrine to his achievements in the ring. He'd had a shot at the British middleweight title in 1976 and had been knocked out in the fifth by Alan Minter at Wembley. He was still involved with the Boys Club and went to watch training and give talks to the groups of disadvantaged kids, who were brought there from all around the world.

Ruby stood by the fireplace. Cheryl thumped herself down in an armchair.

'You don't know whose seat that is,' said Ruby.

'Whatever,' said Cheryl.

Ruby froze her with a gimlet stare and Cheryl slowly eased her enormous buttocks out of the chair, just as Joe Shearing came into the room. He wasn't a middleweight any more. If he'd had to get in the ring now, he'd have found himself up against David Haye. The lightness had gone out of his feet decades ago, but it had not left his touch. He took Ruby's slim hand in his hard slabs of stone as if he were showing a butterfly to a child.

'I'm sorry for your loss, Ruby,' he said. 'Jack did not deserve to go like that. He was a good man. I'll miss him. If there's anything I can do, you be sure to let me know.'

He did the same for Cheryl, finding something to say about Vic Scully, who he knew from the Repton Boys Club. He showed them the armchairs and Cheryl plonked herself down with a huff, while Shearing, whose hips were a menace to him, eased himself down onto a cushioned upright chair.

'How are you for money, Ruby?' asked Shearing. 'You need any help with expenses, it goes without saying ...'

'That's very good of you, Joe,' said Ruby, 'but that's not why we're here.'

Shearing nodded, breathed in through his broken nose, loudly.

'I want you to find out who killed Jack and Vic,' said Ruby.

'You know it was nothing to do with me,' said Shearing. 'He wasn't on one of my jobs.'

'You haven't given Jack anything for years, Joe,' said Ruby, not meaning it to come out quite so bitterly.

'Young man's game,' said Shearing, not taking offence. 'I

thought he was doing fine with the sheep trade I gave him and the office furniture.'

'He was too generous,' said Ruby, through the slash of her mouth. 'Gave too much away. Felt sorry for them. Wanted them to be able to send some back home.'

'That was Jack, though, wasn't it, Ruby?' said Shearing. 'I heard he was badly broken up by those two lads getting it.'

'That's why he took Vic along with him on Sunday night for the pay-off,' said Cheryl. 'He hadn't done that, Vic would still be here.'

'So what do you want me to do when I've found out who's responsible?'

'Tell us.'

'I can do that now,' said Shearing, 'but I don't know who pulled the trigger.'

'Go on, then,' said Cheryl.

'Archibald Pike. He runs a crew out of Bermondsey,' said Shearing. 'What was Jack doing with *him*?'

'All Jack told me was that he'd been approached for a job because his black cab was still in full working order.'

'But why did he need to do the job? He wasn't short of money.'

'She's up the duff,' said Ruby, cocking her head at the morose Cheryl. 'Needs a roof over her head. Scully said he'd do the work at cost on the Grange Road house, but there were a lot of materials to pay for, a new roof ...'

'What was Jack getting for this job?'

'Ten grand.'

'That would have been all right, wouldn't it?' said Shearing. 'Nobody gets money like that these days without taking some sort of risk, though, Ruby.'

'It wasn't that kind of job, the way it was described to him.'

'I heard what happened to the two sheep Scully sent along. Once you've seen something like that, you want to find yourself a shooter with a bit more experience than young Vic.'

'So what's this mean, Joe?' asked Ruby, her derision getting the better of her. 'You going to do anything or you going to let this Archibald Pike walk all over you?'

'I'm told, by the size of him, that would not be a wise thing to do,' said Shearing. 'What I'm doing, Ruby, is seeking some clarification from Mister Pike. When I've heard that, I'll hold a meeting and we'll decide what action to take.'

'So there will be some action?'

'Let's see what Mister Pike has to say for himself first.'

They slept apart having agreed, after the intensity of Isabel's guilt the last time, that they wouldn't sleep together until after Alyshia's release. Boxer had been up early, done his circuit training routine and had taken a swim in the basement pool. He was sitting in the kitchen drinking coffee when Isabel came in fully dressed. They kissed.

She spooned out some muesli, cut some apple and banana into it and sat down across the table from him, flipped open the *Guardian*.

'You know Mercy's still in love with you, don't you?' she said, as if she was reading it from an article in the newspaper.

Boxer poured another coffee, blinking that statement in.

'I don't think so,' he said. 'I told you. We'd been through that one and come out the other side, years ago.'

'*You* might have done, but I can tell you she hasn't.'

'How do you know?'

'I can tell,' she said. 'The same happened to me. I split from Chico when I still hadn't got over him. That's why you're the first man I've been to bed with in seventeen years. What about Mercy: has she had any affairs?'

'Not that I know of,' said Boxer, shaking his head slowly, thinking about it.

'And you would know, wouldn't you?'

'So what are you saying?'

'There's unfinished business,' said Isabel. 'She knows about us. She's hurting. Why do you think she came round last night?'

'She's the co-consultant on this kidnap. We have to update each other on all developments.'

'Really?' said Isabel. 'I think she came to take another look at us together. To see what we were like. To confirm to herself. To find out what she was up against.'

'Up against?'

244

'She's been living in hope.'

'I think you're seeing things that aren't there,' said Boxer. 'I haven't caught a whiff of anything like that since we split up.'

'She hides it because she knows that to show it would be the end of the thing,' said Isabel. 'But she can't hide it from me because I've already been there.'

'What about Sharmila?'

'Sharmila was and is a trophy wife. Their intimacy is restrained.'

'Does that mean *you're* living in hope?'

'I was, for some time, even with what I knew about Chico. That's why I hung around for three years before we got divorced,' said Isabel. 'It's very difficult to shake off your first love. That intimacy is long-remembered. You'll see. Once Chico realises what's happened between us, he won't take it lying down.'

There were two things about Archibald Pike, apart from the obvious one, that even the most unobservant members of his crew couldn't miss. The first was the constant motion, the second was the constant noise. And these were secondary, but necessary, to the one thing that needed no observational skills at all, which was Pike's colossally evident hyper-obesity.

When Pike was given the news that the morning security shift had turned up at eight o'clock to find two dead bodies in the old refrigeration unit, the viewing panel shattered, the girl gone and a total absence of Skin and Dan, a frightening stillness settled. There was no more reaching out, rustling in, chewing over, brushing down, dabbing off or sucking up. The two fingers he'd just licked stayed in front of his livid lips and his eyes, deeply encased in the fat of his face, looked out with the wariness of a gazelle that had just caught the horrible catty whiff of a cheetah on the plain. Even the subterranean gurgling of his digestive system was momentarily paralysed. Radio 2 was playing Roxy Music's 'Do The Strand', which seemed such an unlikely exhortation that Pike's right-hand man, Kevin, turned it off. The silence buzzed for a further thirty seconds before Pike swallowed, which kick-started his peristalsis, and the incessant business of food passing through his system recommenced.

'Am I to understand from this,' said Pike, in his high-pitched, almost falsetto voice, 'that Skin and Dan shot these two blokes and ran off with the girl?'

'Nothing's confirmed yet,' said Kevin. 'But we're assuming that if it had been an outside job, we'd have found Skin and Dan dead on the floor 'n' all. So we're working on the assumption that it was an inside job.'

'And what work *are* you doing?' said Pike, not looking him in the eye, blinking, and expecting a very good answer.

'I've got the whole crew out looking for them,' said Kevin. 'I told you Skin was trouble. Plays it dumb, but he's looking and thinking all the time.'

'And Dan?' said Pike. 'What about Dan? I can't see him getting involved in that sort of stuff. Doesn't have it in him. He's a nurse. Thinks things through. Doesn't take risks. And who's going to give me my insulin injections now?'

Kevin said nothing. He'd never liked Dan. Didn't trust him. He wasn't from London. He spoke with a nancy's accent. He had qualifications. He had a full head of hair. He was probably a poof. One of those things was normally enough for Kevin to stove your ribs in. All together, they made him murderous. Only Dan's special nurse/patient relationship with Pike had protected him from Kevin's boot. Now, though, Kevin was greatly looking forward to finding Dan and taking him down into the basement for some Tudor England re-enactments, involving a red hot poker.

'Where are the two dead bodies?' asked Pike. 'What's been done about them?'

'Nothing yet.'

'Clear the warehouse. Clear everything out immediately. Clean it. Wipe it down. Don't stop until it shines. When does their next shift start?'

'Not until ten,' said Kevin. 'There's blood soaked into the concrete floor.'

'Chip it out. I don't want anything left.'

'And the bodies?'

'Bring them here. Put them in the freezers downstairs.'

The doorman came in, looked at Pike and Kevin, saw the messiness of the air between them.

'This a good time?'

'For what?' said Kevin.

'Bethnal Green are at the door,' he said. 'They're calling themselves a deputation from Joe Shearing, seeking clarification on an incident in Grange Road on Sunday night.'

'What the fuck are they on?' said Kevin.

'They're old school, are Bethnal,' said Pike, sighing and reaching for a huge bag of Kettle Chips. 'When it rains, it fucking pours.'

He reached for his pint glass of milk, found it empty and rattled it on the tabletop. The doorman filled it from the fridge. Pike drank down half of it and stopped. His mouth came away with a white moustache. He'd had an idea; the doorman could see it come on in his head. Pike's cheeks flushed, which was what happened when he was inspired.

'Send them in,' he said, wiping his moustache away with the sleeve of his England tracksuit top.

The doorman came back with the two men. The smaller, grey-haired one was dapper in a camel coat and a brown pin-stripe suit, white shirt, red tie and a chocolate coloured trilby in his hands. His companion was huge, with a heavy, melancholy face under dark hair, and eyebrows and ear hair that needed to be trained, but with pliers. He was wearing a heavy blue coat that looked pre-war and made his shoulders sag with its weight. He didn't speak and smiled only once, to reveal a graveyard of discoloured teeth in diseased gums, with an ox tongue nestling behind.

Before the dapper one could even introduce himself and state his business, Pike started up, breasts juddering, so that the ENGLAND emblazoned across his chest trembled.

'*You're* seeking clarification?' he said, and pointed with his pudgy fingers to his own chest. '*We're* seeking clarification. Don't know what the bloody hell's got into those two. Gone rogue, that's what. Brains frazzled by drugs. Sent them down to Grange Road to pay Jack his second five grand, they shoot him and some other bloke and walk off with the money. Don't tell us. No, no. We only heard it on the radio. Haven't seen them since. Just heard from Kevin here, they done another two in Deptford and run off with *our* merchandise. Don't know what it is about the youth today. The recession killed something in their noggins.'

'They're not that young,' said Kevin.

'We're looking for them now,' said Pike, killing Kevin with a knife thrower's aim. 'We find them and we'll give you your clarification just as soon as we've got ours. Kevin will make them dance the quick-step on hot coals.'

'Why don't you give us their names,' said the dapper one. 'Maybe we can help.'

'Not sure that would be much help to you,' said Kevin. 'One's called Skin, the other, Dan.'

'Haven't we got their full names somewhere?' said Pike.

'I'll just check them up on their P45s,' said Kevin drily.

'Where are they from?' asked the dapper one.

'Your neck of the woods,' said Kevin. 'Stepney. Skin's born and bred. The other's an out-of-towner.'

'They have a vehicle?'

'A white transit van.'

'Got a reg for it?'

'Call Beadle's Garage,' said Kevin. 'They had the MOT done there last month.'

The doorman disappeared. The four men exchanged awkwardness around the room.

'You find them before us, we'd like to have first crack,' said Kevin. 'We're very concerned about the merchandise they've run off with.'

The dapper one looked at his hang-dog companion, who didn't appear to react, but must have done.

'We'd like to be present at the interrogation,' he said.

The doorman came back with the registration number of the van.

'Your best chance is with Skin,' said Kevin. 'Shaved head, baby face, blue eyes, spiderweb tattoo up his neck and right cheek. Can't miss him. The other one looks like a poof and talks la-di-da.'

'He was a nurse,' said Pike, almost wistful.

The two men nodded and left.

'What are we going to do with those bodies from the warehouse?' said Kevin. 'We can't keep them in the freezers for ever.'

Silence, while Pike worked his way through two Chelsea buns, licked the stickiness from his fingers and thumb.

'Pike?'

'I'm thinking,' said Pike.

'We have to get the girl back.'

'Stop telling me shit I already know,' said Pike. 'Who turned the radio off?'

Pike's face screwed up like a spoilt child. He rattled his glass for more milk. The radio came back on playing 'Somewhere They Can't Find Me' by Simon and Garfunkel.

20

Martin Fox and DCS Peter Makepeace had just been issued their security passes and were heading up to the third floor, accompanied by a uniformed officer. They moved in silence, minds too full of what was going to come out of the meeting, which Makepeace's call to MI5 had provoked and which, to their surprise, had been anticipated.

They were ushered into a boardroom with more people than they'd been expecting. Titles, names and departments flashed past: Joint Intelligence Committee, Joint Terrorism Analysis Centre, MI5 and MI6. But the two key personalities conducting the meeting were Joyce Hunter of MI5 and Simon Deacon of MI6.

'Just so no one's in any doubt as to why we're here, a quick intro,' said Joyce Hunter, running her hand through her short dark hair, looking around the table with her green eyes, no make-up, no jewellery apart from her wedding ring. 'Martin Fox and Detective Chief Superintendent Makepeace contacted us last night, concerned at possible links Mr D'Cruz might have to international terrorist organisations.

'Mr D'Cruz revealed that he'd worked for a gold smuggling gang operating between Dubai and India in the 1980s. He also declared that he was in a powerful position to aid terrorist organisations with intentions to attack the UK. He insists he does not help them, but is concerned that his obduracy could be seen as obstructive.

'The kidnap of his daughter, therefore, could be an attempt

by a terrorist organisation to pressurise him into assisting them. Simon.'

'Last night, during a follow-up enquiry on an ex-employee of Mr D'Cruz, named Deepak Mistry, my agent was shot dead in the Dharavi slum in Mumbai for reasons unknown. The Indian police say that our agent was caught in crossfire between two rival gangs. One of these gangs' leaders happens to be Anwar Masood, who supplies "an alternative security apparatus" for Mr D'Cruz. While the other gang was, nominally, headed up by a Hindu called Chhota Tambe, who is known for his antipathy to the Muslims.

'It's also been revealed that both Anwar Masood and Chhota Tambe belonged to the old gold smuggling gang called D-Company which Mr D'Cruz worked for between Dubai and Bombay. This gang was run by the Muslim boss of bosses, Dawood Ibrahim.'

'If they were originally in the same group, what happened to split them up and why do they hate each other?' asked Fox.

'Religion,' said Deacon. 'In retaliation for the destruction of the Babri Mosque in Ayodhya by Hindus, Dawood Ibrahim organised the 1993 bombings in Mumbai. It split his gang along religious lines. They've hated each other ever since.

'We have had no confirmation that Chhota Tambe's outfit was actually hiding Deepak Mistry; all we can say is that my agent was hoping to find him there. Mr Mistry has still not been found and his importance to this case is not clear.

'We've also been investigating possible links between Mr D'Cruz and unsavoury elements within the Pakistani Inter-Services Intelligence agency. Mr D'Cruz was selling steel in Pakistan and receiving contracts from senior ISI officers, and Lt General Abdel Iqbal in particular. While this intelligence establishes some sort of link between Mr D'Cruz and the ISI, it does not show any terrorist connections.

'It is well known in the intelligence community and the international press that Dawood Ibrahim's old D-Company gang has since been incorporated by the ISI into the terrorist group Lashkar-e-Taiba. Confirmation that Mr D'Cruz was under the wing of Dawood Ibrahim in his gold smuggling days shows that there may be a, possibly defunct, link between the two men. So, as far as our terrorist concerns go, the most important link to establish would be between any of these ISI officers that Mr D'Cruz does business with, and Lashkar-e-Taiba.

'So far the only link we *have* been able to establish is between Lt General Abdel Iqbal and his fellow ISI officer, Lt General Amir Jat, now retired. Jat has a complex web of loyalties, amongst them: the CIA, the Afghan Taliban, parts of the Pakistani Taliban, al-Qaeda and, we suspect, Lashkar-e-Taiba.'

'You said the CIA?' asked Hunter.

'The CIA have always been grateful to Amir Jat for helping them mobilise the mujahideen as a fighting force against the Russian occupation of Afghanistan in the 1980s. Amir Jat has maintained that relationship with carefully managed intelligence from the Pakistani border region. A lot of senior CIA officers haven't got a bad word to say about Amir Jat, but the younger officers in the field will tell you about his control of the heroin smuggling business to finance Taliban insurgency and that he is the prime suspect for hiding Osama bin Laden in the Abbottabad compound. So he's a complicated individual.'

'Heroin smuggling,' said DCS Makepeace. 'Amir Jat is beginning to sound like a linchpin to me. And if a direct link between him and Mr D'Cruz could be established, that would give all of us grounds for grave concern.'

'It would certainly go some way to explaining the nature of this kidnap,' said Joyce Hunter. 'No financial demand, only a show of sincerity being asked for. It could be that pressure is being applied to Mr D'Cruz to perform in some way.'

'It also implies that he should know *how* to perform,' said Makepeace. 'That he knows what the demonstration entails.'

'We think that Mr D'Cruz might know something of what is going on,' said Simon Deacon. 'It's possible that this "demonstration of sincerity" is actually a demand that he just continues to keep his mouth shut. At this stage we are inclined to trust him, that he has too much at stake in this country to betray us to terrorists. We are also hoping that if we allow Mr D'Cruz some freedom of supervised movement, we could pull off a major intelligence coup.'

'And what the hell does that mean?' asked Makepeace.

*

252

They went into the bedroom, hoods on, shook Alyshia awake, got her propped up, sleeping mask off. She was groggy from the drug. Dan patted her about the cheeks. She slapped his hands away.

'Hold this newspaper up under your chin,' said Skin.

Dan stood back and framed the shot with the mobile phone he'd found on Jordan and took it.

'Shouldn't I be in there with her?' asked Skin. 'You know: hooded man, gun to her neck. Scare them a bit.'

'With a green and white al-Qaeda bandana, maybe?' said Dan. 'And a bread knife for extra horror? Let's just keep it calm for the moment. We can build up to the more lurid stuff later.'

Dan walked the half mile to Old Street tube station and went down to Bank. He got on the Docklands Light Railway, out towards Canary Wharf and across the river into Greenwich. He made the call from Greenwich Park. He was nervous. His skin prickled and would probably have sweated if it hadn't been so intensely cold. He had some notes written down. He sat on a park bench. People walked past him on their way to work, paid him no attention.

'Isabel Marks?' he said.

'Hello? Is that Jordan?'

'No, Jordan is no longer in control of this kidnap. Your daughter Alyshia is now in our hands.'

Silence.

'I don't understand,' said Isabel. 'Who are you?'

'We have taken over the kidnap of your daughter. That's all you need to know. To prove this I am sending you a photograph of Alyshia holding today's newspaper.'

'I don't believe this.'

'Get used to it, Mrs Marks,' said Dan, finding a bit of confidence now that he sensed she was rattled. 'Can you see the photo?'

'I don't know how to work this bloody thing.'

'Don't try and string this out, Mrs Marks. I'm only going to talk for a minute.'

'Right. I can see her now,' said Isabel. 'What did you say?'

'We want five million pounds in cash. I will call again in two hours' time.'

'What sort of cash?'

He hadn't thought that out. Ridiculous.

'Pounds. Used notes,' he said quickly, because that's what they always asked for in the movies. 'Twenties. In five separate sports bags. We'll call you again in two hours' time with the delivery details.'

'We'll need more than two hours to get five million pounds together,' said Isabel.

'That's your problem, not mine,' said Dan, and hung up.

He took the train back to London Bridge, dropped the SIM card he'd just used in a bin and got on the Northern line to Old Street. He was nervous about being followed. Pike's crew would be looking for them by now and they weren't that far from Stepney. He didn't fancy ending up in Kevin's hands. Skin was a liability. That shaved head and stupid tattoo. He'd only let him out after dark.

The round trip had taken him over an hour. He should have given himself more time before the next call. He'd go west for that one, get away from the East End. Maybe this unit on Branch Place hadn't been such a great idea. He'd rushed into it. And now, with Pike's crew probably bleeding across from Bethnal Green into Haggerston and Shoreditch, time didn't seem quite so available anymore.

Dan let himself into the flat silently. The murmur of voices reached him. He listened at the door. It sounded like a conversation that had been going on a long time.

'That's why I persuaded him we should take over the kidnap,' said Skin. 'We all need to make some money but there's no need to treat people like shit. I mean, what was that all about? All those questions he was asking you?'

'He knew everything about me. He knew more than my parents. He knew more about me than I did myself.'

'Like what?'

Skin was never going to make it as an interrogator.

'Like things from my past that I'd rather forget.'

'And what have you got in your past that you'd want to forget?' said Skin. 'You haven't killed anyone. I had to do those two back in the warehouse. We reckon one was CIA and the other SAS.'

Laying it on a bit thick, thought Dan.

'How many people *have* you killed?' asked Alyshia.

'This week?' said Skin, and they laughed, which sent a chill down Dan's spine.

He put on a hood and went in to Alyshia's room. They seemed to have been unaware of his movement around the flat. She was lying on the bed, Skin was at her side as if it was a hospital visit. At least he was wearing his hood, because he'd allowed Alyshia to raise her sleeping mask.

'This looks cosy,' said Dan.

'Just getting to know each other,' said Skin, looking round.

'A word,' said Dan. 'She still cuffed to the bed?'

Alyshia rattled the manacle, smiled. No fear there, thought Dan. Skin brushed himself down. They'd been having coffee and biscuits. Dan closed the door on her.

'What's all this, then?' asked Dan.

'I'm just getting on with her,' said Skin. 'Finding out shit.'

'Go on then, tell me what you've found out that's going to make it easier for me to get a couple of million quid out of her dad?'

'We're not there yet. You can't rush these things. I'm just—'

'Chatting her up? That's what it sounded like. The fucking CIA and the SAS? Coffee and biscuits? Fuck me. Just tell me you took over this kidnap because you fancied her. Let's get that one out of the way, at least.'

'She's all right,' said Skin, shrugging.

'And when you have to get nasty with her because her dad's not playing ball? How's that going to go? Biscuits are cancelled for break? No cut flowers today?'

'You were the one who *bought* the fucking biscuits.'

'They're rewards for good behaviour,' said Dan. 'She's winding you 'round her little finger. I can tell.'

'How do you know I'm not winding her 'round mine?'

'In your fucking dreams, Skin. She's so far out of your league it's like watching Barcelona versus Barnet,' said Dan.

'You're a cheerful little bastard, aren't you?'

'Try getting yourself *out* of the movie of your life and back *into* the reality. You said it yourself: nobody's going to give us a million each unless we, at least, look like we deserve it.'

'So how did the phone call go?' asked Skin. 'You asked for two mil and she said there's a cheque in the post?'

*

Boxer left a voice message on Frank D'Cruz's mobile and called Martin Fox, to be told he was out of the office. He sent a text: 'Major development. Call me.' He sent a copy to the Ops room and listened to the recording several times on the way to the newsagent, where he bought the *Sun* and compared the front cover to the shot on the mobile. He called Mercy.

'You all right?' he asked.

'Yes,' she said. 'Why shouldn't I be?'

'You sound tense.'

'I'm all right,' she said, brittle, getting on for fragile.

'Someone else has taken over the kidnap,' said Boxer. 'I've tried calling Martin Fox but he's in a meeting at Thames House with DCS Makepeace.'

'Do you know who the new guys are?'

'Not yet,' said Boxer. 'I've sent a copy of the call to the Ops room. Listen to it. We've had a demand for five million quid from a middle class Englishman, who's sent us a photo of Alyshia with a copy of today's *Sun*. I think they're amateurs. We need to act quickly.'

'Leave it with me. I'll get hold of the DCS,' said Mercy and hung up.

Isabel hadn't moved. She sat on the edge of the sofa, staring into her lap, her shoulders rigid with worry. She'd wanted Boxer's instant opinion but he was too professional for that. Nothing worse than for a consultant to be seen backtracking after giving the benefit of his experience. The family's confidence would disappear in an instant. He listened to the last recording of Jordan's voice. He sat down in front of Isabel.

'What?' she said, fingers clasped so tight they'd gone bluish-white.

'He's telling the truth,' said Boxer. 'That's today's *Sun* front cover. He hasn't used any voice distortion and I can tell his speech pattern is totally different to Jordan's. His set-up doesn't feel as professional, either. He's made no threats. His voice doesn't sound like the kind that would make any threats. He sounds like an opportunist. An English middle class opportunist. I also think that because he's made an immediate financial demand, he must be feeling the pinch of time. "I'll call you back in two hours" is from someone who wants to get down to business. But he didn't sound as if he'd quite thought everything through. The money, for instance. I also reckon he doesn't know how big a million pounds in twenties is, nor how much it weighs. This is all good news for us, Isabel. The reason I want to speak to Frank and Martin Fox so badly is that, for once, we have to act really fast. These are the people we want to do business with.'

'What do you mean?'

'Normally under these circumstances we'd start to string out a negotiating process, with the twin aims of frustrating the kidnappers and driving down the ransom. As time marches on, they become more prepared to accept less and less.'

'And why wouldn't you do that here?'

'One of the time pressures on this new lot is that they've "taken over the kidnap". To me, that means they've incapacitated the original kidnappers and "stolen" Alyshia. The one thing I felt about Jordan from the beginning was that he was a consummate professional – the psychology of his threats and knowledge, his aggression and intelligence, his patience and research – it was all energy-draining stuff. Somehow he got caught out, by whom we're not sure, but it must have been by someone who was close enough to—'

'Kill him?' said Isabel. 'Then why isn't this new guy as professional as Jordan?'

'He might be professional in a different way. In charge of security, for instance. That would have given him the perfect opportunity. But Jordan was a leader and a planner. This guy is feeling his way forward. I think he was somebody who got lucky and we have to act quickly because Jordan is the sort who'd have very dangerous backing. They'll be out there and after them with the advantage of knowing who they're looking for. Believe me, we want to do business with these new guys. We also don't want to put Alyshia in harm's way. If one group starts fighting it out with another, over a hostage in the middle …'

'I'm not sure how quickly Frank can get hold of five million.'

'We wouldn't need anything like that amount of money,' said Boxer. 'Just something significant enough to make these amateurs want to do a deal.'

21

Just from the tension during the standard greeting procedure, Lt General Abdel Iqbal could tell that Amir Jat was in a heightened state, could feel it in his hands. He knew then that the task given to him by Mahmood Aziz would be easy: do nothing to assuage this man's fears.

The military flight from Lahore to Karachi had taken Amir Jat two hours, but the airbase was close to the Jinnah International Airport, allowing enough time for a meeting with Iqbal before he had to catch the 12.10 p.m. flight to Dubai.

They were meeting in a prefab building close to the runway, within sight of a camouflaged C130 Hercules being loaded. There was a table and two chairs. The ceiling fan did not work. It was already hot.

'Did you manage to speak to Frank D'Cruz?' asked Jat.

'I spoke to him earlier this morning, but only for a few minutes and the line was bad. He was very tired; it was in the small hours for him. We had a coded exchange, in which I told him we were making enquiries and he told me that something bad had happened to his daughter, but it wasn't terminal. Other than that, there had been no further developments.'

'And what about Anwar Masood?'

'I called him back for a meeting earlier this morning.'

'First, tell me about the meeting you had with him, when he told you the girl had been kidnapped,' said Jat. 'What do you think the design of that information was?'

'The design?' asked Iqbal.

'Why didn't he come directly to me?' asked Jat. 'I have far better access to the sort of information he wants.'

'But here, in Karachi, I am closer. This is not the sort of thing you discuss over the phone.'

'Do you think that's all it was?'

'Are you implying that Anwar Masood might have thought that you were in some way responsible for what has happened in London?' said Iqbal.

'Anwar Masood knows that you will come to me. I am the centre of all operations,' said Jat. 'And yet, for something as important as the kidnap of his master's daughter, he goes to you. There's something not right about that.'

'I can't quite see what it is.'

'It's not transparent behaviour,' said Jat.

'What is transparent behaviour in this world?' asked Iqbal.

'That Anwar Masood comes directly to me,' said Jat. 'What his action has done is to plant doubt in our minds.'

'Not in my mind,' said Iqbal, who was quite stunned at the level of paranoia this incident had engendered in his comrade. 'Frank D'Cruz made an enquiry using Anwar Masood, whose nearest access point to our intelligence operations is me, here, in Karachi, not you up in Lahore, two hours flight away. I have the ability to get an agent to you with the necessary information and back-up intelligence within hours. Don't read anything more into it than that, my friend.'

'There's something not right here and I'm going to find out what it is.'

'Has someone carried out an operation in London?' asked Iqbal.

'Not to my knowledge. I have made my initial enquiries and it's thought to be unlikely, what with the Olympic Games so close and inland security operations tightening up by the day,' said Jat. 'I'm awaiting confirmation, but only the powerful organisations can perform internationally, not the splinter groups. And I'm ninety-nine per cent certain our people are not involved.'

'Then that is what we will tell Anwar Masood,' said Iqbal.

'What concerns him, or rather Frank D'Cruz, is something he mentioned to me just this morning: the kidnappers have made no demands. That is, no *financial* demands. What they have asked for is somewhat abstract, shall we say, and that has raised concerns in Frank D'Cruz's mind because he doesn't—'

'Abstract?' said Jat, neck lengthening in indignation. 'What sort of a kidnapper deals in abstractions? They are the most physical criminals in the world. What on earth are you talking about?'

'The kidnappers asked for a "demonstration of sincerity".'

'What is this?' said Jat immediately. 'I don't like this at all.'

'Frank D'Cruz himself doesn't know what it means, what it is alluding to. He's worried that someone is moving against him, undermining his power. The feedback he's had from his Indian enterprises indicate that he has nothing to worry about from that direction, so he naturally thinks of his more dangerous allies.'

'Dangerous? Is that what he called us? Did he use that word?' asked Jat.

'No, I used that word. Perhaps I should have said: "his allies who are engaged in the more dangerous theatre of operations, with international networks capable of pulling off such a thing as a kidnapping in London". I'm sorry if I misled you.'

'We have to get to the bottom of this,' said Jat, disappointed that he hadn't caught D'Cruz out.

'You don't think we're there already, I mean, from our point of view? Frank D'Cruz has made his enquiry and you've just told me there are no operations currently in progress,' said Iqbal. 'That's the end of it, surely? Why couldn't this just be a London gang taking the opportunity to make a great deal of money out of kidnapping a billionaire's daughter?'

'Because, as you've just said, they've made no demands in four days,' said Jat. 'And the only demand they have made is oddly abstract. Surely you must be able to grasp that an attack on Frank D'Cruz is potentially an attack on our organisation.'

'Potentially,' said Iqbal, who now realised what a masterstroke it had been to mention "the demonstration of sincerity".

'And to answer your question: no, I do not think we're there already,' said Jat. 'I think we're like a stone skipping across the surface of a deep, dark lake.'

*

It was a dark day on Bethnal Green Road, of the sort that brings first light but nothing much brighter. Mercy and George Papadopoulos sat on one side of a table in E Pellicci's, drinking strong, sweet tea while Nelson sat on the other side, filling his fork with bacon, sausage, egg and beans. The light in the room was warm and yellow, which made it look like night outside. Italian flowed over their heads from the till area to the kitchen. Mercy, face propped up on her hand, closed her eyes and, for a brief moment, imagined herself elsewhere.

'Can't you hear it?' asked Nelson. 'It's bloody humming round here.'

Mercy, eyes still closed, wound her finger round.

'Get on with it, Nelson.'

'No, I'm telling you, in the last couple of hours, this place has come alive. You know what that means?' said Nelson. 'Joe Shearing's on the hunt and that's not all I've heard.'

Pause for effect, while the admiral filled his face, chewed it over. Mercy's eyes clicked open.

'Don't string it out, admiral. This is important. We need to know. Time is marching on.'

'The two geezers they're looking for have gone rogue from a south London gang run by Archibald Pike from Bermondsey. Do you know him?'

'I know Pikey,' said Mercy. 'You can't miss him. What do you mean by "gone rogue"?'

'What I've heard only comes from Joe's lot; I don't know Pike,' said Nelson. 'What they tell me is that the two who shot Jack Auber and Vic Scully and ran off with Jack's five grand have also shot another two and taken off with some of Pike's merchandise.'

'Merchandise?' asked Papadopoulos.

'Don't know what they're talking about,' said Nelson, his face a mask of innocence. 'Nor did my informer.'

'We got any names for this rogue duo from Pike's crew, apart from Bonnie and Clyde?'

'Not very helpful ones,' said Nelson. 'Skin and Dan.'

'I suppose that first one's got a shaved head, like a million other blokes in London,' said Papadopoulos.

'But he has got a distinguishing mark,' said Nelson. 'A spider web tattoo that goes up the side of his neck and over his right cheek.'

'He's going to regret that.'

'You want to see it, you'd better be quick,' said Nelson. 'They're going to flay him alive when they catch him.'

'Anything on the other one?'

'Oh, he was a nurse, that's it,' said Nelson. 'And a poof.'

'In whose opinion?' asked Mercy, giving him the dead-eye.

'The nature of an intelligence coup is that the fewer people who know about it, the better,' said Simon Deacon to DCS Makepeace and Martin Fox.

'We are just trying to alleviate your concerns,' said Joyce Hunter. 'We've been watching Frank D'Cruz very carefully since the assassination attempt, which means we follow him wherever he goes, monitor his mobile and fixed line calls, his internet use, go through his rubbish and put agents as close as possible to people he meets, as well as maintaining a Level 2 surveillance on them.

'What I can tell you from the reports I've seen is that the kidnappers have made no direct contact with Mr D'Cruz. That is not to say that he hasn't been complying with the kidnappers' veiled demand by keeping his mouth shut.'

Silence, while the two sides considered whether this was the impasse moment: the point of no further information.

'Who has Frank D'Cruz been in contact with since he's been in London?' asked DCS Makepeace, seeing if he could warm them up a bit more.

'Outside of your immediate circle, his property consultant, Nicola Prideaux, who doesn't do much for him in the way of finding residential property anymore, but does occasionally keep him warm at night. She's his mistress,' said Hunter. 'And he seems to have taken the opportunity to involve himself in the launch of these new electric cars he's proposing to manufacture in the Midlands, so he's been in touch with the events organiser in the City and Goldman Sachs, who are the underwriters for the Initial Public Offering.'

Fox and Makepeace turned on their mobiles. They could tell

the meeting was over. The phones immediately started to vibrate. They excused themselves and went into the corridor. Fox walked one way, Makepeace the other. They both turned at the same moment.

'Are you getting what I'm getting?' asked Makepeace.

'This is Charlie, telling me the girl has changed hands.'

'This is Mercy, telling me the same and that she's since found out from her informer that the two men responsible for the Grange Road killings have gone rogue from a Bermondsey gang, killing another two men and taking Alyshia with them.'

'Any names?'

'Just Skin and Dan.'

'That's good,' said Fox. 'Charlie can use those. Anything else?'

Makepeace repeated Mercy's descriptions of the two men given by Nelson.

'That's great. I'll see you back at the office,' said Fox. 'Can you explain what's just happened to that lot in there? I have to listen to this phone call and brief Charlie.'

Dan bolted out of sleep with a child's cry, as if he'd just pulled out of the big dive into oblivion.

'Shit,' he said, looking at his watch. The research notes he'd been reading fell to the floor.

'What?' asked Skin, pulling the buds out of his ears. 'You should listen to this shit. Fucking dynamite.'

'Why did you let me sleep?'

'You looked all in. Got to be sharp to negotiate a couple of mil.'

'I had a bad dream,' said Dan, still wild from it, getting to his feet.

'Cheer up, me old son. You look scared shitless.'

'What did she say to you back in the warehouse?'

'About "doing something very stupid"?' said Skin. 'Well, it's done now, innit? There's no undoing it.'

He took out his gun, unscrewed the silencer, stood it up on the table.

'If we go down, we might as well go down with the volume up.'

'Do not leave this place,' said Dan, staring at the silencer. 'Keep

263

an eye on the girl. Look out the front regularly. I might go out that way but I'll come back over the canal.'

'Run along, Nurse, and let's get this done,' said Skin. 'It doesn't have to be a million each, you know.'

'So what would you accept now?'

'The way you look, I'd take a fiver and run,' said Skin. 'Suck it in, Danny boy. Feel the part. You can do it.'

Dan took one of the mobiles from the box, put a SIM card in it, found the number, entered it into another mobile.

'Your own mobile's turned off, right?'

'Yeah, I didn't fancy hearing Pike's dwarf telling me what he's got in mind for us.'

'Bin it. I'll only call you on this mobile. And I'll only use it in an emergency,' said Dan. 'If I tell you to run, just do it; leave the girl and get out over the canal. Turn left and you'll end up in the Angel, turn right and it'll take you down to Haggerston and all the way to Limehouse if you want.'

'You sound as if you're not coming back.'

'I am. I've got every intention, but listen, Skin, this is real. We've left a trail of destruction: the two illegals, the cabbie and his friend, and now the two guys in Pike's warehouse. We've got a hostage. But we've got no transport. We've got Pike after us, two mercenaries and soon we'll have the police.'

'You said it would take three days to match my DNA.'

'We're almost through the second day and you know what the cops are like. They've got people everywhere. Somebody from somewhere will have told them who's looking for us,' said Dan. 'You think people love you so much they'd never snitch on you?'

Skin didn't look in the slightest bit worried. Dan thought he couldn't wait for him to leave so that he could get on with doing what he wanted to do: think with his cock.

'If I don't see you,' said Dan, whacking him on the shoulder, 'it's been all right, Skin. Thanks.'

He made for the door.

'You forgot somebody,' said Skin, to the back of his head.

'Who?'

'The cabbie's lot. They'll be after us 'n' all.'

*

Pike's office and warehouse was in a double arched property under the railway line on St James Road in Bermondsey. The office was on a mezzanine above one of the arches and light came in through a semi-circular window at one end. Pike didn't like too much daylight. He'd created another room with a stud wall behind the office, in which there was no natural light, only a mixture of yellow, green and red lighting. This sometimes made Kevin feel as if he was inside the cavernous Pike himself, listening to his noisy, noisome and restive habits, which were the same as those of a grossly obnoxious hound, meticulously lapping its parts over and over again.

There was no sense of the outside world in this room. They had no idea who came into the parking area even, and had to rely on the doorman coming upstairs to tell them, because the intercom had broken down. Normally this wasn't too much of a problem as there were always people around, either in the office or down in the warehouse, where there were cooking and washing facilities. However, everybody was out on the streets, on the hunt for Skin and Dan in Stepney and Bethnal Green.

It was past midday when Kevin's mobile rang. He took the call, listened intently and hung up. Pike's motion had been arrested, with tortilla chip laden with Tesco's guacamole inches from his glistening lips.

'We're not looking for the van anymore,' said Kevin. 'Shearing's lot have found a breaker's yard in Bethnal who crushed it earlier this morning.'

'Tricky,' said Pike. 'That might mean they're still local, though. Better call around. Don't want people wasting their time looking for the transit.'

As Kevin started texting the crew, a cream Toyota Hiace panel van turned off Jamaica Road and headed south, down St James Road and into the parking area in front of the two arches. Two men got out. The Irishman, McManus, was dressed in a denim jacket with a thick black rollneck sweater and blue jeans; the other, Dowd, was in a fleece-trimmed leather flying-jacket and black jeans. They were both wearing black ribbed woollen beanies pulled down over their forehead and ears. They'd come directly from the old refrigeration unit in the deserted warehouse on

Convoy's Wharf, where they'd seen the shattered glass panel and, despite the clean-up attempts, the remains of blood from their two comrades. They rang on the bell. The doorman took his time getting there and opened up, keeping the chain on.

'We've got information about the girl,' said McManus.

'Which girl?'

'The one Mr Pike is looking for.'

'Wait.'

The doorman went upstairs, explained to Pike.

'Who the fuck are they?'

'Didn't say.'

'Did you ask?' said Kevin.

'Send them up,' said Pike.

'Hold it,' said Kevin. 'Let's just find out who they are first. They could be fucking anybody.'

'Ask them how they know we're looking for a girl.'

The doorman went back down, opened the door the same crack to the two faces, hard and cold, eyes barely open, breath coming out in streams of white. He asked the question.

'We used to work as porters in the hospital with Dan,' said McManus. 'We saw your people in the street asking about him; thought we'd come here and tell you what we know. For a return, of course.'

'Like what sort of return?'

'We can talk that through with Mr Pike.'

The doorman went back up. The two men outside listened to his footfall, memorised each trudging step, more infuriated the higher he got. The doorman relayed the dialogue.

'Send them up,' said Kevin, moving to the corner of the room, gun at his side.

The doorman went back down, unhooked the chain, pointed them up the stairs and turned to shut the door. Dowd hit him on the back of the head with a tight leather bag filled with ball-bearings, caught him by the collar before he fell into the door. McManus cupped the forehead with one hand and the back of his head with the other and twisted violently. There was a dull snap and they let him fall to the floor.

McManus started trudging up the stairs, imitating the

doorman's footfall. At the top, he saw the empty office and a door in the stud wall to his right. He had a gun in his right hand by now and, without missing a beat, he ducked to waist height and went through the door at pace, flinging himself on the floor, while Dowd moved across to the stud wall, also with his gun drawn.

A bullet came through the doorway at waist height and went through the arched window and into the grey beyond. McManus pointed his gun up from the floor and shot Kevin in the shoulder so that he dropped his gun. Dowd knelt, swivelled into the doorway and, holding the gun out with both hands, put a further two bullets into Kevin, who'd been thrown back into the corner. The first hit him in the cheekbone, the other in the lung.

Pike was unmissable. A cubic metre of target with ENGLAND emblazoned across it. In his moment of terrible fright, the tortilla chips went everywhere. Kevin slid to the floor and in the ringing silence, they could hear the blood bubbling in his lung and throat. McManus got to his feet, checked Kevin for life, found some and shot him again in the head with his silenced gun. Dowd went to Pike, who was covered in tortilla chips, with a smear of guacamole down his front. He asked him what had happened in the refrigeration unit. Pike told him what he'd heard.

'And where are the bodies from the warehouse?' he asked.

Pike swallowed hard; his goitrous neck shook.

'Downstairs in the freezers.'

McManus moved Dowd aside and shot Pike twice in the chest, once in the head.

'I'm stuck in traffic,' said Fox. 'I've had the operations room patch the recording of the call through to me.'

'He's missed his deadline by a couple of hours,' said Boxer, alone in the room. 'I'm worried now. I thought this would be our big opportunity. I think somebody's got to them. Where's DCS Makepeace?'

'I left him at Thames House. We'd just got to the end of a briefing on Frank. I wanted to get back to the Ops room.'

'According to Mercy, the Met are going to go public with these two as soon as they've traced some photos.'

'Have they got confirmed identities beyond Skin and Dan?'

'Mercy tells me they're ninety per cent certain that Skin is called William Skates. He's been inside, got a long record, shaved head, blue eyes and, most important, he has a spiderweb tattoo. They just want to confirm that his DNA matches the blood sample they found in the Grange Road house. It might take a few hours. They could make the early evening news with him. The second one, Dan, is more of a problem. At the moment they're assuming he's got some sort of history, so they're pulling all records of all male nurses who've done time. So far there have been no Dans. Now they're looking to see if there have been any male nurses who've done time in the same prisons as William Skates, or any other gang members belonging to Archibald Pike's crew.'

'Have you got a strategy for the next call?'

'It's all worked out. I want to move hard and fast on this one. When/if he calls, I'm going to get Isabel to do the deal.'

'You said they're at five million at the moment.'

'Believe me, with all the forces ranged against him, he'll accept a hundred grand and kiss me on both cheeks,' said Boxer.

'Have you had the OK from D'Cruz?'

'He says he's on his way. I've asked him what funds he can access now and he's confirmed that a hundred grand is feasible and he'll bring it with him.'

'Our concern is still for Alyshia,' said Fox. 'Do you know who you're talking to out of the two men?'

'The audio team did some work on the phone call and confirmed that it was made outside with people walking past. They can hear wind in trees, which means a park. So it looks as if one of them leaves to make the call, distant from where they're keeping Alyshia. He's either paranoid about the call being traced, or there's no network, which seems unlikely if they're in London. Our caller is not a Londoner. His accent is middle class, Estuary English. What we know about William Skates is that he's Stepney born and bred, so we're pretty sure we're talking to Dan, the nurse.'

'If Skates is left with the girl, what do we know about him?' asked Fox. 'Is he volatile? Is he likely to harm or kill her if he comes under pressure?'

'He's got a long record of violence, starting with football

hooliganism in the 1980s and stabbing one of his teachers. He's done time for GBH. But there's no record of any violence against women and no sexual offences. I'm still waiting on a fuller profile from Mercy.'

'OK, we'll assess that risk when we've got the additional information,' said Fox. 'Tell me how you're going to handle Dan in the next call.'

'I'll get Isabel to tell him what he probably already knows, that by taking over this kidnap, he's upset a lot of people. If we need more pressure, we'll tell him the police are on his tail too, but I don't want to give him the feeling there's no way out. I still want them thinking they can get away with it, so that they'll do the deal with us.'

'And you're going to do the ransom delivery?'

'That's my intention,' said Boxer, reading something else from Mercy as it came through on the computer. 'I've just heard that their transport ended up in a breaker's yard crusher this morning.'

'That means they're local and running out of options,' said Fox.

'Especially if they're expecting to tear off with five sports bags with a million apiece, each weighing in at 50 kilos,' said Boxer. 'A hundred grand is going to look very nice and portable now.'

22

Amir Jat arrived in the busy Sheikh Rashid Terminal with hand luggage only. A driver took him to a house on 14A Street in the Al Waheda district, close to the airport. They did not speak.

'We don't have much time before your next flight,' said Jat's agent, serving him a glass of boiled water. 'Mahmood Aziz has asked me to confirm to you that none of the major groups within the al-Qaeda network are carrying out operations of any kind in central London.'

'What about splinter groups, or unknown opportunists trying to get al-Qaeda recognition?'

'That's more difficult to ascertain. He's working on it and he hopes to have some more information for you by the time you arrive in Paris.'

'You must tell him that the kidnappers have issued no financial demand. They have only asked for "a demonstration of sincerity".'

'What does that mean?'

'That's the point,' said Jat. 'Nobody knows.'

'All right, I'll do that,' said the agent. 'In the meantime, here are your directions from Mahmood Aziz for the contact he promised you in London. You are to make your way to the Al Hira Educational Centre on Plashet Road in the London Borough of Newham. The nearest tube station is Upton Park. At the centre, you should ask for Saleem Cheema.'

'What if it's closed before I get there?'

270

'You mean, you want to take action immediately?'

'It might already be too late,' said Jat. 'You must tell Mahmood Aziz that his group in London have to start looking *now*.'

'What for exactly?'

'Anything they can find out about the kidnap of Frank D'Cruz's daughter, Alyshia,' said Jat, frustrated by everyone's apparent indifference. 'They have to find out where she is being held and be prepared to take action. By that I mean, take over the kidnap.'

'What further information do you have for this group to act on?'

'None.'

'I've checked all the news channels about the kidnap,' said the agent. 'And there's nothing. They must have a news black-out in place.'

'Mahmood Aziz assured me that this group was fully capable.'

The agent looked a little uncertain. He had no idea of their capability but he knew, like everyone else, that London was a huge city and for any group to find someone hidden in it, with scant information, an impossible task. He was also aware that this was not something to be discussed with Amir Jat. He gave orders and they were followed.

'I will get that message to him,' he said.

'I need a number to call Saleem Cheema when I arrive in London,' said Jat, taking out a UK mobile phone.

The agent gave him the number and handed Jat a German passport. Jat checked that it had a valid entry stamp for Dubai and studied the photo. He went in to the bathroom where a set of clothes was laid out for him. He removed his *sherwani*, *shalwar kameez* and white *taqiyah* and put them in a black plastic bag. He shaved off his beard and changed his hair style to match the passport shot. He dressed in the black trousers, white shirt and black V-necked sweater provided. On his way out, the agent gave him a sports jacket, a wool coat and an airline ticket in the same name as his new passport.

By 1.45 p.m. the driver was taking him back to the airport, and at 2.00 p.m. he checked in, still with hand luggage only, for his flight from Dubai to Paris.

*

Dan couldn't remember a time when he'd been so paranoid. Even when he knew he was going to be busted for stealing drugs from the hospital, he hadn't been as scared as he was now. It wasn't the thought of death that frightened him. Death itself would be a fine thing and he'd seen enough of it in his time as a nurse to no longer fear it. What terrified him was the thought of how he would arrive at that death. Being caught and then in whose hands would he be? He'd never been present at one of Kevin's sessions, but he'd heard about them and he'd been inside the specially sound-proofed room Kevin had in the basement of the St James Road warehouse. There was something a little homo-erotic about Kevin's tastes that made Dan suspicious of what he got up to in his spare time.

Then there was the police. Just the thought of the whole process of being arrested, taken down to the station, interrogated again and again until they'd heard and seen the story from every angle, made him feel exhausted. Then there was the trial, the sentencing and back to HMP Wherever, with all its power struggles, infighting, drugs, pettiness, violence, relationships and crap food. And this time it would be for life: at least twenty years.

The two possibilities made his guts sweat that horrible, cold black ooze that filled the peritoneum with dread.

A couple of black kids were playing footy behind blue railings, in front of a long block of council flats at the end of Branch Place. He envied their unconscious joy at the heroic dribbles and rifling shots. He crossed the bridge on Bridport Place and dropped down onto the towpath on the north side of the canal. He walked fast past endless new developments of smart residential flats in glass and steel – the City workers bulldozing their way across the East End through Dalston and De Beauvoir Town. He felt safer off the streets. No one was walking along the canal in this cold.

He came up off the tow path just before the thousand-yard-long Islington Tunnel, headed down Duncan Street, and turned left into Angel tube station.

He'd been going to head west but now, in a moment of inspiration, decided to go up to Hampstead. He would make the call from the heath. It would relax him. He'd be on his home turf, having done his training at the Royal Free Hospital.

The lift regurgitated him out of the Hampstead bowels in more or less the same state as he'd gone in. A bitter wind was blowing down the high street and here there was a totally different class of Londoner, leaving an upmarket bakery with their wholemeal bread and boxed cheesecake. He ducked down the narrow lane of Flask Walk, past the pub. Wouldn't have minded a pint of Young's to give him courage. In fact, what the hell? He went up to the bar, ordered a Bushmills and a pint of bitter. He sunk the whisky and sucked down half the pint. This had been a good idea. His nerve started to creep back. He ordered another Bushmills, threw it down followed by the other half of bitter. He now felt as if he had a whole platoon of mates with him and they were going to take on all-comers, and win.

It was 4.00 p.m. by the time he crossed East Heath Road and headed down the tree-lined path onto the heath. Here there were people, insulated by big, puffy, quilted coats, walking their dogs. A muscly Jack Russell in a red woolly jacket trotted jauntily past him, while a heavy black lab staggered ponderously behind its owner, who was in no better condition. Two women joggers with pony tails and legs reddened by the cold huffed past, the one telling the other how kundalini yoga was changing her life.

How had he got himself into this state? Why wasn't he still a nurse, heading for a new shift and the certainty of doing good, and pay day with pints in the hospital bar with the lads? Putting a bullet into the back of the cabbie's head flashed sharp in his mind. His father, a postman, had told him at sixteen years old, after a run-in with the police: always resist the temptation to take the first step down, because that will give you your momentum.

That first step down had been stealing drugs to make a bit of money, and now he'd killed two people. But why? He looked up into the cathedral roof of bare branches above his head. He'd asked to work with Skin. That was it. And, by then, he knew what Skin was about. There was something in him that had been inexorably drawn to Skin's aura of indestructability.

Maybe he should call it all off. Disappear into a new life. He had that bit of money from the cabbie, two grand as he stood now. That would fly him somewhere else, away from the madness.

But he didn't stop and turn. It seemed to have been established somewhere that he was going to make this call to Isabel Marks and he was powerless to arrest the momentum of fate, even though it seemed to have disaster written all over it. As he arrived at the park bench on Parliament Hill, overlooking the city lights thrown out across the horizon, glinting in the gun-metal blue-grey of the finishing day, the setting sun dipped below the cloud cover and shed a pink-orange light across the city. In the east, on Canary Wharf, the skyscraper of One Canada Square picked it up in its glass frontage and stood there like a vertical gold ingot, saying: 'I'm yours, claim me.'

Possibly it was that inspirational sight, plus the two Bushmills and the pint of Young's, that jogged Dan's elbow. He sat down on the bench and made the call.

'Isabel Marks?' he said confidently. 'I just wanted to tell you that your daughter is not only alive and well, but in very good health, given the strain she's been under.'

'I'm so glad you've called,' said Isabel. 'I've been worried sick. I couldn't think what had happened. You're more then five hours past your last deadline. Has there been a problem, Dan?'

'What did you say?'

'Dan. You *are* Dan? The nurse?' said Isabel. 'I'm so relieved my daughter is in the professional and caring hands of an NHS nurse.'

Silence. The confidence trembled in his guts. He could feel its inclination to dissipate like a bad dose of diarrhoea. He clasped his right side with his left hand as if this might keep him psychologically together.

'Did you get the money?' he asked.

'We haven't been able to raise five million pounds, even with the extra time you've given us. I told you that was going to be difficult. My ex-husband thinks that would take another five working days to put that sort of cash together.'

'What have you got now?'

'So far we have eighty thousand pounds.'

'You know what that means, don't you?'

'We're doing everything we can, but, you know … banks.'

'That means you're four million nine hundred and twenty thousand short.'

'At the moment. We just need more time,' said Isabel. 'But I suppose you're not in a position where you can wait, are you?'

'I'll tell you what I *can* do that might make the process move on a little quicker,' said Dan, the pressure bringing out some nastiness in him. 'Something that might encourage your ex-husband to be a little more demanding when he goes to see the manager of his extensive funds.'

'Tell me.'

'Give me your address.'

'Why?'

'I want to send you something.'

She gave the address.

'How are you going to send it?' she asked. 'I mean, the mail these days. We're not going to get that before Thursday, and if you courier it, you're going to expose yourself to all sorts of dangers.'

Dan couldn't get over how rock-solid she was. Nothing was getting through to her. He felt a tremendous desire to slap her down. Could just imagine her as the sort of person who'd come out of that stupid bakery with a fucking box of cake in her hands.

'You don't seem to be interested in what I'm going to send you to help you speed up this business of getting the money together to save your fucking *daughter*?'

'*I* don't need *any* motivation to speed up the process. Nor does my ex-husband,' she said, gabbling with fear now, not wanting to know under any circumstances what he was going to send her. 'It's just that he doesn't have liquid funds in the UK at the moment. He has to sell assets and he has to find buyers for them, which isn't always easy. Once they're sold, the money has to be transferred. That takes three working days in this country. When the funds are available, they have to be made into actual cash, the used twenties you've asked for, not just numbers on a computer screen. That means that Securicor vans have to go all over London picking up the money and bringing them to a central location. Each time the cash goes from one place to another, it has to be processed. That means counted and verified. That's not going to happen before the weekend. So, you see, it's not me dragging my feet. I want my daughter back more than anything else in the world. It's just that the world of finance doesn't move at the same speed as my maternal longings, or your needs.'

'But,' said Dan, enraged by her uninterruptible gibbering, 'if I sent you her finger in the post, or I arranged for it to be dropped at your house, not her little finger, but the index finger of her right hand. I mean, it wouldn't be an act of butchery. I know how to do these things. I've been a theatre nurse. I would give her a local anaesthetic, cut it off at the knuckle neatly and I'd cauterise the wound and give her antibiotics. Do you think that might just persuade your husband to go to his bank and say, I have to BORROW this fucking money NOW?'

Dan cut the line. He had no idea if they had the ability to track him, but he wasn't taking risks. Now he'd let her stew for a bit, calm himself down, too, and then see if he couldn't squeeze a bit more out of her than eighty measly grand.

'Listen to you,' he said, out loud. 'Eighty fucking grand. That's better than the poxy shit you were getting for selling your prescription drugs. The hundred quid here and there that you did three years for in Wandsworth. Thank fuck for Bushmills.'

He jumped to his feet with both arms raised as if he'd won something. There was nobody on the heath, only the ravens crashing through the darkening sky on their way to some rooky wood. His face was hot, even in the bitter wind, and his fingers fumbled numbly with the mobile as he changed the SIM card, chucked the old one in a bin nearby. He breathed back the stress, looking out over the city once more. The gold ingot on Canary Wharf had disappeared. Night was falling and it made him feel bolder. He wiped tears from the corners of his eyes and clenched his fist, punched the air as if he was delivering killer blows to someone who was already down.

'That was brilliant,' said Boxer. 'Absolutely perfect. I'm proud of you.'

Isabel said nothing. She was lying back on the sofa, totally spent. Her stomach muscles had gone into a strange spasm, as if her emotional state, with no vocal outlet, had chosen to erupt from her quivering guts.

'I'm done,' she said. 'I'm completely wiped out.'

'No, you're not. You've only just started. He's going to call back. In minutes. I promise you. And you're going to show him how strong you are. Again. No backing down. You can give him the next twenty grand if you want to. Just remember: he's desperate. He might sound bold but we know the time pressure he's under. I think he might be a little drunk, too. There was a thickness to his voice that wasn't there before. Now sit up, Isabel.'

She sat up straight, looked him in the eye.

'Where is fucking Chico?' she said murderously.

'Exactly, that's more like it. I'll call him.'

Boxer tried D'Cruz's mobile: not available, left a message. He sent a text, too. WE NEED YOU HERE WITH THE MONEY NOW!

Isabel sobbed quietly to herself, hands holding her forehead, occasionally blurting great hunks of emotion that came out as if she were choking on them. He held her by her shoulders at arms' length.

'There isn't a chance in hell that he'll carry out his threats. He's built himself up to be bold and aggressive, but it is not in his nature.'

'You said he'd killed somebody already. I saw the draft press release. They've both killed people.'

'They've killed other criminals, under orders from Archibald Pike. You don't know the circumstances. He might have felt he *had* to do it, and he would have been under pressure from Skin, who's probably a different animal altogether,' said Boxer. 'There's a big difference to dealing with a hostage. First of all, you want a hostage alive in order to get your money. Second, in looking after your hostage, as Dan has told us he's been doing, you form a re-lationship, which means, third, carrying out your threats becomes more difficult and, anyway, takes time. You were brilliant to point out how he would expose himself by using a courier.'

'That's what you told me to say.'

'But you said it. You brought it into your spiel as if it was yours *and* under extreme duress,' said Boxer, releasing her shoulders, taking her hands in his. 'You're doing better than I could possibly have hoped.'

'I should have listened to you.'

'You did and you stepped up to the plate and delivered.'

'I mean, you were right. Somebody else should be doing this. It's too … too … visceral for me.'

'But you *are* doing it and you're going to finish it,' said Boxer, looking into her eyes. 'Remember, you're acting a part. It's a tough role, but you've found the resilience in yourself to carry it off. Take a grip of the iron bar of will in your middle and don't let this little shit, Dan, get the upper hand.'

The phone rang. Boxer gripped her hands to stop her from reaching out. He kissed them, let them go. She didn't leap for the phone.

'You can tell him about the other gangs and the police now if you feel you have to.'

She looked at the phone with practiced cool and let it ring twice more.

'Hello, Dan,' she said, staring into Boxer's eyes.

'I'm just limiting my call times in case you're tracking me.'

'We haven't got that sort of equipment here.'

'Yeah, I'm sure,' said Dan. 'Your husband must have a triple A credit rating with any number of banks. All he has to do is go and see the manager and arrange for a temporary loan until he can sell whatever he has to sell. I'm sure someone who's worth four and a half billion dollars has heard of that. I mean, I'm a penniless ex-nurse and *I've* heard of that.'

'He just called after you rang off. He's raised another twenty thousand and he's on his way here with it,' said Isabel. 'That's money he's taken from current accounts and borrowed from friends in London and it's the limit for what he can do tonight. I realise it's difficult for you to give us more time considering the pressure you're under.'

'Who said I was under any pressure?'

'I understand there are a lot of people looking for you at the moment. The East End gang you stole Alyshia from, and friends of the two men you shot in Grange Road. Somebody's also told me that you should take a look at the evening news. If not the six o'clock on BBC, then the seven o'clock on Channel Four, or maybe Sky News, at any time. What I'm offering you is one hundred thousand pounds right now. You tell me the place and I'll have a family friend deliver it to you. It could all be over in an hour or two if you'll accept—'

'Don't worry about us, Mrs Marks. We're *very* safe. Your daughter is in a place where nobody, not even the London rat population, could hear her scream. So don't go concerning yourself that we might be found by anyone,' said Dan.

'Wait,' she said, but he'd already gone.

Boxer was relieved that Dan had hung up. He could feel Isabel edging towards cracking point. One more exchange and she might have fallen. Now she lay on her side, facing into the sofa, shoulders heaving. Boxer called Fox. The calls were being automatically transferred to the Ops room.

'You sound tense,' said Boxer. 'I thought I was the one who was supposed to be tense.'

'You're not here,' said Fox quietly.

Boxer heard his breathing and footsteps as he moved away from other voices in the background.

'Problem?' he asked.

'DCS Makepeace has just done what he wanted to do from the outset. He's taken over the kidnap. He says the circumstances have changed and that this is now a SCD7 operation. I've just had the Commissioner of the Met on the line to confirm it to me. They still want you involved, but you're no longer the official consultant on this case.'

'Even though we're in the endgame here?' said Boxer. 'You've heard the latest exchanges?'

'Even though.'

'And you won't be able to use Mercy as Isabel doesn't know she's with the police, so the DCS will have to brief a completely new consultant from scratch.'

'They're doing it as we speak.'

'What's the protocol for this?' said Boxer. 'I mean, do I tell Isabel Marks? Do I just walk away? DCS Makepeace better give me some guidelines.'

'He will, Charlie,' said Fox. 'But how do you feel about playing second fiddle?'

'I'll do it for Isabel Marks' sake. I'm not going to leave a client in the lurch like that. I'll do whatever's asked of me,' said Boxer. 'How she'll take it is a different matter. I haven't just been the consultant here, as you know. I've been everything.'

'Well, perhaps she could appoint you as her Crisis Management Committee,' said Fox. 'That might resolve things very nicely.'

23

'What we have to do,' said Saleem Cheema, 'and this is from the highest level from our brothers in Pakistan, is find where the kidnappers of Alyshia D'Cruz are holding her.'

He sat back in the ensuing silence and sipped sweet tea flavoured with cardamom. He was in his late twenties, slim, wearing a cream crocheted cap and stroking a wispy beard.

He'd called this council meeting in the workshop at the back of the Pride of Indus restaurant. The room was spotless. White paper overalls hung on coat hangers on a rail, electronic laboratory scales were lined up on one of the work surfaces, boxes of plastic bags were stacked in the corner. On the shelves were jars of white powders, labelled: caffeine, chloroquine, paracetamol and phenolphthalein. This was where two hundred kilos of heroin was cut, mixed, weighed, bagged and sent out to dealers all over the East End of London every month.

The council was not an organised group, neither was it part of, nor did it have any affiliation to, any underground jihadist cell, although all the members were supportive of al-Qaeda's aims. They saw heroin dealing as a way of undermining the Christian West and delivering funds to deserving causes back in Pakistan and to the poverty-stricken farmers of Afghanistan. None of them had been trained in any military activity, although this did not mean they were strangers to violence or weapons. Two of them had shot people, but this had been out of necessity to protect their patch against the local white gangs, who carried names like

Beckton Man Dem or the JC Boyz, and not out of any religious fervour.

'That's it?' said one of the young men. 'You want us to find these kidnappers, in a city of eight million people, with just the victim's name?'

'Who's to say they're in London?' asked another.

'The population of Greater London, including the suburbs, is probably more like *twelve* million.'

'But who's to say they're *in* London?'

'I am just telling you the instructions we've received from our Muslim brothers in Pakistan,' said Cheema. 'This is urgent. It is our duty, even with so little information, to find these people. I want ideas. That means positive thinking.'

There was a precise series of knocks at the door. Cheema jerked his head back and one of the junior members left the table to let in the latecomer, who took his seat. His neighbour briefed him while the others sat in silence.

'I think I can help you with that,' said the latecomer, who was a quiet, shy man with a squarish head, hair shaved up the back and sides with the top gelled into sharp spikes. He was in his early twenties and his name was Hakim Tarar.

All heads turned to Tarar, who rarely said anything in these meetings.

'Tell us, Hakim. Nobody else has had any ideas.'

'As you know, I live in Bethnal and train as a boxer at the Repton Boys Club,' said Tarar. 'My sparring partner is a local boy, English. He was telling me the latest in the changing room after our workout. Bethnal Green and Stepney are being turned upside down because a couple of gangs are looking for two men who've stolen a girl.'

'Which gangs?'

'White gangs. Old style. Nobody we know.'

'Stolen a girl?'

'What does that mean? Is this a sex thing?'

'He wasn't sure. He thought it was something to do with a shooting, or a kidnap. He didn't have the story quite straight, but there was the police in it, as well,' said Tarar. 'And there's been a lot of plain clothes guys around. It's true: I've seen them. I thought it was a drug sweep, but they're all after the same two guys.'

'This shooting? Is that the one they're all talking about in Grange Road?' asked one of the other members. 'They were talking about that on the radio.'

'Have we got any names?' asked Cheema.

'The only name I've got is of one of the gang leaders,' said Tarar. 'Someone called Joe Shearing, who does a lot of work at the Repton Boys Club. I know him because he brought some kids over from Pakistan after the floods in 2010.'

'Get back to your sparring partner, or maybe Joe Shearing himself, if you know him well enough,' said Cheema. 'Get some names. Let's listen to all the local and national news. If the police are involved, they might go countrywide asking for information. We need photos, we need addresses. And fast. Anybody gets any information, I don't want you to talk about it on your mobiles, even your throwaway ones. You send me a text with this week's code and I'll make sure I am by my landline at home. Everything else stops until we've found this girl.'

Dan was in the back room of the Flask pub in Hampstead for the six o'clock news. He was pursuing his successful strategy of Bushmills and Young's and sitting in one of the quieter back rooms. The news passed without incident.

'Bullshitters,' he said to himself. 'Fucking bullshitters.'

A meanness tempered inside him at the thought that they were stringing him along. They had the money, maybe not five million, but a fuck sight more than a hundred grand. The address she'd given him was in Kensington. Let the rich bitch sweat. That's what he was going to tell Skin.

His knees creaked as he got up from the table. His whole body ached from having been out in the cold on the heath that afternoon. The beer and whisky had done something to his muscles, and had left his brain feeling slapped about. He came out of Flask Walk, turned down the high street away from the tube station. Thought he remembered an Indian down the hill where he could get something to eat. He glanced into upmarket clothes shops, peopled by women for whom money didn't seem to be a consideration.

The Shahbagh Tandoori was more his level. He ordered some chicken, rice and a vegetable curry with a pint of lager. He wasn't quite admitting it to himself but he was enjoying this freedom. There was a large part of him that didn't want to go back to Skin and Alyshia in the Colville Hyatt.

After a long pee in the Shahbagh toilet, he came out into the same icy wind blowing up Rosslyn Hill. He drifted down towards Belsize Park tube, even though it was a longer walk, but it would take him past the Royal Free Hospital. He even entertained the notion of going in there, looking up some old mates, take them out for a drink, tell them about his new life, of killing and kidnap.

It was gone seven o'clock when he pulled up unsteadily in front of the exclusive electronic goods shop of Bang & Olufsen on Rosslyn Hill. Jon Snow was talking silently to the shop window on the Channel 4 news from a television priced at £6,000. Abruptly the image changed to a young woman, who seemed to be giving a different type of news. Then he was looking at a picture of himself with the name Gareth Wheeler underneath, aka 'Dan', and next to him a shot of someone called William Skates, aka 'Skin'.

A couple joined him at the window. They, too, stared at the television and, after a moment, the guy leaned across to him slowly and said out the corner of his mouth: 'I think we'll be going to Dixons in Brent Cross.'

The new consultant sent from Specialist Crime Directorate 7 introduced himself at the front door.

'I'm Rick Barnes, from the Met Kidnap Unit,' he said.

Boxer shook hands, took his coat.

'We've met before,' said Barnes.

'Have we?'

'In the pub, with Mercy.'

'Don't mention Mercy being a cop to Isabel,' said Boxer, who remembered him now. He'd taken a fancy to Mercy and she'd asked Boxer along to make sure it didn't go anywhere.

He led Barnes through to meet Isabel, who wasn't interested in him, her mind too full of the afternoon's phone calls to fit another person in. Barnes sat opposite her. He had dark, short hair, thinning on top, blue eyes, sharp cheekbones and a thin-lipped mouth. He was lean and hard, as if he trained a great deal. He was dressed in a grey jacket, red tie and white shirt. He leaned slightly as if he was about to suddenly leap forward and hurdle Isabel and several pieces of furniture around the room. His intensity filled the air, crowded Isabel out of her own home. Boxer started to brief him on the afternoon's developments.

'If you don't mind,' said Barnes. 'I'd rather hear this from Ms Marks.'

'I've just appointed Charles as my Crisis Management Committee,' said Isabel. 'He will brief you on everything you need to know.'

Barnes took a long, hard look at Boxer and remembered how much he disliked him. The feeling was mutual. Five minutes into the briefing, Isabel cut in.

'Why hasn't he called?' she said. 'It's been more than an hour since his last call. You said he would get back to me in—'

'He seemed a bit drunk,' said Boxer.

'How did that manifest itself?' asked Barnes.

'This morning he was nervous and tentative, said he was going to call us back in two hours' time, which turned into something like seven, and he was considerably bolder, with a thickness to his voice,' said Boxer. 'You've heard the recordings?'

'But why hasn't he called back?' asked Isabel.

'By now he will have seen the Channel Four news. He's paranoid about using mobile phones. I think he's going back to where they're holding Alyshia to talk to his partner. Because he's had a few drinks and is on his way down from a high after securing a hundred thousand pounds from us, he might have lost some of his focus.'

'He threatened to send me her finger.'

'That was just the frustration talking.'

'And where the FUCK is Chico?!' shouted Isabel, hammering the glass table top with both fists.

'That's the ex-husband, Frank D'Cruz.'

'I *have* been briefed,' said Barnes.

'I presume Martin Fox is no longer the director of operations,' said Boxer. 'Can your boss find Frank D'Cruz? He's supposed to be bringing us the money, so …'

'They're working on it,' said Barnes, not enjoying this situation, having his professionalism picked over by a fellow consultant. 'Are you going to be the delivery boy?'

'Isabel Marks has entrusted me with that task,' said Boxer, ignoring the slight.

Saleem Cheema came out of his armchair like a rocket when he saw the Channel 4 news. He went straight to his computer, found the shots on a news website and printed them off.

He sent a text to Hakim Tarar with the code. Five minutes later, Tarar called.

'Did you see the piece on Channel Four?' asked Cheema.

'I saw it.'

'Do you know either of those guys?'

'No. Should I?'

'They're from your part of town: Stepney, Bethnal Green.'

'They're not anybody I've ever dealt with.'

'One of them used to be a nurse. Gareth Wheeler, aka "Dan". He got struck off for stealing drugs, selling them in clubs, did some time in Wandsworth.'

'OK. I'll ask around, see if he's in the business. But I don't think he's in my area. I know them all, even the ones who don't deal our stuff.'

'Start checking in other areas: Haggerston, Hoxton, Shoreditch, Dalston. The police think they're still local. They had their van crushed in a Bethnal Green breaker's yard.'

'They both did time,' said Tarar, 'so there's a chance they're users rather than dealers.'

'If you need to, you can make some promotional offers: buy two get one free. That sort of thing might help jog your dealers' memories.'

'You're making this sound really important.'

'I've been told it is, but I don't know why.'

Dan bought a torch and came in the way he'd gone out, down the canal, except that he carried on a bit further and came out on the other side of the tower blocks of the Colville Estate. The wind was bitterly cold and whipped up the rubbish in the street, sending it flashing across the road, where a paper plastered itself against a set of railings. Dan lunged at it, peeled it away, took a while to get it into focus. It was a police flyer with shots of Skin and himself, face on and in profile. Skin's tattoo was unmissable. He stuffed it in his pocket, trotted through the estate and into Branch Place, let himself in through the double doors and sprinted up the stairs to the flat.

Outside the flat door he calmed himself and eased the key in silently. He heard voices as he closed the door, walked down the corridor, veered off into the living room, put on a hood and listened outside the bedroom door.

They were laughing.

He pushed the door open.

Skin had no hood on. He was lying on the bed with Alyshia, both of them smoking weed.

'It's the masked man,' said Skin. 'Fancy a toke?'

'What the fuck's going on here?'

Skin looked around, as if to check on unusual disturbances that had escaped his notice.

'Not a lot.'

'Why aren't you wearing your hood?'

'Too fucking hot.'

'Surprised you didn't send her down to the shops for a take-away.'

'Not when there's all those ready-cooked meals you bought.'

Dan saw the two empty plates on the floor by the bed, four fag ends and a dark, oily weed butt stubbed out in the remnants of a white sauce. Two cans of Stella.

'If she had gone, she could have bought one of these back for you to look at,' said Dan, throwing the balled-up flyer at him.

'No need to get the hump,' said Skin. 'Have a toke of this mate and ... chill.'

Skin picked open the ball of paper, smoothed it out on his chest and stretched it out over their heads.

'Gareth Wheeler?' he said. 'What's the Dan shit all about?'

'One of the old lifers I was treating inside said I looked like Dan Dare and it stuck. And I hate being called Garry.'

'Who's Dan Dare?' asked Alyshia.

'Before your time,' said Skin. 'Before mine 'n' all.'

'Why are you still wearing your hood?' asked Alyshia. 'Now that we all know you're really Dan Dare.'

'Sounds like Cockney rhyming slang,' said Skin. 'I'm feeling a bit Dan Dare.'

'Let's talk,' said Dan, tearing off his hood.

Skin hopped over Alyshia. They went into the other room.

'You've been gone for fucking hours,' said Skin. 'And I can tell you've had a few. So what's the game? My turn to step up, yet?'

'The family know we're in trouble,' said Dan. 'They know Pike's gang and the cabbie's lot are looking for us. *And* the police. We made it on to Channel Four. So ... we're fucked.'

'You're telling me you've been out all this time and you haven't even come back with an offer?'

'Oh no, I've had an offer.'

'Is it more than the fiver I said I'd take?'

'It's a hundred grand.'

'Fuck me,' said Skin, hitting him on the shoulder. 'That's fifty grand. That's fifty grand more than I had this morning. What you looking so sick for? Get back there and accept it. We can't move with her, and we've got to get out of here, so we take what they're offering and leg it. You didn't seriously think we were going to get a million each, did you?'

'You're high.'

'Not so high that I don't know the difference between fifty grand and fuck all,' said Skin. 'Where are we going to get them to do the drop?'

'I've been thinking about that,' said Dan. 'You don't want to be seen on the street, looking like you do, so you stick to the canal.'

'Small problem,' said Skin. 'No boat.'

'You want to go down there on a boat you might get to Limehouse Basin by the weekend. There's about ten locks to get through,' said Dan. 'You're going to walk it.'

'How far?'

'About three and a half, four miles.'

'That's an hour.'

'You got anything else to do, apart from your duties as page boy to the court of Princess Alyshia?'

'I'm just saying, it'll take me an hour. We need to build that into our timings.'

'All right, sorry. I'm just a bit stressed, with London on red alert for our arses.'

'Take a hit,' said Skin, handing him the last dark inch of spliff. 'What's the worst that can happen?'

Dan took a huge toke, held it in until he squeaked and his eyes filled and streamed. The drug slipped into his blood and suddenly he didn't feel hounded anymore.

'The worst that can happen,' said Dan cheerfully, 'is that we die horribly long, tortuous deaths in the hands of one London gang or another.'

'I'll shoot you before it comes to that,' said Skin. 'Promise.'

'That's a very fine thing for you to say, Skin,' said Dan. 'You're a true friend.'

'Don't mention it,' said Skin. 'Tell us about the drop.'

'Limehouse Basin is like a marina surrounded by blocks of fancy flats, full of people who work in Canary Wharf and take home more in their bonuses than we're going to get for putting our lives on the line for this fucking kidnap.'

'Let's get to the detail, Garry.'

'Don't fucking Garry me, Mister Skates.'

He showed Skin the route down to the Limehouse Basin on the A-Z guide, talked him through the details.

'How do you know all this shit?'

'I go walking. I've been up and down this canal a hundred times.'

'You're a sad fucking case, you know that?'

'But now, finally, my sadness pays off,' said Dan. 'I'll get Alyshia's mother to drive her car down to the Basin and leave it under the arches of the DLR with the money in the boot. You should be able to see it from the tunnel under Commercial Road, which means you'll be able to see her leave the car and walk away. I'll get her to go back up the slip road and wait by the DLR station. You pick up the money and, either go back up the canal, onto Commercial Road, or around the blocks of flats, down to Narrow Street. From there you can walk along the Thames towards Shadwell, or the other way to Canary Wharf. You could get the DLR back to Bank from there, catch the tube to Angel and back here down the canal.'

'Why the fuck would I want to come back here?'

Silence.

'Kiss the princess goodbye?'

'You're drunk and stoned,' said Skin. 'As soon as I've got the money and checked it, I'll call you. You call the mother, tell her the address, release her and get out.'

'Where shall we meet?'

More silence.

'That's good,' said Skin. 'We've got nowhere to go.'

'Out of London.'

'What time are we going to do the drop?'

'Midnight?' said Dan. 'There won't be any DLR or tube, so we'll be on night buses.'

'Fucking ridiculous,' said Skin. 'We're not making our getaway with fifty grand a piece on the fucking night buses. No fucking way. I'll steal a car.'

'You can steal cars?'

'I was brought up on twocking and ram-raiding.'

'Twocking?'

'And finally, I've found something you don't fucking know,' said Skin. 'Taking Without Consent. Joyriding, to you.'

'When did you last do that?'

'It's a kid's crime. Twenty years ago.'

'Things have moved on in the car alarm business since then.'

'So you don't want me to nick a transit, it's got to be a Porsche fucking Cayenne now, has it?'

24

'I'm sorry about the death of your friend,' said Chhota Tambe, sitting at the vast desk in his house overlooking Regent's Park, smoking a Wills Insignia cigarette and indicating a chair to the American, who was dressed in black jeans and a fleece-lined flying jacket.

'Quiddhy knew the risks of the business we were in,' said Dowd, who'd been drawn here by the promise of money, his eyes not leaving the cash in neat blocks in front of the Indian.

'And you've found a satisfactory way of dealing with the bodies?' said Tambe, brushing ash from his blue pin-stripe bespoke suit, which he believed made him look at least two inches taller than his four foot ten.

'McManus had some Irish contact from way back. He's taken care of them for us,' said Dowd, who showed him a photograph he'd taken of the two dead men on his mobile phone. Chhota Tambe grimaced.

There was calculation in showing Tambe the bodies. Dowd wanted him to know he deserved his money. He refused an offered cigarette and smirked at Tambe's tie with its bands of orange, lime green, gold lamé and pink, which diminished him, if not in stature, then in the eyes of his tailor.

'And where's McManus now?' asked Tambe, sitting back in his gilt-edged velour chair, finger and thumb plastering his pencil moustache over and again, out to the corners of his mouth.

'He left town,' said Dowd.

'And where will you go now?' asked Tambe blandly, glancing over Dowd's head at the wall beyond, inwardly seething with a torrential rage.

'I thought I'd lose myself for a few months before heading back to Dubai.'

On the wall behind Dowd, in a huge gilt-frame, was a portrait painted from a photograph of Tambe's elder brother Bada Tambe – Big Tambe. There was no family likeness. Big Tambe had been everything his younger brother wasn't: tall, good-looking and charismatic. It was this portrait of his elder brother, which was replicated in Chhota Tambe's houses in Dubai and Mumbai, that had been his mind's focus for nearly twenty years. He'd loved his big brother and he could still feel the stab of grief as fresh as the day when he was told that Bada Tambe had died back in 1993.

However, there was one other person who had occupied Chhota Tambe's thoughts besides his elder brother over the same period of time: Frank D'Cruz. With the same passion that Tambe had loved his brother, he hated Frank D'Cruz. It was one of the great balancing factors in his life.

'The girl?' said Tambe. 'You said the glass panel was shot out. But you're sure she survived.'

'There was no blood in the room where she was being kept.'

'The police are on their tails, you know: the ones who shot your friends,' said Tambe, straightening the cigarette packet, aligning it with the money, as he was a man of great order. 'It was on Sky news.'

'I'd better get going then,' said Dowd, standing.

'This is for you,' said Tambe, easing the block of money across the desk.

Dowd accepted it with a nod, put it in his holdall.

'My men will take you to wherever you want to go,' said Tambe, coming round the desk, no bigger standing than he was sitting. 'Can I suggest the Eurostar to Paris? It's the quickest way out of the country.'

Dowd shook the small, soft hand. The two heavyweights who'd been standing by the door took him down to the garage.

'You mind me asking a question?' said Dowd, as they stood

crammed into the small lift. 'How long's this been going on between your boss and Frank D'Cruz?'

The two heavies looked at each other, grinned, couldn't resist it.

'Depends who you're asking,' said one.

'I'm asking you,' said Dowd.

'We'd tell you it was on the day Sharmila left Chhota Tambe and went to work for Frank D'Cruz.'

'And what if,' said Dowd, thinking about it, 'I was to ask the man himself?'

'Then you'd get a very different story,' said the heavy.

They both laughed as the lift door opened. There were three cars in the garage. They went to a Range Rover, opened the back door for Dowd, who got in. The two heavyweights got in either side of him. No driver. He didn't know what it was at first, this strange pain in both sides that seemed to take his breath away. He looked from one man to the other. They were leaning in on his shoulders, pushing into his rib cage and he had the odd sensation of life draining away inside him.

Dan felt safer in the dark. He didn't need to travel so far afield now. He went down the canal as far as Broadway Market and walked the few hundred yards to London Fields, where he disappeared into the central darkness, sat on a bench and made his call.

'Hello, Dan,' said Isabel Marks, as if he'd made no threat to amputate her daughter's finger, nor that any protracted interlude at a vital moment of the negotiations had occurred. He was stunned by the strength in her voice, cowed by it.

'Good evening, Mrs Marks,' he said.

'I haven't been able to raise any more money,' she said. 'If you want more, you'll have to wait until tomorrow.'

'We're prepared to accept one hundred thousand pounds in cash, but it has to be tonight.'

He could hear the emotion clutch at her throat. It sounded as if she was about to say 'thank you' but couldn't get it out, or maybe she'd thought *fuck you* and had stopped herself from saying it just in time.

'I'm going to hand you over to a family friend,' she said. 'His name is Charles. He will deliver the ransom to you. You should work out the exact details with him.'

'No, no, no, no, no,' said Dan. '*You* will deliver the money.'

'I don't think I can do that on my own,' said Isabel. 'I might not sound it but I'm exhausted.'

'I'm not doing business with someone different at this stage,' said Dan. 'I trust you.'

'I can't do it on my own. I need help.'

'You have to be present in the car,' said Dan, and after some thought, 'I will accept one other person with you.'

'I would rather you sorted out the details with Charles. I don't want to get anything wrong,' said Isabel. 'He's a trusted friend of the family.'

'All right. Good night, Mrs Marks,' said Dan, suddenly feeling immensely sorry for what he'd put this woman through. 'Your daughter is very well and sends you her love. She has not been harmed by us in any way ... unlike the last lot.'

'Thank you, Dan. Here's Charles.'

'Hello, Dan,' said Boxer. 'We haven't had any proof of life from you since you first took Alyshia. We're going to need that before we hand over the money.'

'Five minutes before you make the drop we'll let Alyshia call her mother. She will confirm her physical well-being and then we'll proceed with the drop.'

'What time?'

'Midnight.'

'Why not before?'

'We need time.'

'Where do you want us to make the drop?'

'Give us your mobile phone number and make sure that you're parked outside the Rich Mix Cinema on Bethnal Green Road. Be there at eleven and I'll give you the directions to the drop site.'

'Where do you want me to keep the money in the car?'

'In the boot,' said Dan. 'And I'll want to know the make, model, colour and registration of the car you're going to use.'

'I don't have that.'

'Get it,' said Dan, and hung up.

293

He jogged around the bench for five minutes, trying to keep warm. He switched mobiles and called back.

'I'll be driving a silver VW Golf GTI, registration LF59 XPB,' said Boxer, who also gave the mobile number he would be using. 'Tell me how we're going to get Alyshia back safely.'

'I will stay with her. My partner will pick up the money. As soon as he's verified that you've given us the correct amount, he'll call me. I'll call you and give you the address where she's being held. I'll release Alyshia and leave her with a mobile, just in case.'

'Will you be asking us to leave the car somewhere with the money in the boot?'

'Yes. When I call you back with the address, you can reclaim your car. I will tell you where to wait in the meantime,' said Dan. 'I want you to wear white overalls too, so you can easily be seen. Both of you.'

'Can we have a phone number in case we need to contact you?'

'No,' said Dan, paranoid about the damn things, which he saw as nothing less than tracking devices. 'The money should be packed in ten bundles of £10,000 each. The bundles should be in a zip-up sports bag, soft, no hard casing. If any tracking device is found or any of that explosive dye shit, then Alyshia will not survive the night and you will never hear from us again.'

'Don't worry. It'll be clean.'

'No police,' said Dan. 'And nobody following you. If we get the slightest suspicion you've got others in tow, the deal is off. I'll ask you to drive around a bit so that we can check you've got no tail.'

'How much time will you need between receiving the money and telling us where Alyshia is being held?'

'A maximum of two hours, hopefully less.'

'I'd like an interim proof of life to be given at ten-thirty,' said Boxer.

'Like what?'

'You call us, we ask a question, you get the answer and call us back.'

'Why do you need that when her mother's going to talk to her an hour or so later?'

'It maintains a level of trust,' said Boxer. 'Your contact with us has been pretty erratic. Now we're getting to the crucial moment,

294

Isabel wants to be sure that you're absolutely serious.'

'We're serious,' said Dan. 'I'll call you at ten-thirty. That's it until then.'

Boxer hung up, looked at his watch: just gone 8.30 p.m. He turned to Rick Barnes.

'We've got two hours to find Frank D'Cruz, make sure the money is in order and in the required sports bag,' said Boxer. 'I'm going to pick up the Golf and get some white overalls from Pavis.'

'We can do that.'

'No offence, but I want to be sure that everything is clean.'

'He's bluffing, isn't he?' said Barnes. 'There's just the two of them. He referred to "my partner". They're not going to follow you on your route; they haven't got the manpower for it.'

'Does that mean you want to jeopardise the smooth handover of the hostage by trying to make an arrest at the same time?'

'These guys are wanted for murder.'

'How long do you think they're going to last out there?' asked Boxer. 'They're probably going to have to steal a car, or a number of cars, now that they've dumped their van. They've got two gangs, plus the Met, looking for them. There's been a national news alert. I'd give them maximum twenty-four hours' survival time, even if they do have a place to hole up.'

'We want information from them as quickly as possible on the original kidnap,' said Barnes. 'There are national security concerns.'

'Then nothing I say is going to make any difference,' said Boxer. 'These are decisions that will be made by your boss, and the people in Thames House. But my position is that I'd like to get Alyshia safe first. She might have the most important information of all, unless I've read it wrong and Skin and Dan aren't a couple of likely lads, but, in fact, highly professional operators.'

Barnes said nothing, called DCS Makepeace, told him about the offer and the drop details, asked about Frank D'Cruz. He listened and hung up. Boxer sat back, waiting for Barnes to give out.

'Frank D'Cruz was under MI5 surveillance,' said Barnes.

'I don't like your use of the past tense,' said Boxer.

'He hasn't been seen since four-thirty p.m.'

'And where *was* he last seen?' asked Isabel, hammering away at that past tense.

'He appeared to be doing some pre-launch checks for the electric cars he's going to manufacture in the Midlands. Giving talks, taking potential investors to the sites where the prototypes have just been unveiled.'

'Where's that?'

'There are two in the City, one outside the Royal Exchange, in front of the Bank of England, and the other in St Mary Axe, between the Gherkin and the Lloyd's Building. The other two are outside the main stadium at the Olympic site in Stratford.'

'Yes, he told me about this,' said Isabel. 'He wants to create awareness and bring potential investors on board. So what happened?'

'MI5 lost him somewhere between the City and Stratford,' said Barnes. 'Mr D'Cruz's limousine arrived but he wasn't in it and he hasn't been seen since. His mobile has been turned off and cannot be traced.'

'Was anybody in the car?'

'His UK personal advisor, a young Indian guy, who was wearing Frank's coat, and the woman who runs his residential property portfolio, Nicola Prideaux.'

'And the money he said he'd raised for the ransom?' asked Boxer.

'Neither of the two people in the car seemed to know anything about that,' said Barnes. 'The driver had seen him earlier with a briefcase, but not its contents.'

'What is he playing at?' said Isabel.

'Let's hope whatever it is, he's being very careful,' said Boxer. 'Given that someone's already tried to kill him.'

Hakim Tarar was working with his team of five people. He'd been methodical, starting in his own territory of Bethnal Green, then moving north to Haggerston and Dalston, then west to De Beauvoir Town and now south to Hoxton and Shoreditch. So far, only the dealers in Bethnal Green seemed to know anything about the two kidnappers wanted for murder, but that was because they were a cut above, supplying investment bankers and other City folk who'd moved out east. By the time Tarar got to them, they were edgy as hell after visits from the members of two gangs and feeling the heat of the police all over the area. Nobody else had seen the news, and remained largely unaware of the flyers scudding about in the cold night air.

The Muslim team was not happy. They knew they still had to go through their dealers in Spitalsfield, Whitechapel and Stepney before Tarar would let them off for the night. But Hoxton and Shoreditch was a big job. There were more heroin users amongst the young crowd of these two areas than in the four they'd just been through.

There were two dealers in the Colville Estate alone: Delroy Dread, the huge Jamaican, who catered to the black crowd, while MK supplied the whites. Tarar took Rahim with him, a six foot three hard man, whose family originated in Peshawar and who was used to carrying firearms and discharging them at people.

Tarar decided to see MK first, as Delroy Dread didn't have any white people among his close associates. He sent two of the other gang members to have a talk with the Jamaican, just to make sure.

MK lived off the estate in a sixties block. They went up to the third floor and knocked.

A white-faced kid with explosive hair opened the door, knew who they were just by the way Tarar stood with the looming presence of Rahim behind him.

'We're here to see MK.'

'You'd better come in,' he said, well-spoken, not local.

It was hot in the flat, the kid was barefoot, wearing a Vampire Weekend T-shirt and black faded skinny jeans. He led them into the living room, where there was a girl in her teens, with long blonde hair in a curtain over her face. Her head was bobbing to some music she was listening to on the MP3 player in her lap. MK was lying back on the sofa, black shirt, jeans, trainers and curly hair. He was staring up at the ceiling, listening to the music playing in the room, which was electronic trance. When he saw Tarar, he came off the sofa as if it had gone live.

'Hakim,' he said, shocked that he was getting a visit from the man himself, which could only mean trouble. He used the remote to turn off the music.

Tarar glanced at the girl and the kid. MK footed the girl, who pulled out her buds and came out of the curtain of her hair. She got the message. The kid was already pulling on his grey converses, had his jacket on and was out of the flat in seconds, dragging the girl with him.

'Can I get you some tea?' asked MK.

Tarar shook his head, sat down. Rahim stayed by the door with his terrifying Pashtun stare fixed on MK.

'Seen the news?' asked Tarar.

'Don't watch much telly,' said MK. 'Depresses me.'

Whereas dealing heroin to junkies, who have to steal or prostitute themselves to afford it, doesn't, thought Tarar. He had a very strong antipathy to all the dealers who bought his product. They were unbelievers with no moral core, making money out of misery. He despised them.

'Been outside?'

'Don't go out Monday or Tuesday. I work long hours at the weekend. It's my chill time.'

'There've been these flyers in the street,' said Tarar, taking one out, unfolding it. 'The police are looking for two men who've killed people. Rahim and I would like you to tell us if you know either of them.'

'Are they in the business?' asked MK, reaching for the paper, which Tarar withheld.

'They might be,' said Tarar. 'But not necessarily our business.'

'If the police are after them, what's your interest?' asked MK, finding some confidence now that he knew the visit wasn't directly linked to his heroin dealing.

'They've stolen something which an important friend of ours believes is his,' said Tarar.

'And if I can find these two guys?' asked MK.

'Then we will show our appreciation.'

'How exactly?'

Tarar had to control his loathing of this man. It only ever came down to money with him. The concept of honour was as strange to him as Arabic script.

'Some free product.'

'What are we talking about?'

Now, you see, he was already negotiating, weighing up in his mind how much effort he should expend in return for what.

'Two for one on the next deal,' said Tarar, barely masking his contempt.

'Can I see?' asked MK, holding out his hand.

As Tarar handed over the flyer, he and Rahim searched MK's face, looking for the tell-tale signs, the little tics, because they knew that dealers were as practiced in human nature as poker players.

MK blanched inside as he saw his old friend's face looking back at him.

'Can I keep this?' he asked, needing to say something that might bring back blood flow to his internal organs.

'You don't know either of them,' said Tarar, 'never seen them on your rounds?'

'They don't buy from me, I can tell you that,' said MK, careful not to lie, making sure each step was on the solid ground of truth. He'd learnt things in his time.

'You sell tabs, right?' asked Tarar.

MK shrugged, as if he was embarrassed by this lowlier trade.

'The guy on the left used to be a nurse,' said Tarar. 'Did time for stealing drugs from hospital. That's why we're going around the dealers in the area. Maybe he's got his hand in that business or he's a user. We know he rents a flat in Stepney.'

'You tried talking to the dealers there?'

'There's been a lot of heat already in Stepney. We're waiting for things to cool down before we go in there.'

'I have three chemists from up north who supply me with what I need for my tab trade. They work out the formulae and test the prototypes and then I get them made in China and sent over,' said MK. 'I'm not in any open market for that stuff. The kid who just left moves most of my gear around the parties and clubs in London. I don't deal in any prescription drugs, which is where you might expect to find a nurse, or an ex-nurse, operating.'

'Do you know anybody in that business?'

'The only guy I know lives up in Dalston. I'll call him, tell him you're going to drop by.'

Tarar nodded. MK made the call, wrote down the name and

address. They got up to leave. Tarar turned at the door, Rahim's hairy fist around the handle.

'As I've just told you, our friend will show his appreciation to those that help us find these two men. You know the reward. What I haven't told you is what he'll do if he finds anyone in our dealer network who's been holding out,' said Tarar. 'He has a special sound-proofed room in a basement he's had dug out below his house in Upton Park. The people who go in there never come out with the ability to speak. They've done all the talking they'll ever do in that room. You understand me?'

Rahim nodded that into him, opened the door.

Neither of them spoke as they went down the stairs and out of the building. They walked down the street in silence and only spoke once they'd turned the corner.

'He knows something,' said Rahim in Urdu.

'I'm sure he knew one of them; the nurse, maybe,' said Tarar. 'Did you see how still he went?'

'We should go back there,' said Rahim. 'Before he warns them.'

'I'll call Saleem.'

Rahim stood at the corner, kept an eye on the block's entrance, while Tarar called Cheema. A few minutes passed and MK came out of the building. Rahim tapped Tarar on the shoulder. They watched as MK walked away from them, towards the Colville Estate. Tarar hung up on Cheema as they jogged after him. MK turned left into Branch Place and walked around the corner to some buildings that looked like workshops. He searched his pockets for a set of keys.

'Take him,' said Tarar.

For a big man, Rahim moved fast and with extraordinary stealth. Tarar saw MK's legs give way with fright as he felt the hardness of Rahim's .38 in his kidneys. He put an arm round him, guided him back to Tarar. They pushed him round the corner, out of sight of the workshop.

'I thought you didn't go out Mondays and Tuesdays?' said Tarar.

'It's my workshop,' said MK shakily. 'I was going to do some painting.'

'Got any interesting models in there for us?' asked Tarar,

nodding to Rahim, who kicked MK in the side of the leg so that he went down hard on the tarmac. He got his arm in a lock, rammed his foot into the shoulder joint and started twisting the wrist so that the shoulder started to pop. MK screamed.

'They're in there, aren't they?' said Tarar.

MK couldn't speak with the pain in his shoulder, face against the icy ground. He nodded.

'You know where we're going now, don't you?' said Tarar.

Rahim released him, pulled him up to his feet, which drew a shout of pain from MK, who held onto his shoulder, bent double. He burst into tears, sobbed with fright, so that Rahim swatted him across the back of the head in disgust. They walked to the car while Tarar called two of his team, posted them at either end of Branch Place, told them to call if there were any movements in or out of the unit.

Rahim sat in the back with MK. Tarar got behind the wheel. MK collapsed against the window and wept harder than he had as a child, going back to boarding school.

25

Still no Frank.

The three of them sat around the table with the empty sports bag as the centrepiece, Isabel strung so tight Boxer could hear the tension humming along the wires stretched within her. He wanted to say something to relieve the pressure, but he'd learnt early on in his career that humour never worked in kidnap situations. He wanted to put his arm around her, kiss her neck, say something intimate, but Rick Barnes was there, earphones on, although Boxer couldn't be sure he was listening to the recordings.

The silver Golf GTI was waiting outside, ready to go.

Time moved inexorably towards 10.30 p.m., which was the latest they could leave it before they would have to head for the rendezvous at the Rich Mix Cinema in Bethnal Green.

Boxer was used to this, never allowed it to get to him. He'd spoken to Martin Fox and asked him to do his best to raise the money from other sources.

Rick Barnes sat with his hands splayed out on the arms of his chair, staring straight ahead, doing breathing exercises, listening to the words playing through his head. He'd taken no part in the money problem. The public purse was never open for ransom payments.

The doorbell rang, which jolted Isabel, as if she'd come unwound by about half a yard before retightening.

Barnes didn't react.

Boxer went for the door.

D'Cruz. Finally. He looked shattered, his charismatic swagger shot to pieces.

'Here it is,' he said, holding out the briefcase.

'How much?'

'Two hundred and fifty. That's all I could get in the time.'

'That's good,' said Boxer. 'Isabel and the Met's kidnap consultant can count it out and pack it. You'd better come and have a drink with me. You look done in.'

Boxer put him in the kitchen with a bottle of scotch and a tray of ice, took the money into the sitting room, dumped it on the table. Barnes had his earphones out now, was standing, almost crouched, ready to pounce.

'I'll *kill* him,' said Isabel.

'That's why you and Rick are going to count out a hundred thousand from that money and pack it in ten bundles as per Dan's instructions, and I am going to talk to Frank in private.'

'I'm calling the DCS,' said Barnes.

'I imagine MI5'll want a debrief, too,' said Boxer.

Back in the kitchen, D'Cruz hadn't moved, not even to the whisky bottle. Boxer broke ice into a tumbler, poured three fingers of scotch over it, rattled the glass in front of D'Cruz to break his concentrated stare into the table.

'Drink, and let's talk.'

D'Cruz socked it back, put the glass back on the table, clasped his hands between his knees. His shoulders shook; he was sobbing.

'Apart from what you've just put Isabel through,' said Boxer, 'MI5 are, to use the least exaggerated vocabulary possible, concerned. What have you been doing and why did you do it without their surveillance in place?'

'I had to find out what this was all about,' said D'Cruz. 'I had to make connections to the sort of people who, if I brought MI5 to their door, would annihilate me, my family, my business ... everything.'

'Are we talking about organised terrorists?'

'No, just people who are in the know. I suppose you could call them intermediaries,' he said, nodding and beckoning more whisky into his glass. 'Are you joining me?'

'I'm driving tonight,' said Boxer, pouring the whisky, suspecting that D'Cruz was overacting.

'You've got to get my little girl back for me,' he said, suddenly desperate, as if to confirm Boxer's suspicions. 'You've got to make it work with these people holding her now.'

'That's my intention,' said Boxer, 'and you've arrived just in time. Another half hour and I couldn't have guaranteed it. So what did you find out in your little interlude from MI5?'

'There's a man on his way to London,' said D'Cruz. 'A very powerful man. His name is Lieutenant General Amir Jat. He is a retired but very active officer from the ISI, living in Lahore. He arrived in Dubai under that name on an Emirates flight EK601 from Karachi at one-fifteen local time this afternoon. There has been no Amir Jat on any outgoing flights from Dubai International, but I am told that there was a man travelling on a German passport, who landed at Charles de Gaulle airport at seven-thirty local time this evening and answers to the description of Amir Jat, although he is wearing different clothes, has changed his hair style and has shaved off his beard. He was met, and it is thought he has been given another identity, probably a British passport and a ticket for onward transportation to London. His arrival time here is unknown.'

'And what is Amir Jat here for?'

'I'm not sure, but I have been given the impression that the kidnap was ordered by him,' said D'Cruz.

'Has he come here to rescue the situation now that Alyshia has changed hands?'

'He wouldn't have known that by the time he left Pakistan,' said D'Cruz. 'Although I'm sure he will have been informed by now and it will be high on his list of priorities.'

'Why was he using a London gang and not ISI operatives to run the kidnap?'

'Because the kidnap was designed as a personal attack on me for a reason that he would like to remain unknown.'

'Are you going to tell me that reason?'

'If you want to do business in Pakistan, selling the kind of heavy-duty industrial material that I am manufacturing, then you have to have contacts in the military. The kingpin is Amir Jat. If he recognises you, then all the other senior military officers will fall into line.'

'How does he have so much power?'

'He controls funding ostensibly from the Pakistani government; enormous amounts of it.'

'Ostensibly?'

'There's so much of it and it moves down so many different channels that we have to assume that some of it comes from his powerful relationship with the Afghan Taliban.'

'Opium?'

'We don't actually know this, but we think it is the case.'

'So how did you develop a relationship with Amir Jat?'

'Even to get an audience with him takes time. You only get to him by coming through one of the approved lines of communication. In my case, this was through Lieutenant General Abdel Iqbal in Karachi.'

'And what did you have to do to persuade Iqbal that you were worthy?'

'I knew his brother in Dubai. We were on the same team in my earlier ... career. He is the reason I am so strong in the Mumbai Muslim community,' said D'Cruz. 'And when Abdel Iqbal's eldest son developed a very rare brain tumour, I was on hand to find an American surgeon in Los Angeles who would perform the necessary surgery that nobody else would. I paid the two hundred and fifty thousand dollar bill. It was the best investment of my life.'

'And that brought you into Amir Jat's orbit,' said Boxer. 'He doesn't sound like someone who gives things away for free.'

'I don't know how much you know about business relationships,' said D'Cruz. 'Putting it simply, they are all about power. It sounds obvious, but if you allow a person to maintain a more powerful position over you, it will forever weaken you in that relationship. So what you're trying to do in developing a business relationship is to bring the power of each individual into balance.'

'It sounds as if you're describing the rationale behind corruption,' said Boxer. 'But Amir Jat's probably a very devout Muslim if he has a strong relationship with the Afghan Taliban.'

'Yes, and although he controls a great deal of money, he is not interested in having any of it for his own account. He only uses it to demonstrate his far-reaching power. His personal needs are extremely limited. He drinks boiled water. He behaves as if it's Ramadan every day, eating only in the morning before daybreak and at night after sundown. He prays, of course, five times a day.'

'So, not an obvious candidate.'

'But I succeeded in corrupting him,' said D'Cruz. 'I found his most vile weakness and exploited it.'

'And what would that weakness be?' asked Boxer.

'You don't need to know,' said D'Cruz, dead-eyed.

And Boxer could see that it would be an admission that would take a heavy toll.

'It's something I learned very early on,' said D'Cruz. 'No man is incorruptible.'

Boxer didn't like the way D'Cruz was looking at him. He began to understand how Amir Jat, and Isabel Marks, and all the people who'd ever come into contact with the beguiling charisma of Frank D'Cruz were made to feel. He stared back at him, unblinking.

'And what was the demonstration of sincerity he was asking from you?'

'That, I still don't know for certain. It could be that I just have to keep my mouth shut, but about what, apart from his vile weakness, I do not know. I think maybe he's just rebalancing the scales of power in his favour,' said D'Cruz. 'I am well-protected among the Muslim community in Mumbai, and he wouldn't have been able to pull it off there unless he'd gone to one of the Hindu gangs, and that was never a possibility. In London it's easier.'

'But normally people instigate kidnaps for particular reasons,' said Boxer. 'To earn a ransom is the most obvious. Or to guarantee someone's silence, but only until a crucial moment has passed. Buying your silence about how you corrupted him sounds too general a reason for a kidnap. How long is he supposed to keep Alyshia in order to ensure you keep your mouth shut? For life? There has to be something specific as well, something like, say, an imminent terrorist attack.'

'No. My intermediaries assured me that is not the case. The heat is too intense in the run up to the Olympics. The established terrorist organisations don't want to risk a failure and compromise their networks.'

'Well, Frank, to me there's a logic breakdown in this scenario and if I see it, you can bet your life MI5 will see it, too.'

'Look, Charles, because Amir Jat is a man I do business with, I make it *my* business to know everything there is to know about him. He doesn't operate in a vacuum and I have the means to draw information from those around him. I won't name my sources, not even to MI5, but I can assure you I have them,' said D'Cruz. 'It is the nature of these kinds of relationships that you are always trying to reach beyond the level you have already achieved. So, as soon as I'd brought Abdel Iqbal onside, I reached for Amir Jat. When I attained him, I looked for the next man in the chain. Amir Jat is a man who keeps his enemies as close to him as his friends. I'm not sure that he differentiates between them. I was able to find out which of his friends were, in fact, his enemies and, to my great misfortune, he was also able to find out who one of them was. Yes. *Was*. Amir Jat is not a man who tolerates traitors.'

Boxer was entranced by the spiralling logic of what D'Cruz was saying. It seemed to make some sort of sense, but gave him no hard information to hold on to.

'So you think he's had Alyshia kidnapped in retaliation for you turning one of his "friends" into your spy?' said Boxer. 'That still doesn't make sense.'

'Unless, as you said at the beginning, he's out to punish me,' said D'Cruz, 'for corrupting him and for turning his people against him.'

Silence. D'Cruz poured himself another shot, downed it without taking his eyes off Boxer.

The doorbell rang, which broke the spell between them. Barnes went for it and a moment later appeared in the kitchen.

'It's Mr D'Cruz's limo to Thames House,' he said. 'And it's time for you to go, Charles. The money's ready.'

Dan walked back to the unit, taking a different route in. He was excited; he'd been having some ideas about how the drop was going to work. How they could do it better. He took a different way in by going up Canal Walk, crossing the bridge and coming in to Branch Place from the west. He saw nobody. But one of Tarar's men, hiding behind a low wall topped by the council's blue railing in front of a block of flats, saw him. He watched as Dan let himself into the unit and then phoned in his report.

The studio area was dark, with a curious silence to it. Dan padded up the stairs, wondering what he would find this time. As soon as he entered the flat, he knew something was wrong. There was no chatter, no laughter, no flirtation. Skin was sitting on his own next to the table, smoking a joint, looking at the blank wall. Dan checked on Alyshia; she returned his stare, said nothing. Her other wrist was handcuffed to the bed head. Her hair was wet. He closed the door, went back to Skin.

'What's happened?' asked Dan.

Skin shrugged.

'I thought you were getting on?' said Dan. 'So what's the score?'

'Not a lot. I let her have a shower.'

'Fucking luxury round here.'

'Water was cold,' said Skin. 'She complained. That's it.'

'That's it?'

'Yeah,' said Skin, looking for a new chapter now, his blue eyes gone to black. 'What's the latest?'

'I've just been rethinking how we're going to do this,' said Dan.

'Glad you're here,' said Skin, taking a huge drag, closing his eyes, 'doing the thinking.'

More silence.

'Are you with me, Skin?'

'All ears,' he said.

'I hope the walk down the canal clears that shit out of your system.'

'Don't worry, I'll drop a dexy and get there in half the time.'

'All right, listen carefully. These are *instructions* I'm giving you now,' said Dan. 'When you get to the end of the canal, you'll go through the tunnel under Commercial Road. At that point you'll find yourself between the road and the arches of the DLR in front of the Limehouse Basin marina. There'll be a lock there. I want you to go up the steps on the left and on to the south side of Commercial Road. Got that?'

'Got it.'

'I want you to look over the bridge wall and down onto the tow path where you've just come from and give me a marker.'

'A marker?'

'Something on the bridge. A mark. Where I can tell Alyshia's mother to stop, get out and throw the sports bag with the money over the wall. And where you'll be down below, waiting to catch it. That way nobody sees you and if they have got people following, it's going to be more difficult for them to chase you. They'll have to stop, find their way down there and then find you. It'll give you a few minutes head start to sprint to the car you've already stolen and get your arse through the Blackwall Tunnel.'

'The Blackwall Tunnel?'

'You'd better hope the car you've nicked has got SatNav.'

Skin looked at his watch, began to understand what he had to do in the time.

'Don't worry about the time too much. I can delay them until you're ready,' said Dan, and handed him a phone. 'This is the mobile you're going to use. I've put my number in there already. Check it now.'

Skin found the number, called it. Dan's phone vibrated.

'Good. We're all systems go,' said Dan.

Skin got to his feet, slapped his abdomen. Dan watched him carefully, wondering now if he was solid enough for the job.

'What you looking at?' asked Skin, aggressive.

'Something's changed. I'm trying to work out what it is. That's all.'

'Don't.'

'There was chemistry before and now there's—'

'What?' said Skin nastily. 'Geography?'

'Now you put it like that, yeah.'

'That Alyshia,' he said, 'I saw it from the off. She likes bad guys. I know the type.'

'But what?' asked Dan.

'But not me,' said Skin.

Dan shrugged. Their eyes connected. He saw the hurt in Skin's, which surprised him.

'Just say your *Khuda Hafiz* and fuck off then,' said Dan. 'Remember, she's making you fifty grand richer.'

309

'Say my what?'

'*Khuda Hafiz*. It's Urdu for "goodbye".'

'You know fucking everything.'

'You'd better unlock the other handcuff while you're at it,' said Dan. 'I haven't got the key for that one.'

'Good thinking,' said Skin.

'Don't want her dragging that bed around with her 'til tomorrow morning.'

'You do it,' said Skin, giving him the key. 'And bring back a coat hanger.'

Dan went to Alyshia, unlocked the extra cuff, with her looking at him as if he might have an exploitable weakness. He went back into the living room with the coat hanger. Skin was checking his handgun, put the hood over his head and rolled it back up over his face so that it was just a wool hat. Dan made sure he had the mobile and some paper and a pen.

'What's this for?'

'You're going to give them the run around before they make the drop.'

Skin went downstairs, rummaged around in the studio until he found a pair of long-nosed pliers. He left.

Dan made the call to Isabel Marks at just before 10.30 p.m.

'What's your question?'

'Alyshia and I went to Granada for a weekend last Easter,' said Isabel. 'Ask her where we stayed.'

Dan put the question to Alyshia. He heard the noise of traffic coming over the phone and knew they were already on the move. He held the phone up.

'In the Parador,' said Alyshia.

'You hear that?' asked Dan.

'I heard it,' said Isabel, as the tears came.

26

'What did Chico tell you?' asked Isabel.

'He lost his MI5 tail so that he could go and talk to some "intermediaries", as he called them. They could be people he knows through the underworld or they might be his connections in the ISI – or possibly both.'

Boxer talked her through a less spiralling version of Chico's explanation. She stared out of the window when he'd finished.

'It didn't come across quite as clearly as that,' said Boxer.

'It never does,' she said.

'I'm not sure what's real and what's acting,' said Boxer. 'Was Amir Jat responsible for the original kidnap? I don't know. There were too many logic gaps for my liking. But Frank's desperation to get Alyshia back seemed sincere and it is possible that Amir Jat wants to punish him for what he's done.'

'That's Chico's way: to send you down a single channel. Get Alyshia back. Never tell anybody too much. They'll create their own picture and it'll give them ideas beyond their capabilities,' said Isabel. 'That's his theory, anyway.'

They came onto the Embankment, followed the great black snake of the river coiling through the city. They moved in the peristaltic traffic, amongst cars containing the vague forms of others. Boxer glanced across at her unmoving face, wondering if they were on their way to something more permanent; wanting it, but fearing what he had growing inside him, willing it to obscure that other thing that could just as easily expand in his chest.

'Tell me about Frank,' said Boxer, searching for clues, but also trying to keep her from getting nervous. 'Was he different when you first met him?'

'I used to think he was, but not now,' said Isabel. 'Only by getting free of him, or as free as I could possibly be of him, did I see his real nature, which I think was always there at the centre of his being. It's a curious thing about humans ...'

She drifted away, lost in her ghostly reflection in the window.

'What?' said Boxer, pulling her back to the moment.

'We have an irresistible attraction to something strong,' said Isabel. 'The sad thing about goodness is that it's bland. Evil has the power to provoke extraordinary emotions. And we're drawn to the excitement of the extreme, rather than the dullness of the everyday.'

'And you?'

She looked across at him in the darkness of the car, the outside lights flickering in the cockpit to reveal an eye, a cheek, a mouth, a nose.

'Me?' she said. 'I think I've been very clear. Or did you really mean you?'

'All right, what do you see in me?'

'You've had a traumatic childhood. Your father leaving you like that, so young, and with this terrible accusation hanging over him, which inevitably hung over you, too. That would be enough to lodge something dark inside anybody. But then, terrible things happen to lots of people and not all of them turn to the dark. You have taken the next step, I know that. I don't want to know what you've done. You've been in war, so you've probably killed people, but that was twenty years ago. There's something present in you now that I haven't seen in a man since, well, Chico.'

'Is this why you haven't had a relationship with anybody since Frank?'

'Do you seriously think, after being with Chico, I could be drawn to someone like that sleek little banker who lived next door to me in Edwardes Square?' she said, derisive. 'I did try, just by putting myself in the way of a normal person and, believe it or not, my soul withered in the face of it. I couldn't bring myself to

312

kiss such a man on the lips. It would have been like an exchange of life for death.'

'And with Alyshia?'

'I've been in denial about that,' said Isabel. 'I see in Alyshia what I see in myself. I never met this guy, Julian, but I saw a photograph of them together and I could see he was bad and that she was lost in him. I was determined to break the cycle. I knew something had happened in Mumbai at an emotional level, which had changed her in a more permanent way than her experience with Julian. After Julian, I thought she could be saved. After Mumbai, I was worried that she was lost, but I didn't give up. I was still trying to fix her up with normality, even last Sunday, only a couple of days ago, which feels like a different life now.'

'Do you think the Mumbai problem is to do with Deepak Mistry?'

'Yes, *he* worried me. Deepak was so like Chico. He didn't have his charisma, but he was more dangerous for the lack of it,' said Isabel. 'Chico lived amongst people who fed off his charisma. Deepak was the loner.'

Boxer came off Upper Thames Street, just before London Bridge. At Bank he turned down Cornhill and slowed.

'What are we looking at?'

'Frank's cars,' said Boxer, pointing across her. The City was empty at this time of night but the lights were still burning money all the way up the buildings.

The car was a silver saloon mounted on a stage and striking a dynamic pose as if it had just taken off after a leap over a small rise. INVEST IN THE NEW DECRUZ ELECTRIC CAR was the banner headline on a speeding news bar. Four security guards hung around the podium, which at this hour was unlit.

They carried on through the City and turned onto St Mary Axe. In the open square in front of the Aviva building was the second car, a sporty-looking estate with the same electronic banner and another four security guards.

'That's so typical of Chico,' said Isabel. 'Getting permission to put his cars in front of the Bank of England and between its two most iconic expressions of wealth – the Fabergé egg of the

Gherkin and the industrial might of the Lloyd's Building. You've got to hand it to him: he knows how to show off.'

They headed north, past Liverpool Street station, crossed over onto Bethnal Green Road and parked outside the Rich Mix Cinema, with five minutes to spare.

Skin had dropped his dexy and was jogging down the Regent's Canal, thinking what a good idea it was to be using the empty towpath. He ran past the moored narrow boats next to the railings of Victoria Park. Steam was rising from them, the smell of cooking and muted voices.

He passed underneath Commercial Road, went up the steps, walked back and looked over the brick wall to the towpath below. He stepped back to find a suitable marker and saw what the council had painted along the wall. He called Dan.

'I'm on the bridge over the canal on Commercial Road,' said Skin. 'There are numbers painted on the bridge. She's to drop the bag over the wall between one and two.'

'You got a car yet?'

'Give us a fucking break.'

'Get one. Call me back.'

Skin walked the streets off Commercial Road, found an old white transit. He took out the wire coat hanger, unwound it and straightened it out. With the pliers, he fashioned it into a rough hook. Still using the pliers, he gripped the rubber seal around the window and tore it out. He slipped the coat hanger wire in between the door and the window glass. First yank and the door lock came up. He got in, bust the steering wheel lock, hot-wired it and drove back down Commercial Road. He called Dan.

'I got a van, a transit, so we'll feel right at home.'

'I want them to think we're checking that they're not being tailed,' said Dan. 'Park off Bethnal Green Road near Brick Lane and call me.'

Skin drove. The traffic was light. His adrenaline was high but he was careful. He didn't jump any lights, kept to the speed limit. He parked up, called Dan.

'Write on a piece of paper: "Go to Stepney Green Tube", and

314

tell some kid to give it to the passenger in a silver Golf GTI by the cinema.'

Amir Jat was at Upton Park tube station where he'd arranged to meet Saleem Cheema. A boy in a furry-hooded parka with a *salwar kameez* underneath approached him and led him by the hand up Green Street, past the Pakistani clothes shops, women's shoe shops, jewellery stores and a large DVD emporium. It was all closed at this hour, but Amir Jat felt strangely at home in this anglicised version of Lahore, with its pavements and Belisha beacons, its pubs and Duncan's jellied eels. The boy took him down past the terraced houses of Boleyn Road to a semi-detached house behind a low wall, which had a red garage down one side. The boy had a key. They went to a door under the stairs. The boy pressed twice on a concealed buzzer and the door opened.

They went through another padded door and the boy pointed Amir Jat down some brick steps into the basement and left. There were three men in the room and, amongst them, a fourth, who was naked, blindfolded, with headphones on and tied to a chair. He looked completely broken down. There was a pool of urine at his feet. His legs were trembling. Amir Jat could hear the tinny sound of the heavy metal music that was being thrashed into his ears via the headphones.

The three men greeted Amir Jat with a display of great respect.

'Who is this?' he asked.

'One of our dealers. He rented a workshop to the two men who've taken over the kidnap of the girl you want. It's in another part of town, a few miles from here,' said Cheema. 'We're watching the place as we speak.'

'How many people holding the girl?'

'Two, but most of the time there's only one. The lookout just called to tell us that the one known as Skin has just left, which means the girl is with the ex-nurse, called Dan,' said Cheema, kicking MK in the leg. 'This one's friend.'

'Has he shown you the layout?' asked Jat, looking down at MK, who was crouching and shuddering.

'The workshop has big windows overlooking the canal,' said Cheema, nodding. 'On the street side there's only one window, high up, which belongs to the kitchen. He thinks they'll be keeping the girl in a small flat upstairs.'

'Keys?'

'We have them both, to the workshop and the flat.'

'We'll have to cover the canal side as well as the street side,' said Jat.

'How do you mean?'

'The canal provides an escape route. It will have to be covered.'

'No, what I mean is, we do not carry out this sort of operation,' said Cheema. 'There are trained teams for that sort of work.'

'Can you contact them?'

'No, I can only contact the people who contact me.'

'And who are they?'

'People who've approached me through my suppliers,' said Cheema. 'They call themselves the UK Command Centre.'

'We haven't got time for that,' said Jat. 'We have to act now.'

'But we haven't been given any training for this kind of operation,' said Cheema, 'and we must get clearance from UK Command.'

Jat wasn't used to people answering him back. He looked around him, at the young men in their modern clothes and styled hair, and was dismayed by what he saw.

'You are no different to the people we are trying to defeat,' said Jat. 'You have developed a Western corporate mentality, with politics to match, and it has paralysed you. You have to learn to take the initiative.'

Nobody spoke.

The paranoia was working on Jat. He stared into his own complex world of associations and networks and wondered where things were breaking down and who was responsible. He no longer felt as if he was operating the levers. He couldn't throw himself clear of the vortex of thought that told him no one could be trusted. And yet there were people he still had to rely on.

'What about you?' said Jat, pointing at Rahim, who was hunched under the low ceiling of the basement. Jat recognised where he was from, spoke to him in Pashto, excluding the others, asked him if he was ready and willing to carry out such an operation.

316

'There's only one man and the girl,' said Jat. 'How many of you are there?'

'We are six,' said Rahim.

'Two in the street. Two on the other side of the canal. And two go in. You …' said Jat, casting around and finding Tarar. 'And what about him? He looks like a fighter.'

'He's a boxer. He's never fired a gun.'

'Any of the others fired a gun?'

'Just two.'

'Take one of them,' said Jat. 'Show me the layout and I'll tell you how we're going to do it.'

'What are you saying to him?' asked Cheema.

'He's agreed to carry out the operation,' said Jat.

'These are *my* people,' said Cheema. 'They operate in *my* network. They're not trained for this kind of thing.'

'They don't need any training with me to plan the assault,' said Jat. 'This isn't a complicated operation like the Mumbai attack in 2008 which *I* was responsible for planning. These boys are only up against a nurse and the girl, who will be handcuffed.'

Rahim and Tarar were clearly impressed by Jat. They started talking, off to one side.

'But they are valuable members of my network. What happens if one of them is hurt or killed? We will lose the ability to fund other operations.'

'How much funding do you want?' asked Jat. 'I'll give you all the funding you need. I guarantee it.'

'We'll do it,' said Tarar.

They looked at Cheema.

'We'll do it on condition that we keep the girl and take the ransom. That will give us the funding we need,' said Tarar.

Cheema nodded his agreement at him from behind Jat's shoulder.

'I want to interrogate the girl, once we have her in our hands,' said Jat. 'I need answers from somebody and she will give me the ability to apply pressure. Once I have those answers, she's all yours. Is that agreed?'

They all nodded.

'What do we do with him?' asked Tarar, pointing at MK.

'There's only one thing *to* do,' said Jat.

'No more mess,' said Cheema, disgusted by the pool of urine.

A teenage girl in a black puffy coat walked along the pavement towards the Rich Mix Cinema. She stopped by the silver Golf GTI, knocked on the window. Boxer lowered it. She handed him a note, moved off.

Boxer read it, gave it to Isabel. They set off down Bethnal Green Road. Seven minutes later they were outside Stepney Green tube. Boxer searched the night. Nothing. He sat back. A kid walked past, slapped a piece of paper on the windscreen. GO TO MILE END TUBE STATION AND WAIT. Boxer turned left onto Mile End Road, pulled up outside the tube a few minutes later.

'I was Frank's conscience for the first ten years of our marriage,' said Isabel. 'Until we fell apart. For the next fifteen years he had no conscience. Anybody who came into his orbit, he corrupted them.'

'What about Sharmila?'

'She's from that world. She left a gangster to be with Chico. He put her in charge of his "escort agency". She provides whores for his clients. And, this is Chico for you: he'll make her do terrible things until she's as black as he. The corruptor is only satisfied when his corruptees have been totally immersed in his darkness.'

'But you're out of that now.'

'Am I?' she said. 'What am I letting myself in for this time?'

'I'm not rich. I don't want power over others. I don't corrupt.'

'Are you ruthless?'

He checked himself before he answered that one. Didn't want to lie to her.

'Yes, but only with those who've done wrong.'

An old man in an overcoat, long grey hair spreading out over his shoulders from under a woollen hat, crossed the road in front of them with a limp. He stopped by the car.

'Where to?' asked Boxer.

'You got a cigarette?' he asked, until he saw Isabel and leaned in further. The alcohol and tobacco were fierce on his breath. 'Are you married?'

'No, I'm not,' she said, smiling.

318

'You should be,' he said. 'You're a fine-looking woman. Is *he* married?'

'No,' said Boxer.

'Are you sure you don't have a cigarette?'

'We don't smoke.'

'A fine-looking woman,' he said, staring intently. 'Where do you want to go now?'

'We don't know,' said Isabel. 'We're waiting to be told.'

'Have you got a message for us?' asked Boxer.

He switched his gaze to Boxer and said, 'Qui nunc it per iter tenebricosum illuc, unde negant redire quemquam.'

'Sorry?' said Boxer.

'"Now he goes along the darksome road, towards that place from where they say no one returns",' said the old man. 'Good night.'

He moved off. They turned to the middle of the car, looking out of the rear window.

'Loony?' asked Boxer.

'I think so,' said Isabel. 'Or perhaps a revenant.'

'A what?'

'A ghost, sort of. Someone who comes back to tell you something.'

'Let's hope he was talking about himself going along the "darksome road",' said Boxer, a little shaken at the thought that he himself might have gone beyond the point of no return.

They turned back in their seats. One of the Metropolitan Police flyers fluttered under the wiper, slightly damp. Boxer retrieved it.

'The most important thing to remember in this country,' he said, showing Isabel the flyer. 'Never lose your sense of humour.'

The flyer showed the photos of Skin and Dan, except that Skin now had scribbled bouffant curly black hair and a moustache and Dan had glasses. Underneath it said: 'GO TO SHADWELL STATION, Yours Cannon and Ball'. Isabel started giggling, half involuntary, half hysterical. Boxer did a U-turn.

'By the time we get to Shadwell, there'll be some bloke playing the next destination on squeaky cats,' said Boxer.

Ten minutes and they were outside Shadwell DLR station. It was just after 11.30 p.m.

'Why are you checking the rearview all the time?' said Isabel.

'You never know with the Met,' said Boxer. 'They have ideas of their own. We don't know what information they're operating on, but it's likely to be more than ours. I just don't want them to screw things up for us. I want to get this over and done with before anybody else catches up with Skin and Dan.'

'But wasn't this the idea, to make sure we weren't being followed?'

'It's been more for show than real,' said Boxer. 'There's only two of them and one is with Alyshia. They're making us think they're checking us out. The Met know that. I saw Rick's mind at work.'

They sat in silence in the darkness of the Golf under the yellow lighting on Cable Street. Boxer held out his hand palm up. She placed hers on top and he enclosed it and brought it to his lips.

Isabel's phone rang, making her start.

'Your friend: what's his name?'

'Charles Boxer.'

'Tell him to get the money out of the boot and put it on your lap. Go.'

The phone cut.

They sat in silence again. The sports bag on her lap. The tension occupying too much of her mind to allow conversation. Barely any traffic. The car's computer telling them the outside temperature was now zero.

The phone rang. Dan gave the next batch of instructions to Lowell Street.

'Wait there until I call you again.'

'We're getting close now,' said Boxer.

'How do you know?'

'The phone calls are from Dan. Skin's gone to the drop point to receive. He's not around to get people to stick messages on our windscreen.'

Boxer pulled up on Lowell Street. Empty. No parked cars even. Below freezing now. The tension building as they came to the moment of releasing the money. The terrible point when the kidnappers had everything and the family nothing.

'We've still got to have our proof of life,' said Boxer. 'Don't let him forget it.'

The phone rang.

'Hello, Mum, it's me,' said Alyshia brightly.

'Oh my God,' said Isabel. 'It really is you. Are you all right?'

'I'm fine, Mum. Just do as Dan says and everything will work out. They're all right, these two. You can trust them.'

'Listen very carefully, Isabel,' said Dan, taking over the phone. 'I'm going to give you all the instructions now and you must obey them to the letter.'

Dan talked her through the drop in detail.

'When you've let go of the sports bag, don't look over the wall, just go straight to the car, no looking back. Your friend, Charles, stays behind the wheel. He'll drive you back to the Rich Mix Cinema. You wait there until the money's been counted and I'll call you with the address. Everything understood?'

The wait at the traffic lights at the end of Lowell Street was interminable. They turned onto Commercial Road, found the drop point and pulled over. Isabel got out, gasped at the sub-zero wind that cut straight through her thin white paper suit. She clambered over the railings and walked quickly back over the bridge to where the numbers were painted on the wall. She dropped the bag into the darkness. No sound came back. She jogged back to the car. Two men came running towards her, really sprinting, at full pace. She flinched as they flashed past her. She vaulted the railings, looked back to where they'd gone. One went down some steps at the side of the apartment building while the other ran across the bridge and disappeared through the gap in the wall to go down to the towpath. Boxer was out of the car watching them, leaning on the roof, shaking his head.

Two cars shot past on the other side of Commercial Road; one pulled up in front of the Tequila Wharf development. Two men got out and ran down the steps to the canal. The other car shot across the road and went down the street on the other side of the canal, heading for the blocks of flats around the marina.

'What's going on?' asked Isabel.

'The Met,' said Boxer. 'Going for their big moment.'

27

'Anybody accompanying the girl must be shot immediately,' said Amir Jat.

Jat had drawn up a layout of the buildings, roads and the canal around the workshop on Branch Place. Tarar's other two men had not been recalled from their lookout points. Jat was addressing the four men who were going to perform the operation, describing the best way to mount a successful assault on the flat, how they should move from room to room.

'What if he grabs the girl and holds a gun to her head?' asked Rahim.

'You will have the advantage of surprise so you must move quickly to ensure that does not happen,' said Jat.

'But if it does?'

'Are you a good enough shot to kill the man without harming the girl?'

'He's good,' said Tarar. 'He just doesn't want the responsibility if it goes wrong.'

'And I haven't been trained in assault situations,' said Rahim.

'Nor has this ex-nurse,' said Jat. 'He will be in such a state of shock, I doubt he will be able to react. It's possible, too, that the girl will still be secured in another room. We must put our faith in Allah for a beneficial outcome.'

Jat asked to see their weapons and had them check the mechanisms and load with a round in the chamber. He asked for any more questions. Silence. They left the house in pairs at intervals.

Jat and Cheema met at the VW van they would use for the operation. They picked the others up at prearranged points and headed west.

Only two people in the van weren't nervous: Amir Jat and Rahim. The rest were hyped up, Cheema more so than the rest of them. The steering wheel was skidding through his sweating hands. He was just the driver, but only he knew what he'd been instructed to do the moment this operation was over.

As soon as Skin had caught the bag, he'd turned and sprinted back towards Limehouse Basin. He wasn't taking any chances, not with a hundred grand, which was the most money he'd ever held in his hands at one time. He turned left at the basin and ran in front of the blocks of flats, up some steps, along a walkway and through a small park, which took him to Narrow Street, where he'd parked the van. He got in panting, ducked below the dashboard and hot-wired it. He pulled away and weaved through the narrow streets to join the traffic on Commercial Road. He headed south through the Rotherhithe Tunnel and made his way to the Old Kent Road. He parked up in a side street, got into the back of the van over the front seats, opened the sports bag.

It was nearly unbelievable. Ten packs of ten grand each, just as they'd asked. He counted through one of the packs. Spot on. He riffled the other nine to make sure they were genuine. He clenched his fists, punched the air and did a little hobbled dance around the back of the transit.

Dan was in the living room with Alyshia. He'd removed the remaining handcuff and they were sitting at a table. Dan had one hand on the gun in between them while he played with the mobile in his other, willing it to vibrate. She'd dressed in the tracksuit, T-shirt and trainers he'd bought and she had a blanket from the bed around her shoulders. He'd called Skin several times but the phone was switched off. Dan sat back, tried to relax. Didn't like the feel of Alyshia's eyes constantly on him.

'So what happened,' he asked, going on the offensive, 'between you and Skin?'

'Nothing.'

'I could see that,' said Dan. 'But you were getting on and then …?'

'We weren't.'

'He tried it on?'

She shrugged, as if this happened all the time.

'In the shower?' said Dan. 'That was leading him on a bit too much, maybe.'

'I hadn't had a shower for five days. I was filthy. I've been stripped down to my underwear all that time. I had nothing to hide,' said Alyshia. 'I drew the line when he asked to help, to get in there with me. I told him where to go.'

'And he didn't get … physical with you?'

'No, I'll give him that, he's not a rapist. I just slapped him down verbally and that was it.'

'I told him you were out of his league.'

'It's easy when you're not interested,' said Alyshia. 'You're not gay, are you, Dan?'

'No, just careful,' said Dan. 'I've ended up in prison because of women like you.'

She smiled. He leaned back in his chair, looking at his watch.

'Come on, Skin.'

'What time is it?' asked Alyshia.

'Half an hour past midnight,' said Dan. 'And as usual, I don't know what the fuck he's playing at. Mind of his own, that boy, and not all of it properly wired.'

'Where are you going to meet him?'

'We didn't decide that,' said Dan. 'He was going to see where he ended up.'

'You think he's going to call?'

'What do you mean?'

'Once someone like him sees a hundred grand, they get used to it being theirs. Don't like the idea of sharing it.'

'What's your game, Alyshia?' asked Dan, looking at her out of the corner of his face.

'No game. Just telling you how greed works.'

'You an expert?'

'Yes, I am,' she said. 'I've watched people operating around money all my life. Very few don't succumb.'

It annoyed him, because that was the little worm that had gnawed its way into his brain over the last hour. He hadn't wanted it to, but that was the nature of little worms. It made him angry and nasty.

He waved the gun around a little in her general direction. She didn't take her eyes off his.

'You better pray he calls, because if he doesn't, I'm walking out of here on my own and you'll be—'

The phone rang.

'I've got it, Nurse. I've fucking got it. It's all here. One hundred grand. Get out of there. I'm waiting—'

'Don't tell me,' said Dan quickly. 'I'll call you again in half an hour. Your phone was switched off.'

'I didn't want calls during the drop, and after the dexy my brain was still whizzing. Didn't turn it back on until just now.'

They hung up.

'He called,' said Dan. 'You're free to go.'

The VW van pulled up in Branch Place. They'd checked the unit from Canal Walk and seen shadows moving in the room above the workshop on the canal side. They'd left Tarar there with one other. They'd picked up the lookout at one end of Branch Place and driven around the block. Now they were parked just around the corner. They all got out. The second lookout confirmed that no one had come in or gone out. The four men walked towards the unit, with Rahim out front. He unlocked the main double doors. The four went in, pulled the door closed behind them.

Isabel had her face in her hands, couldn't stop crying; the pressure of the drop and the thought that it might have been for nothing because of the Met had been too much for her. Boxer stroked her back while he made phone calls, trying to find out what had happened. He'd already been outside to inspect the car, couldn't find any tracking device. He hadn't expected to. The money had been clean, he'd checked that. Nothing in the boot, or the back seat. He called Fox.

'The Met were at the drop,' he said. 'You heard anything?'

'What do you mean they were there?'

'They tracked us. Isabel made the drop and guys and cars appeared out of nowhere.'

'I'll talk to Makepeace, call you back.'

Boxer called Rick Barnes.

'I didn't think you'd be able to keep your noses out of it.'

'Don't worry,' said Barnes. 'That's all I can say, Charles.'

'I'm already worried. Isabel's in tears,' said Boxer. 'We've heard nothing from the kidnappers.'

'It's all under control. Just don't rock the boat. As soon as you get the address—'

'You broke the deal, Rick. You said you wouldn't follow and you did. So why should I keep my end up and give you the address, *if* they give it to us.'

'They will,' said Barnes. 'It's just a surveillance operation. No armed men. We want them alive and in possession of the money.'

'Where did you put the tracking device?'

'In her handbag. The old tricks are always the best.'

Boxer hung up. Stupid, he thought. Hadn't even seen the handbag, too preoccupied with the sports bag and what D'Cruz had been saying. The handbag was under Isabel's legs. He got out, emptied the contents onto his seat, found the device, hurled it across the road.

'My fault,' he said. 'I lost concentration.'

The phone rang. Isabel snatched at it.

'Your daughter is waiting for you at Unit 6b, Branch Place, London N1, just off Bridport Place. Good luck. Here she is.'

Dan handed the phone to Alyshia and left the room, gun in hand. He opened the door to the flat, looked downstairs and came eye to eye with Rahim, who, having thought he would have the advantage of surprise, now found it savagely torn from him. His fraction of a second hesitation was enough. The man behind knocked into him. The shot from his gun hit the brickwork and Dan fired as he fell back into the corridor, which ricocheted off the brick wall high above Rahim's head. Dan slammed the door shut with a wild bicycle kick of his feet.

Staying on the ground, he crabbed his way up the corridor back into the living room, where Alyshia was standing rigid as a statue, wrapped in her blanket, phone just off her head, mouth open, stunned by the gunshots. Dan came up off the floor and ran at her. As he collided with her, the phone span out of her grasp and he heard Isabel's crackly voice shouting.

He picked her up off her feet, kept running and turned at the last moment as he smashed into the floor-to-ceiling panes of glass, his back crashing against the lattice work. The old and weathered wood cracked and splintered, the glass shattering, and they were through it and out into the freezing night air and falling, with Alyshia kicking out her legs in desperation at finding them no longer connected to the floor.

The splash was colossal and catastrophic for Dan, who landed first, with Alyshia on top of him. The force of the impact slammed all the air out of him and ripped them apart. The icy water closed around Dan's head, filled his lungs. His chest felt slashed by machetes. The shock seemed to have arrested his heart and paralysed all motor reflexes, so that he found himself trying to remember how to breathe. He struggled. The water peeled back from his face for a moment and he saw the hole he'd made in the window, with a man standing in it. He mouthed to the night like a fish. He heard shouts and another splash, before the water closed back over him and he sank back down into the freezing darkness, his new friend.

Rahim hurtled back down the stairs and crashed out through the double doors, bringing along the two lookouts, still with the door breach between them. They hailed the VW van, which came towards them with a lurching screech. They piled in and took off with the side door still open, legs hanging out, Rahim pulling them in against the G-force. They rounded the corner, crossed the bridge and tore down the slope to the towpath. They all piled out. Cheema and Jat had torches. They scanned the canal.

'Hakim is in the water,' shouted a voice.

They ran down the towpath.

'Where's the girl?' roared Jat.

'She's here, she's here,' gasped Tarar, barely able to speak from the black iciness.

He had her hair wrapped around his fist and he was pulling

her towards the bank. Two of them grabbed the girl, hauled her out, carried her straight to the van, laid her down on the floor. Jat followed, pushed them out of the way and, grabbing her around the abdomen, pulled her upright and gave her a jolting squeeze. Water shot out of her mouth into the back of the van. She coughed and more water followed. He let her down to her knees where she coughed and retched up more of the foul canal.

'Put a blanket around her and get her into the recovery position,' said Jat. 'Stay with her.'

He went back to the towpath, where they were pulling Tarar out of the water.

'Where's the nurse?' asked Jat.

'He's in the water,' said one of the boys, shining his torch into the middle. 'He's not moving.'

'Is he dead?' asked Jat. 'Did Rahim shoot him?'

'No,' said Rahim.

'Let's go,' said Cheema. 'We have the girl.'

'Make sure he's dead,' said Jat. 'He must have seen Rahim.'

Tarar dived back in.

'Everybody back in the van ready to leave,' said Cheema.

'You stay with me, Rahim,' said Jat.

Tarar swam back, dragging Dan's body by the collar. Jat felt for a neck pulse. Nothing. Rahim hauled Tarar out. They ran for the van. Cheema pulled away with no lights on. Tarar shivered uncontrollably in the back.

Boxer drove at terrifying speeds, along roads with no traffic. By the time they pulled up into Branch Place, he could hear the sirens coming from all directions. He pulled up outside Unit 6b. The doors were open, the lights on. He left Isabel in the car, stepped into the parallelogram of light on the pavement and looked around. He had his FN57 handgun in his right hand.

The studio was empty. He went upstairs to the flat. A deathly quiet and an icy wind greeted him. Only the whoop of approaching sirens came walloping through the night. He put the gun down the back of his trousers, covered it. He looked into the living room, saw the broken window. He stood in the jagged hole in the shattered panes and stared down into the canal, where the vague light cast across the water showed a humped body close to the far bank.

He turned to find two armed policemen pointing guns at him.

'We're too late,' he said.

The officers of the Serious Crime Command, who'd sprinted into the Limehouse Basin in pursuit of Skin after the drop, were intent on one thing only: the make, model, colour and registration of the vehicle Skin was using. They telephoned it through to central command and melted away. A number of motorised units took over, handing the vehicle over to different squads, who took it in turns to follow the white transit until it came to rest in a side street off the Old Kent Road.

At that point they called in CO19, the armed response squad, who sent in two teams. Both parked up in an adjacent street and prepared themselves – one on the ground and the other in their vehicle, in case Skin suddenly moved off.

They picked up Skin's call telling Dan the money was all accounted for and that he should release the girl. A report went back to central command, but still the armed response squad were not activated. Only when the four units that had converged on Branch Place confirmed that the girl had not been found, and the other kidnapper had been killed at the scene, was CO19 activated, with the express instructions to bring the surviving kidnapper in alive.

Despite Skin's speeding brain, he had not been stupid. He had parked his transit with a clear route out – a good ten yards of space between him and the next car. This was where CO19 saw their opportunity. Two officers on foot on the other side of the street moved up level with the transit, while the other team remained two cars back. An unmarked police car overtook Skin's transit and began manoeuvering into the space in front. A nodding dog had been positioned in the middle of the rear window for added distraction.

Skin was smoking with one hand and cuddling the sports bag with the other. His gun was lying on the passenger seat. As soon as he saw the reversing lights, his hand reached for the gun. But the CO19 men were moving quicker than Skin's brain. The door opened and a Glock 17 was plugged hard into his throat.

'Fuck.'

28

Alyshia was conscious but in a state of shock and profoundly cold. Her eyes were wide open, unblinking, unseeing.

Amir Jat had them strip Alyshia down to her underwear and the boys who hadn't been in the water were ordered to undress and put their dry clothing on her.

Her head lolled as they dressed her. Her feet and hands were numb, her arms and legs as cold and hard as marble. A boy was assigned to massage each extremity to warm it up. They wrapped her head in a sweater, covering her eyes, with only her nose and mouth free for breathing. Cheema turned up the heating in the van to the maximum. Tarar, teeth still chattering, changed clothes with one of his team.

Cheema drove back via Bethnal Green and dropped off Tarar and the four boys. Rahim stayed in the van to help move Alyshia. They went to Boleyn Road, where they put her in the basement. Jat ordered a bed to be brought down and for hot water bottles to be prepared, along with a pot of tea. He asked Cheema if he had a thermometer. Alyshia's body temperature was 34.5°C.

'That's OK,' he said, 'she's not going to die.'

Rahim brought down the hot water bottles. Jat put one in each armpit, another between her thighs and the last one between her feet.

'Where's the tea?'

'It's coming,' said Rahim.

'Lots of sugar,' said Jat.

Cheema followed Rahim upstairs into the kitchen where they made the tea.

'Give me your gun,' said Cheema.

Rahim frowned.

'Don't question me,' said Cheema. 'I have my orders.'

Rahim handed over his gun.

'Is it ready to fire?'

Rahim checked, found a round in the chamber, flicked off the safety, nodded.

'Do you have a silencer?'

Rahim reached into his jacket pocket and pulled out a thick cylinder, took the gun from Cheema and screwed it on the barrel. Handed it back.

'What is this?' he asked.

'We don't know. We don't understand,' said Cheema. 'We just do what we're told. These are orders from the highest authority. Direct from Pakistan.'

'You gave Hakim your word about the girl,' said Rahim.

'I know,' said Cheema. 'That was before I gave my report. Bring the tea. We mustn't be too long.'

Rahim went downstairs first with the tray. Cheema shut the doors. Held the gun behind his back.

'Good,' said Jat, who was immersed in his project. 'Pour her some tea. Put six teaspoons of sugar in. She's going to be fine.'

Rahim did as he was told.

'You'll have to help her drink it,' said Jat. 'She won't be able to hold anything yet. It's not too hot, is it?'

Cheema was standing next to Jat, looking at Alyshia, whose head was still swathed in the sweater. The gun was now at his side.

'What are you waiting for?' asked Jat.

Cheema turned, put the barrel of the gun to Amir Jat's temple and fired. Rahim dropped the mug of tea. Jat keeled over sideways, the wound smoking as he fell. Blood bloomed over the rough concrete and mixed with MK's urine stain.

Alyshia's scream came out as a dog's yelp and a whimper.

'What have you done?' said Rahim, aghast.

'Those were my orders,' said Cheema.

'But he is one of us,' said Rahim, stating the obvious. 'He … he … he … planned the Mumbai attacks. He is a hero. I thought … you were going to shoot the girl.'

Cheema handed him the gun. His hands were shaking. He didn't know where to put them. He'd never had killer's hands before.

'What have you *done*?' repeated Rahim, staring at his guilty gun.

'As required by the UK command structure, I reported the operation we were being asked to carry out by Amir Jat,' said Cheema, falling into an official-speak he'd never used before. 'They called me back, having received instructions from the highest authority in Pakistan and told me that we should follow Amir Jat's orders precisely and, as soon as the operation was complete and the girl safe, I was to kill him.'

'But why?' asked Rahim, clearly upset, nearly in tears, which was strange to Cheema, who'd never seen any emotion in the man's face before now.

'I asked the same question myself,' said Cheema. 'All they would say was that it was a complicated situation which could jeopardise another operation. They said it was imperative that I follow their orders and report back as soon as … as soon as the deed was done.'

'And the girl?'

They looked at Alyshia, who was still trembling.

'We will be given further instructions about the girl.'

'And this body?'

'We have been given a specific place where we are to leave it,' said Cheema. 'We must do it tonight.'

Boxer took Isabel back to her house on Aubrey Walk. Rick Barnes was waiting there. He had news. Boxer held up his hand, took Isabel up to her bedroom, gave her a sleeping pill, put her to bed. He picked up his computer on the way back down.

'We got him,' said Barnes.

'Well, we didn't get Alyshia, seeing as you asked.'

'We got Skin,' said Barnes. 'He's been taken to Rotherhithe Police Station.'

'You're staying here,' said Boxer, and left the house.

He got back into the Golf and called Mercy as he drove.

'I hear you got Skin,' said Boxer.

'Homicide are talking to him at the moment,' said Mercy. 'I'm on next.'

'Can I observe?'

'I don't know,' said Mercy. 'I'll have to ask DCS Makepeace. What are you going to get out of it?'

'I thought I might be able to help.'

'Like how? This isn't your work anymore.'

'I always felt that the guy, Jordan, was a professional and, if he was, that means he's been trained somewhere and is making himself available in the private sector. I'm talking military-trained. And that *is* my world. I think I've got a better chance of tracing him than you, especially if he's a mercenary in the black.'

'In the black?'

'The type of mercenary who's prepared to work on dodgy projects, like privately sponsored military coups in West African states, for instance – or arranged kidnaps.'

'I'll talk to the DCS. Call you back.'

Half an hour later, Boxer pulled up outside the police station on Lower Road. An officer took him down to the interview rooms, where he was met by DCS Makepeace. They went to the observation window to see Mercy interviewing Skin. He was relaxed, hands clasped on the table, feet stretched out towards Mercy, who was getting annoyed with his attempts to play footsie.

'You've only missed the intro,' said Makepeace.

'Is he talking?'

'So far,' said Makepeace. 'By the way, we found his boss, Archibald Pike and his Number Two, Kevin Heep, a few hours ago. Both shot. We searched the premises and there were two big chest freezers, which had been left open. Human blood traces in both of them.'

'Good enough for DNA?'

'We're not hopeful,' said Makepeace, who turned to look at Skin, 'We're getting to the interesting bit now.'

'So you picked up Alyshia D'Cruz from Jack Auber's house in Grange Road and …?'

'Dan put her out with an injection.'

'And you took her where?' asked Mercy.

'To a disused warehouse of Pike's in Deptford,' said Skin.

Mercy asked him to point it out to her on the map on the wall. Makepeace took down the details and called them through to a mobile unit.

'Can you describe that situation for me, please?' asked Mercy, keeping it polite.

'One half of the warehouse was empty. The other half was an old refrigeration unit,' said Skin. 'Pike's contract was to keep the outside of the warehouse secure. So Dan stayed in the empty part and patrolled the outside every now and again. There were some CCTV cameras 'n' all.'

'And you?'

'I was brought into the refrigeration unit, because there was only one security guy and sometimes they needed two to deal with Alyshia.'

'Deal with her?'

'Take her for a piss, dress her, that kind of thing.'

'And there was just one security guy supporting the interrogator?'

'Only one at a time,' said Skin. 'There were three in all, but I only met two of them. The one who called himself Jordan, he was an American: the group leader and interrogator. And once during a shift change, I heard the Irish guy call his friend Reecey.'

'Describe Jordan for me.'

'He was short and squat. Bit of a gut on him. Long, greasy hair, reddish and thinning on top and at the back. That was the view I had of him most of the time. Hunched over the microphone, talking. Oh yeah, he limped, too. His left leg was bad. I asked Reecey and he said it was a shrapnel wound from a roadside bomb in Iraq. Yeah, and his voice didn't match the way he looked.'

'Meaning?'

'His voice was very soft, you know; he sounded as if he cared,' said Skin. 'Mind you, Alyshia wouldn't have known. I listened to some of the recordings after and his voice had been messed about with electronically.'

'Can you describe his face?' asked Mercy.

'I didn't see much of it,' said Skin. 'He was pudgy. Bad skin.'

'Spotty?'

'No, just not very healthy. Red, but in the wrong places.'

'Beard? Moustache?'

'No, nothing.'

'What about Reecey and the Irish guy?'

'Reecey was in ace condition. Physically, I mean,' said Skin. 'Worked out regularly during the sessions. I got the feeling he'd been hired by Jordan to do the kidnap and he'd subcontracted Pike for the warehouse and cabbie.'

'And Reecey was British.'

'Yeah, and he was mates with the Irish fucker, who Jordan told me was called McManus.'

'What about the one you didn't see?'

'I was told he was American,' said Skin. 'Never got a name. They weren't a very sociable lot. Reecey read a book most of the time when he wasn't working out.'

'Size, height?'

'Tall. Six foot something. Big, too. Fourteen, fifteen stone. Blond hair, cut short. Light eyes, maybe grey. Capped teeth. Looked army to me. Don't know why I say that, but he did.'

'And it was Jordan and Reecey who you shot when you took over the kidnap?'

Skin hesitated for a moment as if, perhaps, he'd better not confess to something so serious, so easily, but by then he knew that homicide had already matched his DNA and he was going down for good, so he might as well go down for everything. It turned him cocky and he twitched his pectorals at her.

'Yeah, that's right,' he said.

'Can you describe the other security guy? McManus.'

'You wouldn't want to go anywhere near him. I didn't.'

'Why?'

'You could tell he was a killer and that he liked it too much. He was the one who volunteered to do the mock execution. "Wouldn't have missed it", he said. "Pity I can't follow through." Nasty bastard.'

'What did he look like?'

'Nothing. Medium height. Five ten, maybe. Black curly hair

cut close to his head. Thin moustache. Brown eyes, I think, but I can't be sure because you didn't want to look in there for too long. Went straight to black, know what I mean?'

'Why did you decide to take over the kidnap if you were aware of the professionalism of the people in charge?' asked Mercy. 'You were risking a lot for a hundred grand.'

'It didn't start out as a hundred grand.'

'So, money was the motive?'

'That wasn't all of it.'

'So what was the rest?'

'We didn't like what they were doing to her ... Alyshia.'

'It sounded to me as if you were involved in what they were doing to her. Helping her to go to the toilet. And what about the mock execution? Were you involved in that?'

'That was too fucking much. That was going too far. That's when we decided.'

'So you were being the good guys,' said Mercy. 'Or did you just fancy her, Skin?'

'Get away,' said Skin, pursing his lips at her in a mock kiss.

'Yeah, right,' said Mercy, shrugging. 'Bit out of your league I'd have thought.'

'What they were doing to her,' said Skin, suddenly animated, jabbing his finger at her across the table, 'was too fucking much. And that's why we went in.'

'All right, Skin, keep your hair on,' said Mercy.

'That's enough for me to be going on with,' said Boxer, watching from the observation room.

'You'll let us know,' said DCS Makepeace. 'Won't you?'

After the shootout in the Dharavi slum, Deepak Mistry was moved out of Mumbai and taken north by car to a village outside Bhopal, where one of the gang members had family. Yash gave him a British passport in a different name. He also bought him a ticket from Delhi to Frankfurt.

The following day, Mistry boarded a train to the capital. In Delhi he stayed in a cheap hotel and blended in with some German hippies. He spent the night smoking grass with them and they left together the next morning for the airport, where they boarded the plane to Frankfurt.

It was freezing in Frankfurt and Mistry discarded his hippie garb and bought a warm coat, a woollen hat and some ski gloves and, later, a ticket to London at the coach station. He'd been told that passport checks on coaches were slacker than on other routes into the UK. He arrived at Victoria coach station at 11.00 p.m. on 13th March. He took a cab to an address in Southall given to him by Yash. Two hours later he got another cab, this time to Notting Hill Gate. Just after 1.00 a.m. he walked down Holland Park Avenue and up the hill to Aubrey Walk. He knew the house from his earlier visit. He just wasn't sure who was in it. He watched and waited in the cold.

At about 1.30 a.m., a Golf GTI arrived and parked outside the house. A man got out and opened the passenger door for a woman Mistry recognised as Alyshia's mother. The man put his arm around her and guided her up to the front door. Ten minutes later the man came out again, got into the car and left, talking on his mobile phone.

From Rotherhithe Police Station, Boxer made his way to Pavis's offices on Buckingham Palace Road in Victoria. He let himself in and set up his computer under a single desk lamp, which was the only light he turned on. He had some phone numbers, which he kept in two places – an encrypted file on his computer and under the floorboards in his flat in Belsize Park. The man he was calling usually resided in Worcester, Massachusetts and his name was Dick Kushner. His day job was running a retreat and rehabilitation centre for war veterans, for which he raised money by finding work for more able-bodied ex-soldiers, who might be described by the press as mercenaries. Boxer used the hotline number that Dick only gave out to a chosen few who he believed shared his ethical view on the business.

'Charles Boxer,' said Kushner, in his soft American accent. 'An unexpected pleasure.'

'Hi Dick, I'm sorry it's been so long.'

'I know you don't need me to find you work, so what can I do for you?'

'I'm looking for somebody.'

'Has he got a name?'

'No, but I have a description.'

'Why do you need this name?' asked Kushner. 'You know my rules, Charlie.'

'We need it so that we can put it on the man's grave. He's been shot in London.'

'I'm sorry to hear that. In London? Was he doing something bad?'

'I can tell you he was running with the wrong crowd, that's all,' said Boxer. He gave him Skin's description of Jordan.

'You think PsyOps?' said Kushner. 'There's only one man it could possibly be and I don't mind telling you his name. I never liked him, or his friend.'

'You know the friend as well?' said Boxer. 'American?'

'Sure. They were interrogation specialists. Ex-CIA. They were involved in the darker end of the extraordinary rendition programme until it was wound up at the end of the Bush era,' said Kushner. 'They ran one of the Black Sites near Rabat. The short, fat guy is Sean Quiddhy, and his friend is Mike Dowd. They're Boston Irish, met at high school, went to Virginia Tech and then on to the CIA.'

'They always work together?'

'As far as I know, but I've never given them anything. They're not my kind of people. I don't have them on my books, so names is all you get.'

'That's great, Dick, you've been very helpful.'

Boxer hung up, called DCS Makepeace, gave him the two names.

'And Reecey and McManus?'

'I'm going to work on those two now.'

He hung up, kicked the chair back and wandered through Pavis's darkened offices, thinking about Skin's description of the English guy: 'he looked army'. Boxer stood on the threshold of Martin Fox's huge office, thinking Pavis must have a recruitment file with CVs of all hopeful employees. Pavis was not like Boxer's previous employer, GRM, with salaried members of staff only. This was a freelance operation where a lot of CVs would get sent,

338

from both good and bad people. He switched on Fox's computer.

Boxer entered the password for access to the Pavis system. He clicked on the recruitment file. The screen demanded another password, which he did not have. He looked at his watch: 3.30 a.m. A bit early to be calling Fox's PA, but there was no one else but the man himself and he would not take kindly to such an early call. He woke the PA on the third ring. She was groggy with sleep but gave him the password.

'Once you get in, you'll see there's just a list of specialisations. Once inside there, you'll find it broken down into languages spoken. Finally, you'll get to a list of names.'

'Are they names from all CVs that Pavis has ever received?'

'No, they've been sorted by Martin and categorised,' she said. 'There will still be files you can't open – the ones with confidential information in them. Martin's the only one with the password for those files.'

'What about CVs from unsuitable candidates?'

'They're trashed immediately.'

Just as the PA had said, the recruitment file was broken down into specialisations. By far the biggest file was Pavis's bread and butter: Physical Security. Companies needing security for their personnel working in dangerous places: telephone engineers in Chechnya or software programmers in Iraq. That file was broken down into the languages spoken, mostly 'English speakers'. The names were in alphabetical order. He glanced down to see if any leapt out. The first was a friend from the Staffords and the second was in the Ds – Michael Dowd. He opened it. First thing: no photo. Second thing: only six lines of CV.

Born: 1967, Boston, Mass., USA
Mathematics Major, Virginia Tech
CIA: 1990–2005
Languages: English
Contact: Schwab
<u>Read more</u>

Boxer clicked on 'read more' but another password was required. He closed the file, went back to the list of specialisations and scrolled down, but found no PsyOps. He went through the specialisations one by one, thinking you really could take over a small country with this level of expertise: Consultancy, Corporate Due Diligence, Investigative, Kidnap, Maritime, Pathfinding, Physical Security, Research and Intelligence, Risk Consultancy, Security Systems and Technology, Specialist Training. And it was in that last category where he found the name Sean Quiddhy, under 'English speakers', and with the same six-line CV as Dowd and again, no photo.

Born: 1966, Boston, Mass., USA
Psychology Major, Virginia Tech
CIA: 1989–2005
Languages: English, German, Russian, Arabic, Urdu and Pashto
Contact: Schwab
<u>Read more</u>

Again, 'read more' needed another password. He went back to the main file. What were these names doing in the Pavis system? Martin Fox was always banging on about what a clean ship he ran, the governments he wouldn't work for, the personnel he wouldn't even keep on file. And yet here were the names of two people that Dick Kushner wouldn't have touched.

He had a thought, went back to the Physical Security file and found his old colleague from the Staffords. He clicked on his name and up came the full CV, with photo attached. He closed up and went to the 'Kidnap' file, opened up 'English speakers', scrolled down to Reece, Gerry. He opened the file: no photo and a six-line CV. He scrolled back up to his own name, clicked on the file: no photo and the tell-tale six-line CV. Fox knew. This was where the leak was coming from about his special service.

'Found what you're looking for?' asked Fox, standing in the doorway, a dark presence, no light on him from anywhere.

He came in, sat in the chair on the visitor's side of the desk.

'Didn't expect to see you up at this time,' said Boxer.

'Technology,' said Fox. 'I get an SMS alert if my computer is turned on without me being here.'

'I've always been a bit of a Luddite in that respect.'

'You worked it all out yet, Charlie?' he asked.

'I'm getting there.'

'How?'

'Sean Quiddhy and Michael Dowd,' said Boxer. 'Skin gave a very good physical description and I went to Dick Kushner.'

'Yes, I heard from DCS Makepeace that they'd caught that idiot,' said Fox. 'Had a look at your own file yet?'

'That's where I am now.'

'So you've found out. I know about your … special service,' said Fox. 'Click on "read more" and enter "CBE" in caps and "sme" in lower case and the numbers "7042". I used your mother's Christian name, because you're already using her maiden name.'

His file and photo came up. The complete CV, including the jobs he'd done for Zhang Yaoting and Bruno Dias, as well as a comment from the Russian businessman.

'So what is this?' asked Boxer.

'There are certain jobs for which I will only use people I can absolutely rely on to keep their mouths shut right into the grave.'

Silence.

He didn't like Fox knowing this about him; worse than someone knowing about a sexual deviancy.

'Why?' said Boxer. 'You're always telling me and the rest of the world how squeaky-clean Pavis is.'

'I'm paying the bills,' said Fox. 'Until the special risks underwriters recognise Pavis, I'm picking up scraps. Some of those scraps are very well paid, if you're prepared to … provide a special service.'

'Right,' said Boxer. 'Are we going to put our cards on the table, Martin?'

'If you like,' said Fox. 'But I'd rather see yours first.'

'We know about Quiddhy and Dowd,' said Boxer. 'There's an English guy that Skin heard the Irishman call Reecey. I presume that's Gerry Reece. Skin reckoned Quiddhy had hired him and that he'd subcontracted the Bermondsey gang leader, Archibald Pike, to provide facilities and security for the kidnap, if not more.'

'I've never used him,' said Fox, holding out a reassuring hand, 'but Gerry's work is organising kidnaps. Mainly in South and Central America. And I'm sure he'd like me to tell you that he's not all bad. He won't take anybody under the age of twenty-five years old, for instance. He's also kidnapped some very bad people in his time: dodgy politicians, drug smugglers, mafia thugs and the like. I'd have to check on this, but I should think the only problem he had with this one was that he's never done a London-based job.'

'Reece's Irish partner? Quiddhy gave his name to Skin as McManus.'

'I know. James McManus. Not a pleasant character, by all accounts. He was ex-UDA; got a taste for killing during the Troubles.'

'Reece got it in the end – you know that, don't you?'

'Skin and Dan,' said Fox, shaking his head. 'What a pair.'

'Not the consummate professionals,' said Boxer, 'but they still managed to do what none of us could. They got Alyshia away from some highly trained operatives who were going to kill her.'

'A couple of lucky chancers, if you ask me.'

'Part of their motivation, apparently, for taking over the kidnap was that they didn't like what Quiddhy and co were doing to Alyshia: heavy interrogation, mock execution. So what did they have to get out of her to set about breaking her down like that?' asked Boxer, drumming his fingers on the table. 'Why the brutal escalation of tactics? Quiddhy was winning on the psychological front; he didn't have to frighten us half to death with that mock execution. I mean, not at that particular moment.'

They sat in silence, thinking.

'Time,' said Fox. 'Maybe time suddenly became an important factor.'

'Time?'

Mahmood Aziz was waiting in his brother's auto electrics and engine parts shop in the Sher Shah Kabari Market in West Karachi. At 4.30 a.m., most of the other workshops and traders were still closed up, but his brother had got in early to start work on stripping down an old truck that had arrived late the night before. Aziz was in the back office, which had a view onto the adjoining street where towers of used tyres had been stacked to the eaves. After some minutes, his guest arrived in this street and

Aziz let him into the back office, unseen by his brother and the other workers.

Aziz made some tea and they sat on the rickety furniture and commented on the coolness of the night.

'You probably haven't heard it yet, but I can confirm that our mutual friend had an unfortunate accident late last night in London,' said Aziz.

'Amir Jat is dead?' asked Lt General Abdel Iqbal, wanting it confirmed in words rather than between the lines.

'He was shot in the head.'

'And where is his body?'

'It will turn up somewhere in London tomorrow.'

'And Alyshia D'Cruz?'

'She is safe.'

Iqbal had been anticipating this news and had expected to be pleased by it, but now that he'd been confronted by the reality, he was suddenly aware of the power vacuum left by Amir Jat's absence.

'There's no need to be nervous,' said Aziz. 'You have our full support and your steady hands will be much appreciated by our Afghan friends, especially after the ferocious tenacity and para-noia of your predecessor, who they had begun to regard as, shall we say, unhinged.'

'I took a call from Frank D'Cruz earlier this afternoon. He was still very concerned about his daughter, even though she was out of her original kidnapper's hands.'

'You told him about the imminent arrival of Amir Jat?'

'Yes, and that he could inform the British authorities of that.'

'Does he believe that Amir Jat was responsible for taking his daughter?'

'I don't know.'

'But you pointed out to him how he had weakened Amir Jat's position by corrupting him and infiltrating the people around him?' said Aziz. 'Amir Jat could never feel safe again.'

'I did, but that didn't seem to convince him. It's possible that their relationship is well-balanced on that front. I don't know what hold Amir Jat had over him from when they first met in the early 1990s,' said Iqbal. 'What Frank D'Cruz was most concerned about with the arrival of Amir Jat was the prospect of an imminent terrorist attack.'

'I hope you assuaged his fears.'

'Of that I did manage to convince him.'

Lt General Abdel Iqbal finished his tea and the two men shook hands and embraced before the ISI officer took his leave. Aziz sat down in the quiet of the office. His brother came in, wiping his hands on an oily cloth.

'Everything all right?' he asked.

'All we can do is hope that this unexpected interference has not damaged the original plan,' said Aziz.

'When will you know?'

'Very soon now. In less than thirty-six hours we will gain our greatest victory over the forces of evil and the Ninth Greater Sin,' said Aziz. 'And then, finally, the world will have another name to think about now that Osama bin Laden has gone.'

'What hour did you set the timers for?'

'Tomorrow morning at the busiest possible moment: eight-thirty London time.'

29

A soft knock at the front door, not using the bell, raised Boxer's gaze from the grain of the table.

He was sitting in Isabel's kitchen, alone with a glass and bottle of whisky. He was exhausted. Not by the rollercoaster but by the knowledge that Martin Fox knew of his special service. It gave Fox power over him. He'd been naïve to think that it could remain a secret. People talk: the business elite with their art collections showing off to each other about another inside track that nobody else has. And yet it was something so intensely personal to him that having someone like Martin Fox know about it, and use it for commercial purposes, drained him.

Another soft knock. He got up, looked through the peephole: young Indian guy, wool hat, cheap heavy coat. He opened the door.

'I am Deepak Mistry,' he said, holding out his hand and ducking his head in a polite Asian bow. Boxer shook his hand, drew him in.

'I've been waiting a long time for you to turn up,' said Boxer.

'I had no idea,' said Mistry, smiling. 'And who might you be?'

'I was the kidnap consultant until the police took over. Now I'm a friend of the family. Charles Boxer,' he said. 'I'm not sure this is the best place for you to be.'

'Is Frank here?' asked Mistry quickly, fear in his eyes.

'No, he's in a suite at the Ritz, but he's looking for you. I'm not sure why, but it doesn't look good.'

'Do you work for him?'

'I did,' said Boxer, grabbing a coat, taking Mistry by the arm. 'But not anymore. I'll give you the full story in the car. I think we should leave now.'

'And why should I trust you?' asked Mistry, tearing his arm from Boxer's grip.

'Why did you knock on this door?'

Silence.

'I'm not going to wake Isabel so that she can vouch for me. She's been through hell tonight.'

Mistry nodded. Boxer led the way to the car and they took off down to Holland Park Avenue.

'Where are we going?'

'Somewhere safe,' said Boxer.

'And Alyshia?'

'That we don't know anymore,' said Boxer. 'We got very close to getting her back tonight but we were pipped at the post.'

He drove past the Royal Crescent, onto the Holland Park roundabout with the Thames Water Tower, half-full with blue water, traffic just beginning to materialise.

'It looks like you're the key, Deepak,' said Boxer, turning into Holland Road. 'I don't know what you know, or whose side you're on, other than it doesn't appear to be Frank's. So maybe let's start with some history.'

'I left the village with my only friend, Yash, in 1994. He went to Mumbai and joined a gang. It was run by a guy called Chhota Tambe, who had been a friend of Frank's in the 1980s. I went to Bangalore. When I needed money to set up my IT business, Yash approached Chhota Tambe on my behalf. He agreed to invest and, seeing as it was my only chance, I took it. But I didn't know what I'd let myself in for.'

'Chhota Tambe wanted something in return?'

'Nothing much to start off with. He seemed content with half my business, and making money,' said Mistry. 'Then, one day, I was flown to Dubai to meet him. I was an innocent, not street-wise like Yash. We talked. We watched a lot of movies and cricket. At the end of the stay, he gave me a contact name in Konkan Hills Securities and told me that he was a good man to sell into. I went back to Bangalore, made the call. Four weeks later, I signed a contract with Konkan Hills.'

'The start of a beautiful relationship,' said Boxer.

'One thing led to another,' said Mistry. 'Frank ended up buying my company and making me head of IT at Konkan Hills. It was only later, when I made it to the inner circle, that I began to realise that Chhota Tambe did not like Frank D'Cruz.'

'And why's that?'

'It dates back to the 1993 bombings in Mumbai.'

'But that was a Muslim attack and Frank's a Catholic.'

'Yes, but I think you can tell from Frank's underworld connections, like Anwar Masood and his network amongst the military in Pakistan, that although he might not bat for the Muslims, he is a faithful supporter and receives rewards in return.'

'So what sort of information was Chhota Tambe looking for?'

'Anything that might bring Frank down,' said Mistry.

'So you're a spy?' said Boxer.

'I'm a late developer,' said Mistry.

'You must be a natural to have fooled Frank for so long.'

'Chhota Tambe might be obsessed but he isn't stupid. He made sure I didn't start spying for him until Frank and I were already close,' said Mistry. 'Once you're as close as I was to Frank—'

'Are we talking father to son?'

'Something like that.'

'So Frank's hurt, as well as betrayed?'

'No question.'

'So how did you get so far in?'

'The houseboys,' said Mistry. 'I should have been one myself coming from Bihar, India's poorest state. It means I know them.'

'And they told you things?'

'No. That was my rule. I didn't want them to tell me secrets. Once you've betrayed your master, he will see it,' said Mistry. 'I found out where the secrets were being told, which was in the Juhu Beach house, close to the airport where people could go without being seen and be made to feel comfortable, if you're the sort of guest who finds being corrupted comfortable.'

'So what was Chhota Tambe interested in?'

'He wanted all Mumbai to know the extent to which Frank was

in bed with the Muslims. How his whole business empire was based on the support he'd given to them, and what he'd received in return,' said Mistry. 'And what the houseboys told me was that there were times when Frank cleared the compound. No servants. Only the gateman outside. When the house was in lockdown, nobody could get in – except Alyshia.'

'Was that why you started an affair with her?'

'Don't make it sound so easy,' said Mistry. 'Alyshia had the pick of Mumbai society. Cricketers, actors, sons of the best families, all of them eating out of her hand. And she wasn't interested.'

'What did the poor boy from Bihar have that they didn't?'

'A total lack of interest,' said Mistry. 'That, and the accessibility to constantly show it to her. Although I'd met her in London with Frank one time, we worked in the same plant for a year or more before we came across each other again.'

'Taking your time is only a good strategy if you sense some interest.'

'I found out that Alyshia had started going to Juhu Beach at the weekends, so I started going there myself whenever I could.'

'Until you met her.'

'By chance. It was the perfect accident.'

'And that was when the affair started?'

'Oh, no; you see, I knew she wasn't interested in men by then and it was making Frank nervous. He'd put the most beautiful cricketer that had ever graced the field in front of her and she'd just walk straight past. So when I met her on Juhu Beach, I said hello, exchanged a few words and left her there. No man in his right mind would have been able to do that.'

'So how did you make it happen?'

'I felt her watching me. Then she started putting herself in my way. From that moment, it was just a question of taking her to the limit of her patience before striking.'

Mistry's forearm had come up with his hand cupped and swaying like a cobra in threat display before darting forward and striking at the dashboard.

'That sounds a little cold-blooded to me, Deepak.'

'I had to protect myself,' said Mistry, opening his hands. 'You know what happens to spies in the end. If I'd fallen for her, how

348

long do you think I could have betrayed her? If she'd ever found out what I was doing to her father, do you think there would be any chance of forgiveness or reconciliation? No, I knew from the beginning. This was a game that had to be played.'

'And?' said Boxer, nearly amused.

'I failed,' said Mistry. 'I fell for her completely.'

Boxer glanced across the dimly lit cockpit of the car, the streetlights revealing Mistry in yellow flashes, his face set, the flat black of his pupils seeing nothing but holding the concentrated desperation of a man who'd lost everything.

'Alyshia and I reconnected after I gave a talk to the sales and marketing teams. This time it was different. There was no reticence. She suddenly seemed to want something from me. I didn't have to keep my distance, and so it started. She trusted me instantly – and I her. We started telling each other things that we would never have told anyone else.'

'Did she tell you what had happened in Mumbai?' asked Boxer. 'Something happened that she wouldn't even talk to Isabel about.'

'Oh, yes. That was why she'd become so vulnerable suddenly,' said Mistry. 'She'd gone to the beach house one night when it was in lock-down. The gateman was especially reluctant to let her stay, but eventually he gave in. There was a very important client of Frank's staying that night.'

'Was it Amir Jat?'

'She was intrigued,' said Mistry, nodding. 'She'd already met him on one of her business trips to Pakistan with Frank and knew his power. At midnight, a car turned up at the beach house, which Alyshia recognised. It was Sharmila's. It pulled up in front of the house and stayed there until the gates closed. Only then did Sharmila get out of the driver's side, which was surprising in itself because she never drove anywhere. She was always driven.

'She went to the back door of the car and let two children out. Girls. Alyshia said it was difficult to tell their ages, but their heads were around Sharmila's waist. Maybe six or seven. She took them by the hand and led them up the stairs to the front door, which opened before she got to it. Sharmila fed the children into the crack of the door, turned and left. In fact, Alyshia said, she turned and *fled*.

'The car's courtesy light was still on as she passed Alyshia and it was the look on Sharmila's face that Alyshia knew would stay with her for the rest of her life. Sharmila's eyes were wide open, lips parted as if to scream but, as in a dream, unable to produce any sound. It was as if – and Alyshia thought about this a lot afterwards – it was as if, rather than driving away from the scene of her total corruption, Sharmila was eternally driving towards it.

'And that was when Alyshia realised the sort of man her father was,' said Mistry. 'Not just someone who finds weaknesses and exploits them, but who's also prepared to use corruption to bind those close to him even closer.'

Mercy finished the first interview with Skin and slept for a few hours in a police cell. She woke with a jolt, sat up, back to the wall, feeling desolate. This is my life, she thought: destined for loneliness, her job the only thing that had meaning. No man. No daughter. And no sooner had she thought it than her mind shifted onto the case to find the terrier in her brain worrying at every detail. She called George Papadopoulos, who was not happy to be disturbed; nor was his girlfriend, who rolled over, taking the duvet with her.

'Mercy, it's … it's four o'clock in the morning,' said Papadopoulos, pulling on his girlfriend's dressing gown, padding into the sitting room.

'I can't sleep,' she said. 'I want to go and have a look at this unit in Hackney where they were keeping Alyshia.'

An hour later, they were being let into the taped-up unit by a uniformed policeman, who told them that it was owned by the Rosemary Works Early Years Centre and was rented out to a local man, Michael Keane, who used it as an art studio. Mercy called the local drug squad, asked if they knew MK. They did.

'We're looking for him,' she said. 'Does he have any known associates locally?'

'Associates is a nice way of putting it. He runs the Colville Estate with a Jamaican, Delroy Dread, and he pushes pills through a kid called Xan – Alexander Palmer.'

'Any addresses?'

They gave her the addresses and told her to be careful with Delroy Dread, who was a yardie and known for his brutality.

'Could you bring Xan in for some light questioning?' asked Mercy. 'Find out when he last saw MK?'

'It'll be a pleasure.'

Mercy and Papadopoulos headed into the tower blocks of the Colville Estate, found Delroy Dread's address and the stairs blocked by a posse of young black youths, who didn't seem to have an emotion between them, but recognised cops when they saw them. Mercy asked to speak to Delroy Dread.

'He sleepin'.'

'We're not the drug squad,' said Papadopoulos. 'We just want to talk to him about MK.'

'Come back the afternoon. Den he be awake.'

'It can't wait that long,' said Mercy.

'It goin' 'ave to.'

Mercy moved forward and the posse tightened, blocked her way.

'You don't want the whole drug squad down here, falling on Delroy, because you wouldn't let us in to ask a few questions, would you?' asked Papadopoulos.

'Disrupt your business just for the sake of a couple of questions?' said Mercy.

Silence. Not a flicker between them. A boy at the back of the group loped up the stairs. Silence and dead-eyed stares until he returned. The posse loosened. Mercy and Papadopoulos squeezed past. Two youths went ahead, two followed behind. They escorted them to an open blue door. One of them put a hand to Papadopoulos' chest, showed him where he could wait outside.

'He not likin' white people.'

Delroy Dread was sitting on a large cream leather sofa wearing a black and white Ska T-shirt and a pair of black jeans in his overheated living room. The smell of weed was strong. Reggae was playing at low volume, the walls aching with it. The room was lit by red glowing lamps. Delroy Dread was close to six foot five and weighed in at sixteen stone, and none of it was fat. His huge, handsome head looked as if it represented a tenth of his bodyweight. He ran a flat hand over his close cropped hair and a huge, veined bicep jumped under his skin. He lit a cigarette. He spoke out of the corner of his mouth as if the other side had been stitched up, which it had, after a knife attack in his hometown of Kingston when he was a boy.

'Sorry to wake you so early,' said Mercy.

'Haven't been to bed yet,' he said, giving her a lop-sided smile, as if there was a new possibility.

'I don't want to take up too much of your time,' said Mercy.

'You a very nicely spoken lady,' said Delroy Dread. 'Where you from?'

'I'm Ghanaian. My name is Mercy Danquah.'

'Black Star,' said Delroy, and held out his huge hand, gave her a finger-clicking Ghanaian handshake, nearly broke her finger off. 'How can I help you, Mercy?'

'I'm looking for MK.'

'In that particular case, I can't help you,' he said, looking genuinely disappointed.

'He disappeared last night.'

'Still can't help you.'

'You know there was some trouble here, just off the estate?'

'I heard.'

'In a unit on Branch Place.'

'I said I heard.'

'It was MK's workshop.'

'So?'

'Some people were keeping a girl in there as a hostage.'

Delroy Dread lifted his huge head up as if something had occurred to him. He reached across the sofa, picked up a discarded paper, twitched it in his fingers.

'These two on the police flyers been floatin' around, litterin' up the place?'

'That's right,' said Mercy, nodding, thinking he knew something.

His sharpness flickered in his black eyes. He slumped further into the corner of the sofa, sizing her up, measuring her for some kind of deal. He clasped his hands over his head; the T-shirt strained against the slabs of his pectorals. Mercy was astonished to find that she'd unconsciously leaned back and crossed her legs.

She told him what they thought had happened last night. He smoked his way through it without comment.

'Somebody else up here last night lookin' for these two,' said Delroy, turning the paper towards himself, inspecting Skin and Dan.

'Who would that be?'

'What's it worth?'

'I'm not drug squad,' said Mercy. 'I'm not sure how I can help you.'

He thought about it for a while.

'You go to church?' Dread asked.

'When I can. It's not always easy in my job.'

'I like church,' said Delroy Dread. 'I like the singin'. My father was a preacher.'

'Do you still go?'

'Not as much as I should, given my capacity for sinnin',' he said, smiling.

'Sin a little less, go to church a little more.'

'Maybe you right,' said Delroy, laughing wheezily to himself. 'The people lookin' for these two, they from a Muslim gang in Bethnal supplyin' heroin. It run by a little boxer fella, Hakim Tarar.'

30

'When I told Chhota Tambe that Alyshia had seen Amir Jat at the house, I could see immediately that he considered it a very significant piece of intelligence,' said Deepak Mistry. 'That was when he told me to put a recording device in the Juhu Beach house.'

'How did you get it in there?' asked Boxer.

'I had access to the compound through Alyshia and I could always go off and chat with the houseboys, get myself a little space,' said Mistry. 'My big problem came when Frank wanted to change his home cinema set-up. The electrician went into the ceiling cavity to do the rewiring and found the recording device.'

'How long did it last?'

'A couple of weeks or so.'

'Did you get anything for Chhota Tambe?'

'As far as I could tell, there were quite a few parties and some business discussions with foreigners, but nothing involving Amir Jat.'

'And why did Frank suspect you of being the spy?'

'The house boys. They had to tell him. They all know what Anwar Masood is capable of.'

'So why does Chhota Tambe hate Frank so much? It sounds like it's something more than just envy.'

'It's an obsession borne out of tragedy,' said Mistry. 'His elder brother and mentor, Bada Tambe, was killed in the 1993 Mumbai bombings. Bada Tambe was unlucky, as far as I can tell. He just happened to be walking past the Stock Exchange on the day of the explosions.'

'And what did Frank have to do with that?'

'They were all part of the same gang at that stage: D-Company, run by a Muslim gangster called Dawood Ibrahim, based in Dubai. He was the brains and money behind that bombing campaign and it caused a religious rift in his gang.'

'And Frank sided with the Muslims?'

'Being Catholic, he could play both sides, but Chhota Tambe, who led the Hindus, thought he was with the Muslims. All Frank's big breaks came from his Muslim connections.'

'So Chhota Tambe had grounds for suspicion?'

'Frank was still working for D-Company, but they weren't gold smuggling anymore; that business dried up when the government opened up the Indian economy, and by 1992, gold could be freely imported,' said Mistry. 'Frank was employed in Dawood Ibrahim's new business, which was smuggling heroin.'

'Now *that* is not something Frank would like to be in the public domain,' said Boxer. 'That would certainly ruin him. Nobody in the West would go anywhere near him. Does Chhota Tambe have any proof?'

'It's not like there's a bill of lading with Frank's name on it,' said Mistry. 'When I told Chhota Tambe about Amir Jat, he was really excited because he knew Jat had close ties to the Afghan Taliban and that he'd been the main conduit of heroin out of Afghanistan back in the 1980s and 1990s. Amir Jat had rewarded D-Company with the heroin business when gold smuggling was no longer viable. Chhota Tambe also knew, as everybody else does now, since a CIA report was published in the *Times of India*, that in late 2007 the ISI merged D-Company into Lashkar-e-Taiba, who were the terrorists responsible for both Mumbai attacks, in March 1993 and November 2008.'

'So Chhota Tambe puts two and two together and assumes that if Frank knows Amir Jat then he must be involved with Islamic terrorism in some way?'

'Not necessarily now, but certainly then, in 1993. The explosive used in those bombings was a military type called RDX – Research Department Explosive – and the quantity required, which was three tons, meant that it could only have come from Pakistan and the person who probably supplied it would have been Amir Jat.'

'And how does Frank fit in?'

'Chhota Tambe is convinced he smuggled it in by boat.'

'Any evidence?'

'None,' said Mistry. 'Doubt is a very powerful thing and obsession a very dangerous condition. It clouds your judgement. And that's what *both* Chhota Tambe and Frank D'Cruz are suffering from. Chhota Tambe is obsessed by who Frank is and what he's done to get there; and Frank is obsessed with what I know about him and Konkan Hills.'

'Well, that's enough motivation for Chhota Tambe to have had Alyshia kidnapped,' said Boxer. 'Did you hear about a plan of that sort in any of your dealings with him?'

'No. The kidnap was a complete surprise to me,' said Mistry. 'The first I heard about it was from someone masquerading as a representative of Alyshia's mother's lawyer. He was very clever. He came through the High Commission. But I'm sure he'd been sent by Frank because he brought Anwar Masood's men to my door. There was a shootout. I think he was killed. At first I thought the news of the kidnap might be another trap set by Frank to bring me out into the open. Then, after talking to Yash, we realised it was Chhota Tambe.'

'So Chhota Tambe ordered the kidnap to draw Frank out of his schedule, tried to kill him on his first night in London and, when that failed, he continued with the kidnap in order to punish him?' said Boxer.

'No, it was Yash who organised the hit on Frank,' said Mistry. 'He didn't ask permission from Chhota Tambe. He did it just to protect me. I'd been in hiding for months. When Yash found out Frank was going to London, he contacted a gang in Southall.'

'The only demand we ever got from Chhota Tambe was for "a demonstration of sincerity" from Frank.'

'I can't believe he was expecting an admission of guilt from him. I mean, not after all this time, but you never know; maybe his obsession had driven him that crazy. I'm sure he had no proof of Frank's involvement in the 1993 bombings or the heroin smuggling, so he might have had some vague hope of a confession,' said Mistry. 'But no, I think it's more likely he was just torturing Frank. Holding his daughter with no interest in a ransom, giving him a riddle that he couldn't hope to solve while escalating the brutality. All that must have driven Frank mad.'

At 6.00 a.m., Mercy got a call from the drug squad saying they'd picked up Xan Palmer.

'He says he and his girlfriend saw MK last night. They left when a couple of Asian guys turned up to talk to MK. He hasn't heard from him since. Tried to call MK's mobile, got no answer.'

'Ask him if one of those Asian men was called Hakim Tarar.'

She heard the officer ask the question, didn't catch the reply.

'Says he doesn't know his name but he'd recognise both of them. One was a small, hard-looking guy and the other was a big, scary fucker, with eyes that turned you to stone.'

'Would you mind bringing them down to the station? Bethnal Green's the nearest. I'm going after Hakim Tarar now.'

Mercy asked for some local police back-up before she called on Hakim Tarar, who lived on the fourth floor of a big block of flats on Nelson Gardens. She wanted all possible exits of the building covered before she knocked on his door. Six officers came with her, two with a door breach in case Tarar was feeling shy.

A neighbour came out of his flat on his way to work, just as the law turned up.

'You know if he's in?' asked one of the officers.

'I heard somebody in there earlier this morning,' he said, eyeing the door breach before he shot downstairs.

Papadopoulos did what he was good at: hammered on the door.

Mercy nodded at the two officers with the door breach. They swung it and the door flew open.

Papadopoulos went in first, checking each room as he went. The bedroom was dark. He turned the light on.

'He's in here, in bed.'

Hakim Tarar was curled up in the foetal position under the bedclothes, running a fever. Above his head was a poster of Amir Khan, World Light Welterweight Champion, and on a shelf below, a few small trophies.

'You don't look too clever,' said Mercy. 'Where've you been?'

'Got the flu, that's all,' said Tarar. 'What you want?'

'That's funny, because I heard you were out and about last night, went to visit your friend MK, took a look at his unit on Branch Place,' said Mercy. 'Did you find anybody in there, Hakim?'

'I don't know what you're talking about.'

'Mercy,' said George, from the bathroom.

She called one of the officers in to keep an eye on Tarar, went to the bathroom. George was pointing at a pair of sodden under-pants on the floor in a pool of dirty water.

'I think our friend ended up in the canal last night.'

'Get an evidence bag, run it down to the lab with a comparative sample from the canal outside the Branch Place unit,' said Mercy. 'I'll take Hakim down to Bethnal Green for a chat.'

Boxer and Mistry came out of Hammersmith onto the Great West Road and drove in silence to the Hogarth roundabout.

'So what are you doing in London, Deepak?'

No reply. Boxer could see the complications from the intensity in the man's face.

'Hoping for reconciliation with Alyshia?'

'I just want to help.'

'Somehow you're going to have to appease Frank.'

'Impossible,' said Mistry. 'He's spent the last three months try-ing to kill me.'

'How would you describe your relationship to Chhota Tambe now?'

'It's finished. It's one thing for him to attack Frank, but Alyshia? A mock execution? That's unacceptable.'

'Do you know where Chhota Tambe is now?'

'Yash told me he's in London, hoping for some kind of victory.'

'Do you know where?'

Mistry nodded.

'So tell me what you're doing in London, Deepak.'

Another long silence.

'You're right,' he said finally.

'And you hope that by giving up Chhota Tambe to Frank, he'll stop trying to have you killed and allow you to see his daughter again?'

They reached a traffic light and went into the right hand filter lane. They crossed the road into Turnham Green.

'Where are you taking me?'

'Some friends who live in the States have a big house in Chiswick with a small flat at the bottom of the garden. It's quiet and nobody knows about it.'

'You're going to put me there and do what?'

'I'm thinking,' said Boxer. 'We have to be careful how we do this.'

'How we do what?'

'Achieve what you want to achieve.'

'And why should you help me?'

'Maybe it's because I'm a romantic,' said Boxer. 'Do you have any of the recordings you made in the Juhu Beach house with you?'

'No.'

'Where are they?'

'Some of them are with Chhota Tambe and the rest were in my flat in Mumbai.'

'Can you remember what was in those recordings? Any names?'

'I listened to them all several times. I supplied notes to Chhota Tambe so he could understand what was going on. I remember everything pretty well.'

'Maybe you heard something that wasn't significant to you or Chhota Tambe, but which Frank doesn't want anybody else to know about.'

'But only Frank would know that.'

'Maybe. I'm thinking that if I get a friend of mine from MI6 to come and talk to you, he might be able to clarify if that's the case.'

31

Boxer jerked awake. Only four and a half hours' sleep, but brain instantly sharp. Isabel was standing at the door, fully dressed, cup of tea in hand.

'I didn't know if you wanted to be woken up.'

'I did. That's good.'

'There's been no news,' she said, sitting on his bed, giving him the tea. 'Total silence since she disappeared again last night. No contact. Nothing.'

'It'll come,' said Boxer.

'Rick Barnes said he saw you leaving the house with someone last night. You didn't come back until after six this morning.'

'Deepak Mistry turned up,' said Boxer. 'Frank's been looking for him. He'd been spying on Frank and using Alyshia to do it.'

'Is this the Mumbai problem? Why it all fell apart?'

'More or less,' said Boxer, and gave her the full story about Chhota Tambe and what Alyshia had seen at the Juhu Beach house. Isabel's face was locked in horror, mouth slightly open, eyes unblinking.

'He made Sharmila do *that*?' she said in the ensuing silence. 'You see what I mean about him?'

'You said Sharmila was from that world. You described her as a "gangster's moll". Do you know which gangster?'

Isabel was shaking her head, looking at nothing, barely listening.

'Chico's downstairs, you know. He's been asking me what happened last night,' she said. 'There's something wrong with him.'

'Physically? Mentally?'

'Both. He looks as sick as a dog on green meat. He's depressed and I think he's scared – which is scaring me.'

'And he's still not talking?'

She shook her head. Boxer kissed her on the mouth and could feel all her worry in the tension within her lips. He hugged her and she clung to him.

'Just tell me it's going to be all right.'

'Everything is going to be fine,' said Boxer, with all the remembered confidence he could muster.

He showered and dressed, went downstairs to the kitchen. D'Cruz watched him eating his breakfast in silence.

'How did it go with the MI5 debrief last night?' asked Boxer.

'It was long and exhausting.'

'Did you tell them anything interesting?'

'Only what I told you about corrupting Amir Jat and how he hated me for it.'

'I don't want you to disappear again,' said Boxer. 'I'm going to need to talk to you later today. It's important; you'll want to know.'

'Talk to me now. I'm here.'

Boxer wiped his mouth with a piece of kitchen roll, shook his head. He went into the drawing room and called his best friend, Simon Deacon.

'We have to talk,' said Boxer. 'I have new information that could help. I think you know what I'm talking about.'

'I'm on my way somewhere,' said Deacon. 'In fact, it could be interesting for you to see this. Let's meet in London Fields. You'll see where I am. Near the lido. The police have taped it all off.'

It took Boxer well over an hour to get to Hackney. He'd always imagined, with such a name, that there would be something significant about London Fields, but it was just a large, flat piece of greenery with big bare trees, a cricket pitch, a lido, tennis courts and some playgrounds all empty of people. He wasn't sure what else he'd been expecting: the sheep still grazing before going to market? He saw the police cordon and Simon Deacon standing within it. He went over and called to him. Deacon beckoned to him; a constable lifted the tape.

White-suited, masked forensics were working around a body. Deacon was looking down at it, hands in his coat pockets.

'Good to see you, Charlie,' said Deacon, shaking hands. They grabbed each other by the shoulder, genuinely pleased. 'Takes me back to the good old days. It's been a pleasure working with you again, even if it has been at one remove.'

'I've felt your hands on the controls, which has been very reassuring,' said Boxer. 'Who have we got here?'

'This is Amir Jat,' said Deacon. 'You've probably heard of him.'

'A little more in the last day than in the rest of my life.'

'We were rather hoping he wouldn't be in this state,' said Deacon.

'Did you know he was coming?'

'Only after debriefing Frank D'Cruz last night,' said Deacon. 'We'd begun to suspect this kidnap of Frank's daughter might have some sort of terrorist connection. We gave him some freedom of movement yesterday in the hope that he would take us to a valuable intelligence source, but ...'

'He told me he was in contact with people he described as "intermediaries".'

'We don't know who he spoke to. He went through some complex series of internet relays to a scrambled line. We suspect he might have been talking to his Pakistani friend, Lt General Abdel Iqbal.'

'So what do you think happened here?'

'It's difficult to say, but I think we might be looking at the end result of a power struggle within the Pakistani intelligence service,' said Deacon. 'Perhaps Amir Jat was holding too tightly to the reins and not prepared to let go. We know he was becoming an embarrassment to the Pakistanis in their relationship with the Americans. CIA field agents have not been happy about him for some time. Pressure has been applied at the very highest level since they suspected Amir Jat's involvement in the NATO fuel convoy bombings and hiding Osama bin Laden.'

'Are the Pakistanis saying anything?'

'We've told them what's happened. I imagine they're putting together a very involved statement, which will tell us very little.'

'Can we go and talk somewhere?' asked Boxer. 'Like in the middle of the park.'

They set off towards the roped-off cricket wicket. Boxer gave Deacon a compressed version of his discussion with Deepak Mistry from earlier that morning. Deacon stood in silence for some moments afterwards.

'Well, the news about the assassination attempt and the first kidnap is welcome. We were very concerned about that,' said Deacon. 'But we're no less concerned by what happened last night and the appearance of Amir Jat's body this morning. We still think there's something going on. One of the preliminary forensic inspections here has revealed that Amir Jat's clothes were wet but not soaked through. His front was stiff with partially frozen water.'

'You think he was involved in taking over the kidnap down by the canal last night?'

'Too early to say, but that's one of the theories we're developing.'

'And that leads you to believe that Alyshia is now being held by some sort of terrorist organisation, or by people controlled by one?'

'I'd like to talk to Deepak Mistry,' said Deacon. 'Even if he can't tell us very much, I'd still like to know what happened in the shootout in the Dharavi slum. The person who he says was pretending to be Isabel Marks' lawyer's representative was one of our agents in Mumbai.'

'I've seen Frank this morning,' said Boxer. 'I think there's real pressure being put on him now. He's saying even less than he was before and he's frightened in a way that he didn't seem to be during the first kidnap, which he always thought was going to be about money in the end.'

'Yes,' said Deacon. 'We saw that in our interview with him last night. The shining inner light of unfounded confidence has finally been snuffed. Nice to see him taking some punishment at last. But yes, we're concerned that this new threat to his daughter seems to have genuinely frightened him and made him even less forthcoming.'

'On the way to the drop last night, I drove through the City and saw Frank's cars,' said Boxer. 'I think you could call that the ultimate central position to create maximum awareness.'

'I hear what you're saying, Charlie, but look: *because* those cars were being positioned in such sensitive areas of the city, they have been *very* carefully checked over. They went straight from the port to a police warehouse, where they were the subject of a close inspection by two Explosive Ordnance Disposal squads,' said Deacon. 'There was no trace of anything suspicious at all. The cars don't even work. The batteries have been disconnected.'

'Are the batteries still in the vehicles?'

'Yes, because eventually they're going to be reconnected and driven all over the country through various temporary switching stations that have been set up to show off the concept.'

'What sort of work did the EOD squads do on the batteries themselves?'

'I don't know. I'd have to ask for the report they gave to the police and MI5 on that.'

'I imagine the batteries are sealed units,' said Boxer. 'I doubt they would have taken them apart. Would they be able to detect a substance like PETN in a container within a sealed battery cell, from the outside?'

'I'll have to check,' said Deacon. 'I think I really would like to talk to Deepak Mistry now.'

Working with the local police and drug squad, Mercy and George Papadopoulos picked up the other four members of Hakim Tarar's gang. They were all taken to Bethnal Green Police Station, where Mercy briefed an interviewing team who took the gang members off into separate rooms and worked them. Within an hour they'd come up with the name of the final member of the gang and Mercy telephoned her report to DCS Makepeace.

'There's only one member of the group missing now. His name is Rahim and, by all accounts, he's the dangerous one, and armed. None of them will divulge his whereabouts, if they even know it. We still haven't got any intelligence on where they're holding Alyshia, but we've definitely picked on the right guys and we'll keep banging away until they talk,' she said.

'Have you any suspicion of the possibility of a terrorist attack associated with this group?'

'I can't say,' said Mercy. 'We're not that far in with them yet.'

Papadopoulos came in with a report he'd just torn from the hands of the lab technician. Mercy read it, nodded.

'I've got to go now, sir,' she said, and hung up.

She went back to the interview room; Hakim Tarar was flushed, his throat rasping. He had a temperature of 102 degrees. She organised two aspirin for him.

'We've just had the analysis back from your underpants, the soaking wet ones we found on your bathroom floor,' said Mercy. 'The water extracted from them is an exact match for the canal water outside Unit 6b on Branch Place, where Alyshia D'Cruz was being held hostage. That must mean you were there last night.'

'Yesterday afternoon I went for a run. It's part of my boxing training. I tripped and fell in the canal. I got cold. I went to bed. I woke up this morning with a fever. I don't know any Unit 6b. I don't know any Alyshia D'Cruz.'

'You supply the drug dealer known as MK with heroin.'

'So *you* say.'

'No, so says another dealer on the Colville Estate: Delroy Dread.'

'Never heard of him.'

'Delroy Dread said that two of your gang members went to see him last night and asked him if he knew anything about an Indian girl being held hostage somewhere on the estate by two white guys,' said Mercy. 'He even showed me the Met police flyer they left with him. Now why would two of your boys do something like that?'

'Ask them. I don't know.'

'You ever met someone called Xan Palmer – Alexander Palmer?'

'Never heard that name.'

'Twenty-two years old. Pale face, big hair. He deals pills for MK in the clubs.'

'Sorry, I can't help you.'

'He remembers you, and the blonde girl who was with him clocked you, too. And that big guy you brought along for support. Rahim "with eyes that could turn a man to stone". You all met in MK's flat last night. I'm surprised you have no recollection of all this, Hakim. You know what the desk sergeant just told me? They found MK's body snagged in Bow Creek in Canning Town. He'd taken quite a beating before being strangled and he had some cigarette burns to the skin around his eyes. That ring any bells with you?'

Tarar looked up into his head.

'None,' he said. 'And I know a bell when I hear one.'

32

'I've heard the report from the EOD squads. The batteries were X-rayed in position and found to be normal, which meant they didn't feel the need to remove them, dismantle them and give them an internal visual inspection,' said Simon Deacon. 'Now the EOD guys concede that the batteries *are* big enough that something explosive could be disguised to look like a cell, which would not show up clearly on an X-ray.'

'So what now?' asked Boxer.

'You know what intelligence work is all about, Charlie,' said Deacon. 'We have disparate pieces of information and all we're trying to do is put the right pieces of information together to achieve the correct picture. Deepak might be able to verify or clarify one of those pieces.'

'Can I ask you what it's to do with?'

'A break-in at D'Cruz's car plant in early January this year.'

They went through the garden door at the side of the house and down the path to the small flat. Boxer knocked on the door. No answer. He took out his key, opened up the flat, which was empty.

'Shit,' said Boxer, as they walked through the empty rooms.

'Too nervous,' said Deacon. 'Maybe, given that Frank's after him, he started to feel like a sitting duck.'

'Put your hands on your head,' said Mistry, from the front door, gun in hand. 'Don't turn around. Just put your hands on your head. That's both of you.'

367

Mistry crept forward, put the gun on Deacon's spine and frisked him, found nothing, withdrew back to the door.

'Turn around slowly, hands on head,' said Mistry. 'You sit on the sofa in the middle. Charles, you stay where you are.'

'I can understand why you're nervous,' said Deacon, lowering himself onto the sofa. 'All I can say is that we are who we say we are and we believe that you might have valuable intelligence—'

'I need proof.'

'I can only show you my ID card, which gives me access to the MI6 building.'

Mistry nodded. Deacon slowly produced his ID.

'How do you know each other?'

'He was my commanding officer in the 1991 Gulf War,' said Boxer.

Silence. Mistry gave the ID back, lowered the gun.

'I'm sorry,' he said. 'I've been on the run now for a few months. I just got paranoid, that's all.'

Mistry sat down, put the gun on the table.

'You want to talk to me about Alyshia and Frank D'Cruz?'

Deacon produced a voice recorder, set it on a table between them. Boxer made some tea, put out a plate of biscuits.

'You worked in the Konkan Hills steelworks,' said Deacon. 'Did you ever visit other companies that were going to take your steel; the car factories, for instance?'

'Yes. I had close contacts with the various line managers to make sure that I was producing the right quality steel for them.'

'Did that include the electric car business?'

'I was given a tour of that facility and we had discussions.'

'Were they producing the batteries in the same facility?'

'Yes, but in a different building.'

'The cars they were manufacturing for the European market, were they any different?'

'There were some style differences, that's all. The platform was the same.'

'And the batteries?'

'They were the same.'

'Were those cars selling in the Indian market?'

'Yes, but to an exclusive minority. They were expensive compared to the fossil fuel cars.'

Deacon and Mistry talked at some length about the recordings he'd made in the Juhu Beach house in November and December of last year. Nothing seemed to interest Deacon particularly until Mistry started talking about a meeting between Frank D'Cruz and an Afghan called Jawid Sahar.

'Do you know how Frank had met Jawid Sahar originally?'

'Interesting,' said Mistry. 'His was one of the few names that caught Chhota Tambe's attention, too. Frank knew him through Amir Jat. He was a businessman with connections to Hamid Karzai's family in Kabul. Frank was looking to sell his steel in Afghanistan.'

'What did they talk about?'

'They didn't talk very much about steel. They spoke about Frank's deal with the British government to set up the electric car factories in the UK,' said Mistry. 'There seemed to be no detail too small for him. I think Frank felt compelled to be so revealing because Jawid Sahar was a contact of Amir Jat's. He wanted to be in there at the beginning of the rebuilding of Afghanistan, and a direct route into the Karzai family was very appealing.'

'Did they happen to talk about the prototypes?'

'They talked about everything,' said Mistry. 'Frank was very pleased with himself because he'd just got permission from the Mayor of London to install the advertising pitch for his cars in the middle of the City and out at Stratford, in front of the Olympic stadium. It gave him the opportunity to brag about all his ministerial connections.'

'Did Jawid Sahar ever come back?'

'Not in the following two weeks while I was still at Konkan Hills.'

'Did you ever hear the name Mahmood Aziz mentioned in any conversation with Frank or any of the Juhu Beach house tapes?'

'No.'

Deacon's mobile rang, he took the call and listened for some minutes, hung up.

'I think I've got all I need for the moment,' he said. 'You've been very helpful. Just one last thing, Deepak. Do you know who shot the Englishman who came to see you in the Dharavi slum?'

'I assume it was one of Anwar Masood's men. They were looking for me and they'd shoot anybody.'

'He was my agent and a good man.'

'Then I'm sorry for that,' said Mistry.

They exchanged mobile numbers in case there was a need for any further contact. Deacon left. Boxer walked him back to his car.

'What was the significance of Jawid Sahar?'

'He's a known associate and supporter of Mahmood Aziz, who is Amir Jat's main contact with the Afghan Taliban. Aziz is responsible for a number of bombing campaigns. He also has UK connections. He was born and lived here until he was twelve. And he has international ambitions on the scale of Osama bin Laden.'

'And all those questions about the car factories?'

'We're still waiting to see the Indian police report about that break-in. We've been told that the warehouse holding the electric car prototypes for the UK market was accessed and that nothing of value had been stolen.'

'You need to get your bomb squads back on the job,' said Boxer.

'The positive thing is that if any devices have been planted, they haven't been detonated, which probably means they're on a timer and they're waiting for a specific moment,' said Deacon. 'And if there's an override, they haven't exercised it because they don't know what we know.'

'What do you think Frank knows about any of this?'

'Everything and nothing. He obviously knows who he's been speaking to but not necessarily their connections. He probably knows about the break-in to his car plant but not what it was about. I'm sure he doesn't know detail because it would be too risky to have him out there knowing anything specific. I think he's just been told to keep his mouth shut in a general way about anything potentially sensitive and if he's lucky, they'll release his daughter.'

'I'm off her case now, but Alyshia still feels like my responsibility,' said Boxer. 'And I'm aware that eight million Londoners are more important than one young woman.'

*

Mercy went to the interview room door, knocked, sat back down. A few seconds later, the desk sergeant opened it. Xan Palmer and the girl were standing there, looking even paler and more panic-struck, having just been shown MK's body.

'Is this the man you saw last night in MK's flat?' asked Mercy.

They both nodded.

'I can't hear you,' said Mercy.

'Yes,' they said.

'Thank you, that will be all,' said Mercy, and shut the door in their faces.

'I'm not interested in sending you down for your drug dealing, Hakim. All I want to know is where the girl is. You don't tell me that and, now that we have MK's body, you'll be sent down for the max. You'll never meet Amir Khan in the ring and you'll be boxing for the veterans by the time you get out.'

'I can't tell you.'

'That's progress,' said Mercy. 'Not, I won't tell you, but I *can't* tell you. Why can't you tell me? Against your religion?'

'You could say that.'

The door opened, the desk sergeant came in again, timed it so that four members of Hakim Tarar's gang walked past and looked in, eyes connecting. He put a piece of paper down in front of Mercy, backed out. She read it, smiled.

'Know what this is, Hakim?' she said. 'This is the report on the footage from the Rosemary Works CCTV camera at the end of Branch Place.'

'What do I care?'

'It shows the registration number of the VW Transporter you were using last night. It belongs to Ali Wattu of the Pride of Indus restaurant on Green Street. Now that's a Page One mistake. You've got to know that every inch of London is scanned by CCTV these days, even somewhere as insignificant as Branch Place. Whoever planned that action last night wasn't thinking straight. You got anything you want to add now? Anything that might mitigate your horrible circumstances?'

*

'What are my chances of success here, do you think?' asked Mistry, sharing a takeaway curry and a bottle of beer with Boxer in the Chiswick flat.

'Probably better with Alyshia than they are with Frank,' said Boxer. 'At least Alyshia knows Frank for what he is: a corruptor of men, and women. As you said, that scene with Amir Jat, Sharmila and the very young girls is not one she will ever forget. You've betrayed Frank, but you had no option but to comply with Chhota Tambe's demands. I think even Isabel is well-disposed towards you, and she's someone who's grown to understand the dark side of Frank D'Cruz. No, your main difficulty is with Frank. Unless you get his support, he will find ways to make your life difficult, if he doesn't manage to terminate it.'

'He seems to trust you,' said Mistry. 'Can you talk to him?'

'I can try,' said Boxer, 'but don't expect Frank's forgiveness to come for free. There'll always be a price to pay, and it won't be in cash.'

'He'll want to have a hold over me.'

'And you'll have to decide whether Alyshia is worth it,' said Boxer, looking at his watch. 'I've got to go and check on Isabel. You going to be all right now?'

'I'll be fine,' he said, picking up the gun.

'Where did you get that from?' asked Boxer.

'Yash arranged it for me from one of the Southall gangs. I picked it up this morning.'

'Used one before?'

'Once.'

'Be careful then.'

'Yash told me I shouldn't get caught with it,' said Mistry. 'This was the gun they used when they tried to kill Frank three days ago.'

Saleem Cheema sat in the basement room with Rahim. He was looking at Alyshia, with her head still wrapped in a sweater. She now seemed comfortable, whereas he was in a state of extreme tension. An SMS arrived on his phone with a loud beep that, in his highly anxious state, brought him out of his chair. Rahim stared straight ahead, unmoved. Cheema had no idea what was going through his mind. The coded SMS told him to call the UK command from a fixed line. He went upstairs. His hands were sweating and shaky. Every time he'd called UK command, the orders they'd given him had pushed him further beyond his moral boundaries. He made the call, gave his code name.

'You are to kill the girl.'

'What?'

'I think you heard me.'

'But why?' said Cheema desperately. 'She's served her purpose. Why do we have to—'

'It is seen by the high command in Pakistan as an appropriate punishment for Frank D'Cruz and that's all you need to know.'

'I don't know whether I can do that.'

'There is also the danger that she may compromise your network if she's released at a later date,' said the voice. 'Where was she when you dealt with our friend?'

Silence from Cheema.

'I think you see my point now,' said the voice. 'The decision has been taken that this is the best course of action.'

More silence from Cheema as he struggled with himself.

'I am surprised at you. I would have thought your earlier task far more difficult.'

'Is there a deadline?' asked Cheema.

'Before midnight tonight.'

33

'The purpose of this meeting is to devise a strategy for dealing with a potential terrorist attack on the City of London,' said Natasha Radcliffe, the Home Secretary, as chair of the COBRA emergency meeting. 'Now that we've all seen this report about the D'Cruz cars, does anybody have any suggestions on how to approach the matter?'

'The first thing we should try is a remote inspection of the two cars in Stratford,' said Joyce Hunter of MI5. 'Those cars are under a canopy in front of the stadium in the south of the Olympic park, which is closed at night. They're not visible from the outside. The EOD Ammunition Technicians can send in a remote control-led vehicle, which will tell them if they've got anything to worry about. If there's anything unusual, they can remove the batteries to a safe place and dismantle them.'

'And if you do find something ugly out at Stratford, what are you going to do in Bank and St Mary Axe?' asked Mervin Stanley, the Mayor of London. 'If we have army bomb disposal units out on the streets of the City, it's not going to look good. Markets could crash. This could have global consequences.'

'We'd have to have a media black-out, for a start,' said Barbara Richmond, the Minister for Counter Terrorism. 'An evacuation procedure in place.'

'We're concerned about the batteries only, aren't we?' said Natasha Radcliffe. 'I understand from the report that the cars themselves were given the all-clear. What sort of devices would we be talking about if they were contained in the batteries?'

'Given that they didn't show up on the earlier EOD inspection, which checks a whole range of device attributes, they would be small, contrived to look like the cells of an electric car battery, odourless and with no obvious energy supply,' said Simon Deacon. 'What particularly concerns MI6 is that we've now been able to establish an information chain about these cars, from Frank D'Cruz to a known terrorist operative called Mahmood Aziz, who used to be a UK citizen and now wants to be the next Osama bin Laden.

'As you all know, there have been hundreds of breaches in security with radioactive material since the breakdown of the old Soviet Union. The one that particularly concerns us was found on an arms smuggling mule train, going from Tajikistan to northern Afghanistan in January this year. Fortunately the Americans were able to get the material on a flight to Kabul before an insurgency attack on their post, which killed all of the smugglers they'd just captured. These arms were destined for Mahmood Aziz in his stronghold of North Waziristan. The CIA confirmed that the phial taken from the arms smugglers contained radioactive material.'

'So we're talking about the makings of a dirty bomb,' said Mervin Stanley.

'That's our concern, at the moment,' said Deacon.

Silence.

'The devices, *if* they exist,' said Joyce Hunter, trying to strike a positive note, 'will probably have timers and, in the event of those being discovered, also mobile phone triggers.'

'So someone would have to have to be able to see the cars in order to establish that they were being tampered with by police or army, and then trigger the bomb with a mobile?' said Stanley.

'That's correct,' said Hunter. 'Electronic jammers will be installed around the Stratford podiums before the EOD Ammunition Technicians start work. If the EOD squad detect anything unusual, I would advise closing down the mobile phone network before they go into their render safe procedure.'

'That might not mean much out in somewhere like Stratford, although I'm sure the contractors who are still working, night and day, wouldn't be too happy about it,' said Stanley. 'But if that was done in the City, I think it could set off a panic and we might see a catastrophic market reaction. The one thing the City of London could do without, after all its been through in the last three years, is a run on the market.'

'If a dirty bomb goes off in Bank, St Mary Axe or Stratford,' said Natasha Radcliffe, 'there will *be* no City of London, no Olympic Games. That will be the end of the market and the end of billions of pounds of revenue for London and the UK, which is why, Mervin, we'll learn as much as we can from the Stratford cars first and only move in on the City cars if the EOD technicians express their concern.'

'This may sound like a stupid question but, if there is a timer, will they be able to determine the date and time that the device is supposed to explode?' asked Stanley.

'Bombs in the real world don't come equipped with Hollywood timers with big visible red numbers counting down,' said Hunter. 'The EOD Techs would have to locate the timer and take it from there.'

'I would imagine that the timers for the Stratford cars would be set for the same time as the City cars, for simultaneous explosions,' said the Met Police Commmissioner. 'If we knew what time they were set for in Stratford, that would tell us how long we've got to deal with the City vehicles. In the meantime, we should establish which rooms in all the buildings in the area of Bank and St Mary Axe have a line of sight to the cars. We should also put plain clothes officers on the ground to see if there are any obvious interested observers within range of the cars.'

'At the beginning of this report, we're told that Alyshia D'Cruz is now in the hands of an Asian drug gang, which Counter Terrorism tells us could possibly have links to al-Qaeda,' said Mervin Stanley. 'But you don't tell us whether there's any link between her being held and these bombs going off in the City.'

'That's because we don't know, which is why we have to be very careful,' said Barbara Richmond. 'If they do have links and they get wind of a rescue attempt on Alyshia D'Cruz, they could alert the bombers and the devices may be triggered.'

*

Boxer went back to Isabel's house. The overcast day was beginning to get darker as Rick Barnes opened the door for him.

'Any news?'

'Nothing from the kidnappers.'

'How's the investigation going?' asked Boxer. 'I've heard they picked up some suspects. You must have some leads by now? CCTV footage?'

Barnes said nothing. Blanked him.

'Where's Isabel?'

'In the kitchen,' said Barnes. 'You're not going to tell her anything, are you? It'll just make her even more anxious.'

'You're getting that close?'

Barnes nodded. Boxer brushed past him. Isabel was in the kitchen, staring into the table, nothing in front of her. She looked up, dazed.

'It's you,' she said, the hope gone from her face.

'It's going to be OK,' said Boxer.

'I don't know how you can say that after what we've been through.'

'It's the rollercoaster, but we're going to get to the end of the ride and it's all going to work out fine.'

'Where've you been?'

'Putting intelligence sources together,' said Boxer. 'Do you know where Frank's gone?'

'He's at the Savoy now. Their Royal Suite was given a makeover a couple of years ago and, at three hundred and twenty-five square metres, and ten thousand pounds a night, he prefers it to the Ritz,' she said drily. 'You've been with Deepak?'

'I introduced him to MI6. He's been helpful.'

'Is this anything to do with Alyshia?'

'Not exactly,' said Boxer. 'He's come to London because of her, but the information he's brought with him is to do with something else.'

'You're not telling me things again.'

'Only because it doesn't concern you,' said Boxer. 'It's not material to Alyshia's release.'

'So, Deepak's in love with her,' said Isabel. 'That's why he's here, isn't it?'

'Have you got any objections to him?'

'I liked him, but that doesn't mean anything. It's whether Frank likes him that matters.'

'I'll work on that.'

'Always the negotiator.'

'Think positive, look to the future,' said Boxer. 'I told you, I like being where things matter.'

'Have you spoken to Amy yet?' she asked, and the question sliced through him.

'She refuses to speak to me. I called her at my mother's; she cut the line.'

'That's what matters, Charles; nothing else,' said Isabel. 'You're just concentrating on things that you *can* control, while what matters to you spins away.'

Once he'd seen the other members of his gang in custody, and Mercy had played the CCTV footage of the VW Transporter in Branch Place, and his fever had edged up another degree, Hakim Tarar's resolve finally cracked. He gave Mercy the Boleyn Road address of Saleem Cheema's house. Mercy was glad. She didn't want to have to bring in the owner of the vehicle, Ali Wattu. That would have been dangerous, because she'd assumed that the Pride of Indus restaurant was close to where Alyshia was being held and she didn't want any possibility of the new kidnappers being alerted.

At 6.00 p.m., a blue transit with *Jack Romney Decorators* on the side entered Boleyn Road and drove past the house where Saleem Cheema lived. It pulled into an open space, just beyond the house on the other side of the road. The driver got out, threw a coat on over his paint-spattered overalls and walked away. In the back was a Metropolitan police surveillance team.

The two men sitting in the back watched a monitor, which showed images from a camera mounted in the 'O' of Romney. Nothing happened for half an hour. Then the front door opened and Saleem Cheema came out, turned right. The surveillance team called in a ground force, taking it in turns to follow Cheema, who went to the greengrocers and bought a selection of fruit and vegetables. Nobody went anywhere near him.

Mercy's caution was rewarded because Saleem Cheema's next move was to go around the corner into the yard behind the Pride of Indus restaurant and pick up the VW Transporter he'd driven last night. A mobile unit was called in to follow the van, but it only went as far as the house on Boleyn Road, where Cheema reversed it up to the garage doors, turned off the engine and went into the house.

At 6.15 p.m., the four members of the EOD squad got dressed in G4S security uniforms, miked up and, carrying electronic jammers, walked out to the two cars mounted on podiums under a canopy outside the Olympic stadium. They had a quick chat with the previous shift of security guards and positioned the jammers.

They had decided on simultaneous inspection of the two batteries. The two EOD teams were linked to each other and to an operations room in an EOD vehicle at the entrance to the Olympic Park. They opened the front doors of the cars and pushed the seats forward. They opened the rear doors, unlocked the back seats, folded them forward and once more into the footwells. This revealed the batteries, which powered the cars. A visual inspection revealed nothing extraordinary and they retreated to the command post.

Two technicians sitting next to each other in the command post began operating the remote controlled vehicles, known as Wheelbarrows. These were mobile laboratories mounted on narrow caterpillar tracks. From these Wheelbarrows, each technician had four images displayed on screens, as well as a whole range of detection monitors, ranging from radioactive material to electronic pulse, sound, radiowave and odour.

'Let's take some more X-rays first,' said the supervisor, 'and run a comparison between the two. See what that throws up.'

The new X-rays came up on the screens. The technicians and supervisor looked them over. One of the techs pointed to a central part of the battery in the car on the left.

'These batteries should be exactly the same,' said the technician. 'Isn't that right?'

'That's what we've been told,' said the supervisor. 'Have we got the images from the battery manufacturers?'

The images were brought up on the monitors and again the technician pointed to the central part of the battery in the car on the left.

'The battery from the car on the right is exactly the same as the image sent by the manufacturer,' he said, 'but this one, that central section isn't quite right.'

'What was that?' said the other technician.

'I didn't see anything.'

'On the electronic monitor. There was a pulse.'

They replayed the digital recording from the Wheelbarrow and, sure enough, there was a small electronic pulse from the battery in the car on the left.

'These batteries are supposed to be completely uncharged,' said the supervisor.

The technician checked the output terminals. Nothing.

'So there's something in there,' said the supervisor. 'Let's get her out.'

Boxer went up to the Royal Suite in the Savoy, which occupied the whole of the fifth floor. D'Cruz's Indian assistant took him through the wood-panelled office to the sitting room. D'Cruz was standing at one of the windows, looking out over the Thames. There had been no improvement in his state of mind. His face was flaccid and dull. He looked immensely lonely. Boxer had no intention of giving him any of the intelligence he'd gleaned from Simon Deacon. The pressure was clearly on D'Cruz, who might be inclined to pass anything on to his 'intermediary'.

'I met an old colleague of yours last night,' said Boxer.

'Who would that be?' asked D'Cruz, not turning round.

'Deepak Mistry.'

Now D'Cruz's face came alive. Boxer saw it in the window's reflection: the eyes narrowed, the lips tightened, the facial muscles trembled with rage under his slack skin. He turned, looking murderous.

'And what is he doing here?' said D'Cruz quietly.

'He told me who was responsible for the first kidnap, and why.'

'Go on.'

'Chhota Tambe.'

Silence. D'Cruz blinked, confused.

'Chhota Tambe? I haven't seen him in twenty years.'

'He's been following your career very carefully – and obsessively.'

'I'll tell you who *does* know Chhota Tambe, or at least used to know him very well, and that's Sharmila.'

'Right, the gangster's moll,' said Boxer. 'Isabel mentioned that.'

'They met in Dubai. He pursued her. There was some financial enticement until she realised his intentions, which she wasn't interested in. She came to me. I gave her a job. We got involved.'

'So, a double obsession.'

'Double?'

'You stole his girlfriend and he thinks you were responsible for the death of his elder brother.'

'Bada Tambe?' said D'Cruz, puzzled. 'Is he mad? Bada Tambe was killed by a bomb outside the stock exchange in the 1993 Mumbai attacks.'

'That bomb was made up of a military explosive known as RDX, Research Department Explosive, from Pakistan. He thinks you landed it when you were working for Dawood Ibrahim.'

'I didn't work for Dawood Ibrahim in 1993. I was already in the movies.'

'Chhota Tambe begs to differ. He said he knows you were involved in heroin smuggling out of Pakistan. A business that had been given to Dawood Ibrahim by Amir Jat, who I understand you also know quite well.'

'Was that what he meant by the "demonstration of sincerity"?' said D'Cruz. 'Was he looking for some kind of admission of guilt? Because if he was, I wouldn't have got there in a million years.'

'Deepak thinks he intended to punish you,' said Boxer.

D'Cruz seemed to get locked in position. His face was in the dark, with only a low lamp on in the room. Behind him the lights of the Royal Festival Hall and the National Theatre glittered in the ceaseless black flow of the Thames. He couldn't seem to move his feet, as if too much processing power was being used up elsewhere.

'You know, Frank, the one person you can confide in is me. I'm not going to talk to anyone,' said Boxer.

'Why should I?' said D'Cruz, reanimating himself.

'Because it might make you a happier man.'

'You think *happiness* is important to *me*?' said D'Cruz, stabbing himself in the chest with his finger. 'Happiness is for people who believe in dreams. It's for people who are content with the deluded life. It's just something that's written into the constitution of the United States of America.'

'And Alyshia is what to you?'

He turned back to the window, his breath fogging the glass.

'Look at yourself,' said Boxer. 'You look like that because you think you might lose her.'

'I lost her when she left Mumbai.'

'Why did she leave Mumbai?'

'Because I found out the son-of-a-bitch she was having an affair with was spying on me.'

'And you told her that,' said Boxer. 'Did you tell her that Deepak didn't love her? That he only got involved with her because it made spying on you easier?'

D'Cruz nodded, his whole body juddering.

'And did she tell you what she'd seen?' asked Boxer. 'Sharmila delivering children so that Amir Jat could abuse them.'

'Shut up!' roared D'Cruz, arms raised, thumping the window with both fists. 'SHUT UP!'

He turned away from the window, walked into the room, sat down in front of Boxer, hands clasped between his knees, searching the air in front of him for answers.

'Chhota Tambe,' he muttered to himself. 'Chhota Tambe. You know, I assumed that Deepak was spying for someone really important, like the Mahale family, but Chhota Tambe? He's just a small-time crook. A hood. A *goonda*.'

'Envy and jealousy are big emotions in a man,' said Boxer. 'Remember what I said to you at the very beginning about women?'

'But all this was so long ago. It's like ancient history after what India has been through over the last twenty years.'

'You take his woman, you're a movie star, you become successful through your connections to the Muslim community, while a grieving Chhota Tambe sits in Dubai, hitting the arm of his chair with a clenched fist,' said Boxer.

'He's right,' said D'Cruz, suddenly looking up, catching Boxer's eye. 'He's right about the heroin. I did one shipment for Dawood Ibrahim. I had no choice. It was my payment to him for being given a break in the movies.'

'Your first lesson in man-management,' said Boxer. 'That should help you understand why Deepak Mistry had to do that work for Chhota Tambe.'

'Deepak Mistry betrayed me. I gave him everything and he betrayed me,' said D'Cruz, jabbing the air with his finger. 'He betrayed my daughter, too.'

'What about Chhota Tambe's allegation about landing the Pakistani military explosive?'

'The RDX? I had nothing to do with that. Dawood Ibrahim only used Muslims for that work. It was a religious battle. *Jihad*. There's no way they would have let a Catholic anywhere near the RDX. Chhota fucking Tambe.'

'When Alyshia gets out of this, she's going to need someone,' said Boxer.

'She was crazy about Deepak,' said D'Cruz. 'She wouldn't believe me. She thought I'd cooked the whole thing up. The electrician finding the recording device, Deepak going into hiding, all the recordings on his computer, his handwritten notes. She thought *I*, her father, had fabricated the whole thing. And, yes, she told me what she'd seen at the Juhu Beach house. No, that's not quite right, she didn't just *tell* me, she *lashed* me with it. She whipped me to the bone. That was how much she loved him. That was how much she hated me. After all I'd done for her. And after the lie he'd perpetrated to bring her close.'

'Do you want your daughter to love you again?'

'She will *never* love me again.'

'No, not like before, but that's the nature of knowledge. You both have to come to terms with it.'

'And what are you proposing?'

'That when Alyshia is released, you won't stand between her and Deepak, if that's what she wants.'

'No, no, no. That is not acceptable. *He* will never go near her again. I've already saved her from one son-of-a-bitch; I won't let another destroy her.'

'Then you will never be happy and nor will Alyshia. There's

nothing more destructive than the love that could have been. She'll just be waiting for you to die.'

Silence.

'Why are you doing this?' asked D'Cruz, suddenly baffled by the level of intimacy in this conversation. 'What do you want out of it?'

'To be happy myself.'

D'Cruz gave him a grunt of recognition.

'I've warned Isabel about you; you know that, don't you?'

'What did you say to her?' asked Boxer, going cold at the possibility he might have told her his dirty secret.

D'Cruz saw it, realised his power.

'Don't worry,' he said, smiling. 'I just told her not to get involved with a man whose problems are worse than her own.'

'For the second time, you mean?' said Boxer, hating him now.

D'Cruz looked up; they locked eyes.

'Sometimes I don't like you, Charles Boxer.'

D'Cruz suddenly seemed livelier. The charisma wasn't turned on yet, but some shape had come back into his face. Boxer had seen this before, playing cards with players who'd suffered a long losing streak before finally getting a couple of winnable hands.

'Do you know where Chhota Tambe is now?' asked D'Cruz.

'Deepak says he's in London.'

D'Cruz stood, walked back to the window and looked out over the river, with his hands clasped behind his back. He nodded to himself.

'If Deepak wants my forgiveness, then I'll want my own "demonstration of sincerity" from him,' said D'Cruz. 'If he wants to see Alyshia again, you tell him, he has to kill Chhota Tambe.'

34

The COBRA meeting was reconvened with the same people present. Natasha Radcliffe gave a summary of the EOD Ammunition Technician's report.

'On finding some visible differences between the two X-rays of the batteries in the Stratford cars, the EOD squad decided to remove the suspect battery from the car. They took it to a protected warehouse for dismantling and found a small device, using PETN explosive attached to an enclosed metal phial, which they have not opened, but which they are concerned might contain radioactive material.

'The explosive was sufficient to have blown the car apart and disperse this radioactive material, in the current weather conditions, over about four square miles. The detonator was connected to a timer set for eight-thirty a.m. tomorrow, but with a mobile phone override, so it could be triggered manually. They're working on the SIM card now. They've moved their command post to the City and are awaiting our instructions. Simon?'

'The CIA have confirmed that the metal phial is a physical match for the one found on the arms smugglers' mule train in northern Afghanistan in January this year.'

Natasha Radcliffe turned to the Met Police Commissioner.

'All rooms with a line of sight to the City cars have been identified and I've been assured that they will all be empty by midnight tonight. I have officers on the ground and a number of CO19 armed response teams in the event of any attempt to trigger the devices.'

'Joyce?'

'Electronic jammers have already been installed under the podiums of the cars during the shift change of the security guards in the City, and the mobile network will be shut down at midnight.'

'What's your problem, Mervin?'

'The Tokyo market opens at midnight UK time,' said Stanley.

'There are no traders at their desks after nine p.m.,' said Joyce Hunter. 'I checked.'

'Just one other thing,' said Stanley. 'You gave the order for the Stratford bombs to be defused at three-thirty and this report is timed at eleven-oh-five. That means it took them just over seven hours to deal with one bomb.'

'I understand that bomb disposal is not a rush business,' said Barbara Richmond.

'But now they've got two bombs in the City and only eight and a half hours.'

'First of all, they've learnt a lot from dealing with the Stratford bomb,' said Joyce Hunter. 'Secondly, there will be two teams, one working on each car, and we don't yet know whether both cars contain devices. Thirdly, the first four hours of the operation were spent analysing the two batteries, removing the suspect one and transporting it to a safe warehouse for dismantling.'

'So you're saying that the bombs will be out of the City by four o'clock in the morning?'

'*Inshallah*,' said Hunter.

'Any news on Alyshia D'Cruz?' asked Natasha Radcliffe.

'We have identified her whereabouts. We know the number of people holding her. We're just waiting for the right moment to go in there and take her,' said the Met Police Commissioner.

'We want to ensure that we have the best possible chance of taking the gang leader, Saleem Cheema, alive,' said Barbara Richmond. 'The intelligence rewards could be enormous.'

'The EOD technicians will be told to start work at midnight,' said Natasha Radcliffe. 'The mobile phone network will be shut down from now until the batteries are out of the area.'

*

At 11.15 p.m., Saleem Cheema couldn't bear the tension anymore. He'd put off this moment for as long as he could and all he'd discovered in those hours was just how inexorable time was. He handcuffed both of Alyshia's wrists to the frame of the bed.

'I'm not going anywhere,' she said, blindly.

Neither of them responded. Cheema told Rahim to follow him and they went up to the kitchen, where they made tea.

'I've spoken to the UK command centre again,' said Cheema. 'They've told me that we have to kill her before midnight.'

A long silence ensued, during which Rahim looked at his watch, blew on his tea and sipped it.

'I've never killed a woman,' he said.

'I'd never killed anyone until Amir Jat last night,' said Cheema.

'I could tell,' said Rahim.

'They've asked me to do it,' said Cheema. 'No, they've ordered me to do it. They say it's a punishment for the transgressions of her father, who has consistently received support from our brothers in Pakistan but never given anything in return.'

'What if we don't do it?'

'She could be dangerous to us. She was in the room when I killed Amir Jat. It's possible that she's seen us when we dragged her out of the canal.'

'I've never killed a woman before.'

'You've already told me that, Rahim,' said Cheema, annoyed. 'But *I* can't do it. I can't kill a woman in cold ... I'm ... I'm begging you to do it.'

Rahim put his mug of tea down on the sideboard, stared into the floor.

'I will tell the UK command that you completed the task,' said Cheema, taking him by the arm. 'I'm sure they will reward you.'

'I will do it,' said Rahim, shaking off Saleem Cheema. 'But then I am finished with this. We will have killed the hero of the Mumbai attacks and a woman. That, to me, is not what the Islamic revolution is supposed to be about. So I will kill her for you, but then you must never contact me again.'

'And Hakim?'

'Hakim is his own man,' said Rahim. 'I'm going out for a walk now. You wait for me downstairs. When I come back, I will do it, but you will be there when I kill her. You will take visual responsibility.'

Boxer drove back to Chiswick, the black hole expanding in his chest, thinking about what Isabel had said to him about Amy. On his way out of the Savoy, it had hit him with such force that he'd had to pull over. This is what his life had been since his father had disappeared: expending great effort to control the manageable but remote, while letting the more intimate but complicated things spin away from him. It had been some minutes before he could continue, and even then he'd driven like someone recovering from a stroke – or was it an epiphany?

He parked up and went to the flat at the bottom of the garden in Fairlawn Grove. He gave Mistry Frank D'Cruz's proposal, which was greeted in total silence.

'That's the way Frank is,' said Boxer. 'It's how he's been brought up. He doesn't know any other way.'

'No,' said Mistry.

'No?'

'I'm not going to do it. The man is sick in the head if he thinks I'm going to restart my relationship with Alyshia on the back of Chhota Tambe's murder.'

'You said you'd used a gun once before. When was that?'

'I had to show my allegiance to Chhota Tambe. It was part of my initiation into his gang.'

'Do you think that's any way to start a relationship?'

'With a gangster, it's the only way,' said Mistry. 'But with the woman I want to be my wife, who I've already lied to once, I don't think I can do it and keep a clear conscience, however much I hate Chhota Tambe for what he's done to Alyshia.'

More silence. Boxer contemplated the darkness growing inside him. He knew the only solution.

'And what if I was to do it for you?' he said, enjoying the irony of it, knowing that this was the work he should have been paid for by D'Cruz.

The two men stared at each other. Boxer with quicksilver running through his veins again, the excitement clutching at his throat.

'Why would you do such a thing?' asked Mistry.

388

'Because it's the only way that Chhota Tambe will ever be brought to any kind of justice for what he's done,' said Boxer. 'What do you think he had in mind for Alyshia after that mock execution?'

'Yash was convinced he was going to kill her. It was the only possible punishment for Frank, as far as Chhota Tambe was concerned: Frank's daughter for Chhota Tambe's brother. It was the most destructive thing he could think of,' said Mistry. 'So, what do you want me to do?'

'Get me close to Chhota Tambe.'

There was tremendous tension inside the Jack Romney Decorators van. The ground forces were in constant contact now that the VW van had been backed up to the Boleyn Road garage of Saleem Cheema's house. The officer in charge of the CO19 squad, sitting in an unmarked van in a parallel street, was convinced that they were about to kill the girl. He was desperate to go in, but that presented its dangers, too, and he was constantly weighing up Plan A versus Plan B. He was also under pressure from the operations room to wait for the right moment. They still had no idea if there was any link between these kidnappers and the people who'd planted the bombs in D'Cruz's cars.

The surveillance team in Boleyn Road sat in their van, chewing gum at triple speed now, looking at their screen, waiting, ever hopeful. At 11.30 p.m., they finally got their break. The front door opened and Rahim came out into the road and walked towards the shops. The surveillance team relayed the information to CO19.

As Rahim turned the corner, they were waiting for him and came up on either side. He felt the uncomfortable pressure of a gun in each kidney. They walked him to the parallel street and put him face down in the back of the CO19 van, stripped him down to his underpants. They cuffed him and searched his clothes. They found the front door key to the house, which they handed over to an Asian officer, specially selected because of his similar height and build to Rahim. He dressed in Rahim's clothes, put on his trainers.

They questioned Rahim to find out where Cheema was in the house. He refused to speak.

The officer walked to the house on Boleyn Road, let himself in and went to the back of the house, checking the rooms. He found the secret buzzer in the wall that Hakim Tarar had revealed to Mercy. The door clicked open. He took out his Glock 17 and calmly went down the stairs.

Saleem Cheema was looking up and saw Rahim's trainers and jeans coming down the steps.

'You were quick,' he said, and made the mistake of looking down, unconcerned.

When there was no reply, he did look up and that was when he found himself looking down the Glock 17's barrel. He reached forward for the gun Rahim had left him and the bullet hit him in the right arm, knocked him off his chair. The officer went down to the basement floor, picked up the gun. He cuffed Cheema's hands, reported back into his lapel mike.

Alyshia was shaking on the bed, her head was still wrapped in a sweater, which covered her eyes, the handcuffs were rattling against the frame of the bed.

'You're OK,' he said. 'I'm police.'

35

At 11.30 p.m., the jammers were all in position under the podiums and the mobile phone network in the City was shut down. Police diverted the traffic away from Threadneedle Street, Cornhill and Leadenhall Street. Office cleaners trying to get to work were turned back.

The two EOD teams of technicians, still posing as security guards, moved in on the cars in front of the Royal Exchange and on St Mary Axe and exposed the batteries to their colleagues operating their mobile Wheelbarrows. In front of the Royal Exchange, they installed a CCTV camera on the plinth of the Wellington equine statue. In St Mary Axe, the CCTV camera was clamped to a nearby tree. They left the scene.

Plain clothes officers and MI5 agents moved through the streets, looking into the small courts, lanes and dead ends, checking that they were empty of people. Two mobile CCTV units monitored the area around the two podiums. One team of firearms officers from CO19 were stationed on a flat roof behind a balustrade on the Bank of England building, with a line of sight to the podium behind the Wellington statue. Others were on the ground, behind the pillars of the Royal Exchange, at the mouth of Pope's Head Alley and on the steps of Bank tube station. Another CO19 team were based on the side roof of the church of St Andrew Undershaft on St Mary Axe, with a view of the podium in the square in front of the Aviva Building, while others looked out from an outdoor staircase on the Lloyd's Building and from a narrow passage by the church.

The technicians moved their Wheelbarrows into position and took the first X-rays of the batteries and scanned them for any electronic signals. Nothing was coming off them – no odour, no sound, no radioactive warning. They studied the images, comparing it to the car battery in Stratford that had contained a bomb.

'I can't see anything suspicious,' said the supervisor.

'Maybe they did a better job on these two,' said the tech.

They looked at the output of the electronic signal detector. Nothing.

'More sophisticated, or harmless?'

'Let's take a shot from underneath the vehicle,' said the supervisor.

The techs pulled out the Wheelbarrows, repositioned them, took another two X-rays.

'What the fuck is this?' said the supervisor.

Into the frame of the two screens showing the feeds from the CCTV cameras came two men in long dark coats, running at the podiums, holding their right hands out in front of them.

The Met police mobile CCTV units picked them up, too. The order was given immediately.

'Take them down.'

That was what the CO19 teams heard in one ear. In the other was the wild shout of *Allahu Akbar*. There was no hesitation. Four shots rang out. The two men fell to the ground, their mobiles skittered away from them across the paving stones.

'I think we've just been given our answer,' said the EOD supervisor. 'Let's get those batteries out.'

Deepak Mistry and Charles Boxer were heading for a meeting with Chhota Tambe. Boxer had already stripped down and cleaned the gun Mistry had been given by the Southall gang and found more ammunition for it. This was the weapon he'd decided to use. It would be confusing for the police to find the gun used in the earlier incident, where he and D'Cruz had been on the receiving end.

Boxer was going to drop Mistry off near Chhota Tambe's house in Regent's Park. The story was that Mistry had found someone close to Frank D'Cruz who was prepared to kill him for a fee of £2,000. They were relying on the intensity of Chhota Tambe's obsession and his need to take action against Frank D'Cruz before he realised who had been responsible for the initial kidnap. Once D'Cruz had worked that out, there would be an all-out war on Chhota Tambe's interests in Mumbai from the likes of Anwar Masood.

'How are you going to persuade Chhota Tambe to leave the comfort of his warm house in Regent's Park and venture out in the cold and dark onto Primrose Hill for an assignation with your proposed hit man?' asked Boxer.

'In this particular case, I know he would like to be involved, to actually give the order,' said Mistry. 'And he still trusts me. He knows what this business has cost me.'

'How did you meet me? How do you know what I do and that I'm willing to do it?'

'You found me. You were the kidnap consultant appointed by Frank.'

'Why am I willing to kill him?'

'Frank found out you were having an affair with his ex-wife and wouldn't tolerate it,' said Mistry. 'I think that's something Chhota Tambe will identify with.'

Boxer gritted his teeth at Mistry's improvisation. It had the horrible ring of truth about it.

They drove past the house on Park Road and continued to Primrose Hill, where Boxer showed Mistry where to bring Chhota Tambe. He dropped Mistry back at Chhota Tambe's house, parked the car and walked to Primrose Hill, up to the bench with the view of the BT Tower. His mobile rang; he must remember to turn it off. Deacon.

'How is it going, Simon?'

'I just thought you'd want to know that Alyshia has been rescued and D'Cruz's cars have been rendered safe.'

'That's good. Has Isabel Marks been told?'

'Yes. She's heading to the hospital now to see Alyshia,' said Deacon. 'You don't sound particularly elated ...'

'Just a few things on my mind,' said Boxer. 'That's all.'

'The frightening thing, Charlie,' said Deacon, 'is that if Alyshia

393

hadn't been kidnapped, I'm not sure how close we'd have got to discovering the bombs. It focused our minds.'

'Sometimes you have to believe, Simon.'

'Let's meet for a drink soon.'

'Any time,' said Boxer. He hung up and turned off the phone.

He stood in the darkness, away from the lamp light shining down on the bench, with the cold running through him, the black hole in his chest widening at the notion of Amy, and now possibly Isabel, turning away from him. He saw two men approaching up the lit walkways of the park, recognised Mistry as one of them. He was surprised by his companion. Even though he knew his name meant 'little', he hadn't expected him to be quite so small – barely five foot, and tubby with it.

Boxer kept to the shadows, waited. Rather than the task in hand, he found himself thinking of his father. But this time the thought came with a question, one that so many others had asked him and which he'd never answered: at what point did you stop looking for your father? And the answer was that he'd stopped looking for him on the day he'd thought for the first time that his father might have been guilty, and not just of one killing.

The two men arrived, sat down on the bench. Boxer looked around the empty, freezing park. He didn't think about it. He walked calmly out of the darkness and into the light, fired, dropped the gun and carried on walking.

36

Alyshia had been taken to Newham General Hospital emergency department, where she'd been given a full check-up. When her father heard about the rescue, he immediately organised an ambulance to take her to a private room in the Bupa Cromwell Hospital where Isabel would be waiting for her. Frank D'Cruz was not able to make it as he was undergoing a debrief at Thames House.

Isabel didn't get to see her immediately as the doctor D'Cruz had hired at great expense to give Alyshia a thorough examination did not want any interruptions. He came out to give her exactly the same findings as the NHS doctor at Newham General: Alyshia was in very good physical shape, considering the extremes of her ordeal. However, mentally there could be repercussions: the dreaded post-traumatic stress syndrome.

Isabel didn't know why, but once the doctor had left her in the corridor, she knocked on her daughter's door before going in. An etiquette had established itself in her mind. This disappeared on entry as Alyshia, connected to a saline drip, held her arms open and cried out something that Isabel hadn't heard for many years.

'Mummy!'

For the first few minutes they didn't speak and just held onto each other: Isabel hugging her, breathing in her hair, kissing her head, rocking her child while Alyshia inhaled the familiar warmth of the cashmere sweater, the perfume, the deeper, atavistic mother scent.

'I'm sorry,' said Alyshia, over and over again. 'I'm so sorry, Mummy.'

'Don't be ridiculous,' said Isabel. 'You've got nothing to be sorry about. If you weren't here, that would be something to be sorry about. But you are. You really are here.'

She crushed Alyshia until she squeaked.

'I meant I'm sorry for all my cruelty,' said Alyshia. 'For pushing you away when I came back from Mumbai. I should never have done that. You are the one true person, the only really true person I can trust more than anybody else. And I didn't know that until I thought I was never going to see you again.'

Isabel said nothing, just crushed her so hard that Alyshia whimpered like a kitten.

They held hands, looking at the miracle of each other, unable to speak, a whole lifetime to exchange in one sitting.

Over the next fifteen minutes, they calmed down. A nurse brought some tea. Isabel went to the window while she checked the drip, temperature and blood pressure. She told Alyshia that D'Cruz wouldn't be able to come until after his debrief.

'I don't want to see anybody except you,' said Alyshia, shaking her head. 'I've been surrounded by men for a week. Bad men. Let's just have some time together, the two of us.'

'Deepak's here, too,' said Isabel. 'He's desperate to see you.'

'I can't do Deepak now,' she said. 'I might never be able to do Deepak.'

Saturday midday, Boxer was sitting with his mother, Esme, at the kitchen table, drinking coffee. He'd come to pick up Amy, who was getting her things together in the bedroom. They still hadn't actually spoken to each other since the ugly phone call he'd made at Heathrow.

'How's Amy been?' asked Boxer.

'She's been good; great, in fact. We've had a nice time together,' said Esme, lighting up her fourth cigarette of the morning, Marlboro, full strength. 'I like her. She has spunk, as my bloody father used to say. She reminds me of me, when I was her age. She can take the battering. She's strong inside. And she's learnt to protect herself.'

'Maybe you're getting childhoods muddled up,' said Boxer. 'Your father beat you up. We've never laid a hand on Amy. Mind you, she's aggressive enough to make anybody think we *have* laid a hand on her.'

'You and Mercy are making parental demands on her, which Amy doesn't think you deserve to make when you've already fallen short in your parental duties,' said Esme. 'When you've already built up such a deficit of love.'

'A deficit of love?' said Boxer. 'But, Christ, doesn't she understand that we've done everything we possibly can, given the jobs we've got?'

'Why should she? She was just a kid when you went globe-trotting, saving people in Mexico, Pakistan and Japan. Why should she have to grasp the reason her parents don't come to see her play football, act in the school play, do her stand-up session at the Comedy Store —'

'Do her what?'

'You didn't know that, did you? They had a school's night at the Comedy Store. She did a set. It went down a storm. She did it for me a couple of nights ago. She's good. As you say, a lot of aggression to work out there.'

Boxer sipped his coffee, rocked in his chair, watching his mother smoke her cigarette in the most luxuriantly enjoyable style.

'I'm no different. I haven't exactly been there for her as a grandmother. Had my own problems, as you know,' she said, wiggling her cigarette, tilting her wrist. 'But I don't make any demands on her. She doesn't call me granny. I don't expect her to. I just see her as another girl, or rather, a young woman. I like her when she's being attractive, and dislike her when she's being unpleasant. But I've recognised that I don't have the right to expectations. That's the destructive thing about families. If the child doesn't live up to your expectations, then you're unhappy and so is the child.'

'But we weren't, I mean aren't, a destructive family,' said Boxer. 'Not like your crazy dad.'

'You weren't violent, that's true, although it sounds as if Mercy can be threatening.'

'Probably under a lot of provocation, and she had a destructive father, too,' said Boxer. 'My father didn't do anything to me. He murdered *your* business partner and ran away.'

And killed something in you in the process, thought Esme, but for once didn't say it.

'And you didn't take that as a rejection?' she said. 'I know I did. And that's what you're handing down to Amy. You were away a lot, but that was your choice. You could have decided to be there for her, but you weren't, probably because your father abandoned you.'

'She seemed very happy when she was small,' said Boxer, aware that he sounded defensive, reeling with the guilt. 'It's only since she became a teenager she's been so impossible.'

'You decided to spend more time with her, but it was too late, Charlie. She'd already started protecting herself. You weren't around, Mercy had her own problems and she'd chosen a certain career path. What's a child supposed to do? And once those barriers are in place ...'

'So what do I do now?'

'Try to form a relationship with her with no fatherly expectations. Don't expect love when you've done very little to engender it. Treat her like any other young woman. See if you like her. See if she likes you. Take it from there. I reckon it's your only chance.'

Frank D'Cruz was pacing the corridor outside Alyshia's room. He was nervous in a way that he'd never been before. He'd been told, even when Alyshia had heard his debrief was over, that she still hadn't wanted to see him. Isabel had been able to persuade Alyshia to give him a hearing, only after she'd told her about a three hour discussion she'd had with her ex-husband once he'd got out of Thames House.

But there was another reason D'Cruz was finding it difficult to go into the room. He knew Deepak Mistry would be there at her bedside. Part of that three hour discussion had been about Deepak and how he'd successfully made his case to Alyshia, which hadn't reflected well on D'Cruz.

D'Cruz hadn't seen him since the day before he'd fled from Konkan Hill Securities in December last year. On Thursday morning, three days ago, as he was being driven to Thames House, he'd heard a news report about a suspected gangland murder of an Indian mafia don on Primrose Hill. Now he had to go into this room, look Deepak Mistry in the eye, accept him, and then win over his daughter.

He knocked, went in. Deepak Mistry stood, not as if ready to flee, but more as her protector. D'Cruz looked at his daughter in her hospital gown and realised that he hadn't seen her since December last year either, and it came to him in that moment how much he'd missed her. How much he'd sacrificed in his rage.

He went to her and she accepted a kiss, but did not embrace him. Her restraint was palpable and painful to him. He shook hands with Mistry, made eye contact, let him know that there should be nothing between them now.

'Maybe I should leave you two to talk,' said Mistry.

'No,' said Alyshia. 'You're part of this. We're both going to listen.'

D'Cruz went to the window, peered through the blinds for a moment and turned to face them, hanging his head.

'I realise I've done some great wrongs,' said D'Cruz, with total solemnity. 'Great wrongs. And the greatest of wrongs I have done have been to those closest to me. I am sorry. I can't undo what I've done, but I would like to try to put some things right. I have decided to set up a charitable foundation to look after street children in Mumbai,' he said, ignoring Alyshia's raised eyebrow. 'And I would like you to come back with me to Mumbai to run it. And if it would suit you, I would also like Deepak to be involved in some way.'

'It sounds as if you've been talking to Mum.'

'As you know, she is the centre of all goodness in my world. She has spoken and I have listened,' said D'Cruz. 'I have also decided to stop the escort agency and encourage Sharmila to work with the Mahale family's AIDS awareness programme.'

They looked at him. He stood with his back to the window, held out his hands, palms upwards, the charisma streaming out towards them from his fingertips.

'What?' he said.

*

Driving Amy back to Mercy's house in Streatham, Boxer found himself trying to work his way into this new idea of a relationship: *not* being a father.

'I'm thinking of having a dinner tonight with Mum in an Iranian grill just off Edgware Road. I'd like you to come, if you're up for it?' he said, thinking how odd that sounded.

'Yeah, that sounds good.'

'I know you haven't seen much of your friends while you've been staying with Esme, so if you want to see them first, that's fine. I'll tell you where the restaurant is and you can make your own way there. The place is nothing special, but the grilled meat is fantastic. It's bring your own booze, too, so it's cheap, cheerful and relaxed.'

'OK, great,' said Amy, nodding while texting Karen.

They arrived in Streatham. Amy took her case upstairs. Boxer joined Mercy in the kitchen. It struck him now, after that merciless conversation with his mother, just how sterile this house was. It was brightly painted, nicely furnished and very neat, but it didn't feel lived in or welcoming. There wasn't the usual crap around that he associated with family life. He realised with a pang that Mercy had never had a real home. Her father's house had felt like a barracks while her own had something of an aparthotel about it.

'What you looking at?' asked Mercy.

'Nothing,' he said, taking a seat.

'What's the scene with Amy?' she asked. 'Her greeting was almost civil.'

'A new strategy,' said Boxer. 'I'm pretending *not* to be her father.'

'Is this some counselling from that great expert on family matters: the drunken hag?'

'She wasn't drunk, hasn't been drunk, according to Amy.'

'They're in the same coven, those two,' said Mercy. 'How did I come out in the parental review?'

'We both scored nought out of ten, but with mitigating circumstances,' said Boxer. 'Your brutal dad and my absent one.'

'Right, so we're just acting out the family scenarios we're familiar with,' said Mercy, sounding bored. 'It's easy looking down from the hallowed heights of Hampstead, but I can tell you it's different down here in the mean streets of Streatham.'

'Her theory is that you should treat her like a young adult who's staying with you.'

'You mean I get rent?'

'You'll probably find she could pay off your mortgage.'

'Is she coming tonight?'

'I asked her and she's accepted.'

'We're all so bloody grown up.'

They were upstairs in the Iranian grill. The chair Boxer had kept for Amy stood at the head of the table, empty. Occasionally Mercy glanced at it and then at Boxer, and shrugged. The chair remained like a silent rebuke. Except that, in his new role as 'non-Dad', he refused to allow it to develop into anything as powerful as a rebuke. He decided that she'd preferred the company of her friends. He wasn't going to let it get to him. They ordered their food, drank the wine Boxer had brought. Mercy was looking festive. She had make-up on, which was rare, and the gold stud earrings he'd bought for her on one of his trips. She was wearing some multi-coloured African cloth, which she'd had cut into a mini-dress, with a shawl to match. Her foot nodded against his shin.

'So,' said Mercy, rolling up fresh herbs and yoghurt in flatbread, 'what are you doing with yourself now that it's all over?'

'I'm preparing to move The LOST Foundation into some new offices near Marylebone High Street.'

'And how much is that costing you a month, or are you working out of a shoebox?'

'Zip,' said Boxer. 'And it's two hundred square metres. A satisfied client let me have it.'

'What it is to be in the private sector,' said Mercy. 'Anyway, that's not what I meant. What I meant is: how's it going with Isabel? Or should I say: how's it going to go? Have you seen her since … ?'

'No, I haven't,' said Boxer, pouring more wine. 'I'm giving her space to see if she wants to continue … the thing.'

'Ah, yes, the thing,' said Mercy.

'You know how it is.'

'Do I?' said Mercy. 'I haven't had a thing in ages, although if I'd been as mad as you, I might have found myself having "a thing" with a crack dealer called Delroy Dread.'

'Seriously.'

'Yes,' she said, putting her hands to her face, letting out a high-pitched giggle. 'He flirted with me and I found myself flirting back. You should have seen the muscles on him.'

'I think Skin had a thing for you, too,' said Boxer, 'playing footsie with you in the interview.'

'Pity,' said Mercy wistfully, 'that my only admirers are drug dealers and murderers. Why's it that only criminals think I'm hot? And what does that say about you?'

'Me?' said Boxer nervously, checking her for insight, but she was more occupied by her food.

'What is it about bad guys?' said Mercy, sipping her wine.

'Perhaps they like a bit of strictness,' said Boxer. 'Anyway, what I meant was, now that Alyshia is safe—'

'Oh yes, the gorgeous Isabel might feel very differently about her knight in shining armour.'

'You did a lot more than I did to get Alyshia back.'

'Thanks for the recognition from the private sector.'

'No, Mercy, you did a great job.'

'Yes,' she said, looking at the empty chair, but not shrugging this time, seeing her failure sitting there. 'There *are* things I'm good at.'

They drank more wine.

'So,' said Mercy, unable to leave it alone. 'Isabel?'

'Didn't I say?'

'Not yet.'

'I'm in love with her.'

'That might be difficult for you, Charles Boxer,' said Mercy, hurt, his words slicing through her.

'I know,' he said, 'but I've never wanted a woman more in my entire life than Isabel Marks. She … she's … she'll …'

'She's got all the right tenses, anyway,' said Mercy, annoyed with herself for always hiding her feelings behind humour. 'She must remind you of the mother you never had.'

'When are you going to meet the father you never had?'

'That's our problem,' said Mercy, grinning, reaching across to hold his hand. 'If we hadn't been such lost souls, we might have stayed together.'

He squeezed her hand, thinking: *Jesus, Isabel was right*. Mercy still hadn't let him go. Was she living in hope? He looked at the chair again, as if that, in his mind, was all that was left of their relationship.

'Shall I call her?' asked Mercy.

But, despite the feeling of humiliation trembling at the outer limits of the hole in his chest, he wouldn't let her.

Finally, just as the plate of lamb kebabs arrived, someone asked if they could take the chair. They nodded and saw it removed to a table where it was introduced into another family and was sat upon by a young girl, who turned and smiled at them. And they realised that all their parental expectations were tied up in that wretched chair.

They left the restaurant and went to hail taxis on Edgware Road, where the Lebanese men were sitting outside the cafés, huddled in their coats, smoking their *hookahs*. He put Mercy in a taxi heading south, crossed the road and took another heading north.

His mobile rang. Isabel. His heart leapt.

'How's Alyshia?' he asked.

'She's fine. She's recovering well. She'll be out tomorrow. I've left her at the Bupa Cromwell with Deepak and I'm at home on my own. I'd like to see you. I think we should have a talk.'

He redirected the cab to Aubrey Walk, staring straight ahead, mouth set. He knew what 'having a talk' meant. Maybe Frank's warning about him had finally brought Isabel to her senses and this was going to be the brush-off. He felt sure she would have the lightest of touches, but it wouldn't make any difference to the hole expanding in his chest after two rejections in one night.

He paid the cabbie, made his way past the fake Georgian façade to her door, feeling the emptiness now, both inside and out. He rang the bell.

She opened the door for him and he knew instantly that everything was going to be all right. There was no hesitation. She opened her arms and he walked into them, heard her gasp in his ear as he held her to him and kissed her neck.

They sat with the bottle of scotch and the ice tray, their hands threaded across the kitchen table, smiling, on the brink of laughing.

'How's it going between Alyshia and Deepak?'

'I don't ask. He's still here. They talk,' said Isabel.

'And Frank?'

'I think she was struck by his remorse and surprised by his magnanimity, but under no illusions about his capacity for change,' said Isabel. 'What about Amy?'

'I'm trying a new approach and it seemed to work at first, but now I realise it hasn't. Not for her, but for me.'

His phone rang, he checked the screen.

'Mercy,' said Boxer. 'She'd only call if it was important. I'll have to take it.'

He listened, blinked, said nothing, dropped the phone, looked to the window, where he saw through their cheerful reflection to the darkness beyond.

'What is it?' asked Isabel.

'Amy's gone,' said Boxer. 'She left a note on her bed. The last line was:

"YOU WILL NEVER FIND ME."'

Acknowledgements

I would like to thank everybody who helped me with this book especially my old school friend, Robin Clifford, who introduced me to a number of people working in the private security company industry. Those I spoke to have asked to remain anonymous. What I can say is that, to a man, they were extremely impressive people with what struck me as an unimpeachable moral centre, unlike a number of characters in this novel.

My thanks, too, to my old friend Steve Wright, who reported to me a conversation he'd had with his then six year old son, Calum. This was introduced into the mulch of my cerebral composter and ten years later got worked into some barren patch where it has produced this fruit.

There is no such thing as an unedited book. This one went through quite a few processes even before it saw the light of day. When it did finally come out into the open I was grateful to have Andrew Kidd on hand to give me some very valuable editorial notes. Most of these I incorporated into the text prior to the novel being submitted, which undoubtedly affected its positive reception.

There are days when writing can seem like the most exquisite torture ever conceived by the devil himself. Hours of writhing on a skewer of your own invention to produce a few droplets of sweat, which fall to the page and blur the four words you've managed to wring out of your severely gnawed pen, can seem like a terrible way to earn a living. On the other hand, hitting the vein and getting a gusher, with the brain motoring faster than the ink flows and the stack of blank pages falling visibly as they're filled with wild imaginings, can make it all feel worthwhile. I have paid rare visits to these extremes while spending most of my time in the ground in between and I can tell you that the one thing I'm deeply grateful for is not to be doing it alone. I would therefore like to thank my wife, Jane, for cajoling me back to sanity while I'm writing, for her infinite patience and perceptions in the editing process, for the endless shoring up of the edifice once the work has gone and for her love, which I value above all else and return with all my heart.

What's next for Charlie Boxer?

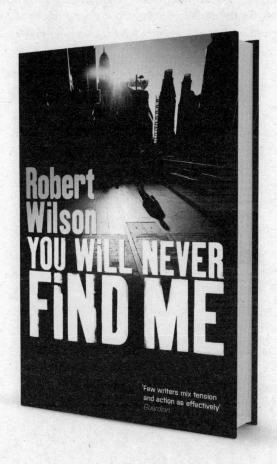

Robert Wilson

YOU WILL NEVER FIND ME

'Few writers mix tension and action as effectively'
Guardian

Available from Orion in Hardback and ebook

February 2014

www.orionbooks.co.uk

Available in ebook